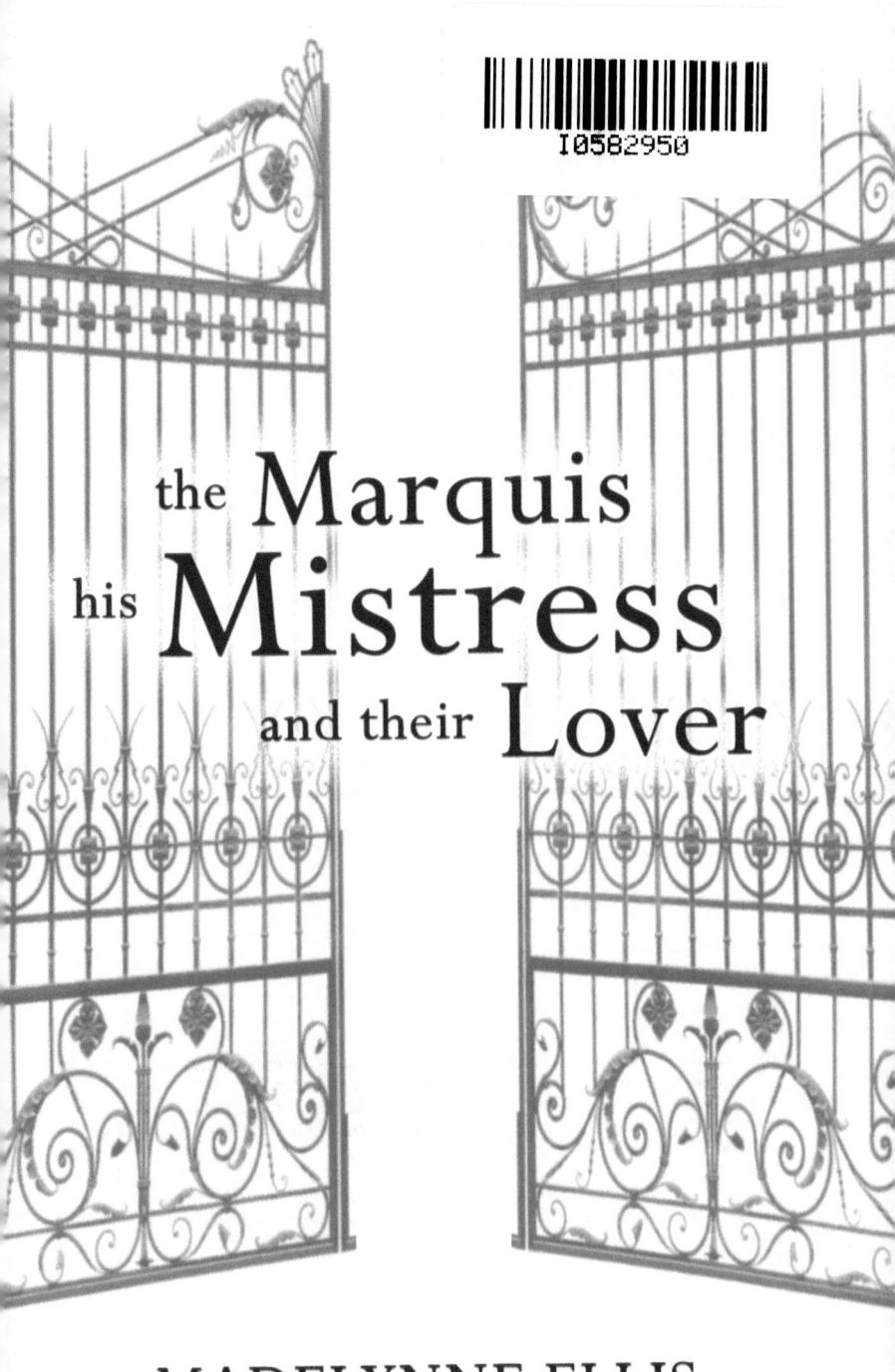

the Marquis
his Mistress
and their Lover

MADELYNNE ELLIS

THE MARQUIS, HIS MISTRESS, & THEIR LOVER

She's the disgrace of the county...

Bella Rushdale has returned home still unwed having eloped with Viscount Marlinscar, and she's now engaged in a scandalous liaison with the Marquis of Pennerley. Remote Yorkshire society is outraged!

Something ought to be done.

Even the untrained observer can see there's something deliciously perplexing about the relationship between Bella and the two rascals responsible for her disgrace. As rumours of unnatural activities, forbidden pleasures and the inevitable repercussions abound, Bella vigorously resists her brother's attempts to strong-arm her into wedlock. But, all too soon everything gets out of hand, putting Bella at risk of losing far more than her reputation. Can three people whose lives and hearts are so inexorably bound forge a lasting bond? Or is their love as ill-fated as society would have them believe?

Scandalous Seductions

Also by Madelynne Ellis

A Gentleman's Wager
Indiscretions
Phantasmagoria
Three Times the Scandal
The Viscount, His Lover & I
The Ghosts of Christmas
Past
The Serpent's Kiss

Wooing the Wakefields
A Devilish Element

Romps & Rakehells
Capturing Cora
Seducing Sophia
Taming Taylor

Forbidden Loves
The Kissing Bough
Pure Folly

The Black Halo Books
Come Undone
All Night Long
Off the Record
Come Together
All Fired Up
Come Alive
Reflex
Replay
Refrain
Revive
Toxic
Reckless Beat
Rock Giant
Rock Solid

Anything But...
Anything But Vanilla
Anything But Ordinary

Stirred Passions

Cherry Bomb
Black Velvet
Soul Kiss
Mint to Be
Screw Driver

Standalone titles
Tempted
You, Him, & Me
Don't Mess with my Relic
Sharing Adam
Gabriel's Naughty Game
Confessions of a Greedy
Girl
Crazy Love
Washed Up

Gothic Urban Fantasy
Blood Moon in
Possession: Three Tales of
Shapeshifting &
Possession
Prophecy
The Demon Way
Shadow Queen

CHAPTER 1

BELLA

21st July, 1801, Yorkshire, England.

O H, LORD! "Stop the carriage. I'm going to be sick!"

Miss Annabella Rushdale slid across the cushioned leather seat towards the door as Lord Pennerley's carriage jerked to a decisive stop. It was not a moment too soon. Rather than await the aid of a footman, she flung open the door, and if the ground had been a little closer, she would have jumped. As it was, she buckled at the waist and promptly cast up her assets. In hindsight, neither tansy nor caudle had been wise choices when they'd stopped for nuncheon some hours back. The one left her mildly intoxicated and the other, contrary to her memory of it, tasted rather like warm, gargled phlegm.

Only dimly aware of the movement around her, Bella waited for her head to clear a little before opening her eyes. Both liveried footmen were now down from their respective perches and attending to the carriage steps. The taller of the two, Patrick she thought it was, offered her his assistance in descending onto terra firma, although after hours of being jogged about, it seemed almost as though the road jumped to meet her.

Devilish things, carriages—she'd never liked them. In times past, she'd always eschewed such ungodly modes of transport, preferring the feel of the wind in her hair as she rode, to being jerked and jostled inside a claustrophobic leather-lined box. And this particular example, despite its sumptuous fittings, was particularly airless and hot.

"How very considerate of you to miss the interior, Miss Rushdale."

She turned in time to see Vaughan, the Marquis of Pennerley, descend the steps behind her. He looked eerily immaculate; his dark ringlets resting gently on his shoulders, and not a crease in sight on his black pantaloons or charcoal-grey coat despite the many miles they'd travelled. He'd spent most of them stretched across the rear-facing seat with his head supported by a mound of coloured squabs. She'd believed him asleep, except he'd stirred quickly enough at her prompt.

He fluttered a handkerchief before her nose, which she gratefully accepted. The linen smelled of his rosemary and bergamot pomade. "We'll take the air awhile. And Patrick, fetch Miss Rushdale a drink instead of gawping."

"Yes, milord."

Now that the world was no longer rocking, and she had a lovely fresh breeze blowing in her face, Bella's nausea quickly receded. She offered Vaughan a meek smile as he handed her a glass of Madeira brought to him by Patrick. It did nothing for her stomach, but the sweet, rich liquid did take away the horrid taste in her mouth.

"I think it's the caudle I drank earlier."

"Fool you for drinking such muck." Vaughan had already expressed his distaste when she'd first requested the beverage, but the drink, like the land around them, was part of her welcome home. Three and a half years had passed since she'd last seen Yorkshire.

"Shall we?" Vaughan offered her his arm to lean on. He led her along the grassy verge away from the carriage and the team of chestnut horses. To their right, a ditch bordered the rolling country road, at the bottom of which a narrow brook tumbled over a bank of pebbles.

"Are we close?" she asked, quite certain they must be. They were high up on the rolling moorlands of England's backbone, and now that she'd revived a little, she could taste the special quality in the air that told her she was almost home. She'd almost forgotten the smell in her time away—first in London, and then at Pennerley, Vaughan's estate on the Welsh border—but she recalled it now, the miasma of ancient rock, grass, and earth, of iron-tainted water and heather and ferns. It was quite different to the scent of Shropshire with its glittering quartzite stones and huge hummock like hillsides. "We are," she concluded, as the startling familiarity of the environs finally sunk in. "Why, that's Grinton Church over there, and the river... That's the Swale. We're almost at Grinton Bridge. I had no idea we were so close." She clapped her hands in delight, only for her brow to immediately furrow. She had not anticipated the view around her, because this was not where they were supposed to be. "We're almost at Wyndfell," she laughed in puzzlement. "I thought you said we were stopping at Middleham, but that must be miles back. Whatever are you up to, Vaughan?"

She did not anticipate a direct answer.

Vaughan idly swung his silver-topped cane. "Joshua was most insistent I return you home."

"My brother did?" She had been unaware the two maintained any kind of correspondence.

"Honestly, Bella. You needn't look so horrified. I thought you'd be pleased to see him. He is your only family."

True. She was dearly looking forward to seeing her brother again, and all of her old haunts, and the people who had once been her whole world, even though it was unlikely they'd be nearly so eager to see her. One didn't run off to London with a viscount and return, still unwed, on the arm of a marquis, without sustaining a few black marks against ones name. Quite likely, Joshua would be the first to remind her of that fact, though she prayed not in front of Vaughan. A marriage wasn't on the cards. She couldn't even properly lay claim to the title of mistress. There was no official accord between them, nor any sort of financial arrangement. She wasn't even certain Vaughan liked her all that much.

For her part, the possibility of life without Vaughan was unfathomable. She was besotted in the worst possible way, for she knew he would never return her affection. Vaughan's heart belonged to someone else. It always had, and it always would. Nothing she could ever do or say would change that.

"Is my brother expecting us?"

"Of course." Vaughan graced her with a wan smile, which tweaked the edges of his sensual lips upwards but failed to ignite any sort of fire in his violet eyes.

And Lucerne? Is he aware of our proximity too?

She supposed he must be. Even if Joshua had not made him aware of the visit, he would be well acquainted with the arrangements for the christening. He would know that she was to be godmother to the little mite. It had been Louisa Wakefield's dying wish, though Bella was hopelessly ill-suited to the role of moral guardian, unless to act as a warning of what not to do. At least the child would have two other godparents to deliver sensible guidance.

"If your head's clear now, we might press on."

Bella's gaze drifted towards the flock of sheep dotting the hillside. "Another moment or two. I still feel giddy." This second wave of stomach cramps wasn't due to travel sickness, but anxiety. There wasn't only her brother to face on the road ahead. Once they crossed Grinton Bridge, they'd climb again, pass through Reeth, and head high into the Pennines above Swaledale to reach Wyndfell Grange, but to get there they would first have to pass the gates of Lauwine Hall.

Eight months had passed since Lucerne walked out of their lives and severed the bonds that had once united them. The hurt remained as fresh as ever. And while she appreciated they might pass by the gates today unhindered, there would be no avoiding Lucerne indefinitely amidst such a small community.

Of course, rekindling his acquaintance with his dearest friend was Vaughan's primary motivation in accompanying her to the christening of little Louisa Wakefield. It was certainly not out of any sense of duty or affection that he'd travelled over two hundred miles to watch the squalling babe have its head wetted.

"Did you wish to walk a while?" Vaughan offered, drawing her out of her thoughts. "I can have the carriage go ahead and meet us at the bridge."

"You're being awfully solicitous today." A fact that made her wary. For certain, it implied that something was afoot.

Vaughan acknowledged the remark with a brief lowering of his eyelids. "I have to at least be seen to be taking good care of you."

His remark surprised a smile from her. "You do take good care of me."

He shook his head. "That, we both know, is an outrageous lie. I'm almost always vile to you."

Bella waved the remark away. "If I didn't care for your actions, I wouldn't stay. After all, I'm not obligated to do so."

"Yes. There's no denying you're an oddity."

She smacked at his fingers, an act that in times past might have led to a tumble. Now he merely gazed at her, faintly amused.

Twenty or so minutes later, Vaughan drew the curtains across the carriage windows as they neared the entrance to Lauwine. Bella wasn't fooled by the display, nor did she require any sort of visual clue to know the precise moment they tramped passed the great wrought-iron gates. Nearing four years was nothing compared to the twenty-three she'd spent living here. She could not pretend she didn't know every curve in the road, or that part of her wanted to lean out of the window and find Lucerne waiting for them. Instead she bit her lip and looked at the floor until they were almost at Wyndfell Grange, and Vaughan opened the curtains again.

Things were about to become uncomfortable, she could sense it with every fibre of her body, but there was nothing to be done save to endure it. She would not turn tail and run from the clouds ahead, but would do her duty to her deceased friend.

Geese squabbled in the lane that led up to the house. The Dalmatians running alongside the carriage sent them waddling off in a panic. Wyndfell itself hadn't changed a bit. It still perched at the top of the valley, a weathered grey refuge, surrounded on all sides by fields full of ling. The garden was neat, but lacking in variety, for only the hardiest plants survived the rains and winds. Still, it was home. Her old swing still hung from the ash tree to the left of the house as it had done since she was a very small child, and the juniper by the front door still encroached upon the threshold.

"It's as if I never left."

Even her brother, standing on the driveway, looked exactly as he had always done; hawk-like in his brown and buff clothing, with his brown hair and beady eyes. On second thought, his jawline was no longer quite so sharp, and he did appear to have expanded a little around the middle. The first signs of grey streaked the wings of his hair.

"Brother." She curtseyed, holding his hand, which made him shake his head. When she stood again, he raked his gaze over her appearance. Her pelisse had been discarded inside the carriage in a feeble attempt to mitigate the early summer heat, and the wind nipped at her bare arms and tugged at the sheer muslin of her dress.

"Bella," Joshua replied, after an insufferably long pause. "I was beginning to fear you wouldn't arrive in time. I've been expecting you all week. What's been the delay, or oughtn't I to ask?" He shot a foul glance over her shoulder at Vaughan, who remained at the top of the carriage steps.

"Ill-maintained roads for the most part." The journey north had been long, dull, and deeply unpleasant. It had not, as Joshua so clearly supposed, been relieved by numerous bawdy games, or in fact, any sort of sexual congress.

"Well, I guess you're here now. I sent word over to Lauwine when I saw you coming up the lane."

The boy would have run the direct route over the fields, which was why they had not passed him. "I expect Wakefield will be along presently. He wants to go over the details with you. I'm not sure what the fuss is. Plenty of bairns get christened every day."

"But not his daughter." Almost a year had passed,

but the poor man was still mourning his wife, Bella's one-time dearest friend. "I expect he simply wants to make sure everything adheres to Louisa's wishes."

Focussing on Wakefield's plight meant she didn't have to think about how the message detailing their arrival would be received by Lucerne. "Shall we go in? I should dearly like the opportunity to revive myself before he arrives." She turned towards the house, and Joshua followed her to the door.

"I've put you in your old room. I thought that's where you'd want to be."

"And Vaughan?"

Joshua came to a halt. He wet his lips and looked at her. "The marquis isn't staying here, Bella. I assumed you knew that and had said your goodbyes."

No, actually. She hadn't realised that.

Hellfire, she'd known there was something brewing.

Bella pivoted on the spot to find her trunk had been unpacked onto the gravel drive, but Vaughan still remained at the top of the carriage steps. At least his expression was one of boredom, rather than maliciousness. For once, perhaps he had not done this out of spite or to cause an upset, but rather to avoid one. That did not stop her words trilling out, "When were you going to tell me?" she demanded. "Were you even going to tell me? If you're not to stay here, then where are you staying?"

Vaughan tilted his head a fraction. The tip of his tongue ticked against one eye-tooth. "I've rooms arranged at the Inn."

"You mean in Reeth? Why would you choose to stay there? Why not here?"

"Bella." He descended onto terra firma and rested one gloved hand against her bare arm. "You know perfectly well why. Don't pretend otherwise, or at least, if you must argue, then do so with your brother. It does no harm to me to have folks know I'm bedding you." He squeezed slightly. "I expect you and Mr. Rushdale have plenty to say to one another, and I will only get in the way. I'll see you on the morrow. Should we need to discuss anything, we can do so then."

He pressed a kiss to her knuckles, thus prompting her to hold onto her waspish remarks. Mr. Rushdale? Since when had they reverted to such formality? She'd feared this return to her childhood home would result in developments she didn't care for, but not that she would be abandoned so soon.

She held tight to Vaughan's hand, refusing to let go.

"We'll see one another at the christening, Bella. I'm sure you're overdue for a break from me, and they do say that distance makes the heart grow fonder."

Yes, that was what she feared. Eight months had passed since he'd last set eyes on Lucerne. Their parting, for all it had been fuelled by anger, had been impassioned, and their reunion, she didn't doubt, would be equally intense. To return to Reeth, Vaughan would have to drive past the gates of Lauwine again, and what was to stop him turning in instead of carrying on? She did not want the two men to meet, and especially not when she wasn't there to witness what was said.

"Until the morrow then."

She relinquished her hold, blinking hard to relieve the stinging of her eyes. She was not the sort of pretty miss who bawled over a brief farewell.

"Pennerley." Joshua acknowledged Vaughan's departure with a tilt of his head. "My thanks for the return of my sister."

A darkling smile stretched across Vaughan's lips, accompanied by a black glint in his eyes. "Oh, I'm not returning her, Rushdale. I'm not in the least bit done with her yet."

The remark startled a squeak of laughter from her, and dampened some of her darkest thoughts. Still, she hated being unceremoniously deposited home like this. Joshua's incredulous expression didn't quite make up for the lump of anxiety embedded in her chest. She watched the handsome black and gold carriage roll away with a sense of foreboding and only turned towards the house once the carriage had become a minute dot on the horizon.

"Is this your doing?" she demanded of her brother. "Did you tell him he had to stay elsewhere? Why would you do that? You know what he is to me."

"Aye, I know it." Irritation dug deep furrows into Joshua's brow, but still he extended a hand towards her. "Come inside, Bella. We can discuss it further in comfort."

Her fists clenched. "I'm not altogether sure I want to come inside. What other nasty surprises do you intend to spring upon me? Do you intend to lock me up?"

"Bella—for all the good it would achieve. Lock you up, good heavens. The window sash would have to be nailed shut from the outside and iron bars installed, and even then, you'd no doubt climb the chimney and shimmy out onto the roof. Oh, do stop pouting and come in. Believe it or not, I am actually pleased to see you, and I prefer not to have such discussions out-of-doors."

Pleased? He had a strange way of showing it. Only, of course, she was being unfair. He was welcoming her home. He hadn't disowned her or disassociated himself from her despite the disgrace she'd brought the family name. Though what difference it made whether they quarrelled in the garden or the parlour she couldn't fathom. The servants would hear regardless. Servants universally knew everything, and the gossip would spread hereabouts in no time. Not that she cared for the opinions of their neighbours. Still, she supposed they may as well sit in comfort. And the prospect of tea and pastries was appealing.

If the exterior of Wyndfell Grange hadn't changed a bit, then the parlour had changed even less, unless it was to appear shabbier and ever more dulled with age. Soot stained the walls around the chimney breasts, and the cushions she'd badly embroidered as a girl were in dire need of a good beating. Likewise the heavy drapes that covered the bay window and her favourite seat of old.

Her former home looked as weary and brown as her brother. The years she'd been away had not been kind to either, it seemed. She supposed Joshua's concerns had been focused upon the mine, and worrying over her behaviour—the latter being entirely unnecessary—and not on the state of the household. He needed a wife, that much was very clear, a topic she would tackle at some point during her stay, but right now, they needed to iron out the riddle of Vaughan's departure.

"If you've driven him away... If he truly leaves—"

"If he meant to turn you out, he would not have gone to the effort of delivering you home. In any case, he made his intentions quite plain to anybody listening." Joshua shook his head solemnly, gaze downcast towards the hearth. "If there'd been any doubt over the nature of your association, he's spelled it out for everyone to hear."

"But—"

"Oh, do sit down, Bella."

Joshua flopped into his favourite armchair.

Bella did not sit as instructed. Instead, she craned

over the arm of her brother's chair. "If everyone is aware of our relationship, then why pretend otherwise. Why send him to the inn? Folks are hardly likely to imagine he's going to swive me right under your nose."

Her brother made a distasteful clacking noise with his tongue. "I'd prefer nobody thought of him swiving you at all. Nor is it something I want to discuss with you. Please, Bella, curb your tongue. I know he's a rakeshame, but that is no excuse for you to speak like one. And before you torture me with a continuation of your tirade, I did not send him anywhere. I expressed the opinion that it might be more appropriate if he were to reside elsewhere for the duration of the visit, but I did not force him to do so. I doubt very much that I could force Pennerley to do anything he didn't wish to do."

"You could have extended an invitation."

"For what earthly reason would I extend such a courtesy to a man who hasn't even the decency to make you his wife? You're no common chit. You're a gentleman's daughter. You can't honestly believe that this is what I wished for you. Or that Mama and Papa would have wished their only daughter to become the mistress of such a devil? I cannot think it's even what you want for yourself?"

"He's no devil, Joshua. And I love him."

The admission only intensified her brother's scowl. "What happened, Bella? You tore off with one man, a decent one I thought, and now you return on the arm of another. Years I've wasted, awaiting the promised letter announcing your betrothal to Lord Marlinscar. Imagine my surprise last November when he finally appeared on my doorstep, but instead of the conversation I hoped we were about to have, he informed me you'd parted ways, and there was no bloody sign of you."

"We did part ways." Though she didn't see why

Lucerne had thought it necessary to inform her brother of that fact. She'd written herself and informed him she was residing at Pennerley. "Things became complicated and uncomfortable between us."

Joshua was only half-listening to her. He straightened himself up, so that his chin jutted out at an angle towards her. "Do you know what Marlinscar had the temerity to tell me when I enquired about your whereabouts?"

Bella glued her lips together and shook her head. She did not need to hear it. She could well imagine.

"That he'd asked you to come home with him, but you'd refused. That it pleased you to take up with Pennerley instead. What the devil are you doing, Annabella? I thought you damn near hated the man, but now, you apparently love him? Is this what you want out of life, to be one man's mistress and then another's? What happens when Pennerley tires of you? Will you find yourself another lord? Or maybe a tradesman, or a chimney sweep? You're no young chit anymore to go fluttering your eyelashes and imagine it's enough. Who is going to keep you when I'm gone?"

"Oh, stop it, please. You've no grounds to lecture me. You may criticise, but you're hardly virtuous. How many times did you prick my maid while I still lived here? How often have you tupped her since, with no intention of making an honest woman of her?"

"I have... I have urges," he blustered. "And it's altogether different. You're the daughter of a gentleman."

"It's not different. It's the same, Joshua. It's exactly the same. As to your question, there won't be anyone else. I don't know that Vaughan loves me now, or that he ever will, but that changes nothing. I don't want anyone else." She quietened, with her arms folded, but her toe still tapping angrily. "Also," she sniped. "I have urges too, and Vaughan happens to satisfy them all. That wasn't necessarily so with Lucerne." She closed her eyes briefly and rallied her thoughts together. "I do hope you're not cross with him. My decision was not his fault. He tried. He asked..."

"But you fancied you'd win a marquis instead of a mere viscount."

"Do you honestly think a title matters to me? Oh, Joshua, nothing good would have come of it. It was not a choice I made to be difficult. Vaughan and I..." She shook her head. There was no easy means of explaining their relationship. She didn't entirely understand it herself, only that to be without him was unthinkable, and that was why she'd turned Lucerne down. In the end, she'd known she would never be satisfied as Lucerne's wife. They might have made a good go of it, but there would forever have been a part of both of them that craved what they'd abandoned. Lucerne might deny that Vaughan's name was etched across his soul, but she knew the truth. Like her, a part of him would always be enslaved to Vaughan's will.

"I hear that Pennerley and Marlinscar are no longer friends. Was that your doing?"

Bella sagged at the shoulders. She turned away from her brother and drifted from the fireside to the window seat. The intricacies of the relationship between the three of them were not easily unravelled, nor did she want to unpick them for her brother's analysis. It was difficult enough to get it all straight in her own head. In any case, Joshua was, no doubt, already acquainted with all the bawdy rumours regarding the two men, and their relationship with her, and even if he dismissed it all as hearsay, he had to realise there was far more to this than a quarrel over which man's bed she preferred to frequent.

A deep sense of weariness drove her down onto the

cushioned window perch. As far back as the winter Vaughan's thoughts had turned north to Lucerne. He wasn't here to watch the blessing of Wakefield's daughter. He'd come knowing that his presence would force a confrontation between himself and Lucerne. What the outcome of that would be was anyone's guess. She couldn't predict it. Hell, she feared most of the possibilities... perhaps all of them.

"Bella, whatever's wrong?"

Joshua appeared right before her and turned the back of his hand to her brow. "You've gone quite pale."

"It's nothing. It has been a long journey that is all. You know how much I detest carriages. If you're done reprimanding me now, please may we have some tea?"

As if the help had been loitering outside the door awaiting a cue, the maid bustled in carrying a tray of china and a freshly baked fruit loaf. Joshua poured. He had always been immensely practical. "I don't wish us to row while you are here, but I do wish you'd show a little understanding of the situation you've put me in." He passed her a cup of tea. "You must realise I've been roundly criticised for my handling of things. There are plenty hereabouts who believe I ought to have galloped straight after you when you first left, horsewhipped Marlinscar, and dragged you home by your hair. The only reason they're not here expressing their outrage that I've allowed you back under my roof without renouncing your sins and swearing a vow of chastity is that they're terrified your wickedness might be contagious. You know how the world works. So much as a whiff of scandal, and everyone is blessed with an opinion on how it could all have been handled properly."

"I don't care what they think."

"Evidently. I, however, have to live among these people. They're my neighbours. Do you think isolation in this place is what I wanted for myself? No decent woman will let me within twenty yards of her person, let alone allow me to court her. The Rushdale name is so soiled that even the Hayes sisters avoid me."

"I should have thought that was a blessed relief." She flashed him a quick smile, which Joshua surprisingly returned.

"Aye, well maybe there are a few benefits to my notoriety, but far more discomforts. I should like a companion to grow old with, and a flock of bairns to pass on my name and the mines to."

Bella curled her hand over her brother's. "I'm sorry. I ought to have made the connection." She'd somehow assumed that he'd simply chosen not to wed, not that he'd failed to attract a wife because of her behaviour. Really, it was hardly fair to blame Joshua for that. "Perhaps it's as well that Vaughan isn't our guest. Although, knowing how fickle the locals are, his presence is just as likely to attract them as see them cowering behind their drapes. People do love a good scandal to give their tongues some exercise."

"True enough. Though I pray he doesn't cause any upset. Really, if you must associate with him, it would probably be best for all if you only remain here in Yorkshire a day or two. Attend the christening, keep your promise to Louisa, and then return to the hellhole you've been hiding in with him."

"You mean his castle," she said.

Joshua squinted at her, probably thinking her fanciful.

"He really does own one, and that's where we've been cosseted, as you well know. Pennerley is the most extraordinary place. You would love it, Joshua. I just know you would."

"Would I? Well, it's not very likely that I'll see it, for reasons that are too obvious to state. In a moment we'll drop this matter, and set it aside until after Wakefield has made his visit, but I beg you before we do that you'll promise me one thing. If Pennerley does offer for you, swear you'll accept. I'll not stand before another peer of the realm and hear him report my sister blithely dismissed his suit. It was hard enough to hear the once."

Bella lowered her cup back to the saucer balanced upon her lap. "It's irrelevant, as he won't, but very well, should such a miracle occur, you have my promise that I'll accept." Vaughan was not inclined towards marriage. He had one true love in the world, and it was not her. However, if for some unfathomable reason his opinion changed, she would readily accept. Her heart would not trouble her over the prospect of marrying Vaughan as it had over the possibility of accepting Lucerne. If Lucerne had proposed in the early days of their acquaintance... Well, things would be different now. Though not, she was unreserved in admitting, necessarily better.

CHAPTER 2
VAUGHAN

V AUGHAN SETTLED AGAINST the squabs and kept away from the windows until the carriage had left both Wyndfell Grange and Lauwine Hall behind. He understood Bella's pain, her fright, but their parting of ways was entirely necessary. Placating her brother being only one reason on a list of many. Better this than having to constantly endure lecture after lecture about his intentions. As for said intentions, they would be to avoid making unnecessary declarations. More importantly, he'd made the decision to retreat to Reeth for his own benefit. He and Bella had been holed up together a full eight months. That time had not slipped by easily. Sometimes it had been damn near intolerable. They were alike in far too many ways, both full of fire, argumentative, and each determined to have their own way. Plus, he liked extremes, and risk taking. Bella brought out the worst of him. She made him crazy. He'd lost count of the number of times he'd tried to send her away. She never went, no matter how mean or cruel he was, or how far he pushed her. That tenacity perhaps explained how she'd wormed her way into his heart. Oh, the majority of it was still devoted to Lucerne—as much as he'd like to murder the man—but Bella kept on encroaching on that territory.

Time apart would definitely do them good, even if it did leave him bereft of a sparring partner and a bed mate. He sighed, and cursed as the carriage jogged over a rut in the ill-kept road. Renewing a dialogue with Lucerne would likely prove tricky, and the route back into his bed fraught with perils. Bella and Lucerne had their own issues to resolve. "I could curse you into oblivion," he mumbled aloud, speaking to the phantom of Lucerne he envisaged occupying the facing seat in the carriage. "Even understanding all your reasoning, I cannot comprehend the choices you made or the actions taken." But then, running had ever been Lucerne's preferred method of dealing—or rather not dealing—with anything that troubled him. He had run from Rome all the way to England, and from the intricacies of their relationship with Bella into Georgiana St John's arms, then most recently from Pennerley to Lauwine. Vaughan had no intention of allowing him to run again. If that meant building fortifications with which to hem him in, then that's what he would do. What he wouldn't do was imprison him. Much as his heart was devoted to the wretched idiot, Lucerne had to accept his love freely, and not only that, he needed to return it with the same level of intensity. He was not interested in a comfortable, insipid affair. Lucerne needed to match him, as Bella did. Matter of fact, Lord Marlinscar could learn a thing or two about loyalty from her.

CHAPTER 3
LUCERNE

L AUGHTER FILLED THE long silent hallways of Lauwine Hall. Squeals and giggles, accompanied by the patter of tiny footsteps now that little Louisa had begun toddling. The arrival of Wakefield's siblings to the hall meant the child's antics were no longer confined to the nursery. They had repealed instead to the salon adjoining the music room, from which came a constant hum of voices speaking, singing... After such silence, Lucerne's ears rang from the near constant cacophony. It wasn't that he disliked the camaraderie. Indeed, quite the opposite, he heartily wished for Lauwine to be forever full of such gaiety and laughter. He and Wakefield had been rattling around its vast rooms for the last eight months, too tied up in their individual griefs to even notice the dearth of company, but the last few days had changed that, and they were both a little brighter for it. Or rather Wakefield was, and Lucerne would have been, if it wasn't that the reason for their arrival meant a particular event was now that much closer.

His decision to return to Lauwine last November

had not been taken lightly. He'd known it would have deep, lasting implications, but with his emotions knotted and tried to their limits, his options had seemed hopelessly few: endure, and end up ever more conflicted inside, or create some space around himself in order to clear his head. Wakefield's plight had provided the motivation to end the stagnation, but if he'd expected time apart from Vaughan and Bella would help him to see things clearly, then he'd underestimated their hold upon him. His thoughts remained as muddled as they'd ever been. He loved and loathed them both. Wanted them with a relentless passion that raged constantly just beneath his skin, yet feared for his sanity if he so much as set eyes upon them again. A normal life, with a sensible, homely woman who could help him fill this house with the voices of countless children, wasn't that a better option, the kind of future he should be aiming for?

Maybe so, but his mind could not hold to the pursuit of such a goal. Instead it tormented him with visions of Bella in places she could not possibly be, and with the insidious whispering of Vaughan's voice in his ear coaxing him to unnameable depravities.

For months too, he had imagined and re-imagined their reunion. In one version, he was welcomed with open arms, in another, his heart smashed and trampled. All manner of possibilities existed in between, but he could not prophesize the true outcome. Tomorrow would provide him with an answer.

Of course, a public reunion was not what he wished for. It would necessitate a degree of reserve that meant none of them could be truly open about how they felt, and with masks concealing the truth, how could he be certain his assessment of the situation was accurate?

A private tête-à-tête would be far preferable, but with neither Vaughan or Bella yet arrived in Yorkshire, and the christening set for the morrow, that possibility had become an outright absurdity. Unless, of course, Vaughan were to climb in his window post-midnight and accost him in his dreams.

Mentally, he made a note to ensure the latch remained unfastened.

Good Lord, how ridiculous was he?

Vaughan was not going to come creeping into his bedchamber. In all likelihood, he had entirely dismissed Lucerne from his thoughts. There had been no communication between them since he'd turned his back and defied Vaughan's wishes by leaving Pennerley.

It had been the right choice. Hadn't he told himself so every night since?

Other choices, earlier choices, he wished he could have made over again, but not the final one. What they'd had was unsustainable.

"Yes, but what have you now, Lucerne?" He heard Vaughan's voice as though he were standing right behind him.

He refused to answer.

"Nothing. That's what. You sacrificed it all for nothing."

"I did not. I stepped aside and gained peace of mind. It was the right thing to do." The only thing he could do. For all the protestations Vaughan and Bella had made to him about one another during the time the three of them had lived together, his two lovers had only truly ever had eyes for one another. Didn't the fact that they were still together all this time after his leaving prove it?

Lucerne steepled his fingers and pressed them to his brow. He would know soon enough. The christening meant that he would have to spend time in close proximity to Bella as they all huddled around the font and swore to undertake the moral and spiritual guardianship of Wakefield's daughter. And Vaughan would no doubt attend. It was too great an opportunity to make a spectacle of himself to miss it, what with near half the county invited, and many of them attending purely to lay eyes upon the wicked marquis. They cared naught for little Louisa's welcome into the church, but did so relish a chance to gawk and gossip.

The gossip that had circulated about him and Bella, well, that alone was enough to turn the air blue. Add the mercurial Marquis of Pennerley to that mix, and what you had was an irresistible lure. It would be diabolical.

And the upshot would be that poor little Louisa would be saddled with two preposterously ill-chosen god-parents. Miss Rushdale, mistress to a Marquis, and he, an outright fool and a known reprobate. But it was Louisa's wish, and Wakefield was determined to uphold it.

At least the little mite would have one morally upstanding guardian to seek advice from in the shape of Miss Caroline Wakefield.

Lucerne started to find the lady not five steps away from him.

"Are my sisters disturbing you, Lord Marlinscar? If you require me to hush them... I know we can be quite rambunctious when we're all together, and little Louisa is proving to be such a delight it's making us all exceedingly merry."

"No. They may make whatever noise they wish."

"If you are quite sure. I did notice you've been lingering a little while."

Had he? He supposed that was true, for he was still level with the door to the Yellow Morning Room and not yet ensconced within the sanctuary of the library. Not that it was truly such. The Misses Wakefield, of which there were four—perhaps it was five— were readers, every last one of them, which made for numerous interruptions. His current companion had a leather-bound tome tightly gripped within her hand.

"I thought perhaps you were questioning whether to say something to your unruly guests."

Lucerne had played host to many unruly guests. The Misses Wakefield barely qualified.

Again he shook his head. "A building this size deserves to be filled with voices. It's been quiet too long."

"Then perhaps you might like to join us for some tea?" she offered, amusing him greatly that he should be extended an invitation to take tea in his own home.

"Perhaps another time. I have some things to attend to." He bowed his head to her, and she dipped into a curtsy in return, only she fell into step beside him when he moved on.

"I really feel we ought to thank you more sincerely for looking after our brother and his dear little one over these past months. I don't know what he would have done. He was so devoted to Louisa. It's quite tragic they had such a short time together."

"Yes," Lucerne agreed. Louisa's death had come as an almighty shock. "Though I fear you overestimate my involvement. I've done little more than provide a roof."

"Oh no." She rested her fingers lightly upon his coat sleeve. "You've done far more. You've provided him with a home. We did fear so that he would march straight into another marriage in order to provide a settled environment for the babe, and that would likely have proved foolish. Matches ought to be carefully considered, don't you think?"

"Definitely," he agreed.

"I believe he ought to marry again, don't you?"

Lucerne bowed his head. Wakefield hadn't expressed a desire to find another wife.

"I don't expect it would be a love match. I think a

person can only ever have one true love. Don't you agree? But he might make a sensible, beneficial union, in order that little Louisa might know a mother."

"I don't think even that sort of arrangement has occurred to him yet."

Her square brow wrinkled in the exact way Wakefield's did. "A man ought not to be alone all his days."

They reached the Grand Chamber and crossed its chequerboard floor to reach the library. Lucerne opened the door and let Caroline enter ahead of him. At least he believed she was Caroline, for she was the one most like Freddy and least like her other sisters, being shorter and plumper. The others were all willowy and possessed of needle sharp elbows with which he'd witnessed them assailing their brother whenever his actions met with disapproval. Hers was also the only name he had managed to remember. Perhaps there was an Eliza, and a Maria, and Josephina... nay, Joanna.

"Will you marry someday, do you suppose, my lord?" she asked, as if that were a perfectly reasonable question to spring upon a man.

He noticed that a vase of flowers had magically appeared upon his desk.

"Don't tell me, you haven't given the matter any thought." Her chuckle filled the room with warmth. "What do gentlemen find to converse upon, if not their futures?"

Anything and everything, he wanted to say to her. And sometimes nothing at all. He had thought about marriage, of course he had. He still possessed the ring he'd bought for Bella. Matter of fact... Well, never mind what he'd done with it. That wasn't an appropriate conversation to have with a respectable lady. It wasn't even thought appropriate. "Are you looking for something in particular?" he asked, heartily wishing she'd hurry up and allow him some peace. Nearly all the restoration work required upon the estate buildings had been completed, but there were several fences he intended to replace with drystone walls. Estate management had helped fill the arduously long days. In addition to the restorative works he'd undertaken, he'd also employed a butler, a housekeeper, and a decent groundsman, who in turn had each employed numerous underlings to make everything about his estate run properly. Despite the expense, he was turning a profit off the Marlinscar lands for the first time in over a century.

Lucerne settled at his desk, leaving Caroline to peruse the shelves. At least someone was enjoying the wealth of knowledge bowing the oak shelving. Besides a few favourite volumes—most of which he kept in his private chambers—he rarely glanced at the books lining the walls.

A knock disturbed him right as he dipped his pen ready to tally some figures for recent purchases.

"Come."

Wakefield entered. "Lucerne, excellent. Ho, what are you doing in here, Caroline?"

The lady hastily snatched a book from the nearest shelf.

"Lord Marlinscar kindly agreed that I could make use of his library. I was just selecting another book."

"The Horrors of Oakendale Abbey," Wakefield said, spying the spine of the red-leather bound tome. "Do not tell me you have succumbed to this gothic nonsense too?"

She jumped, and gave an uncomfortable giggle. "Of course not. I was still perusing. You know I don't care for ghosts and such things, but we should not squabble over our hosts literary tastes."

"Of course not," Wakefield agreed.

Lucerne watched them, torn between bemusement and a desire to seize the book in question and press it to his chest. The book most certainly wasn't his, but it didn't take any figuring out as to how it had come to stand upon his shelves. The book belonged to Bella.

Wakefield took possession of the book, and turned it open at the first page. "In the gloomy month of November," he read.

"Annabella Rushdale," Caroline said, leaning in to her brother's shoulder to see the pages. "Is this book not yours, then, Lord Marlinscar?"

"It would seem not," he replied. "If you leave it here, I'll have to make sure it gets back to its rightful owner."

"Well, regarding that," Wakefield stepped toward the desk, and gently lay the volume down upon the leather top. "There's a laddie come from Wyndfell. Ran all the way, or so he says. Though I'm not so certain of that given the profusion of blackberry stains around his chops. They've arrived. Pennerley and Bella are finally here. I was beginning to fear they wouldn't make it in time. Anyway, I came to say that I'm off to Wyndfell right away to run through the arrangements for tomorrow. If you could spare a while to come along—you too, Caroline—then we might stage a rehearsal. I'm sure Rushdale will stand in as the vicar."

Lucerne's fingers clawed against the blotter. "I'm sorry, Wakefield. I just don't think I can spare the time right now."

"I'll come," Caroline readily agreed. "Perhaps we could return Miss Rushdale's book for you, my lord?"

Lucerne preferred to accomplish that task himself. "Is a rehearsal entirely necessary? Aren't we all primarily required to stand by and observe? I'm certain Reverend Hindes is well practiced in the art of welcoming babes into the bosom of the church. Hasn't he wet the heads of near everyone in the parish?"

"Aye, but Louisa did have some specific requests, and I simply want to ensure everything runs smoothly." Wakefield's brows furrowed at Lucerne, as if he were the primary cause of this excursion.

I'm not the one insisting on luring together a set of people who probably ought not to be in the same space. Considerably better judgment could have been used in choosing the child's godparents, but Louisa could hardly have guessed they'd be estranged at this point.

Caroline watched them as if somehow following the silent exchange being waged. "I'll fetch my bonnet," she said, having clearly decided no progress would be made while she lingered. She sallied toward the door, turning only at the last to remark, "If you could accompany us, then you could return that book yourself."

Lucerne thumped the desktop the moment Caroline closed the door behind her. "You know damned well why I won't go to Wyndfell. I'm no longer welcome there."

"You say that, but I don't know it to be true. Admit your perceptions of several things are rather warped, Lucerne."

Freddy, dear Freddy. He would dearly like to squeeze his hands around the man's throat. Why did he insist on being so blind to the truth?

"I understand that you're riddled with guilt over how things turned out between yourself and Bella, but you're hardly the one to blame over that. Beside, even if it were so, I'm sure Joshua would put aside past indiscretions for an hour or two for the sake of my child. He is the one who sent the runner, after all."

"Aye, to inform you of his sister's arrival, no more. It was not a summons."

Wakefield conceded the point by pursing his lips.

"I know you're only looking out for your daughter, but as I keep explaining, you have things all wrong in regard to what happened between Miss Rushdale and I. It matters not that she chose another over me in the end. It was still me she ran off with in the first place. So, I'm sorry, but no, I won't set foot there without a formal invitation to do so. Joshua Rushdale has not forgiven me, and he won't, not for a very long time." If ever.

Having given this emphatic speech, Lucerne spread his hand over his face so that he covered his eyes. Truly, it was down to Rushdale's practicality that Lucerne hadn't found himself called out over his diabolical behaviour. He'd betrayed the man's trust in stealing his sister away from him, and then added insult to injury by failing to marry her. Matters were only worsened by the fact he'd been quite unable to explain precisely what had happened between them, as doing so would have caused infinitely more trouble. No man wanted to learn how his sister had been thoroughly debauched by two supposed gentlemen, who had also been sexually intimate with one another in her presence.

"Lucerne, I wouldn't ask this of you if it wasn't important to me."

"No, Freddy. I am sorry, but no." He would not be persuaded.

Wakefield slammed his hand down on top of Bella's book. "Goddamnit, Lucerne! Will you not do this for Louisa?"

Louisa was dead and buried. Whatever choices he made would have no bearing on that fact. "She asked only that I be godfather to little Louisa, no more than that, and I have readily agreed to that. Do you think it will be easy for me tomorrow, to stand by Bella in church? It will be the hardest day of my life."

Wakefield clenched his teeth so tightly, his jaw jutted out. "Blast you! It's not Joshua you're afeared of, nor Bella either. It's Pennerley. You're afraid that he's there with her, and that you'll not control your emotions, but that the taunt of seeing them together will strip away the veneer of civility from you. The bastard deserves your wroth, Lucerne. And I, for one, should prefer to see you punch him this evening than fail to control your emotions at the service tomorrow."

"I have no intention of throwing my fists around then or at any other time."

"You say that now, but how will it be when you are face to face?"

"Nothing will disrupt the christening," Lucerne said through painfully clenched teeth. "There'll be no public quarrel between myself, Joshua, Miss Rushdale, or anyone else."

Wakefield laughed at him. "You can't even bear to say his name, can you? What the devil, Lucerne! Why should you be all in knots? The man stole the woman you planned to marry and hasn't even had the grace to marry her. Instead, he openly flaunts her as his mistress. He should be the one afraid of encountering you. He deserves calling out for his behaviour."

Lucerne raised his hands in alarm. Then slowly brought them to his head. This was exactly the sort of talk he wished to avoid.

"I know how you feel about such things after the tragedy of your brothers, but the fact remains, he has slighted you, not insignificantly, and ought to be made to pay for that."

"Oh, Freddy. I should be the loser in any battle we fought." Quite aside from Vaughan being the better swordsman and the better shot, Lucerne inevitably bowed to the other man's will whenever there was conflict. The one and only time that reasoning hadn't held true was when he had rode into the night last Halloween, and the only reason he hadn't capitulated and admitted his error was down to there being several hundred miles between them. That was no longer the case.

Oh dear God. He was scared all right, but not over the possibility that Vaughan might attack him. He was afraid he might fall at the other man's feet and beg for his forgiveness, only to be rejected. The same logic applied to Bella.

He felt certain she would slap him the moment she set eyes on him, but he was not about to share that thought with Wakefield. Mayhap she would contain the urge until after the ceremony, and they could spar among the gravestones. All three of them could parley, and perhaps come to terms. Maybe then, they could reconcile in the best possible way.

Lucerne eased his way out of his seat, and stood awkwardly. Thinking along these lines tended to play havoc with his emotions, and this occasion was proving no different. Part of him desperately longed to suffer the humiliation of having to atone for his sins on his knees between Bella's thighs, and by having Vaughan fill up his throat.

The muscles of his backside clenched tightly, as he imagined the slide of Vaughan's cock into another place too.

Without a doubt, he was afraid, deeply so, but not for the reasons Wakefield imagined, but because everything he'd left behind was right here within his reach again.

He stepped awkwardly toward the door, determined to find privacy in his own chambers. Wakefield doggedly pursued him to the door. "Adhering to your own logic, there's no chance of encountering Pennerley at Wyndfell, as Joshua would not welcome him without the man having formally offered for his sister, and we both know Pennerley won't do so."

Maybe that was true, and maybe it wasn't, both in regards to Joshua's non-acceptance of the situation, and Vaughan's refusal to conform to societal norms. On the other hand, wasn't Joshua just as likely to turn a blind-eye in the hopes of securing a more preferable outcome?

Bemusement over the possibility caused him to smile. If Joshua's thoughts lay in that direction, he was certain to be disappointed. Vaughan scorned the very notion of marriage.

"Lucerne, please."

"It didn't end well, Freddy. I truly am sorry. I will serve you willingly tomorrow, but today I have to decline."

CHAPTER 4
LUCERNE

ONCE WAKEFIELD LEFT, Lucerne circled the library, too agitated to settle at his desk. He had never properly explained to Wakefield or anyone else what had really happened to sour his relationships with Vaughan and Bella. At first, it had simply hurt too much. He could hardly think of them without great pain, let alone speak of them. Then, as the months had flown, he'd realised that even if he felt able to unburden himself, he couldn't, for fear of revolting the listener, not to mention potentially digging a grave for three souls in the process. What they'd done, what the three of them had shared, it was not something society would ever condone. To the majority, an arrangement between three people was preposterous. The world operated on a system of unions between one man and one woman. Yet, variations on that theme were extraordinarily common. How many men of his acquaintance had mistresses in addition to their wives? It would be quicker to count those who did not.

"Aye," he imagined Wakefield replying, "But that is entirely different to the arrangement you engaged yourself in. See, men have appetites a delicate wife can't always be expected to accommodate, and thus other arrangements are made. It is something else entirely for a man to seek the attention of another man and a female lover and for them all to fornicate together. The notion of the men alone interacting thus is diabolical. It's quite unnatural."

Was it? He didn't know if that were Wakefield's genuine opinion, but his friend's animosity to Vaughan meant that it was always Wakefield he imagined arguing a contrary opinion to his former lover.

Vaughan believed in freedom of expression, and that love between men was as natural as that between a man and a woman. Also, that narrowing ones range to agreed societal norms was as sure a way to crush the spirit from a body as dropping a huge rock upon them.

It was true that Lucerne had known true joy while desperately in love with both a man and a woman. Hell, he remained in love with them both. There was no means he'd found of excising either from his heart. Time and distance had not achieved these things, only magnified and clarified them. However, to return to things as they had been, without resolving any of the issues, would be a horrific mistake. That didn't stop him longing for their embraces though.

Perhaps he ought to have gone with Wakefield to Wyndfell Grange and spoken to Bella. If the situation were not so awkward with Joshua and he could have been certain that only Bella would have be present, then maybe... But to risk facing them all three at once?

He clapped a hand to his head. What a fool he was! Facing them all was exactly what he would have to do tomorrow, in sight of the whole parish. And then, what if instead of hostile, stilted greetings, they chose to cut him directly?

What if he found Vaughan and Bella to be joyously happy, with no care for him at all any longer?

He'd left, in part, so that Vaughan and Bella might finally admit how they felt to one another, but hadn't it always been in the back of his mind that once they had done so they would then come and reclaim him? Vaughan had always done so before.

Had that been his grand mistake?

Lucerne swallowed the bilious lump in his throat. When decay set in, you had to act quickly to stop its spread.

"Aye, you moronic baboon, but one does not normally cut off ones own head in order to rectify things."

Lucerne spun on his heels. It seemed as if the marquis were right here in the room with him, his words had sounded so clearly. Of course, he was quite alone.

"Yes, you are, aren't you?"

In his mind's eye he pictured Vaughan lounging in the desk chair, one leg cocked up over the arm, and the sole of his boot pressed against the blotter.

"At least this way, my mind is intact," Lucerne replied snipishly. No matter that his heart lay in shreds.

"That must be why you spend so many hours talking to yourself."

Not so very many.

"It's quiet. There's no one else around with whom to converse." Their conversations tended to run more smoothly now. "Why shouldn't I take the opportunity to address all the things that ought to have been said, but never were?"

"We did say them, Lucerne. Not every conversation is conducted with words. It strikes me that your issue was that you couldn't deal with what was said."

"She loved you, and you... You loved her too. There was no room for me."

"Poor Lucerne. His whole world pivoted on its axis because, like our precious Earth, he'd been demoted. No longer centre of the universe. Yet forgetful of the fact he remained just as precious."

Lucerne raised his hand. "If that were even vaguely true."

"Do you think my heart so tiny that it cannot accommodate loving more than one person?"

"In actual fact," Bella interrupted. There she stood, leaning against the book case, one foot cocked out so that he could see her shoe, while her fingers trailed lightly back and forth over the top of her bosom. "I believe we were still debating whether you had a heart at all, and I, for one, am quite certain that you don't." She paced forward and leaned over the oak desk to reach Vaughan, and push two fingers against his chest. "There's naught but a lump of black coal in there."

Vaughan scowled, but she merely pursed her lips and blew him a kiss.

"You have more affection for your least favourite boots than you do for me. More for that sow Neddy Darleston has taken to walking on a leash."

"Miss Rushdale, you should not say such horrid things about Lady Darleston."

Bella pinkened across her cheeks, but they both tittered at the joke. "See," she said coming around the desk. "There's not a single bit of love in you. Not one tiny bit."

Vaughan grabbed hold of her and wrestled her onto his lap. "Plenty of the sort you like."

She wriggled lasciviously against him. "Not that you noticeably share. It's all talk and tease with you. Lucerne isn't nearly so stingy."

"Hm!" Vaughan pushed her away.

"And that's why I'm going to suck his cock and not yours."

"Are you, indeed?"

"Yes," she announced, twinkling mischief dancing in her eyes. "And you're going to watch."

Vaughan's lips pulled into a tight scowl. "You can't make me."

"I don't need to. But if you do, I'll kiss you afterwards while the taste of him is still all over my mouth."

Vaughan's moue, stretched into a half-smile. "Very well, get to it. Before he spoils the fun and recalls we're mere ghosts, and this is all but fantasy."

Lucerne squeezed his eyes tight shut.

Bella skipped over to him and grasped his arm, turning him so he once again faced the shelves. She sandwiched herself into the space between the books and his body.

"Bella," he murmured.

"Lucerne..." She sank onto her knees. No need for her to unfasten the frontfall of his breeches, he'd already obliged. His cock was standing ready for her. Delicate butterfly kisses teased the length of his shaft. A sly lick brushed the eye, then when he could no longer hold onto his breath, she surrounded him with the heat of her mouth. That alone might have undone him, but it wasn't only Bella he wanted.

Lucerne pressed his fist to his nose and upper lip. He sucked down several breaths, attempting to steady himself as panic threatened to engulf him. He needed them both but dared not confess it aloud.

Good and wound up now, his cock throbbed. How was it possible to simultaneously feel so terrified and aroused? When these visions first started tormenting him, he'd told himself they were his mind's way of eliminating them. But the truth was that he had no eyes for anyone else. There was no woman he wanted more than Bella, and no man who had ever turned his head besides Vaughan. If the latter were to turn up now, Lucerne would fall upon him like a man deprived of water. He'd strip him. Kiss him. Bend over and beg to be fucked. This was what he feared. Not some vague possibility of a row breaking out, but that his longing would put them all in danger.

"I want you," he whispered into the silent air. "I need you."

In his imagination, Vaughan drew up behind him, proud and magnificent, his dark hair curling into ringlets upon his shoulders and his violet eyes gleaming like amethysts. His breath whispered against the back of Lucerne's neck, disturbing the closely shorn hairs. "This craving for us both all of the time. It just won't do, Lucerne. It just won't do."

"Fuck me," he pleaded.

His prick grew stiffer still as he waited for a response.

He ought to take himself off to his chambers where he was more certain of maintaining his privacy, yet he remained rooted to the spot, wrist working furiously, while Vaughan's presence warmed the whole of his back.

When the library door creaked open, he gave a startled groan. Who? What? He froze. His hand still around his cock, stomach muscles cramped, hardly daring to breathe, while still desperate to drive his cock through the ring he'd made with his fingers and finish himself off.

"Begging your pardon, my lord." It was his valet, and not one of the Misses Wakefield. Lucerne gave an audible sigh of relief. "There's a gentleman here to see you."

Lucerne hastily fastened his breeches.

Ivo did his best to pretend there was nothing untoward about his master's actions. He was rather accomplished at the task, but then, he'd seen all manner of wild goings on during the years in London. Not only the antics the three of them had got up to, but the mayhem that abounded from the many guests they'd entertained.

Lucerne stood patiently, as his valet adjusted the line of his coat and straightened Lucerne's neckcloth. "Perfection again." He bowed from the neck and backed out of the library, leaving Lucerne to his thoughts and free to release his straining cock from its hastily constructed prison. He would attend his guest momentarily, but a private moment was necessary first. To ensure it, he turned the key in the lock. Pressed firmly against the bare wood of the door, he stroked his cock urgently. There were no voices in his head this time. His teeth bit into his lip, but beyond that, his entire focus was applied unto his prick and his quest for speedy gratification.

His stroke eased a little as he felt the familiar sensation of his semen rising up from his ballocks. Normally, he employed the aid of handkerchief to restrict the mess, but this time he paid no heed to where his spillings fell, only basked instead in the release of tension from his mind and limbs.

Spent, Lucerne lingered a few moments resting heavily against the door, waiting for the blissful sense of calm to creep over him. He was not so shivery under his skin anymore, but the sense of quiet he normally experienced wasn't there. How could it be, when he knew his former lovers to be so close?

Still, it was necessary to pull himself together. A guest sat waiting. So, he'd best get on with addressing the fellow.

Clothing straightened out yet again and hands

freshly washed, Lucerne headed across the grand chamber to the drawing room, only to discover his guest had escaped. Lucerne located him at the billiards table next door, cracking shots across the baize. He recognised the thinning pate immediately. "Aubury! I wasn't expecting you. Did you send word?"

"Marlinscar." Charles raised his head to reveal a jowly round face. "No, indeed. You don't mind the intrusion, do you? It's quite by chance I found myself this way, and I thought it might be rather jolly to stop by and see how you and Wakefield were fairing."

"Of course you did, Charles. Wakefield's not here at the moment, I'm afraid."

"Yes, your man said he'd gone off to the Grange. I must admit I'm surprised. I thought things between you and the Rushdales were strained."

"Wakefield and I aren't one and the same."

"But he's a friend staying in your house."

"It's his daughter's christening tomorrow. Louisa was quite specific in who she wanted as the child's godparents, therefore an association with the Rushdales is a necessity."

"Annabella?" Charles snickered in the back of his throat, a noise he tried to contain with his coat cuff. "She is here in Yorkshire? I thought..."

"Pennerley is also here."

The remains of the snicker dropped from Charles's face, and his hands clawed around the edge of the billiards table. "Everything I've heard said he was still in Shropshire."

"Everything you've heard is likely weeks out of date. The devil travels fast."

"Aye, but..."

"Faster than idle gossip even."

Charles straightened and smoothed a hand down over a gaudily patterned waistcoat. He'd grown rather more rotund since Lucerne had last laid eyes upon him, which would have been last autumn. Heavens, was it really that long—nearly a year ago. "Yes, I suppose that's true. You and he are still..."

Lucerne lifted his eyebrows inviting Charles to voice the rest of his question, but the other man puffed up his cheeks and bumbled nervously about. Truthfully, not one person of his close acquaintance had asked him directly what had happened between himself and Vaughan. Oh, there'd been rife speculation on the subject, Lucerne was sure, but no one had the nerve to seek the actual truth. Not even Wakefield, who could have done so with ease. In Wakefield's case, they'd rather decided between them, without saying much at all, that it was better if a true explanation of events were avoided, then neither party had to admit any uncomfortable truths.

"You and he, you were close. Everyone was very surprised. I suppose you're still at odds."

Lucerne bent lower over the cue and took his time lining up a shot. Only once he had sent the balls ricocheting around the table did he answer. "Frankly, Charles, I don't know what we are. There's been no communication between us since All Hallows Eve. Nor do I know if he intends to be at the christening tomorrow. We shall see."

Charles backed away from the table and sagged into an ancient leather chair. "Living dangerously there. I shouldn't like to leave any interaction with Pennerley to chance. One never quite knows what he'll do."

"I dare say that I know him better than most. A christening is not the sort of place he'd choose to make a scene. That's assuming he even intends to set foot inside the church. There's no specific reason for him to do so."

"You mean besides the chance to rattle the nerves of everyone hereabouts? Who else of our set is around?"

Lucerne took another shot at the balls. "Help yourself," he waved Charles toward the spirits decanter he was staring at. "No one that I'm aware of. I've not heard much from any of them. They've had matters of their own to engage them I should think, without needing to embroil themselves in my affairs."

"You mean that they're terrified of Pennerley and won't risk his ire by seeming to side with you."

"You make it sound like we're at war, Charles."

"Are you not? Here's the thing, Marlinscar. No one knows a thing. Only that one moment you're bosom friends, and the next, you cut one another dead. You don't even seem sure yourself as to what's going on. I conclude the break was his doing. Cast you aside when he grew bored of you I expect. You're hardly the first."

"You're wrong on all counts," Lucerne said. He watched Charles gulp down a glass of his best brandy. "I chose to settle here at Lauwine. Vaughan didn't dismiss me, no matter what you imagine." As a matter of fact, he'd near begged him to stay. "Nor are we generals of opposing armies."

"You're not fighting over Miss Rushdale? What? It's what I heard, is all I'm saying. Never believed there was any truth to it, of course."

"Of course," Lucerne echoed. He joined Charles in enjoying a glass of brandy.

"I said to them that was saying it, 'There ain't no truth to it. None. Pennerley and Marlinscar fall out over a woman? Utter poppycock. They'd never let a woman come between them.'"

Lucerne coughed explosively, showering the floor in droplets. "Caught me in the back of the throat," he huffed and swallowed. "And you're quite right, by the way. Bella made her own choice to stay at Pennerley when I left."

Charles eyed him sceptically, but nevertheless nodded. He returned his glass to the table and lifted the decanter again. "And as to your leaving being your decision—pish! If you walked away it's because he allowed you to. You're a fool if you believe otherwise. If he's here now, you can lay money on the fact it's because he's decided it's time to take you in hand again."

Lucerne shook his head, unwilling to put his faith in that being true. "I'm as much in the dark as to Vaughan's intentions as you," he claimed. "Are you here to stay? I think you'll find my other company most agreeable." They needed to leave behind the topic of his relationship with Vaughan. Too much speculation in that direction would only feed his insecurities about tomorrow.

"Stay? Don't mind if I do. That's kind of you to offer. What other company?"

"The Misses Wakefield."

Charles paused part way to returning the stopper to the decanter. "Wakefield's sisters are here?"

"All of them."

Charles could hardly keep the glee from his face. His attempt to do so gave him an odd pucker and emphasized the beginnings of crow's feet around his eyes. "Is he set on matching you up?" Charles asked, having given in to the grin.

Until that moment, the possibility hadn't occurred to Lucerne. Wakefield wasn't the sort to thrust one of his sisters at someone, but if a mutual affection just happened to arise through two people being around one another for a significant portion of time... Well, that he would certainly celebrate. "I'm not in the market for a wife, and Wakefield is aware of that."

"Fiddlefaddle," Charles remarked, making a dismissive gesture with his hand. "It's in the man's best interests to pair you off with one of his sisters. Relieves him of the burden, no? And tightens the ties between you."

"He's not attempting to marry me to one of his sisters, Charles. Heavens above, they're here for the christening and no more."

"But with Bella no longer in the picture, you can't tell me he's not aware of the opportunity."

"Whatever opportunity you imagine exists doesn't."

"No, of course not," Charles said, attempting another po-face. "Though I should think you're getting to an age where you ought to consider it."

Lucerne struggled to hold onto the second mouthful of brandy he'd taken. Gads! "By the same logic, you ought to be parading yourself before the society mamas."

Charles shook his head, making his jowls quiver.

He reclaimed the cue from Lucerne, as he was merely holding it rather than using it, and for several uncomfortable moments, concentrated on lining up decent shots, and the clack of balls being pushed into pockets. It was only after all the balls had found their way off the baize that he opened his mouth again. "Actually, there was a lass recently. I thought it might come to something. Decent folks, no pedigree, but I had a mind to ask for her."

"What happened?" Lucerne asked.

Charles shrugged. "We weren't right for one another. She only had a passion for my rhymes, you see, not for me. Words enthralled her, but she didn't care for the burden of living with a true poet."

"Ah, indeed, not everyone has the temperament for that," Lucerne observed. Knowing Charles, she was probably barely aware of his existence prior to him making some overblown attempt at romanticism.

"That's true. Precious few understand us. Anyway, I took myself off to Town after that, but it's all terribly dull there these days, what with Pennerley hiding in his castle, you out here in the wilds, and Darleston lying low. Matrons and chits on parade, that's it. Even Ned's uprooted himself from civilization. Staying with some fellow or other, I'm not sure where. And of course, Giles went and got himself married to that Allenthorpe girl. Can you believe it? And after all his talk of free love and the evils of matrimony. Anyway, they're completely, revoltingly besotted. Quite inseparable. It turns the stomach to see them together. Say, you did hear about Lady Darleston, didn't you?"

Lucerne shook his head. Very little in the way of news had reached him.

"They say she's gravelly ill, unlikely to survive the summer. Rumoured to be mad too. Apparently, she shot someone."

Lucerne stared at Charles aghast. "Poor Darleston," he said, meaning his friend Robert, and not his viper of a wife. He was sorry to hear the lady was ill, but she'd been responsible for a great deal of anguish. All those hideous letters to the newspapers that had left Robert in fear for his safety. He'd write to him, and let him know there was a room here for him at Lauwine if he needed somewhere to lick his wounds. Not that he expected to be taken up on the offer. Leastways, not while he remained at odds with Vaughan. Vaughan and the Darlestons went way back, and much as he'd insisted to Charles there were no sides, he couldn't for definite say Vaughan didn't think that way.

Yet again, he wondered if it might have been wiser to go to Wyndfell with Wakefield and risk Joshua's ire.

Tomorrow was going to be dashed awkward. Maybe it wasn't too late.

"Let me introduce you to the Misses Wakefield," he said to Charles. That would hopefully keep the man occupied, and allow Lucerne to slip away for an hour or so.

CHAPTER 5
LUCERNE

LUCERNE RODE AS far as the boundary wall between Lauwine and Wyndfell Grange before all the reasons he hadn't gone along with Wakefield re-occurred to him, but given he was such a short way from his destination now, he ploughed on, only to stop once the house came into sight. What the hell would he say? He wasn't actually needed. The christening didn't need a rehearsal. Everyone would know his purpose was to engage with Bella. Was that truly what he wanted? He still loved her. What had he to say to her? That he was sorry he'd left? She'd probably laugh in his face and thank him for doing so. It meant she'd got what she really wanted—Vaughan. As for that man, what had Lucerne to say to him? Nothing sensible, that was for sure.

He slipped off the horse and inched along the length of the hedgerow running parallel to the house. Maybe if he waited until Wakefield and his sister emerged, then he could ride up, and his interaction with the Rushdales and any other guests they happened to have would be short. But then, what good would simply seeing them do?

None, that's what.

They needed to talk to one another, freely, openly, without witnesses.

How that could possibly be accomplished he didn't know. He was not prone to climbing in bedroom windows.

The snap of a twig behind him caused him to turn abruptly. Two shadowy figures crept through the undergrowth towards him. "Piss," he muttered, thinking Rushdale's groundsmen had stumbled upon him. It seemed better to simply present himself and be caught on the property than to attempt any sort of action that might result in a chase or draw unnecessary attention.

"My horse has thrown a shoe," he announced, when the first figure emerged fully into view. Hopefully neither of the pair had any knowledge of such things. "I was on my way home. We'll be fine, won't we boy? This route just takes the corner off the journey."

The boy, for now that he'd emerged into the light, Lucerne could see he was just that, started and let out a shriek that brought the second figure running. "What the devil are you howling for? Do you want to get—"

His tirade ended abruptly when he too spied Lucerne. The second fellow was an older man, rake-thin with lank, greying hair that spilled from beneath a severely weathered cap. His cheeks were covered by bushy whiskers that ended either side of his mouth, leaving his chin bare.

"Lord Marlinscar." He dug an elbow into he boy's side and they both quickly doffed their caps to him. "We didn't see you just there. You gave him a proper fright appearing like that. Didn't he?"

The boy nodded.

"This aint be part of Lauwine, is it?" The older fellow asked. His tongue swept nervously over his cracked lips.

"No indeed," Lucerne responded. These pair weren't groundsmen. He'd lay money on them being poachers. It might buy him some goodwill from Joshua if he turned them over, but not enough to straighten anything out between them, and of course he'd have to make an explanation as to how he'd happened upon them in the first place.

"We were just taking a shortcut too, heading down into the village from across..." The skinny fellow turned back to look in the direction from which they'd just come. "From Arkle way. That's right, eh, Tom?"

"Absolutely," the boy agreed.

Lucerne gave them both a nod and led his horse on as if he were headed back to Lauwine. The pair followed a pace or two behind him going along with the ruse that they were all about legitimate business. Lucerne didn't inquire what was in the sacks slung over their shoulders, and they had the sense not to ask why his stallion still had four shoes if it had supposedly shed one. After a yard or two of weary plodding, Lucerne paused long enough to ensure they caught him up. "I hear Miss Rushdale has returned," he remarked conversationally. They were in sight of Wyndfell Grange now. The roughhewn grey stone building stood at the top of a bank of ling. "Is that true?"

Tom scratched his head under his cap. "I don't rightly know for definite, milord, but there was a grand carriage that passed earlier, and my cousin Will who works directly for Mr Joshua Rushdale did say they've been expecting her."

"The swell what brought her home's staying at the Dog & Basin," the other lad piped up. "Saw him go in, I did. While I was fetching back Ma Hicks's hens. Never seen anyone half so grand, not even yourself, milord. Our Annie's eyes near bugged right out of her head she was gawping so hard at him. I think she thought he was a prince out of one of those stories she's been burying her nose in. Begging your pardon, but Mrs Castleton's been teaching her her letters, though me dad doesn't see the point in it since Tom Pickett's already set his heart on her."

"But maybe Annie's not so set on Tom." Lucerne remarked. His mind whirled. Vaughan, as predicted, was not staying at Wyndfell, but in Reeth village.

"Oh, that she ain't." The boy was talkative once he had a subject. "Says he has a noddle like a big fat porker." He pushed up the tip of his nose and made a grunting noise. "But dad and Tom are close, you sees, so it's more or less settled."

He did see. The girl would get little to no say in the matter, not that there was anything to be done about it. The only way to get her out of the situation would be to find her a decent position, and he didn't know any ladies hereabouts, let alone one who would willingly take on an untrained lady's maid. Besides, if Mrs Castleton, she who had the ear of the county, couldn't accomplish anything, then he stood no chance of improving the lass's position. Paying her any sort of attention would work against her, given that he'd become known hereabouts as Lord Libertine—a despicable roué who stole away respectable daughters, only to seduce and abandon them. The only reasons he hadn't been driven out of his home by swathes of peasants was that he'd spent months mending their fences and roofs, and it was well known that Bella Rushdale had always been a wayward miss.

Mentioning her even to these pair would likely prove a mistake. Nor did he dare make any further inquiry about Vaughan, for it would surely meet his ears. Then again, might that not precipitate some action on the part of the marquis, thus relieving Lucerne of some of the burden he was carrying? If Vaughan came to him, then couldn't they reason things out?

He shook his head. There were only two likely outcomes to a meeting between himself and Pennerley: either they'd end up fighting or fucking. His body trembled with desire for both.

They reached the edge of the field and tumbled through a gap in the hedgerow onto the lane. "Evening, milord." The two men doffed their caps again, before turning towards the village, while Lucerne made a show of checking his horse's hooves. He waited until the two men were far ahead so that he might have space to consider his options. Three courses were open to him. He could continue up the lane and arrive at Wyndfell Grange by the official entrance. He could turn tail and head back to Lauwine with no one any the wiser about his actions. Or he could face the beast he now knew was residing at the Dog & Basin. None of which seemed any more sensible than the other, thus he remained idling in the lane by the way marker post, watching his stallion crop the weed riddled verges.

Four or five minutes passed until he was forced off the road by the appearance of a carriage hurtling towards him in the direction of Reeth. Lucerne led his horse onto the verge to allow the landau to pass. It was not, as the initial colours suggested, carrying the Pennerley coat of arms, but a smaller crest incorporating a griffon with a serpent in its maw that he didn't recognise. He watched it pass, only for the team of four to come to a halt a twenty or so yards later, whereupon a young man stuck his head out of the window.

"Marlinscar, is that you?"

Somewhat surprised by the greeting, Lucerne led his mount down the lane towards the speaker, who had already swung wide the carriage door and was issuing commands to the driver and his companion to see to Lord Marlinscar's mount, and for them to secure him access into the mothball scented interior.

"Crakehall?" he asked uncertainly, squinting into the evening sun in an attempt to identify the fellow. They'd been at school together years past, and were acquaintances more than friends, Stephen Crakehall being several years his junior, and a former fag of his at Eton.

"The very same." His grin engulfed his face as he clasped Lucerne's hand and tugged him into the belly of his beast, before shaking it with enthusiastic vigour. He was little changed from the spindly limbed, chinless boy he'd been at twelve, except he now sported neater attire, devoid of the multitude of dinner and boot-blacking related stains that had been a staple of his boyhood costume. "How are you? Whatever are you doing in these parts?"

"The family seat is just over the rise," Lucerne explained. The chimneys of Lauwine were just visible where the hillsides dipped to form the river valley.

"Really? Good heavens, I had no idea you hailed from this far north."

He didn't. The ancestral estate had been abandoned for years before he'd fallen upon the idea of reviving it. While his parents had still lived, they'd resided predominantly in the City, save for twelve weeks each year when they'd retire to a rambling Jacobean farmhouse in northern Herefordshire.

"What brings you this way?" Lucerne settled himself upon the cushioned seat, beside his old friend.

"Oh, ambition, for sure. I'm not one for the wilds," the sandy haired man admitted with a laugh. He applied a stout cane to the roof, to signal the driver to move on. "You know me, I like things civilized, but I'm here to barter my soul for a seat in the house. Sir Thomas Lartington—do you know him?—has a seat to be contested in the upcoming by-election, and he's taken a fancy to having me represent his interests."

"I see," Lucerne muttered, struggling to recall whether Lartington was a Whig or a Tory. He was not personal friends with the man, nor did he recall their paths having crossed, though he was aware of the name, as he was aware of all the notable families in the area. "I suppose you are on your way to Stags Fell?"

Crakehall gave him a cheery nod. "That's correct. To meet a young lady of his acquaintance, though I'm not entirely sure we're on track."

"You've come too far north," Lucerne offered him a sage nod. "Your man would have been best heading west out of Leeming. As it is you've come up to go down again."

"West at Leeming, eh? Do you know, I'm not altogether certain we even passed that way? Is that before or after Richmond?"

"Much earlier. You would have passed the coaching inn there. No matter, your destination is ahead of you now. Another hour should see you there."

"That long? Heavens. The sun will be retiring before we do. Still, it's good to know we're on track."

"You mentioned a lady," Lucerne prompted him.

Crakehall's mouth cracked wide into another smile. "That's right. Matrimonial shackles are the price of my folly." He threw Lucerne a wink. "At least she's a beauty, so I'm told."

"So you're marrying into the family. I didn't know Lartington had any offspring. Is it a niece, perhaps?"

Crakehall squeezed his lips between his fingers. "No, my fortunes are not risen so high as that. The lady in question is the eldest daughter of one of the burgesses. The price of his support, I understand."

"Ah, I see." Clearly Lartington had the borough in his pocket, save perhaps for this particular gentleman, but every man had his price. "Well, I do hope the lady is everything you might wish her to be. You must call upon me at Lauwine and introduce her, once you've made it official."

"That's most kind of you. There's no Lady Marlinscar as yet?"

Lucerne shook his head. "And no plans afoot in that regard." He did not elaborate.

"I must say, Marlinscar, I am surprised. I swear there were rumours you'd been snatched up by some northern heiress at one point. I suppose that must have been a year or two back. Some relation of that friend of yours... Pennerley, that's the fellow. All nonsense cooked up by the gossipmongers, I suppose."

"Many's the gentleman who's been shackled by thoughtless tattle," Lucerne remarked, allowing his gaze to stray towards the window. His name had indeed been attached to a certain lady's, specifically, the one whose home he had just been idling outside. Moreover, this was not a topic he much cared for. Any association of his name with Bella's or Vaughan's instantly put a bee in his breeches. Questions were inevitably asked that he hadn't any answers to. He couldn't rightly confess to having had an intimate relationship with Vaughan, and confessing to one with Bella didn't paint him or the lady in a terribly flattering light. No, it was best he simply avoided the subject with any but his closest friends, and even then... well, Charles's poking his nose into the matter earlier had made him want to flee the county.

"Of course, you're quite right," Crakehall agreed. "I

suppose you've heard that the Pope and Napoleon have signed a concord."

He hadn't. "So France is catholic again."

"In a fashion. At least while it suits Boney's interests." They discussed the continuing quarrel with France until they reached the crossroads, at which point, Lucerne bade Crakehall farewell with a promise that they would catch up again soon.

CHAPTER 6
BELLA

B ELLA HAD BARELY recovered her outward
composure by the time the party from Lauwine
arrived. Still, she was hard pressed not to
release a strangled gasp, when Lucerne was not among
the number of callers. She had no wish to encounter
him, but his absence raised additional concerns. Not
only would their reunion now be in public, rather than
in the privacy of her childhood home, but it was
distinctly possible that he and Vaughan were renewing
their acquaintance at this very moment while she was
not around to witness it. Not that her presence would
change a thing, but at least if she was there, she'd be
cognizant of the facts. Standing in the shadows waiting
for events to unfold did not suit her at all.

Wakefield was gaunter than she recalled. They had
not set eyes upon one another since the day he'd wed
Louisa. The beginnings of salt and pepper wings flecked
his hair, and several deep worry lines had etched
permanent grooves into his brow. Still, he remained
moderately handsome, in a steady, ordinary sort of
way. Distinguished, Louisa would have insisted.

"Rushdale, it's good to see you again." Despite being close neighbours, her brother and the captain clasped hands and shook robustly, as if they'd not clapped eyes on one another in months. Perhaps that was so. After all, if Joshua and Lucerne were at odds, then Wakefield might keep his visits to a minimum, given he was depending upon Lucerne's hospitality. It was yet another means by which her actions had isolated Joshua. It was a wonder he had not decided to lock her away in the attic in order to resurrect his social standing. The folks hereabout would love that. Mayhaps he had it planned for after the christening.

Would Vaughan stage a rescue?

Only perhaps once he'd tired of other distractions.

Except he would never tire of Lucerne.

"Your daughter?" Joshua asked.

"Doing admirably." The joy with which Wakefield spoke of little Louisa, eased away some of the worry lines. "She's getting into no end of mischief now she's walking, and I'm afraid her aunties are quite encouraging it. You'll see her tomorrow. She's the image of Louisa, though a mite more rambunctious."

"Spirited?" Joshua stole a glance in her direction. "You'd best start laying firm boundaries."

"Aye, she's a whirligig all right, but a truer delight there never was."

Louisa had possessed more strength than people gave her credit for.

"How about yourself? Are you well?" Wakefield asked.

"Very. I have the mine to keep me busy."

"Of course. It's still…"

"Productive, yes. Things couldn't look better in that regard, but you're not here to talk industry, but of tomorrow."

"Yes. I thought if Miss Rushdale wasn't too tired

from her journey that we might run through the ceremony. It's unfortunate that Lord Marlinscar couldn't make it, but Caroline is here with me. Forgive me, you've not yet been introduced. Caroline, this is Mr Rushdale, and his sister. And this is my second youngest sister, Miss Caroline Wakefield."

"Pleased to meet you, Mr Rushdale. Miss Rushdale." The lady in question stepped forward and dipped into a polite curtsy. She was much shorter than her brother, but otherwise much like him in both colouring and features. "I've heard so much about you both."

Poor Joshua, a scarlet blush lit up his cheeks. "It's unfortunate that one does tend to get mentioned hereabouts more often that one would like," he huffed.

The attic was looking to be an increasing likelihood.

"Oh, I only mean that you are Lord Marlinsar's closest neighbours, and friends of my brother's, it's a joy to make your acquaintances at last. Although—" She leaned closer so as to whisper. "If there's scurrilous gossip I'd prefer to hear it directly."

"Caroline!" Wakefield tugged her back to a respectable distance. "Please do try to curb your enthusiasm for nonsense. I'm sorry, should we start?"

Bella covered her mouth with her hand to hide her smirk. Caroline Wakefield would certainly liven things up. She endeavoured to like her immediately. "I'm Bella," she said, extending her hands towards the other woman. They embraced lightly and exchanged kisses as though they were old friends.

"I know of you from Louisa's letters. She wrote of you often."

"You were acquainted?"

"Briefly, before that disastrous expedition to India." She quietened and shot a scurrilous glance at her brother. "She really ought never to have gone," she added, having determined that his attention was elsewhere. "She was far too delicate for such climes. But let us not dwell on past miseries. By some twist of fate, we are to be given the moral guardianship of Leesa tomorrow, and you may not be aware of it yet, but Freddy is working himself into all sorts of conniptions expecting a crisis when there won't be one. Christenings are hardly known to be drama filled affairs."

Clearly, Wakefield hadn't enlightened her as to the reason for his worries.

"It's as if he expects a bolt of lightning to halt proceedings, or a riot, or the font water to freeze."

"The latter's not unheard of," Bella remarked. "The tiny church is bitterly cold in winter, and often freezes. But never yet in July. I'm sure everything will be well."

"You don't know of a reason for his anxiety."

Bella shook her head. "I certainly don't intend to cause any discord, and I can't see that anyone else would do so at a christening either." She voiced her opinions loudly enough so that she was sure Wakefield heard. "Let's do this. What is it you want us to practise?"

The next twenty minutes passed rapidly, Bella and the others following Wakefield's instructions to the letter, while Joshua stood in for both the vicar and Lucerne. Really, there was so little required of them that a rehearsal was hardly necessary. Bella was quite certain Reverend Hindes would have shuffled them into order without one, but it hurt no one to humour Wakefield's wishes. It also gave her the opportunity to ensure that Miss Wakefield would be positioned between her and Lucerne.

"Must you hurry off immediately?" Bella asked when the rehearsal reached an end, and Wakefield seemed intent on making haste. "Some refreshment, or perhaps a turn about the garden. It's such a pleasant evening after all."

"I'm not sure we have time for that—"

"I should like that," Caroline interjected. "Would you show me, Mr Rushdale? Don't be so dour, Freddy. We must wander that way in order to reach the horses."

"Yes, well, I guess that's true."

Caroline and Joshua wandered a little ahead, the former making numerous forays off the cracked pathway to point out various flowers amongst the borders. Wyndfell's garden still played host to more wild flowers and weeds than anything deliberately cultivated. There was an overabundance of both common mouse-ear and yarrow, not to mention rather a lot of Yorkshire fog creeping into what had formerly been her attempt at a herb garden. Really, things had suffered at the lack of a feminine hand.

Wakefield stayed Bella's progress as they rounded the corner of the house. "Where is he?" he demanded. "Pennerley. You arrived with him. Where is he now? I'm satisfied that you don't intend to cause any disruption tomorrow, and Lucerne intends none, but I've no assurance that the same is true for that riotous bastard."

"I hardly think he intends to cause a to do in church, Wakefield."

"You might not think it, but I put nothing past the man. What does he intend, Bella? Why is he here?"

"He accompanied me home. Beyond that, your guesses to his whereabouts and purpose are likely as accurate as my own."

"I find that difficult to believe. What the devil happened, Bella? After every letter Louisa received from you, she anticipated word of your betrothal to Lucerne; instead I returned to England and discovered you'd abandoned him for that despicable rogue instead.

I could never understand Lucerne's tolerance of the fellow, but for you to choose him over a good man—"

"Clearly you know nothing of anything. Lucerne abandoned me long before I made my choice." She paused, and grit her teeth in order to resist the urge to let spill the tide of emotions she was struggling to hold back. "I tell you truthfully, it will be deuced awkward to stand by Lucerne tomorrow at the font, but I'll not quarrel with him. What's in the past is done, and there's no changing it. But I cannot speak for Vaughan. What animosity or affection that exists between he and Lucerne is a matter for them to determine."

"But if you spoke to Pennerley..."

"Do you really imagine that would achieve aught? Let me assure you, my influence is minimal."

"I'm sure you are underestimating yourself."

She laughed. How little Wakefield truly knew Vaughan, if he honestly believed that were the case. "If that were so, then he would not have arrived alongside me and departed without me within the space of a heartbeat."

"But you must be aware of his plans."

Bella shook her head, and began walking again, so that Captain Wakefield had to jog to catch up. "I have no knowledge of his plans whatsoever. It would not surprise me if he were to seek out Lord Marlinscar at some point, but I find it unlikely that he'd do so at your daughter's christening. A private tête-à-tête is more likely." Unless Vaughan meant to upset things out of spite, or to intentionally rile Lucerne. He was not one for gossip, but sometimes he liked to create it. "Perhaps they are communing even now."

A look of intense horror washed across Wakefield's face, deepening those already well-worn grooves in his brow. He overtook Bella on the path and reached the stable yard as Joshua was helping Caroline into the saddle. Wakefield wasted no time in getting astride his own mount. "I pray not," he remarked as he turned the horse's nose towards the lane.

Likewise, Bella silently added. She remained heartsore and vexed at Lucerne over his past behaviour, and now he was surely going to steal Vaughan away from her. Nay, there would be no competition between them, for Lucerne already possessed Vaughan's heart.

She had witnessed their separation. She alone beside the two men knew how deep their feelings for one another ran. If their paths had indeed crossed, then surely more than words would already have been exchanged. They had never been able to keep their hands from one another. If Wakefield returned to Lauwine and discovered them together, it was as likely that he'd find them fucking as engaged in fisticuffs, and that was something she really did not want occupying her thoughts. Nevertheless, the possibility troubled her for the remainder of the evening, and well into the small hours.

CHAPTER 7
LUCERNE

ONCE CRAKEHALL'S CARRIAGE was out of sight, Lucerne mounted his stallion again. He had come some distance out of his way, thanks to his unanticipated carriage ride, but the canter back would, he hoped, help him clear his head of all the nonsense swirling about in there. More than ever, he needed to think clearly about what he wanted, and how best to achieve it.

The evening air was clammy and thick, with little in the way of a breeze. Yet heavy clouds were drawing in by the time he reached the little church where the christening was to take place the following day. Lucerne urged the horse over the low curtain wall of the graveyard, intent upon utilizing the short cut, and yet he found himself trotting along at a mediocre pace, rather than riding like the devil to avoid the coming downpour. A storm would leave everything feeling fresher. Not for the first time, he wondered if a similarly violent clash might set himself, Vaughan, and Bella back on the correct path. At the very least, the opportunity to vent everything he was feeling and had felt over the last eight months might rid him of the crippling anxiety in his soul.

As long as that clash didn't occur tomorrow. He did not want little Louisa's christening to be overshadowed by scandal. Thus he had to hope that Vaughan would keep his distance a while longer. Bella would not cause a scene. Louisa had meant too much to her to disrespect her friend's memory. They'd been the dearest of friends since childhood.

With Louisa in mind, Lucerne found himself moving in the direction of her grave. A bouquet of fresh flowers already sat before the headstone in a pewter vase.

It was as Lucerne straightened after paying his respects, that he saw him—leaning negligently against the side of a sepulchre, coat collar raised to offer a little protection from the rain that had already soaked his dark hair.

Vaughan's gaze met his as though this assignation were planned.

Ha – as if anyone would choose to meet in a churchyard in the rain besides a poet. A poet might. They were sufficiently crackbrained.

Lucerne's grip tightened around the horse's reins.

How was he here? Had he been followed from the outskirts of Reeth? Nay, he'd have been aware of someone behind him on the road. The simple answer was that chance—fate, if you will—had brought them together. He glanced down at the grave, and knew at once that it was Vaughan who'd brought the flowers. He'd always held a soft spot in his heart for Louisa.

Their gazes met again. Lucerne swallowed slowly. There was no avoiding this. He couldn't simply turn and walk away. Vaughan would never tolerate such a direct cut. They would have to speak. Lord knew, part of him desperately wanted them to communicate, and on a much baser level than via dialogue, but he would not race forward and swaddle Vaughan in an embrace, nor kiss him so that their lips were left bruised. He wouldn't grab his arse, or pin him tight against the stone casket at his back. Nor fall to his knees, or drop his breeches and offer himself up so they might rut like animals.

Instead, he pulled his shoulders back and plodded over to Vaughan so that they stood face to face.

It had been eight months, yet his heart was galloping and his innards twisted in so many knots it might only have been minutes since he'd stormed out of the solar at Pennerley, having ended their relationship. All the boiling rage, the injustice, turmoil and heartache he'd felt then swelled again. He had done the right thing in leaving. He would not apologise.

Leaving Vaughan and Bella to work things out, coming north, coming home to Lauwine and Wakefield had been the right thing to do – the sane thing to do. Did he have regrets? Of course. There were plenty of things he wished he could go back and do differently, but he wasn't here looking for forgiveness.

"Vaughan." His voice gave way under the strain of even that. There remained too much that needed to be said but couldn't really be put into words.

"Lucerne." He received a nod in return.

They would act like gentlemen. Civil, ordinary gentlemen – exchange pleasantries, shake hands, and walk away, keeping all the turmoil that existed between them locked away inside.

"You're not at Wyndfell with Bella."

The observation met with a predictable elevating of Vaughan's eyebrows. "That would be asking a little much of Joshua Rushdale, don't you think?"

"She's formally your mistress, then?"

Vaughan laughed. He reached up and covered his

lips with his thumb. "Regretting the decision to let her go?"

Every damn minute of the last eight months.

"It was Bella who let me go, not the other way around."

The smirk that lifted the edge of Vaughan's mouth caused his fists to clench.

"Is that why your bed's still empty – still smarting from the dismissal?"

He could almost level a similar accusation at Vaughan, but he refrained. "Who I choose to occupy my bed is none of your concern."

Vaughan's smirk transformed into a sneer. "Wakefield's a dire disappointment, I imagine."

"Leave him out of this."

"All this time living on your gratitude, and I bet he hasn't got on his knees for you even the once."

That was an image he did not even care to have in his head. His interest in Wakefield had never been of that nature. He had never had any interest in any man besides Vaughan. He alone had turned his head and made him question everything he knew.

"He is my friend, and it hurts me not at all to support him and his child. Lauwine is awash with empty rooms."

"Not entirely empty," Vaughan continued to tease. "I did hear that the Misses Wakefield are also in residence. He's moved his whole family in. No doubt one of them will be obliging soon enough, and then they'll be a permanent fixture."

With a half-supressed sigh, Lucerne turned towards his mount. "Neither they, nor their brother, have designs upon my person, and they are respectable ladies. Not the sort to dally with a gentleman in order to secure their future."

"Then they're most unlikely to turn your head. Still,

you must admit, it's the predominant reason a man would surround another with all four of his unwed sisters."

"They're here purely for the christening." That they had arrived three weeks early and intended to remain another four was neither here nor there.

"Of course." Vaughan clapped a hand against his thigh. "How silly of me to think otherwise. I wager one is already ahead in the stakes. Not perhaps the oldest or prettiest, but the one with a modicum of wit and a knack for effortlessly inveigling her way into your company. You'll be trussed up before you know it."

Lucerne shut tight his lips. He would not allow himself to be riled, even while Caroline's name echoed in his head. In any case, he had no genuine objection to the idea of matrimony. In fact, providing it was with the right woman... Well, never mind. The right woman was no longer interested in him, assuming she ever truly had been. He'd missed his opportunity. "I trust you've no plans to attend tomorrow," he said instead.

Vaughan coughed and pushed away from the sepulchre. "It's true. I've no interest in seeing water poured over a baby's head. Although, I suppose there's some entertainment to be had in seeing it cursed with two hopelessly immoral moral-guardians."

"You don't intend to accompany Bella?" Lucerne asked, choosing to ignore yet another slight, because there were merits to the argument.

"That is what I just said."

"It was Louisa's wishes, that we be godparents to her daughter."

Why – why could he not help himself, and keep his mouth closed.

Because you're desperate to drag this impromptu meeting out as long as possible, because you're still hopelessly in love with this devil of a man. There is nothing that you haven't let him do to you, and that you wouldn't like him to do to you over and over again.

Now he was being harsh on himself. He did miss what they'd had dreadfully. There was part of him that would be forever Vaughan's, but he did have limits. He'd proved that when he'd insisted on space.

"Much as I liked her, she did always show questionable judgement. Marrying that dolt of a soldier being a prime example."

"They were deeply in love, and perfectly suited to one another. Besides, you practically made it happen."

Vaughan shook his head as though Lucerne were moon-touched. He wasn't. He might not possess any evidence, but he knew Vaughan had had a hand in manipulating events so that Louisa and Wakefield's marriage had come about. Of course, he'd done it for her and not for Wakefield. Still, while Lucerne couldn't precisely pinpoint where the animosity between his two oldest friends initially came from, he understood well enough that Vaughan considered Wakefield responsible for his wife's death. In less chivalrous moments, he'd thought the same. It had been foolhardy taking such a delicate woman to India with the regiment, but the young couple had been in love, and unwilling to spend what might have been years apart. At least the time they had spent together had been happy. He could not claim to have experienced anything similar. His time with Vaughan and Bella had been tumultuous from beginning to end.

Then why in hell's name do you crave it so?

He'd sought the answer to that question the entire time they'd been apart, and for years and years before they had both become intimately embroiled with Bella and one another. His only conclusion was that there was no rational explanation for how he felt. He was more or less addicted to the man, and there was no weaning himself from him. Avoiding contact didn't lessen his desire. If anything it made the cravings stronger.

"Lucerne."

The soft purr of Vaughan's voice almost right by his ear made him realise he had been staring at the stallion's shoulder for several minutes. The breeze ruffled the back of his hair, but it might also have been Vaughan's breath. Lucerne turned cautiously. Barely an inch sat between them. He looked straight into Vaughan's violet eyes. Time froze for a minute. His chest rose and fell rapidly, straining the fabric of his waistcoat and coat. Still, he remained breathless. He did not recall dropping the reins or the stallion moving out from behind him, but when Vaughan reached out and he jerked backwards, he found himself trapped, pressed tight to an eight foot stone cross.

It was as if every cell in his body became alert at once. Oh God, please! He wanted this with every inch of his being. That made him a desperate, foolish wretch, make no mistake, but... when had he ever been anything else? Please. Lucerne's heart welled up into his throat. His lips tingled with need. The anticipation – lord, the anticipation! Shivers raced up and down his spine, his nipples were like rocks beneath his shirt, and something else was growing increasingly tumescent too.

Vaughan's mouth hovered inches from his own. "It's been good seeing you again. We must indulge in more of these chats. Good evening, Lucerne."

No. No. It was impossible. He couldn't walk away. They hadn't even kissed. Christ and all the angels, they hadn't even kissed!

Only that was precisely what Vaughan had done. He was gone, leaving only the wind-blown church gate screeching on its hinges.

Lucerne did not move. He did not run screaming down the lane after Vaughan, nor tear at his coat or shove him into the hedgerow so that they might tumble amongst the grass. He remained paralysed, the cold of the stone chilling his back.

Suddenly the world seemed frighteningly desolate. The flowers – rain sodden now – no longer looked quite so fresh. Nevertheless, Lucerne bowed to his knees and plucked one of the blossoms from the bouquet and wrapped it inside his handkerchief, before stowing it inside his pocket. He ought to have foreseen this. That in leaving Vaughan and Bella to discover one another, his position in their friendship would become obsolete.

What had he done? Was his future indeed as Vaughan suggested, to wed Caroline Wakefield, and to live a tolerable existence from now until death do us part? That wasn't the future, the life he wanted at all.

He wanted a family; love, lust, exuberance, indulgence...craziness, obsession, monstrousness – sweet searing pain. He wanted those moments of complete connections, no inhibitions, no barriers, three souls, three bodies entwined as if they were one. The highs and the come downs, the nights of no sleep and overindulgence, his throat so hoarse he could barely talk and his arse equally tender.

He wanted gentleness, security, a place inside two hearts that beat to the same rhythm as his own. And offspring... someone to remain after he was gone, a product of all this raw, unbridled passion, someone who would know that it was possible to love more than one person to the depth of your soul, because they'd witnessed it every day. That's who their parents had been.

"I want you, you stupid bastard," he hollered. "I love you. I always flaming did. And I want Bella too."

The rain had soaked through every layer of his clothing by the time Lucerne reached Lauwine, but not even that had dampened the fire Vaughan had lit inside him. After all this time, he had never once thought that Vaughan would simply walk away like that. It was not the reunion he'd hoped for, nor the one he'd feared.

It was crystal clear in his mind now what he did desire. How to get it—that was a dilemma for another time.

Lucerne staved off interacting with his various guests and headed straight into the wing that housed his private suite of rooms. Ivo, his valet, let out a yelp of alarm on seeing him. "I'll fetch towels. Arrange water for a bath."

"Leave me."

"But my lord."

Lucerne ushered his bewildered valet into the corridor, and locked the stout doors firmly behind him. Trembling he might be, but he could peel his own clothing from his skin. Besides, the thought of anyone's hands other than his own upon him right now was intolerable, unless...

There were too many memories burned into the weft of this room. Right there, he had first tumbled with Bella before the fireplace. And there, he and Vaughan had smashed a vase while wrestling for dominance. Vaughan had been the victorious one. Vaughan always was; Lucerne inevitably subjugated to his will.

Don't kid yourself that isn't what you wanted.

Indeed. Why wouldn't he bow to someone prepared to deliver exactly what he wanted? For certain, Vaughan believed in delayed gratification, but he always delivered in the end. The journey, while torturous, was without exception also delicious. All these thoughts, these layers of memories, they weren't helping at all.

Lucerne hurried on, passing into the bed-chamber. Again, he turned and locked the doors behind him. A low banked fire was alight in the grate. Lucerne hurried to it, shedding his outer layers. He left them discarded over various furnishing. Shirt, under-breeches, stockings; every single item he had on was soaked through. He stripped naked. Kindled the flames in the grate, and finally sank onto the floor by the hearth where he lay on his back staring up at the gloom of the ceiling. In his mind's eye, he was back outside in the graveyard, Vaughan before him. Their heads angled, mouths parted, ready to touch. He was so very ready to feel that touch.

Lucerne closed his hand around his risen prick. Vaughan once again pulled away from their almost kiss before it had been fulfilled. Only this time, he didn't vanish into the night, but sank gracefully onto his knees. He spoke no words as he dealt with the layers of Lucerne's clothing. Words were unnecessary. Vaughan's mouth engulfed the whole of Lucerne's shaft. This was how Vaughan had first displayed the depths of his affections. Before that, the idea that two men might find such incredible joy together had been anathema to Lucerne, but that had simply been down to a matter of doctrine. Not everything one was taught was true. And sometimes, one had to experience a thing directly to know its value.

"Yes," he hissed, his strokes quickening, as he imagined pushing deep into Vaughan's throat. His lover showed spectacular skill in this area, a skill Lucerne thoroughly appreciated. Although he made a point of not enquiring into how Vaughan had acquired it. He didn't want to think of him with his sensual mouth wrapped around another man's cock. Right at this moment, he did not even want to imagine him with his mouth upon Bella, an act he had witnessed countless times.

Their first time, all three together, had been in the billiards room downstairs. The pair of them possessing her at the same time. He had never rightly understood why Vaughan had initiated that encounter, but understanding Vaughan was...well, it involved twisting ones mind in strange directions, and he could change his mind on a whim.

"If you're going to poke at me in this way, I won't be giving you the poking you're obviously gagging for."

"You're sucking me, not—Ooh!"

"I'm not what, Lucerne?"

His buttocks clenched, while his prick wept copious pearls into his hand as he imagined Vaughan holding his legs aloft, poised ready to penetrate his arse.

"Confess; a good fuck is what you really crave. You're horny, and you've no means of relieving yourself of the itch other than by your own hand. It's not love you want from me. It's a good arse pounding."

"I'm in love with you."

"All you want is satisfaction." Vaughan's wetted thumb swirled around the puckered entrance to his arse. A single finger penetrated him. Then two... then three.

Fuck, that felt good. His hand slid with possessed fury along his prick.

"Aren't I allowed to love you and want you to fuck me silly?"

Vaughan pushed inside him, and Lucerne began to come at once.

"Oh, fie! You really have missed me, haven't you?"

"More than you will ever realise." He sobbed his orgasm into the air, turning it blue with curses and endearments.

"Or maybe I understand more than you think, and I just enjoy making you suffer."

"Why would you do that?" And, if this was suffering, then he'd take more turns at it than it was possible to count. "That's an odd way to show your love."

"Might I remind you, that you're the only one bandying that particular four-lettered word about?"

Yes, he was. Declarations weren't really Vaughan's style. He spoke via his actions.

"Do you really not love me anymore?" Lucerne was spent; exhausted and breathless, with a sticky hand and a pink haze clouding his vision, but there was still a warm glow inside of him.

"Are you absolutely certain I loved you to begin with?"

Yes. Yes, he was. As sure as it was possible to be.

He fully admitted he'd lost sight of that fact for a time, but deep down he'd still known. All he'd really wanted were reassurances.

And he'd been given them.

Looking back, he could see that too. Alas, at the time, he'd been too blinded by jealousy to recognise them for what they were. His fleeting sense of peace deserted him again. What a dire mess he'd made of everything. He'd feared being alone, and here he was, alone. There was no warm body to snuggle against, no one to hold him close, only the pool of his own spendings drying upon his skin.

Mouth twisted with distaste, Lucerne wryly mopped the mess from his hands and stomach. Good lord, was there ever such an enormous clot as he?

CHAPTER 8
BELLA

B ELLA ROSE TO a dreary grey morning, the thin fissure of green of the surrounding heathland buried beneath a sea of swaddling mist. Even the welcoming scent of hot chocolate, settled upon the little table before the fireside, couldn't quite coax a smile from her. That delicious little treat was courtesy of Joshua, no doubt. He was trying. God help him. She even appreciated his efforts. The chocolate did thaw out her core, and revive her from the lingering lethargy remaining from the journey home, but the niggling prickle of fear running beneath her skin couldn't be so easily overridden. Disaster had struck the last time she and Vaughan spent a night under separate roofs, and though she knew he was only a short ride away in the coaching inn at Reeth, her stomach still churned over the insufferable distance that she sensed growing by the minute.

It would not be for long. Once the christening was over, there was nothing to hold her here. Joshua might claim that Wyndfell remained her home, but it no longer felt that way. While nothing much had changed, and it all remained so achingly familiar, she sensed she was out of step with her surroundings. If anywhere was home now, then surely it was Pennerley, or indeed, wherever else Vaughan laid his head. She would follow wherever he went, near or far, to the ends of the earth if need be.

"It'll brighten, Miss," Tilly, the new maid—Emma, her predecessor, had departed six months back to wed a haberdasher's son from over Castle Bolton way—remarked, mistaking her consternation for concern over the christening. "Don't you go fussing yourself and getting all in a glower. It'll be glorious by ten o' clock. Soon as the sun's up proper, it'll chase all this nonsense away."

If only the arrival of the sun could chase away all her doubts about today. Would the devilish Marquis of Pennerley even put in an appearance? Of course. He would not miss the opportunity to see Lucerne. Her stomach sank into her boots, as she pictured herself huddled around the church font with the vicar and Miss Wakefield, and Lucerne not a foot away from her.

Ever since the night of the phantasmagoria, she'd nimbly pushed Lucerne from her thoughts. She knew what lay in Vaughan's heart. He meant them all to be reunited, but she did not see how that could be. Events had weathered them all. They could not so easily pick up the pieces of the past and begin anew. Truths had been spoken, decisions made. She might sometimes miss the times they'd had together in London, but she did not crave Lucerne's presence in her life again. She had made her choice, Vaughan, and would make the same choice again now, if everything were made over. It was not that she didn't still harbour feelings for Lucerne, of course she did – that's why this upcoming meeting with him would prove so challenging – it was that he had not been who she thought him to be. She'd imagined him loyal to the core, but that was not true. He had sought affection outside of their merry triad. He had broken them all to pieces, and come to them only as the harbinger of death, not as a penitent seeking absolution. Death and destruction, that's what she thought of now when her mind wandered in his direction. Of course, she did not attribute Louisa's demise to Lucerne, and he had clearly done all within his power for Wakefield and dear little Louisa, but, she could not forgive, not so easily, especially knowing how deeply Vaughan's affections for him ran.

They had come here to Yorkshire, and she knew in her guts that Lucerne would break her heart anew. He would not do so intentionally, but it would happen all the same. He would take Vaughan from her, and she would be left with nothing but the blemish to her reputation.

"Miss, are you well? You've gone quite pale."

Tilly was all of sudden right by her, holding onto her arm as if she expected Bella to faint dead away.

"I'm weary," Bella allowed the weathered, wiry little maid to guide her into an armchair. "I do detest carriages, and we were travelling for an insufferably long time."

"I expect that's it, Miss. Pennerley—that's the Marquis's place isn't it?—I suppose it's more than a canny way. Near to the other side of the country I hear. I think anyone would be wrung out by such a journey. Now, I believe cook has made a banquet, but is there anything particular you'd like for me to ask her for, besides the chocolate, that might restore your spirit?"

"Nothing," Bella insisted. Not when her agitation had her in such an iron grip. "And you may leave me and go about your tasks. I'll dress in a little while."

~*~

A bright, disconcertingly yellow sun had burned away the earlier mist, as predicted, by the time Bella slid from the back of her hopelessly ill-tempered mare. In Bella's absence, the horse had clearly been overfed and under-exercised. However, she had outright refused to climb inside another carriage, especially anything as frightfully rickety as the one her brother owned, the interior of which smelled of saddle dubbing and axle-grease. Regardless, the route to the ancient parish church was far more direct upon horseback, thus allowing her to stave off the inevitable meeting with Lord Marlinscar a fraction longer by not departing Wyndfell until the latest possible moment. She had quite decided to cement the dissolution of their friendship by reverting to the use of his formal title. They would refrain from the intimacy of Bella and Lucerne, and she would become Miss Rushdale, and he Viscount Marlinscar. That was proper. Sensible.

The man in question had taken up a position right outside the church door, making it quite impossible to avoid him. His shadow spilled over the worn steps, and the sunlight splashed streaks of pure gold through his blond hair, making him glow like a gift from God. As ever, he was immaculately attired. Lucerne—Lord Marlinscar – she immediately corrected herself – had never adhered to the fashion of affecting a slovenly appearance, but rather one of rigid elegance. Today, he'd dressed in a pale grey cloth, which by rights ought to have drained any sort of colour from his skin, but the effect was quite the reverse. He seemed more alive, more vital then she had ere seen him, save perhaps that first time when she'd spied upon him swimming.

No matter. His vitality and vigour changed nothing.

Bella heaved a sigh. Her nose tingled, a sure sign of her vexation. She didn't want to confront him. She didn't want to have anything to do with him at all, not even pass him by. And she most assuredly didn't want to stand elbow to elbow with him inside the church, but she was here, as promised. Louisa had bid her take care of the moral guardianship of her child, and so she would act as bidden.

"I understand Louisa's sentiments behind this folly, but Wakefield must realise you're ill-suited to this role." Joshua secured her arm around his to walk her to the sunken entryway. Even he had donned his finest for the occasion, including a new dark green tailcoat with a high, turned-over velvet collar. For once he did not look like a dusty house-sparrow.

"You made plain enough your opinion of my morals yestereve, please, let's not retread the same ground now. Your point was made. I'm an appalling disappointment to you."

"Bella, I just wish you to be happy."

"Vaughan makes me so. We went over this point too."

"And I continue to find that assertion highly suspect. The man's a fiendish churl. What joy could he possibly bring you?"

"Take care brother, least I actually verse you in the details."

Joshua looked her in the eye, but never paused or showed a hint of dander. "I expect that would be a rather mortifying experience for the both of us." He deposited her upon the family pew at the front of the church, whereupon Bella found her smile. Perhaps Joshua had only intended to labour his point again, or maybe he had deliberately saved her a deal of discomfort by walking her right into the church without stopping to address, or being stopped by, anyone, as it was apparent they were engaged in a vitriolic discussion.

Their views were at odds, but they had been close friends. Closer than many siblings born so far apart. He'd cared for her after their parents deaths. Had done his absolute best without stifling her. He'd allowed her untold freedom, and by his own confession, he was suffering for it now. How unfair that it was so. Joshua had done nothing but good. He did not deserve to be ostracized, though she was damned pleased to learn it had kept him free of the Hayes sisters, neither of whom she cared to have as a sister-in-law.

"Miss Rushdale, may I sit by you?" Caroline Wakefield blinked myopically. The church interior was rather gloomy after the brilliant sunshine outside. "It's rather crowded on the Marlinscar benches. I'm not at all sure that the regular congregation will fit in alongside us."

"Please, do." Bella shuffled along the pew, nudging Joshua in order that he also make space.

"It is an impressive crowd you've brought together to witness the child's baptism." Bella turned her head to peer at all the people filing into the tiny Norman church. There hadn't been half so many at Wakefield and Louisa's wedding, and that had been the talk of the neighbourhood for months.

Caroline settled in beside her, her face obscured by a straw bonnet edged with a peach-coloured ribbon. She clutched a leather bound copy of the common prayer book unopened in her hand.

"How is little Louisa today?" Bella asked. Striking up a friendship could only make the hours pass more quickly, and at least Caroline was prepared to address her. Every other person in the church averted their gaze when she peered in their direction. Hypocrites to a soul. There were plenty among them unmarried who engaged in illicit bedsports, and twice the number again who were wed and engaged in congress outside of their holy vows. The only difference between them and her was that she didn't conceal her sins, she owned them. More to the point, she did not regard them as sins at all. Love was holy, and she loved Vaughan. Moreover, she accepted that certain things simply were— Vaughan swore he would not wed, and therefore, being his mistress had to be her highest aspiration. Of course, she did not care to have him call her that. Vaughan did not own her in such a way as people might imagine.

"Oh, she's in fine fettle," Caroline replied. "Screamed herself into exhaustion on the way here. I don't believe she cares much for the carriage. It was only when Frederick opened the sash and she felt the air whistling past that she quietened."

"Did she not travel with the nursemaid?"

"He won't hear of it. He dotes upon the girl. She's going to end up hopelessly spoiled. The best thing would be if he were to marry again. He ought to be lavishing such affection on a wife, not a daughter."

"Do you believe that is likely, that he will remarry?" The thought that Wakefield would move on from Louisa at all, let alone so soon, rather shocked her.

"Oh, he must. He's so young, and there's no bringing Louisa back. As dear a girl as she was, the babe needs a mother, and some healthy competition from some siblings. Only children grow into such sickly sorts, do you not find?"

"I confess I've not paid much heed to such things." She could not think of one person wholly without brothers and sisters or multitudes of cousins to keep them smart, which nevertheless wasn't to say that she entirely agreed with Caroline Wakefield's assertion. Caroline, one of so many children would obviously believe multiple siblings most advantageous to a child's well-being, to suggest otherwise would be to disparage her own upbringing.

Reverend Hindes droned his way through the service in the same tedious monotone Bella remembered. At the point where she was required to escort little Louisa up to the font her feet were frozen—a damp, pervasive cold riddled the building. It was no great surprise that so many of the parishioners suffered from rheumatism. She stood to the left of Caroline, who stood to the left of her brother holding his peacefully slumbering daughter. Lucerne took up a position opposite to Bella on the far side of the holy reverend.

"I baptize thee in the name of the Father, of the Son, and of the Holy Spirit. Amen."

"Amen." The congregation droned.

The child startled awake the moment the holy water hit her brow. She squawked, simultaneously proving herself possessed of a monstrous set of lungs and a pair of brilliant blue eyes. She squirmed like an eel in her father's arms, and succeeded in freeing an arm from the swaddling. At a little over two years of age, she was the match of any crocheted blanket. One pudgy arm free, she slapped her hand into the font, sending a spray of water right up into Lucerne's face. He blinked and spluttered, caught off guard. Bella raised her hand before her face to conceal the smile tugging upon her lips.

Not content with one soaking, little Louisa continued to flail, getting herself into a hopelessly damp tangle, all the while continuing her outraged shrieking. The remainder of the blessing was hastily spoken, and the party were ushered out into the sunlight.

"A fine fettle you're in today, Miss Louisa Wakefield." Bella said, taking possession of the still squirming child from her father, and moving away from the gentlemen. "They'll not forget you, that's for certain. Poor Reverend Hindes won't want to see you again before you're wed, I shouldn't imagine. He's old, you know. It's not good at all to give such a man a fright." Deep down, she wanted to congratulate the child.

"Mar-Mar," crowed the babe, reaching out her tiny arms in the direction of her father, though it was not him, Bella realised she was calling out to.

"Lord Marlinscar? Yes, you did rather drown him, you naughty imp." Little Louisa considered her, blonde head cocked to one side. It was hard to see any of her father in her features. She had an upturned button nose, and a gently rounded face, but her mother's eyes and chin. It seemed perfectly clear that she would grow into the spitting image of her mother. Only in their personalities did they differ, that belligerence, that stubbornness in the face of adversity. That was her father.

"Mar-Mar," she said again.

"No, I think not. Enough damage has been wrought already. I think perhaps I ought to deliver you to one of your aunties, or your nursemaid, perhaps?" Caroline had temporarily become muddled in the exodus of people from the tiny church, so Bella ambled up onto the grassy bank with the tot, who quickly settled herself on the grass and began rooting about amongst the wild bilberries.

Bella bent down to the child's height.

"Mar-Mar. Dad-dad," the little girl said imperiously. She stared intently at Bella, whereupon it occurred to Bella, that they had not been properly introduced. "Bella," she said, pointing to herself. "I'm one of your godmothers. The wicked disreputable one."

The girl cocked an eyebrow. "Bwella."

"That's right."

"Bwella and Leesa go see Mar-Mar."

"No, I don't think so. Not right now."

The little girl's face scrunched, and another yell seemed inevitable.

"Stop that," Bella snapped. "Yes, I quite see you've fallen for his charms, but I must tell you that it's not at all appropriate. Also, he's a monstrous rogue, though that is true of most men hereabouts. And in any case, you're far too young to be setting your heart on someone." Bella settled her skirts beneath her and sat beside the babe. "Truthfully, I can't recommend ever becoming attached to one man. It brings no end of heartbreak and woe, which is not to say that it doesn't bring joy too, only that one sometimes wonders if the constant ruffling of ones emotions is worth it." Right now, she certainly wasn't sure of it. Her emotions were all of a dance. Vaughan, as far as she could tell, hadn't appeared, and was avoiding Lucerne – Lord Marlinscar! Heavens, would she ever get that fixed in her head – long term it would be deuced tricky. In fact, it appeared that her time was already up. As she watched, the bulk of the group around Captain Wakefield broke away, and he and several others began ambling up the grassy bank towards her. Bella stood at once, while Little Louisa contented herself with raising her hands, in which were clutched an assortment of weeds and beheaded daisies. Her father graciously accepted the gift, but when he failed to pick her up, another scream filled the air.

"Have her nursemaid take her, please," Wakefield said to the woman on his right, whom Bella guessed to be another of his sisters, whereupon the child was immediately whisked up into the arms of one of her aunties, and carried towards the waiting carriage.

"Bella, you'll join us, I hope. There's a nuncheon arranged, and my sisters insist we must take it down to the river to enjoy."

"A pic-nic," another of Wakefield's sisters declared.

"I do so love a pic-nic, and Lord Marlinscar tells us it is quite safe to paddle, even though the water is rust coloured. Please join us, Miss Rushdale, both you and your brother. You must both come. You must. It is in Leesa's honour."

"Do forgive her," Caroline interjected. "I'm afraid Maria is always hopelessly forward. But do also come along. Lord Marlinscar's cook has provided an absolute banquet, and it would be a pity for it to go to waste."

"Of course, you and Mr Rushdale must join us," added a friendly male voice.

Bella didn't need to turn her head to know it was Lucerne who was addressing her. His voice was as familiar to her as her own.

"Thank you," she dipped a curtsey in the direction of Wakefield and his sister, ignoring the fact that Lucerne had spoken. "Of course we'll join you."

Wakefield beamed from ear to ear. "I'm so pleased to hear it. Louisa would so ardently have wished it so. She did so love to see all her friends together."

"Will anyone else be joining us?" Bella asked, as she fell into step with Caroline

"Only Mr Aubury. Do you know him? He's also staying with us at the hall, but I don't recall seeing him since we arrived. I expect he just lost sight of us amongst the muddle of well-wishers.

Aye, that was possible, or he had deliberately sneaked off knowing that he wouldn't be missed. Church services were hardly Charles Aubury's usual pastime. Quite possibly, he thought he might actually be struck down by God if he even crossed the threshold.

"Yes, we're acquainted," she replied. It was curious, though, that Wakefield hadn't mentioned that he was staying at Lauwine last night. Either it had slipped his mind, or Charles had only recently arrived.

Knowing Charles, he had caught wind of the fact

that Vaughan was to be in Yorkshire, and had set forth immediately so as not to miss any fireworks that resulted. Charles was a hopeless voyeur, in addition to being a compulsive gambler and a horrid tattletale. He was quite the worst gossip she had ever met, and rumour had it he'd been distraught that he had missed Vaughan's phantasmagoria last October. She was certain that was because everyone knew Pennerley and Marlinscar's friendship had ended that night, rather than out of any love of the macabre. Anyone who was anyone had an opinion on the whys and wherefores of it all. Very few of them had any inkling of the truth.

CHAPTER 9
BELLA

THE MISSES WAKEFIELD turned what began as a rather awkward gathering on the riverbank into a merry affair. As promised, Lucerne's cook had provided a veritable banquet of breads, potted meats and salmon, boiled eggs and a ham, as well as macaroons, and an assortment of freshly picked berries, which they spread across three checked blankets. Little Louisa pottered about on the riverbank pulling up weeds and handing out posies to people under the close supervision of her nursemaid, but soon enough she was whisked away for her nap-time much to the disappointment of all her aunties.

"Goodbye Leesa. Goodbye."

"We'll take tea together later."

"I believe Joanna enjoys tea in the nursery, rather more than she cares for dining with the grown-ups. She's there every day," Caroline confided, leaning in to Bella. The sun was shining, and the bank of ferns shielded them from the breeze. Caroline's hair was peeping out from under the brim of her bonnet, and her soft-grey eyes were full of warmth. It was perfectly evident that she adored her family.

"Well she did spend time as a governess," Eliza, the second eldest of the Wakefield sisters remarked. She had dressed in a spotted muslin, with a dashing green spencer. She settled herself parallel to Bella and attacked a hard-boiled egg, tapping it against a handy rock. "What's more—" she elaborated, in a show of friendliness, "—she actually enjoyed it. Can you believe she stayed four extra months with that family, after Freddy told her she could return home and it was no longer necessary for her to be in service."

Of course, Bella had quite forgotten that Wakefield's fortunes had improved immeasurably upon his marriage to Louisa. She had known he was impoverished, but not that circumstances had been so dire for his sisters that it had become necessary for them to work.

"She wants Freddy to allow her to take on that role for Leesa, would you believe?"

"I think he would prefer to see us all married off than fawning over his offspring," Maria, the youngest sister, joined them. She was slender as a twig, and had dark wavy hair, unlike her siblings, who were all a rather more mousy brown. Maria untied her bonnet, causing much clucking of tongues, and cast it aside on the blanket. Then off came her shoes and stockings too, which she tucked under her bonnet. "Of course, it's possible that's exactly what Jo has in mind."

"Whatever do you mean by that?" Caroline demanded, starring aghast at her sister. "And what in heavens name are you doing? We're in company; you can't go taking things off as if you're at home in your boudoir."

Maria turned up her nose and got to her feet. "Stick in the mud. I'm going to paddle. You'll join me, won't you, Miss Rushdale? And I mean that Jo would be right underneath a certain person's nose so that he could hardly fail to notice her."

It wasn't difficult to figure out who they were talking about, not when Maria and Caroline both shot glances in Lucerne's directions. She no longer had any claim to Lucerne, nor wanted that to change, yet this talk of Jo attempting to snatch him up left her feeling inexplicably vexed. Now Caroline was on her feet too, pursuing Maria down towards the pebble-strewn riverbank, and Bella found herself following along.

"You say such horrid things. Jo loves Leesa and wants to spend time with her; she is not attempting to connive her way into Lord Marlinscar's heart."

Leesa? Why ever did they keep calling her that?

"No," Maria laughed. "That would be your game, with your book borrowing, and filling his house with flowers. Here, see this posy I've made, Lord Marlinscar," she fluttered her eyelashes, and then winked at Bella. "And here is a nosegay full of baby's breath and forget-me-nots, I've made for you. Oh, and would it be an awful trouble if I joined you in your library a moment, so I might choose another book from your extensive collection? Here, let me pour your tea, Lord M, from your very own pot." She cackled wildly, much amused by her own teasing, while Caroline's pale cheeks flamed. "I'm so sorry about my family disturbing you, Lord Marlinscar, their boisterous behaviour must be quite trying for you, but allow me to converse quietly with you on whatever topic you desire, and of course I will quieten all the feminine frivolity for you."

Caroline's mouth pursed angrily. If she had been unobserved, Bella had no doubt, that Maria would have caught a smack for her jibes, but as both she and the gentlemen were present, her anger had to be contained. Not that the gentlemen paid them any regard. They were engaged in a stilted conversation about land rights and politics. Joshua and Lucerne were sat as far apart as it was possible to be, and were hardly prepared to look at one another. Wakefield... dear Wakefield seemed wholly oblivious to their discomfort, and Charles... Well, he was drawing naughty caricatures of them on a nearby boulder using a piece of slate.

"I've always found that Lord Marlinscar enjoys frivolity and giddiness," Bella remarked.

Both sisters stopped in their tracks and turned to observe her, Maria ankle deep in the stream, and Caroline just shy of where the foam lapped.

"How so?" the latter demanded.

"I've never seen him laugh," said the younger.

Suddenly the centre of attention, Bella uneasily gnawed at her lower lip. How did she explain? Even the tamest of stories would cause one or the other to faint dead away. Also, did she really wish to isolate herself further? Everyone else hereabouts knew her whole history. They'd kept catalogue of her many faults, hence her current status as county pariah. As soon as the Wakefield sisters were aware of how tarnished a reputation she bore, they too would likely avoid her.

And even bypassing all that, did she wish to relay to them exactly how close she and Lucerne had once been? The answer was a resounding no.

That part of her life was past. Lucerne had ended it last October, and she wasn't here to remake it anew. They'd exchanged no more than nods of acknowledgement so far, and that only because it would have raised more questions not to have done so.

"Do explain, Bella. From all Freddy has said, and what we've seen over our time at Lauwine, he finds any sort of gaiety tiresome."

"I'm sure that's not true." If it were, then Lucerne was no longer the man she knew.

To avoid their questioning gazes, she sat down and removed her shoes and stockings.

"Bella what is it you aren't telling us?" They were united now. Two sisters against her.

Bella refused to lie and suggest it was nothing, but even if she was tactful, she was still likely to drop herself in it. Back on her feet, she waded into the water, with her skirt bunched around her calves. It had been years since she'd paddled in this fashion. She'd forgotten the pure joy of curling her bare toes against the stones, and the tickle of the water as it flowed around them, and even the thrilling numbness that came from the coldness of the water if you paddled for too long.

"I came across one of your books at Lauwine," Caroline remarked innocuously.

"What of it? I must have left it behind. Louisa and I did stay there for a time, before she and Wakefield married."

"Only, Lord M seemed rather reluctant to give it back. I did offer to return it to you last night."

"Well, perhaps he had not finished with it."

"Or perhaps he wanted to return it in person," Maria observed. Her shrewd glare landed upon Bella, and her brows twitched. "You were enlightening us as to his character."

She most certainly was not. If anything, she was doing her best to avoid discussing him at all.

"He virtually creeps around his own house as if he has a perpetual headache."

"You are just too noisy, sister," Caroline said.

Bella sighed. "All I meant was that when he first came to Lauwine, he held a huge ball and invited most of the county. The whole hall was filled with light and music and games. That was not in the least bit dour."

It had been the start of something...

"You must be referring to the ball where Freddy and Louisa met."

The pair had actually grown acquainted on the coach journey north, but to have met one's love at a ball did sound more exciting. "Yes," she agreed.

"Things have happened since then. I don't see any balls on the horizon, and there are never any guests at the hall besides us, and now Mr Aubury, I guess." Maria seemed content to muse on that, but Caroline continued to regard Bella shrewdly, prompting her to wade out a little further. When the water level was low, as it was at the moment, it was possible to cross right over to the other bank.

Maria followed her out towards the centre, where the pebbles gave way to soft silt and the water flowed faster. Caroline tentatively tiptoed behind them, sticking to the slab-like boulders that protruded above the water level in order to stay dry.

"Curious, don't you think, how things are all tied together? If there'd been no ball, then there'd have been no marriage, and we wouldn't all be here celebrating Leesa's christening." Maria said.

"Why do you keep calling her that?" Bella asked.

"Leesa? Little Louisa is too much of a mouthful for her. Leesa is what she calls herself." Maria stumbled, and her eyes widened, only for her to steady herself. Nevertheless, she wrapped her arm around Bella's so they were linked together. "Freddy stopped correcting her right after we arrived. I think he rather likes it. It places a degree of separation between the babe and her mother, so that the one can be something other than just a constant reminder of what he's lost. It's hard to move on when there's a living replica of everything he's lost right in front of him."

"I suppose you all think that's what he needs to do?" It was with grateful relief she took up the subject of Wakefield's future in place of hers and Lucerne's past.

"Of course," Maria beamed. "It's been a year. The best thing would be if he were to marry again. We're all four of us in agreement on that. Leesa needs a mother, not to be brought up in a silent mausoleum by two eccentric gentlemen, or heavens knows how she'll turn out."

Bella sniffed. "I don't know. That might be rather fun."

Her companion's narrow brow wrinkled. "You are a queer one. It would be ghastly. She'd either fade into the woodwork or turn into some hopelessly errant romp. No, my brother must find another wife."

There was such a note of finality about her words that Bella was at a loss as to what to say. "Of course," Maria muttered, after a moment or two. "It's quite unlikely that she'd end up stuck there forever with just Freddy and Lord M, anyway. Even if my dear brother doesn't find another maid willing to have him, then Lord M will get snatched up sooner or later. They all do, lords. I may not have set foot outside the county, but I've read every edition of Debrett's. They're always busy securing their lineages. Practically as soon as they're of age, they're out wife seeking. Is that not what you've observed?"

"I guess so," Bella admitted. Although, with one notable exception—Vaughan. Lucerne had, for a time, shown an interest in her, and she truly had believed he would wed her.

She could not picture him with another woman bound to his side. When she envisaged Lucerne's future, the person she saw there with him was Vaughan.

He would steal him away from her.

She swallowed the lump rising up her throat. She didn't want that to happen, but how could she ever stop it? If she threw any sort of obstacle in the way, it would only incite Vaughan to work harder to gain what he wanted.

Why could he not be content with her?

Why could he not love her as he did Lucerne?

Why had she not been born a man?

"Gracious, am I upsetting you, whatever have I said?"

Bella bowed her head, and made a pretence of trying to spot a fish, while she hastily brushed away the tears that were forming in the corners of her eyes. She was not feeling herself. Tears wouldn't solve anything. She needed a plan of action.

"Unless... Oh, my... Miss Rushdale, do you have a passionate tendresse for him also?"

"What?"

"Are you more smitten even than Caroline?"

"What are you saying about me?" That lady called.

"That you're the direst hag, sister dear."

The jibe prompted Caroline to brave another leap to a more central boulder. "Why are you now whispering? If you have something to say about me, Ma-ry-a Wakefield, then say it to my face, you horrid imp."

"I'm not saying anything of you, but I can make something up if you desire. Shall I holler out your not-so-secret desire to swoon in Lord Marlinscar's arms and have him revive you with a kiss?"

"Oh, you horrid... horrid..." Caroline leaned forward as if to swipe at her sister's arm, but her feet slipped out from beneath her, and down she sat with a mighty splash right in the middle of the river, startling laughter from both Bella and Maria.

Bella leant Caroline a hand and pulled her onto her feet again, outraged and spluttering.

"Ma-ry-a!"

"I'm so sorry," she giggled.

"Look at me. I'm soaked. This was my best dress."

"It'll dry."

Additional splashes and sprays of water announced the arrival of the gentlemen coming to the rescue. Joshua, Wakefield, and Lucerne all reached them more or less together.

"Caroline?"

"Are you all right, Miss Wakefield?" Lucerne asked.

"Allow me to be of assistance."

Caroline had no chance to respond before Joshua caught her up in his arms and carried her back to dry land.

A wave of pure nostalgia hit Bella. When she had been small, she and Joshua had often come here together, and he had swept her into his arms in that manner. He would take her home, grubby and wet, and never once complain. He'd been the perfect elder brother. Had shielded her from the harsh realities of their parents deaths, and what had she given him in return? Nothing, that's what. He wanted a family of his own, but her reputation had tarnished his.

Caroline was promptly swaddled in picnic blankets and escorted over to where the carriages were parked. While her elder sisters fussed over her, Charles took it upon himself to pack up the remains of their feast into the basket, and Wakefield grasped Maria by the wrist and tugged her back to shore.

"What nonsense were you up to?"

"Oh, let go, Freddy. I didn't do a thing. She slipped is all."

"With the aid of a gentle shove, no doubt."

CHAPTER 10

BELLA

"I'M AFRAID THAT, like most siblings, they have their hierarchy and their squabbles."

So intent had her focus been upon Caroline, Bella had not noticed Lucerne standing right beside her. It was with a jolt that his potent familiarity inveigled its way into her senses; his clothing, his scent, the awareness of his height, and his shadow upon her skin. She remembered them all, and her body unconsciously warmed to the presence.

"May I offer you some assistance back to shore?"

Bella brushed off his attempt to clasp her arm. "I'm perfectly capable, thank you. I got myself out here, I can get myself back." Assuming that was even where she wanted to be. Right now, the opposite side of the river looked rather appealing. Caroline had been bundled into Joshua's carriage, along with Eliza, presumably for the sake of expedience in getting her back to Lauwine. It was a swifter, lighter vehicle than the one that had carried the bulk of the party to the church that morning, and of course, the smaller curricle had already departed with Leesa and her nursemaid. A wiry old groomsman still had charge of her mare.

"I only meant to be—"

"It's unnecessary." She turned about and set off towards the opposite bank.

"Bella?"

Lucerne splashed back to where all the activity was happening, waved at the coachmen to go on without him, gathered up Bella's shawl and shoes and caught up with her as she was scrambling up the tufted mud bank.

"Whatever are you up to?"

He easily made it onto the bank, whereupon he stretched out a hand for her to take. Bella ignored the offer and fought her way up with the aid of several firmly rooted sods.

"Bella?"

"The party is over. I'm taking myself home."

"In the wrong direction. Your horse is the other side of the river."

"Maybe I intend to walk."

"Yes, I expect you do. Here then, you'll be needing these." He passed over her shoes and shawl. "We'll have to cross back over at the ford."

Bella gave a humph. "That's assuming I desire your companionship. Did you consider I'd a mind for solitude?"

"I know that ill suits you. Nor am I about to leave you alone in the wilderness. Your brother has kindly taken Miss Wakefield back to the hall, and you've abandoned propriety and your groom."

"I abandoned both long ago. If we're seen together, it'll only worsen the opinion everyone already has of me... and of you."

Lucerne regarded her with his lips puckered and face drawn into a frown. "The damage to both of our standings could easily be swept under the carpet, if—"

Bella raised her hand to stop him. "That time is past, Lucerne. I'm not here with the intention of changing anything. I did not come to see you, or to resurrect anything, and I'd prefer we weren't observed together. Being so will only foster expectations. Joshua is riled and ridiculed enough without provoking him further or subjecting him to further insult. It's over, Lucerne."

"Can we not be neighbours and friends?"

What game was he playing with her? "Did you not hear what I said?"

"Every word," he confirmed with a nod. "But I don't agree that it precludes us from friendship. You're suggesting that your brother is the barrier, but I don't believe that. He has never thwarted you in anything. I believe you fear that you might still feel something."

Of all the high-handed, arrogant... "Our relationship is dead, Lucerne. It is done, finished with. You made your choice, and so did I. My heart is not yours anymore."

"Indeed, was it ever?"

He made her so furious, the words to express her anger didn't exist. How dare he throw that at her? After she'd waited... and waited. She'd loved him, of course she had. It had not been her heart that was divided back in the winter of 1797. It was he who had been caught between herself and Vaughan, unable to abandon one or the other, insisting on having them both. She'd been filled with such joy, such hope when they'd left Wyndfell, and where had it got them? Within eighteen months, he'd been in the arms of another woman, and then when Vaughan had reacted, and raced off to Pennerley, he'd done nothing to heal the wound. Instead, he'd brought everything to a close.

She found herself staring at the toes of his wet

boots, unable to look directly at him, so violent was her outrage.

"Has it been all you expected, Bella? Has he kept you safe and satisfied? Does he keep you warm at night as you always desired he would?"

"What occurs between Vaughan and me is none of your business."

"Then at least tell me that you're happy."

She had been, up until her return to Yorkshire. Now things were in motion that she didn't care for, and happiness seemed out of reach. She had no idea where Vaughan was or when she would see him again. He could ride off at any moment, leaving her here, and she wouldn't know of it until afterwards, and the only thing convincing her that he had not done so was the presence in the county of the man before her. "Why wouldn't I be?" she snapped churlishly. "Vaughan is everything to me."

Lucerne sighed and awkwardly clasped his hands, only to then tuck them out of sight behind his back. "Then I'm glad for you. You deserve happiness, and... Well, I worried. You and he have not always seen eye to eye in the past, nor have you had the courage to admit what you so obviously felt for one another. I'm pleased to hear that's no longer the case."

Not a single solitary thing was simpler. God's truth, she hardly knew from one minute to the next what Vaughan really felt for her. The only thing she knew with any certainty was how she felt about him.

"Things are certainly simpler without you around. There's no reason for Vaughan and I to fight."

Lucerne stumbled but righted himself quickly. "Of course." He gave her a quick tight smile. "Thank you for that timely reminder of why it was best for me to leave."

"Exactly," she agreed. Not that it had been right for him to leave. In fact, it was the most hideous, horrible, inconsiderate thing he'd ever done, even worse than the host of false promises he'd made her. He ought to have stayed at Pennerley and mended things, not run off leaving everything smashed to pieces, and her and Vaughan struggling to piece things together without him. Well, they'd managed.

She raised her head to look at him. They'd worked things out. At least she'd thought so, until yesterday. Now she wasn't half so sure.

"Have you let us go, Lucerne?"

Lucerne paused in the act of turning away. "I left, didn't I? I wintered here. Nearly a year has gone by. A lot has changed. I've had to move forward."

And yet, she could hear the uncertainty in his voice. He was shaking his head, though he probably didn't realise it.

"In body you left, but in spirit..."

He looked right at her. Lord, the blue of his eyes. She'd forgotten the warmth of them, and how they would dance with amusement. There was no merry dart to them now, only sadness—colossal, weighty sadness— like a lodestone dragging him down. He sighed, even as she watched, and shook his head again.

"Bella, I'm sorry things ended the way they did. It was not my intention to cause you pain."

She nodded. "But you did, and you still are."

Lucerne winced, and his skin visibly blanched.

In the absence of any vocalized response, Bella continued. "Things have been good without you, but even in your absence, you've been a constant presence. It probably doesn't need spelling out, but you may as well know that he thinks of you every day. You are still the only thing that really matters to him. Oh, he has some affection for me, but I can't cross my heart and swear to you that it's love he feels, however much I might wish it."

"Bella, I'm—"

"Don't. Don't you dare tell me that you are sorry. Your regrets benefit no one. You ruined everything, and you're going to ruin it again."

He shook his head, and his expression grew darker. "No..."

"You deny that you are going to break my heart anew?"

"Bella, I can't account for Vaughan's actions, only my own, and I have no plans to..." He fell into an uneasy silence. Whereupon, they began to walk again, side by side, but worlds apart. They crossed the stile and a field where the river bent away from them in a wide loop, then re-joined it as it approached the ford.

"Do you truly have the strength to deny him?" Bella muttered under her breath as they crossed the water. "He's in your head, your heart, as much as he's in mine."

"I've moved on." There was no conviction in his words. Another might not hear the desperate longing there, but she did. "He does not want me."

"You're a bigger fool than you appear if you believe that to be the truth."

"Bella, I saw him. He's not... He's no longer interested in me."

"He plays a long game," she laughed. "He's toying with you, as he's always done, as he always does. And he's making you pay." He deserved to pay.

When and how had they seen one another? She wanted every detail of it. All they had said, every action, every half smile and glance shot at one another.

"You offer friendship, Lucerne, but I cannot give it. You're right, this has little to do with Joshua, but it's not because I'm afraid I still have feelings for you. I don't. You rid me of those the moment you brought Miss St

John into our home. I cannot love you, Lucerne. Nor can I forgive you, therefore friendship is impossible."

Bella's nose tingled, but her anger was too hot for tears. Her anger had not bubbled to the surface quite so fiercely for many, many months. When he'd left Pennerley, she'd had time to reflect on all that had occurred. The moment he'd presented her with Georgiana had been the pivotal moment. Until then, things had been salvageable. Afterwards, given the opportunity, she'd have worked to forgive him to salvage what she, he, and Vaughan had together, but Lucerne had chosen instead to rip a hole in Vaughan's heart too.

Yet still Vaughan loved him.

"Why, Lucerne? Why could you not have stayed and worked things out? Was it truly so hard to believe in the three of us? Could you not trust that we could weather any storms?"

Lucerne's frown deepened. "Your actions didn't give me any cause to believe that any of it would last. After Vaughan left, it was perfectly apparent which way your feelings leant, and it was not in my direction. We finally had one another without him around, but it was like all the vitality and warmth seeped right out of you. A man can only fool himself for so long, Bella. It was abundantly clear that you were both far more besotted with each other, than either of you ever had been with me. What choice was truly left to me, other than to give you both what you actually wanted?"

"Do not try and twist things to present yourself as some kind of martyr. You didn't leave because either of us wished it. You knew perfectly well we both wanted you to stay."

Lucerne's jaw clenched so tightly that his pulse showed clearly in his cheek. "Fine," he snapped. "I did it for my own sake. My emotions, my sanity could take no more trampling. I wasn't going to stick around to be slowly ousted."

Bella laughed hard. "You're a damned fool, Lucerne. Vaughan would never choose me over you. He never has and he never will."

"He has chosen you, Bella."

She shook her head hard enough to dislodge several of the pins holding her hat in place. "No, he has not. What he has done is delivered me home to my brother. I don't know where he is, or even if he's still in the county."

"He's at the Dog and Basin in the village."

Her heart soared at the knowledge that he remained close by. Not that she expected him to leave, not without first reclaiming the man before her now, whose blond head was bowed as if a colossal weight sat upon his shoulders. As they stepped into the lane, Bella's groom came trotting around the corner, leading her mare by the reins, and from the opposite fork in the road, a small curricle came towards them from the direction of Lauwine.

"Until next we meet." Lucerne waved at the driver, who appeared to be Captain Wakefield. He immediately swung the vehicle to turn around so that the horses were pointed back towards Lauwine again.

"Let's not hurry to do so," Bella replied.

Lucerne acknowledged the remark with a nod. He was a pace or two away from her when he suddenly turned back. "You didn't believe in us either," he said. "I look back, and I realise I was only ever the means by which you found your way into Vaughan's bed."

Bella blinked hard. Her anger spiked again, sending vicious spears of tension out across her skull. At the beginning, she'd had no designs upon Vaughan. Lucerne had been her entire focus... Hadn't he?

Of course he had.

"I most certainly did believe in us. You and I, it could have been very different, but you never asked, Lucerne. Never made any hint of it, at least, not until it was way too late."

To her surprise he dug into his pocket. "Take it." He placed something in the centre of her palm, and closed her fingers over the top of it. "It was always meant to be yours, so you'd best have it. If you want to know how you never came to receive it before now, then I suggest you ask Vaughan. You imply that I'm the one who was jealous and foolish and who destroyed us, and maybe I am responsible for some of that, but it wasn't purely my actions that kept us apart, Bella. If it had been entirely down to me, I'd have wed you within days of us first leaving Yorkshire together."

"Marlinscar..." Wakefield hollered.

"I'm on my way." Lucerne bowed from the shoulders and stalked towards the curricle. He climbed inside and took the reins from Wakefield. Bella watched him until he was swallowed up by the bend in the lane. Only then did she look down at what she knew lay in her hand. The ring he'd clearly once intended as a mark of their betrothal sat in the centre of her palm. It was a beautiful thing, and perfectly chosen for her.

Unbidden tears filled her eyes, and a horrid, uncomfortable lump swelled inside her throat. He had meant to make her his after all. Only circumstances had swayed him off course.

Nay, not circumstances—Vaughan.

Vaughan had stopped Lucerne from making her his wife.

CHAPTER 11

BELLA

BELLA SIGHED OVER her groom's insistence on talking to her. He'd prattled on, asking inane questions, from the moment he'd helped her astride her mare and she'd nudged the horse towards Reeth village instead of home to Wyndfell. She supposed he was not much accustomed to the whims of young ladies, or following them about, given that she'd been absent for the entire length of his employment. She missed Mark and his stoic silences, though it was probably for the best that her former servant had moved on. There was awkwardness enough associated with her return home without any need for additional embarrassments.

She left the groom to tie up the horses by the water trough outside the blacksmith's yard.

"Will you be long, Miss?"

That rather depended upon whether Vaughan was where Lucerne claimed he was. "I'm not sure. Just wait here, and don't come looking for me."

"Mr Rushdale wouldn't like me to leave you wandering about unattended for too long."

"Do not come looking for me," she reiterated. "Not unless I'm still missing when the sun goes down." It was late July and currently mid-afternoon. If her business with Vaughan had not concluded by sundown, then a rescuer might be a genuine necessity.

Bella did not look back, nor did she head directly to her destination. Instead, she meandered along Silver Street, stopping to peer through the windows of the small collection of shops. There was little of interest to see. However, after the third set of people bypassed her and tittered into their handkerchiefs, she dispensed with her attempt to be circumspect. Why hide what everyone obviously knew to be true? She was a scandalous harlot. On this occasion maybe it would better serve her purpose to act like one.

On reaching the Dog and Basin, Bella walked right in. Her appearance in the gloomy interior was met with a shriek of outrage. Immediately, a balding little man came scurrying out from behind the bar. "Mistress?" he enquired, while wringing his hands upon his greasy apron.

His nervousness convinced her he knew exactly who she was. He was probably calculating the odds of being beaten black and blue for facilitating her sinful behaviour.

"Lord Pennerley is resident here, is he not?"

"Aye, that's so..."

"I wish to see him."

"Aye... Right. Of course you do. Right. Yes."

"Well," Bella sighed. How backwards her home county seemed in some regards. "Is it really so confounding a request? Here is my calling card, if it will serve to expedite your mission. Or maybe you could simply escort me to where I might find him. He is here, is he not? He's not out somewhere else?"

"I believe so, yes Miss." He turned her card about

between his fingers, and visibly paled at the sight of the Rushdale name. A goodly number of his relations were likely employed in her brother's mine.

"You believe he's here, or that he's out?"

"Here." He stowed her card in the pocket of his apron, then seemed to come to a conclusion that it was better to have her out of sight than in the taproom for all to see. "Come, 'tis right this way."

'Here' turned out to be a small sitting room, wood-panelled with smoke-stained blue walls above, and an assortment of crockery on display. Vaughan sat before the unlit fireplace, engaged in a lively discourse with two other gentlemen over the front page of a recent edition of the The Times.

"I'm sorry to intrude my lord, but there's a... Well, there's a lady that wishes to speak to you."

"Another, Pennerley." His compatriots exchanged an assortment of nudges and winks. "There's been a rare stream of them today. You should have taken lodgings in the local whorehouse, not the Basin."

"And you should mind you tongue." Vaughan rose and crossed the room on seeing her. He bowed in greeting and lifted her hand, so that he might guide her into the room. "Miss Rushdale, what a glorious surprise. I was not expecting you."

"Of course you weren't, you made a point of delivering me elsewhere."

A flash of ire filled his bright violet eyes, but he blinked and it was gone. "What can I do for you?" He half-turned so that he was able to keep an eye on both her and his companions. Both men were sat back in their chairs, observing them closely, one with his hands steepled and fingertips pressed together, the other with the now folded broadsheet tapping against the arm of the chair. Bella didn't recognise either of them, but that hardly seemed to matter. It was clear they were, at the very least, acquainted with her name and her relationship with the marquis.

"I would speak with you – in private."

Vaughan's eyebrows winged their way upwards, and he pursed his lips. "I see."

Bella wasn't at all sure that he did. This was no lewd proposition she was making. They genuinely needed to talk. "I know you stopped him," she said. "All the waiting and hoping I did, and nothing coming of it, that was down to you. He told me so. He gave me this."

She opened her palm to reveal the ring. Somehow, she could not bring herself to put it on, no matter how lovely it was. Her heart no longer belonged to Lucerne.

Whatever warmth had remained in Vaughan's face utterly vanished. "Please excuse us, gentlemen." Rather than sending them from the room, he bundled her through a second door to the right of the one she'd entered through, and up a flight of narrow stairs. They emerged in a large room, most likely the grandest in the inn. It was spartanly decorated, as was Vaughan's preference, with only a few tapestries and an large rug to offer some semblance of homely comfort, but the bed was an enormous canopied affair, at the base of which sat Vaughan's own iron-bound trunk. Bella tugged to free her arm from his grip, but his hold remained firm around her wrist.

"I suppose you mean to deny it," she sniped.

Vaughan made a small noise to the contrary. He released her and crossed to a side-table that held a half-drunk bottle of port nestled on a tray amidst an assortment of uncollected dinner dishes. He poured himself a large glass. "Why would I do that?"

"Indeed, why would you?"

Vaughan knocked back the drink, returned the glass to the tray, and then turned to face her, shaking his head. "This is hardly a revelation, Bella. Why the accusatory tone all of a sudden?"

"You don't deny it?" Not that Vaughan was much for squirming and wriggling his way out of situations. He preferred directness. Still... "I could have been his wife. None of this hateful drama need ever have happened."

"Hateful drama? Is that what our time together has been?" His voice was quiet, but the tone lethal. "I rather thought we'd enjoyed one another's company. Something that would never have happened if you'd married Lucerne."

She supposed that was true, but it was true of almost any fork in the path of life. If you took one route, different events unfolded than if you'd gone another way. Still, he had actively prevented them marrying, and she wasn't fool enough to think it was because he'd wanted to claim her for himself. No – rather he'd intended to prevent her from stealing Lucerne away from him. It wasn't about vows or fidelity, but ownership. Lucerne belonged to him, therefore he couldn't go giving himself to anyone else.

"What are you doing here, Bella?" Vaughan stripped off his coat, so that he was in his waistcoat and shirtsleeves, a warning he meant business if ever there was one. Well, she meant business too. Bella opened her mouth to repeat her accusation, but Vaughan waved away the remark before she'd even uttered it. "Please, do me the honour of not lying to me. This is not about what happened or didn't between you and him nearly four years hence. Or even the results of my interference. If he'd truly wanted you then, he'd have wed you despite anything I had to say. He's a grown man, and eminently capable of making atrocious decisions all on his own."

"But you..."

"Did I use my influence to steer him in a certain direction? I just admitted as much. Of course I did. How would it have benefited me to see you both exchange matrimonial vows? I was never going to be the third party in your marriage, but that hardly needs spelling out, does it? You've know it all along. Now, if you wish to continue wasting your breath chastising me for that, then allow me to apologise in advance for my rudeness, because I've no intention of staying to listen to it. If on the other hand, you'd like to tell me what it is you actually want, then—"

"Answers," she blurted explosively. "I'm sick of secrets and machinations. I want to know exactly where I stand in your affections, assuming you hold me in any regard at all."

"Oh, Bella."

"What? You disposed of me yesterday like unwanted baggage and then went to him."

Vaughan pulled her to his side again, so that when he spoke his breath flashed heat against her cheek. "Point one: I dropped you at Wyndfell out of courtesy to your brother, and for no other reason than that. Point two: I did not go to see Lucerne, or seek him out in any way. We did happen upon one another, but not through any design of mine. And in any case, what of it? We barely exchanged a handful of words."

"No doubt you made up for that with actions."

Laughter lines creased his face, though he didn't chortle aloud. Instead, he dragged her closer still, so that she was bound within the circumference of his arms, and his scent played upon her senses. Whenever they were this close, she could not fail to react and warm to his touch. Still, she turned her head away from him.

"Gosh, he has you wound up tight. If our reunion had gone as you suppose, do you think I'd be standing here now listening to your jealous gripes? Do you think Lucerne would have been so eager to seek you out and drive a wedge between us? Think on why that might be to his benefit."

"He was looking to renew our friendship."

"And it's customary when doing so to offer a woman a ring you once intended to present as a betrothal gift?"

"I do not know why he did that, other than to open my eyes to the truth that you're no saint."

He gave another scoffing laugh. "If you are not aware of my extensive list of vices by now, then you're dangerously simpleminded. I think it's perfectly clear that he meant it as a statement of intent. Clearly, he's still in love with you."

Bella stiffened. Was Lucerne still in love with her? Thinking back over their conversation, it seemed that he still possessed some affection for her, but love...She wasn't sure how she felt about that. Surely the fires that had once consumed them were all burned out.

Vaughan ticked a finger under her chin, and lifted her gaze up to meet his. "Should I be concerned that you might run to him?"

She turned her head away from him again. "I made my choice, Vaughan. Nothing has altered."

He gave a slight nod. "Then it might interest you to know that the only noteworthy event of yestereve was that I was forced to retire with a raging cockstand. It troubled me horribly all night. I was of half a mind to steal in through your window."

Bella's gaze dropped down to his loins, to see if it persisted still. "That would imply that you missed me, my lord," she remarked, failing to neutralize a smile from tweaking her lips. He didn't deserve her smiles. She was still mad at him. Motives be damned, he'd still acted against her interests.

"Mayhap, I did, Miss Rushdale. Mayhap I did."

"You missed me?" She raised both brows. That didn't sound like him. He was toying with her for certain. Although she still felt hugely elated to hear him say it.

Vaughan trailed a finger down the side of her cheek. "Is that truly so difficult to comprehend?"

As a matter of fact, it was.

"If you did, it was only because you lacked another to torment."

"Oh, Annabella, there were offers aplenty. Everyone through from the pot boy to your old friend Mrs Castleton. Pleasure was mine for the taking if I chose to entertain such company. Even Lucerne was rather more keen to engage with me than one might suppose him to be."

Was that supposed to imply he had rejected all those offers out of some sort of fidelity to her?

"I don't want to play guessing games, or to be wrapped in riddles," she complained.

"Then let us be straightforward."

Before she could make a reply Vaughan pulled her tight against his body and crushed his mouth down upon hers. It was a quick, aggressive kiss, more demanding than sweetness, but when had that sort of thing ever enthralled her, and when had Vaughan ever been one to offer such? Immediately, her body warmed to his touch, even as she hated herself for allowing him to manipulate her emotions so easily. If not for him, then for good or ill, she would have been Viscountess Marlinscar by now. She'd have been respected in the county, rather than being a source of ridicule. Moreover, Joshua would still be respected too, instead of being ostracized by those whom in the past he'd called friends.

She had to do something to remedy that, though what it might be, she did not know.

"Head in the moment, Miss Rushdale. Head in the moment. My affections are what you came to claim, are they not? And here I am offering them."

Bella pushed him away, but Vaughan spun her around, throwing her balance off kilter, and easily manhandled her towards the bed.

"What I seek and what you offer are rarely one and the same."

"That is because half the time you hardly know yourself what it is you are looking for."

"But you're all-seeing."

"Precisely." He kicked open the lid of his trunk and snatched a cravat from the pile of clothing contained within. In a trice, she was bound to the bedpost, able to raise or lower her hands a little, but quite unable to get free.

"I most assuredly did not come here in order to be bound to your bedpost."

"No, you came hoping that I'd bed you. Has one night apart truly left you so agitated?" He raised the back of her skirts, exposing her bare behind to the air. Then his hand settled warm upon it, and a quiver of excitement rippled through her tensed body in expectation of what was to come. He might thrust his fingers into her, fill her quim or her nethers with his prick, strike her until she screamed out, or make her wait exactly as she was until the anticipation of what was to come became unbearable and her temper quickened to a fury alongside her frustration. Then she would rage, and he would fuck her as she yelled obscenities at him.

"No. It's not why I came. I told you why. Also, there's the matter of you not turning up to the christening."

"Must you always lie to yourself? You want reassuring. What concerns you isn't the past – I've never hidden the fact that I was opposed to you commandeering Lucerne. He was mine, Bella. I couldn't just let you take him – but what concerns you now is whether he'll usurp your position Is that not so, Miss Rushdale?" He rubbed up against her rear.

"Stop that."

"Really?" He pouted. "But Annabella, you're always so delightfully willing."

She twisted her head to look back at him. "And you're predictable."

He stepped away from her. "Leaving you here and sending for your brother it is then. I wonder what he'll make of you sneaking off to meet me after the no doubt long speech he gave you about morality. I hear the Methodists have been courting him."

"That is not true."

"Are you sure? I heard it from several very reliable sources."

"You just made it up."

"Come sing praises to the Lord with us," he teased, putting on a local accent. "You'll be saved, and welcomed into his joyous bosom. Your sister too, if she was to repent her sins and truly seek God's mercy, as he forgives all sinners."

"Even the sins of the flesh?" he posed the question as if she were addressing the preacher.

"All sins?"

"Even laying together unwed?"

"Aye?"

"Even sodomy, and lying with two men at once? What about Onanism, or drunkenness... indolence?"

"Stop it." Her concern for Joshua was too great to make a mockery of it. She fought against the binding around her wrists, but only succeeded in shaking the bed, and showering herself in dust from off the canopy. Bella sneezed violently. "Please, stop. He's been hurt by our actions enough already."

"What action of mine has caused him any difficulty?"

As if he truly needed her to spell it out. "Every damned moment we spend together further blackens his name, because he is my brother and a good man, and refuses to disown me despite the vexation I cause. I do not like that you are making fun of that."

"He could just as easily benefit from our arrangement. It is his choice not to, Bella."

She had not thought of it like that, but obviously a connection to Vaughan could be seen as rather advantageous in many circumstances. Alas, not in the circles Joshua inhabited. If he were to go to London things might be different, but here in Yorkshire his morality was vastly more important than whose dinner table he sat at, or what influence he could muster in the House of Lords.

"Just please do not summon him here."

Vaughan ticked his tongue against his teeth. "Did you really believe I would?"

"Frankly, I never know what to expect of you. Sometimes you are a creature of whim."

"It takes one to know one." His chuckle pulled his lips wide, so that she was treated to a glimpse of his teeth. "I find I'm of a mind to indulge a few such whims now. It was diced inconvenient having you elsewhere last night."

"It's your fault we were apart. Also, you still haven't explained your absence from church."

Vaughan ignored her attempt to bait him. In all fairness, he was not one for constantly re-treading the same ground. His reasons for his actions regarding her delivery to Wyndfell had been given. There was really nothing more to add. As for the christening... "You realise, I was not on the guest list? And in any case, why would I choose to bore myself to tears watching a baby having its head wet? Screech, did it? Gruesome."

"You'd have seen Lucerne."

"Aye, but as we already established, I had already done so with less of an audience. Unless you're suggesting I should have upstaged Wakefield's brat?"

She shook her head.

"Some people are inordinately fond of children; you'll find I'm not one of them, Miss Rushdale. Should I ever have misfortune of begetting any, I shall endeavour not to pay them the slightest regard until they are of age and capable of conversing without setting ones teeth on edge."

She swore at him. "You're hopeless. You'd repeat all the mistakes your own parents made."

"Madam, I dearly wish they had cut me from their lives until I reached my majority. Now, must we continue to converse on this most unappealing subject, or might we return to that which has rather more bearing upon the present? You see, it occurs to me that your brother would be facing the same dilemma now whether or not I had audaciously stolen you away rather a number of years ago. You were a dreadful flirt even before I met you. I should think you'd already tupped half the men of your acquaintance, and therefore, had you remained at Wyndfell, would likely have soon tupped the rest."

It was a minor concession, but at least he implied she'd been the active partner in such actions, and not merely the object of male enjoyment. Not that his accusation was correct. Prior to her invitation to stay at Lauwine Hall in 1797, her exploits had been limited to an uninspiring affair with her groom. Mark had been all brawn, with barely an iota of wit to him. He'd served her exactly as she'd asked, which, while it had alleviated a certain degree of boredom, hadn't exactly passionately engaged her. It was hardly surprising that Vaughan, who was in every respect Mark's opposite, had so captivated her. He offered everything her life until that point had been lacking.

"And they were all superior lovers to you," she remarked haughtily, still cross over the Lucerne situation, and his lack of regard for little Louisa Wakefield, even though it made no sense to be so. It wasn't as if she wished to pick up the pieces of their relationship with Lucerne and attempt to glue them back together. She wanted what, as far as it appeared to others, she already possessed – Vaughan.

"Of course they were." Vaughan tipped his head back and laughed. "Is that the best you can do? Heavens, Bella, you've only been back in this forsaken backwater for a day. I had hoped you might survive a little longer with your wits intact."

So far, her return home had been one lesson in endurance after another. Therefore it was hardly surprising she was wholly out of sorts.

"Let's fix you, shall we?" He plucked open the buttons of her spencer and then unravelled the bib-front of her dress, exposing the swell of her bosom. His hands cradled the weight. Then his index fingers circled her rapidly stiffening nipples. "I'm the best you've ever had and the only man who's ever come close to satisfying you. That's why you're here. It's why you keep coming back, and it's why you turned down Ned Darleston, and Raffe Devonshire, and especially why you dismissed Lucerne."

"He never—"

He sought her gaze, and held it. "We both know that if you'd left Pennerley with him that night..."

They did, and she didn't want to speak of it. The

ring Lucerne had handed her weighed heavy in her hand, but she couldn't quite bring herself to uncurl her fingers and discard it. Whether she liked it or not, he was part of her past, and he still meant something to her, even if that something was a hopelessly muddled mess of contradictions.

"Be honest—he bores you in bed. Always has done, once the novelty of having him ceased. If you had bound yourself to him, sex between you would have devolved into him dutifully poking you once a week for strictly procreational purposes, and you being forced to take a regular lover or three."

"He does not bore me, and that would not..." Why was she defending him? And why was Vaughan even implying such a thing, unless he genuinely feared losing her to Lucerne. It made no sense, not when she knew exactly how besotted Vaughan was with him. Unless he was trying to rationalise his own feelings, put some distance between them. How she wished she knew exactly what the two men had said to one another the previous night, then she might better understand Lucerne's actions, and Vaughan's current agitation.

He was agitated. She could see that now, looking closely at him. It would not have been obvious to anyone else, but she knew him far better than most. It was like a buzz existed beneath his skin, which he was fighting against.

"Lucerne doesn't possess the level of cruel ingenuity you require." Vaughan twisted one of her nipples, making her yelp. Yet when he then sucked at the pulse point on her neck, her womb clenched hard, and an anticipatory thrill of being claimed swept through her making her feel more alive than she had since they'd set out from Pennerley. A sigh escaped her lips. There was no escaping the fact that she was wholly infatuated with this man. Not blindly in love—she was perfectly aware of his faults—but they did not seem to matter.

"Then how is it that he does not bore you also?"

His words were whispered straight into her ear. "Fucking a fellow in the arse never grows old, Bella. And, as luck would have it, I possess more than enough ingenuity for both of us, as you are well acquainted... with." He punctuated each word with a cruel nip that he then soothed with a kiss.

"What is it with you and your obsession with bottoms?"

"What isn't to like about them?" He shifted his attending, stroked his palms in wide circles over her exposed cheeks. His thumbs traced the channel between them, hinting at a more invasive touch still to come. "If you were able, I'm sure you would enjoy pricking them too."

"What is wrong with pricking my quim?"

"The prospect of a bastard squalling in my arms, perhaps."

She scowled, but Vaughan ignored her vexation, choosing to drop to his knees behind her instead. There, the tip of his tongue followed the path his thumbs had just traversed, making the muscles of her lower body clench. She fought hard to contain a sigh, the tension making her stance rigid. Nevertheless, her body quickly warmed to his touch, while her cruelly pinched nipples stood out like beacons.

"I'm a woman, Vaughan. Can't you love me in that way? There are methods we can employ."

"Do I not always make you weep with bliss?"

What he was doing was wrong in so many ways, yet somehow inappropriately right too. They were past her denying she took pleasure in being penetrated thus. The tip of a finger circled her hole, and dipped very delicately inside. It was only for a fraction of a second. He was testing her, preparing her...

"Lucerne never shied from spilling his seed inside me."

"Lucerne was a fool, and planting his seed in you would have given him the perfect opportunity to override my every objection." Vaughan's tongue again swept the spot his finger had just occupied. "Hell's teeth, Bella, I've no desire to see you swollen up like a barrel, and in any case, we've enjoyed plenty such congress. Perhaps you have forgotten Beltane eve?"

She would never forget Beltane eve. Vaughan had made love to her all night, out in the fields surrounding his home with the purpose of enacting some pagan rite to reawaken the earth and make it bountiful. He had not teased or tormented her, only loved her as any woman might wish to be loved. They'd fallen asleep together outdoors and woken at midday when an irate dormouse had scurried up her leg. She was not much for squealing, but she had shrieked that day.

"That was twelve weeks ago. You've not had me in that way since."

Tsk, tsk. "How remiss of me. Maybe after I've availed myself of your derriere."

"Vaughan, please!" Could he not understand that what she needed now was some little reassurance that what they had remained intact, and was not about to end? Oh, why had they come north? They ought to have stayed at Pennerley.

Vaughan ached. Although, he could not precisely say what it was he ached for.

His head told him that it should be Lucerne. It had taken every ounce of strength that he possessed to walk away from him last night. He'd wanted to do more than pin the stupid bugger against a headstone and ravish his mouth. He'd wanted to fuck him until they were slick with one another's sweat, and exhaustion consumed them both. But, he understood Lucerne. Giving in at once without first having to work for it was as likely to cause a backward step as to bring them properly together again.

In any case, things needed to be carefully handled. He wanted Lucerne, but he was in no hurry to give up Bella. His prick was currently hard for her, and a night without her had left him more uneasy than he'd ever believed possible. Truthfully, the moment she'd appeared downstairs he'd wanted nothing more than to pin her against a wall and sink his cock inside her. No other woman had ever claimed his attention thus. There had been lovers aplenty over the years, but they had all walked in and out of his life for the most part in a single night. A few had lasted weeks, fewer still months. Lucerne had been his only constant until Bella came along.

Goddamn her, but he still didn't entirely comprehend how she'd inveigled her way into his life and bed.

While Lucerne had been present, their interactions were easily attributed to rivalry. Now, only a fool would pretend that was the case.

He was not a fool.

He realised it would be no easy task to cast her aside, nor did he wish to. Rather, he hoped to reconcile the three of them, so that he wouldn't have to give up either of them.

Vaughan had hope for Lucerne, given his actions of earlier.

What in heaven's name had he been thinking to give her that ring now? Whatever did he imagine to achieve with such an action?

As for Bella, he knew she would deny it until she was blue in the face, for he had listened to her many extensive rants and rages, but deep down she still cared for Lucerne. Her love for him was not as withered as she liked to tell herself. She just wished it so, for then it was easier to deal with her hurt. In the same way, she attributed Vaughan more pain and anxiety from his separation from Lucerne than existed. That wasn't to say he hadn't craved the bastard with every ounce of his soul. There were nights when it had been hellish torment existing apart from him. However, Vaughan was a patient man. It wasn't as if Lucerne hadn't flown from him before. It wasn't as if he hadn't crossed continents in the past in order to reclaim him. The difference to those other times was that then there'd only been the two of them involved.

"Vaughan," she murmured, pushing her body further towards his, and reminding him of her presence. Her sigh pushed hot and sharp through his skin and into his heart. "Please, Vaughan."

He didn't usually relent, but now, if there were ever a time to do so, seemed an appropriate moment. Besides, he wanted to feel her sliding all over his prick.

Shit!

He found a piece of sponge and doused it in the dregs of the wine he'd drunk earlier, before slipping it into place inside of her. Then, rather than scramble about on his knees, Vaughan pulled Bella away from the bedpost. It meant she was bent forward at the waist, so that her upper body sat parallel to the floor, with her full breasts hanging bounteously downward. Still behind her, he nudged her legs apart, giving him access to her pussy. It was pink and perfect, swollen with need, and wet with arousal. Vaughan lazily speared his fingers forward through her folds to find her clit. The little nubbin was already standing erect. He rolled his index finger back and forth over it, while his tongue teased her opening. As a result, he was rewarded with needy groans.

Bella shuffled on the spot as he continued to work her into a frenzy with his tongue, and then his fingers. He slid two inside of her and fucked them in and out. He needed her to come. Wanted to see on her face, and feel the hum through her body that he'd created. The closer he brought her, the more agitated her stepping became, until she stilled suddenly, and all her muscles tensed.

She came hard around his fingers, her pussy squeezing them in an iron grip. Barely had he let the tremors fade than he stood and pushed his cock into the heat of her channel. She was so slick and smooth. Hot as a furnace, and pleasingly eager for more.

Her cunt stretched to accommodate him. He looped an arm around her waist, while the other encompassed her breasts.

"Is this it? Is this what you need?"

"Yes. Oh, Vaughan. Yes," she rasped. "So much so. Fuck me hard. I want to feel you even when I'm gone from here."

The idea was certainly a pleasing one. He pulled back so that he was almost wholly free of her and then rammed forward again. It meant clenching his teeth to hold himself in check, because the result was a pleasure so sharp it raced in circles at the base of his cock and threatened to ignite fireworks in his brain.

"When I lie in bed tonight, and I touch myself, I want to still feel where your cock has pressed."

"You know diddling yourself is a sin, right?"

"Everything we've ever done together has been

indecent and sure to send me straight to hell. I don't mind. I know you'll be there."

"Are you saying you want to burn forever with me?"

"I've been burning from the moment we met. Oh – you feel so good inside of me, Vaughan."

She felt incredible around him. Really, he had not taken full advantage of what she was so eager to offer him, but it had been difficult to shake off the notion that Lucerne possessed some right to her pussy. It had always been a nonsensical concept, and even more so these last ten months. Why shouldn't he fuck her any way he pleased? Why shouldn't he pour his goddamned soul into her? Her derriere was a sweet taboo, but fucking her pussy felt sweeter and twice as sinful.

Bella had belonged to Lucerne.

Well, no more.

"Bella." Dammit, he sounded as desperate and needy as she did.

She couldn't reach out to him, and he was momentarily sad for that fact, but nor did he want to slow things in order to release the bindings. Instead, he clove as much of her body to his as he could. He held her firmly in his grip and refused to slow down or temper the force of his thrusts.

She was screaming out his name between ragged breaths. Her muscles fluttered around him. It was as if they were made to fit together exactly like this, like she was made for him, and he for her.

Those sparks of lust he'd been fighting to subdue began bursting into flame. Streamers of heat shot through his body. The punishing rhythm was so intense it hurt. He was on the edge of pain when her inner muscles began to flex around him, drawing him deeper as he spilled a portion of his soul into her.

In the quiet that existed in the moment after their climaxes faded, Vaughan reached up and pulled the knot out of the cravat. Bella's hands dropped to her sides, but in a trice she had turned herself about and wrapped her arms around his neck. He could hardly bring himself to look her in the eyes, but there was no avoiding it either. It exposed him, but he wanted to be exposed. He wanted her to know that this meant something.

Love radiated from her body and her expression, but the sadness, the weight on her shoulders hadn't gone. "Why must you love him more than you do me?"

In that moment, he couldn't swear that was true.

"Perhaps there's room in my heart for the both of you."

She gave a slight nod, then pressed their foreheads together. "It's selfish, I know it, but I want you wholly to myself."

"There's not a part of you wishing for another set of arms around you too?"

"You're all I need, Vaughan."

He sealed his lips tight.

"It's all right," Bella stroked her fingers through the front strands of his hair, pushing it back off his face. "I know you don't feel the same. I know you still want him. I know I have to reconcile myself with that."

"He could belong to both of us again."

She thought a moment, then shook her head. "I wish it were as simple as that sounds, but I don't know that I can..." She sighed deeply. "I don't know that I can forgive him for having left."

CHAPTER 12
BELLA

"CRAKEHALL?" said Joshua a full ten days after the christening. "Who the devil is he, and why should I give a damn he's taken it into his head to get married?"

"Because we're invited to the announcement," Bella responded. They were in the back parlour at Wyndfell, as a great deal of soot had fallen down the chimney in their customary sitting room, and everything within was covered in the stuff. Even in here, a room more like a monument to the past century, it was impossible to entirely avoid the filth. Great clouds of it kept whistling past the window – the maids were outside beating the carpets clean.

"Do you not find that odd, that we should be invited to an announcement by people we're unacquainted with, when we can hardly get an invitation from those we do know?"

"Not in the slightest," Bella said blithely. It seemed to her that they should count their blessings. Also, there were two very likely explanations for the invitations. Firstly, the very fact that they were unacquainted meant that Mr Crakehall wasn't privy to the scurrilous gossip circulating, and secondly, Vaughan had somehow engineered the invitation. Quite possibly both factors were at play.

She had seen frightfully little of Vaughan. He arrived at Wyndfell every other morning, but Joshua insisted on chaperoning them for the entirety of his visits, so they were deeply frustrating. It reduced the conversation to pleasantries, and there was no possibility of intimacy. Bella was not sure how Vaughan was tolerating it; she was ready to contemplate murder. Therefore, any invitation that might buy her a few moments alone with the man she loved seemed like a blessing beyond measure.

"Please agree that we can go." Even if Vaughan wasn't in attendance, there would surely be somebody present she could converse with. "It says it's to be held at Stags Fell," she pointed out, taking the card from her brother's hands.

"Does it?"

Bella turned towards the mantle in order to hide her smile. She set the card there, and made a deliberate show of peering intently at the lettering again. "It does."

Of course, the location of the event, a beautiful, stately building not even a century old was not what was enticing her brother's interest. Joshua was no lover of architecture. Houses that contained ten times the number of rooms as residents he considered wildly indulgent. Nor was he interested in formal gardens with pristine walkways – a point on which she admittedly agreed. She missed the rambling overgrown gardens of Lauwine from before Lucerne's occupancy. However, Joshua was an admirer of Sir Thomas Lartington, the owner of Stags Fell. He was a fellow engine enthusiast, and had written several well-received treatises on the subject. Bella had been treated to an excessive number of passages from them that Joshua insisted on reading aloud. As if noisy, dirty machinery interested her. She'd only set foot in the tin mine he owned twice in her life, and the other mines – lead was it? – never. So, why would any sort of noisy behemoth entrance her?

"Is this Stephen Crakehall some family member of his?"

"I don't know, Joshua. As best as I can recall, I've never met him, but I'm bored to tears cooped up here with nothing to do. We've barely seen a soul since I arrived home."

"The silence never used to bother you."

Oh, but it had. She shot an irritable glance at him over her shoulder. Could he not see how that fact had influenced her decision to flee when the opportunity arose? What young lady wouldn't seize the chance to see London on the arm of a member of the nobility over drifting aimlessly about in a landscape comprised almost wholly of mist, sheep, and ling?

"Mayhap this is the first step towards reacceptance? People have seen Vaughan paying court and have realised things are not as licentious as their fevered imaginations suggested."

"Would that I believed that also."

She scowled in his direction.

"I'm no fool, Bella. Tis lip service Pennerley's paying, nothing more. The man has no respect for social niceties. He is merely humouring me. He's not going to suddenly announce decent intentions towards you, and I can't understand why you're not doing a thing to encourage them. Don't you want a respectable life?"

"Mistresses have more fun," she replied flippantly. "And as you said, he's merely indulging you."

When he frowned, she shook her head and crossed to where he was sat in a cracked leather wingback. "Oh,

Joshua, you know I do not mean it. Of course I would like to be his wife. I desire that above most things. How grand to be the Marchioness of Pennerley. But what good will imagining something so far-fetched do me? He is not going to transform, nor do I wish him to. I love him because he is exactly the way he is."

"A dishonourable rogue," he muttered, and sighed, before taking hold of her hands. "Dear sister, I do not understand you. You are a gentleman's daughter. You could have the pick of decent men..."

Bella squeezed his hands. "They would not suit me. We would make one another frightfully unhappy. I'd much rather be happy, wouldn't you?"

"You do not know that, Bella."

They had covered this ground so often now that Bella simply turned away from him rather than restating her arguments. She took up the servant's bell and rang it over vigorously. The fact of the matter was that she was quite unable to even conceive of giving Vaughan up. Not only that, increasingly the thought of ever entertaining another man left her with a sick sensation in her stomach. She may have been willing and wanton in the past, but now there was only one pole on which she cared to slide. It might pain her brother to recognise that, but it was a fact.

"I'd like tea and whatever dainties cook has about," she told the maid, who still looked rather soot-stained beneath a hastily tied fresh apron.

"Very good miss, I'll ask her what she has."

"You've an awfully sweet tooth of late," Joshua observed. "I suppose that's his doing, too. I have a tin of candied oranges here if you would like a piece."

Bella reached out her hand immediately. "Where did they come from?"

Joshua placed a small tin into her hand. "Lauwine."

"From Lucerne?" Her attempt to refer only to him

133

as Lord Marlinscar failed as often as not. "A peace offering?"

"From Caroline Wakefield."

"Ah, a reward for your gallantry. Yes, I should like one, thank you." As a matter of fact she helped herself to three of the tiny pieces, and sucked on them one after another. They were rather sour despite the syrupy coating. "Do you suppose an invitation has been sent to Lauwine also?"

"As we two pariahs are included, it would seem reasonable to assume that every scoundrel hereabouts has garnered an invite."

Bella settled upon a carved wooden backstool, which creaked alarmingly under her weight, causing her to hop to her feet again immediately. "I do wish you would forgive him." While she had no real desire to see Lucerne on a daily or even frequent basis, a warmer relationship between the two households would have provided her with some amiable companions at least in the form of the Misses Wakefield. Never before had Bella craved female companionship so ardently. She had spent the whole of that morning composing letters to various acquaintances in London out of sheer desperation. A usually avid letter writer, she was not.

"Do you promise to behave if I agree?" Joshua asked. The way he looked at her was horribly grave.

"I will be the height of discretion."

"Hm," he grunted. "I suppose it is too much to expect sobriety and chastity."

"When did you become such a dour knave? You used to be far more spirited."

"I am not a horse, Bella."

"I fear you are very much like a wild stallion that has been broken, and now you are odiously compliant and soulless."

Joshua rose from his chair and snatched back his

tin of candied oranges. "Would you prefer that I was inclined towards kicking and biting?"

"I wish you would stop turning every conversation into a discourse on my failings."

His chin jutted out, and he puffed himself up as if a lengthy outburst were on the horizon. Bella looked longingly at the door, and wondered if it was possible to reach it before the tirade began.

CHAPTER 13
VAUGHAN

AUGHAN HAD WORKED the knots out of his limbs with an early morning gallop. The sun over the moor had left him unusually jovial. His spirits lifted higher when he returned to the inn to find the landlord in possession of an invitation for him. He was no young lady, prone to giddiness over the prospect of a ball, but he did love the opportunities such gatherings afforded.

His fellow occupants at the Dog and Basin, Godfrey...Gadfly...whatever it was, and the other fellow, Armitage, were both fully versed on the details of the upcoming occasion, though neither was in possession of an invitation. Nevertheless, it was a matter of mere moments before Vaughan himself was apprised of the facts. It seemed both the residents of Lauwine Hall and Wyndfell Grange were among the invitees, as was the local physician, Doctor Garth, and some of the other local well-to-do families he was as yet unacquainted with.

There was a second missive, this one from his sister, Niamh. Vaughan scanned the lengthy contents, and put it aside for later consideration. There was a swathe of it on the subject of matrimony. It seemed Niamh was still as besotted with Henry Tristan as she'd been when she first left for London. He had thought the exposure to society at large might turn her head in another direction, but it seemed her affection for Mr Tristan was rather more steadfast. He supposed he ought to be pleased. Henry Tristan was at least a vast improvement on the reckless young rogue she had set her heart on last autumn. He was worldly, astute, amenable, and had means enough that Vaughan did not have to fear he was merely seeking his sister's hand in order to secure her funds. It was mildly troublesome that the man had trailed around after him in the past like some lovesick whelp, but thankfully he had never been tempted to share more than a brandy with him.

Yes, matters would have to be settled soon enough. One needed to secure an heir after all, and he had no plans to produce one.

Having drafted an elegant response to the invitation, and dispatched it, Vaughan set out across the village green with the intention of taking himself on a walk to stretch his legs. Endless idling was tiresome, and he thought he might seek out a little something for Bella ahead of the ball. He was absolutely of a mind to escort her there, and arrange several other things besides. Having to pay her court as society, or at least Joshua Rushdale, insisted upon was growing exceedingly tedious. He rather supposed that was the point. Rushdale meant to wear him down until he was obliged to make some rash gesture in order to secure time alone with her.

If it had been any other woman, he'd have cut his losses by now and turned his attention in another direction, but there were multiple reasons why he had not done so, which he did not care to consider too deeply. In any case, Bella was as vexed by Joshua's unreasonableness as he. Not that it was genuine unreasonableness. If Niamh had been in Bella's current situation, Vaughan would not have been half so tolerant. He'd have severed the man's ballocks from his personage by now.

However, he was not going to think on it, for it inevitably brought on a headache. There were other matters to attend. Days had passed, and save for that one interaction, there had been no opportunity to cross paths with Lucerne. He did not want to storm up to the gates, so to speak, and demand Lucerne's attention, rather he wished to insinuate himself into the other man's conscious again, so that little by little, he would feel the tug and return to the place he ought never to have left.

For that to work, there had to be at least some form of interaction. This invitation from Crakehall would surely provide that. He had in his head a tickle of a memory that Crakehall had fagged for Lucerne at school. It would be a perfect opportunity.

Having strolled twice around the green, Vaughan found himself in the vicinity of the small haberdashery as two ladies approached. He was not in possession of their names, but the resemblance was quite unmistakeable – they were clearly Wakefield's sisters.

"I do hope whatever we find in here will be serviceable," the first remarked, as she approached the shop door. She was wearing a horrid straw bonnet with a russet ribbon, which made her seem altogether more round and homely than was considered fashionable. The second was taller, clearly younger, and full of angles. Everything seemed to stick out in some way, including both her chin and nose, both of which were now tilted towards the sky in despair. She stopped in her tracks and planted her hands on her hips.

"Heavens, Caroline, serviceable? I don't want serviceable. We're to attend a ball, a proper one, and my first at that—"

"You have been to several."

"Assembly balls in our village hardly count. One is required to be there, and has to be constantly inventive to find reasons not to endure their tedium. This will be different. There are to be lords and ladies present. I don't want to look like a country bumpkin. If only we had time to visit one of the larger towns, or we had known of the invitation sooner. Then we could have visited the modiste in Harrogate on our way here."

"From what Lord Marlinscar has said, Mr Crakehall wasn't even in the county then."

That confirmed the connection.

"I wonder who it is he's to marry," the speaker continued. "Isn't it rather peculiar that no one seems to know?"

Her sister pursed her lips and wrinkled her distinctly Wakefield-esque nose. "Perhaps it's a surprise, and the lady herself does not know it yet, or he plans to choose someone from among the attendees, and that is why so many people are invited."

"Maria, you say the most preposterous things. Of course he is not going to choose whichever lady catches his eye off the guest list. I'm sure there is no conspiracy, and the lady herself is perfectly aware of the arrangement."

Maria pursed her lips and dove her hand into a box of buttons. "Well, I'm not so sure." She let the buttons run through her fingers. "Perhaps she doesn't care for him. Perhaps he has a wart on his nose or is one of those toad-faced individuals. I shouldn't like to marry one of those. Imagine having to look at him across the breakfast table for the rest of your life. And think of the children. They might turn out toad-faced too." She stuck out her tongue in horror. Although she faced the shop window, her reflection showed clearly in the glass.

Her sister promptly shook her head. "Toad-faced, indeed. You should be lucky to receive any offers at all, and it is said that some toads are truly princes in disguise. Perhaps if you dismiss them all out of hand, then you will miss out on a prince."

Maria considered that for about half a second. "Oh, I wouldn't mind," she confessed. "That is, unless he was a particularly pleasant and elegant prince." Her gaze settled at that moment upon Vaughan, and a spark of vitality seemed to illuminate her features. She winked at him. "The current lot are said to be gluttonous pigs."

Vaughan did his best to suck in his smile, only for the naughty imp to wink at him again. Did she actually mean to flirt with him? Oh, the fun he might have at Wakefield's expense if he weren't preoccupied with other matters.

"Oh my, heavens! Maria, you cannot say such things."

The woman named Caroline looked about in dismay, and on seeing him within hearing range blanched a particularly sickly hue.

"I believe I just did."

"Then take it back."

Maria scoffed. "I can't unsay something. In any case, it is not I who has my eye on such a lofty beau as my future husband."

Vaughan wasn't sure it was possible for a lady to look more horror-stricken, and he delighted in macabre surprises and shocking virgins out of their undergarments.

"Ma-ry-a! Do not begin this again."

Maria laughed, and did a curious jig on the spot, barely able to contain her sheer delight in her sister's torment. "Then admit you're intoxicated by him and are hopelessly doe-eyed in his presence. Joanna might be besotted with our niece, but you are all eyes for Lord M."

So, Miss Caroline Wakefield was developing a tendresse for Lucerne? Interesting. She was not at all to Lucerne's tastes but represented everything Lucerne thought he probably ought to settle for. Good, honest, demure, and lacking every talent Lucerne really cared for. "They would be tolerably suited," he thought, hearing the words as spoken by his harridan of a grandmother. The dowager had held an opinion on everything, and had never shied from voicing them. She had told Vaughan that Lucerne was a man prone to folly and who would cause him a deal of distress. Then again, she had also congratulated him on selecting a special friend with such spectacular calves. The dowager had invested a great deal of energy in the study of men's legs, a fascination his sister appeared to have inherited. His thoughts turned to her letter again, and her insistence that he talk to Henry Tristan.

He would do so, in his own time. There was no need to rush, and presently he had business in Yorkshire that required his full attention. Niamh, London, and her attachment to Mr Tristan would have to wait.

The two Misses Wakefield still remained outside the shop, and Vaughan returned his attention to their conversation. Bella had mentioned meeting them following the christening, and some fall one of them had taken, but she had made no mention of any doe-eyed glances in Lucerne's direction. That perturbed him a little. If anything, a rival for Lucerne's affections ought to have made her realise that she still cared for him. Her continued insistence that there was no spark left to rekindle between them concerned him more than he liked to admit. Everything revolved around the three of them making a solid accord.

"Do you suppose Lord M might dance with us at the Crakehall gathering?" Maria Wakefield said. "I do hope so, for we won't know any of the other gentlemen present, and it will be such a waste if there is not the opportunity to dance."

Her sister didn't respond. She was riffling through a box of ribbon ends set on a table beside the window, her eyes downturned, and her cheeks still flushed with embarrassment. After a moment, Maria clapped her hands, "But of course he will, out of some idiot obligation to Freddy. He'll give us two dances apiece, even if we all exhibit two left feet and tread on his toes."

"Do not tread on his toes, Maria."

Vaughan barely contained a snort of laughter, and decided to seek the lady out himself for a dance. They were right about Lucerne. He would dance with them, and did so moderately well when he had the sense not to wear over tight breeches, but if the minx before him, now smiling secretly to herself under her bonnet were to deliberately set out to trip him, there might be an opportunity for him in that moment to engineer an interaction. He would like it immensely if Lucerne were to fall right into his waiting arms, and then they happened to dance a step or two together. It would naturally scandalize the locals, and be seen as a glorious jape by those more worldly.

"Please, Maria, enough of this prattle." Caroline threw the bits of ribbon she had separated back into the box of oddments. "Might we enter, now? If we don't make more haste the shopkeeper will turn the sign, and then we will all have to make do with what we have brought for there will be no time to venture back again, or for Eliza to work miracles."

Miracles indeed would have to be wrought, if this Eliza was going to turn Wakefield's sisters into something other than the dowdy spinsters they clearly remained.

Although, he conceded, the chit had some skills as a torturer.

"Pennerley?"

Vaughan had taken in all the sights to be found in the little village, and was idling on the stone bridge over Arkle Beck when a horseman approaching from Grinton direction hailed him. He was dismayed to discover the man to be Joshua Rushdale.

"Out for a ride?" Vaughan enquired. The problem with the countryside was that unless one was being entertained, or had gainful employment or an estate to oversee, there was precious little to do besides stroll and gallop, and well, roll in the hay if circumstances allowed it. Thanks to this fellow, the latter was proving difficult.

"I've been attending business. Mines don't run themselves."

"Oh, I was under the impression one employed a captain to oversee the running."

"Quite," Joshua agreed. He dismounted and found a ring on which to tie the horse's reins. "However, it also pays to keep a careful eye on said captain. I don't care for surprises."

"I don't suppose mining produces all that many."

The other man broke into a curious sort of smile. "You'd be surprised," he said. "I'm glad I've happened upon you. There are things we ought to discuss."

"I can't think what about," he remarked, brows raised.

Joshua mirrored the expression. "Pray do me the favour of not being deliberately obtuse. You can't expect me to turn a blind eye to what's going on when you're in my home parish."

"And what is it that's going on?"

"Well, that's what I'd like to know."

Vaughan raised himself onto the side of the bridge and sat with his back to the water. "That's rather circular logic. You want to talk to me about what's going on, but at the same time you'd like me to explain what it is you think that is."

Joshua placed his sun-browned hands on the wall and looked out over the bubbling brook. "I know she's your mistress, and I don't care for it one bit. In fact I'm going so far as to say I'm outraged by it. Disgusted. But what am I to do? I've no wish to alienate my only kin, and I'm hardly able to thwart a man of your means or reputation. You won't have her while she's under my roof though."

"Of course not." Vaughan made a mental note to clamber in through Bella's window at least once before they left Yorkshire. He did so detest people setting him boundaries. The only thing they had ever done was make him want to cross them.

"Now perhaps you'll do me the courtesy of explaining how we arrived at this position," Joshua said drawing his attention back from the water, and up to Vaughan's face. "I tolerated all those seasons in London on the understanding that she would marry and become Lucerne's wife, so how is it that failed to come about, and instead she has thrown her lot in with you?"

"The heart is fickle."

Joshua shook his head, making his brown curls shake. He was overdue a trip to the barber. The fellow could almost pass for fashionable. "There's more to it than that. Something must have happened, or been said. She would not have simply walked away from such an advantageous match for no reason. I saw how she was with Lucerne on many occasions, her heart was his, and I know he meant to do right by her."

Vaughan slipped off the wall again, and paced the width of the bridge. This firm but polite discourse on the subject unnerved him. Anger or resentment would have been easier to deal with. "Surely this is a conversation better had with Bella, or Lucerne."

"Do you not think I have followed that route already? Neither will tell me a thing, or at least nothing that makes a ha'porth of sense. You were there, so please, do me the honour of explaining it. It's the least you might do under the circumstances."

"Where is Bella?" Vaughan asked. He stooped and picked up an array of stones, which he lined up along the side of the bridge. He flicked them, one by one, and watched them drop into the gushing, gurgling brook below.

"At home bottling preserves. At least, that's where I left her."

"Something she has a talent for?" Vaughan little cared either way, but he liked the idea of Bella working like a scullery maid, dressed in an apron and mop cap. Moreover, he enjoyed a brief imagining of leaving floury handprints all over her bottom and thighs. When the opportunity arose, he would have to indulge in that little fantasy, and of fucking her senseless across the kitchen table between the peas in need of shelling and a ball of freshly kneaded dough. "I don't pretend to understand the inner workings of the female mind. Are they not all creatures of whims?"

"Some." Joshua agreed. He came again to Vaughan's side, even going so far as to knock one of the stones off the side. "You know more of this than you are currently admitting. What did you do? What did you say or offer her to steal her from Marlinscar's side?"

"So it's a thief you have me pegged as?"

"Are you not one?"

Vaughan raised his fingers to his lips, and briefly covered them. "I confess, I've stolen a thing or two in my time, but you're mistaken in believing your sister to be one of them, or that I deliberately seduced her away from Lucerne. Whatever choices your sister has made have been entirely her own."

"Then explain to me how it comes to be that you and he are no longer friends?"

"That is none of your business."

"But it is true that you are not?"

"We do not currently see eye to eye on a couple of points." He shrugged as if they were minor things.

"And you expect me to believe that Bella is not one of them?" The lines around Joshua's mouth grew deeper and grim. "For God's sakes, man. One of you, at least, owes me some sort of explanation. I thought I might at least rely on you to be direct. You're not normally one for delicately skirting issues."

True enough, at least in some regards. It was certainly an image he presented to the world, if not an entirely accurate one. There were layers upon layers of things he held close to his chest.

Joshua cleared his throat. "Something happened between the three of you. I wish to know what. Is that truly such an enormous demand?"

Vaughan turned sharply towards the other man. "You only think you wish to know. The truth is, you want an assurance that what occurred is not as bad as you fear. Unfortunately, I have to inform you that your fears are almost certainly justified."

An angry tick pulsed in the side of Joshua's clean-shaven chin. "What the devil are you saying? Spit it out."

Vaughan closed his eyelids, then slowly opened them again. He did not blather as commanded. What had occurred between the three of them was nobody's business but their own, and there was no way of explaining how he and Bella had come to be together and Lucerne estranged from them without revealing the sort of intimate details that no man who cared for his liberty willingly shared. Rushdale had been a willing co-conspirator in the past, a ready and willing participant in a number of japes, but he was not a particularly enlightened being. If he had any inkling about the sort of acts Bella had witnessed Lucerne and himself perform, he'd be beyond horrified. Men just weren't supposed to enjoy the company of other men, and if they were so ungodly as to give in to such urges, then they most certainly weren't to be indulged in the presence of a woman. Of course, no woman had ever been asked her opinion before being subjected to such a decree.

"Please, I have the utmost respect for your sister. What use will this serve?"

"You have no respect for her at all. If you did, you would marry her. There's no impediment to you doing so."

Vaughan allowed his bemusement to curl his lips. Perhaps no impediment that Joshua could see or was likely to understand, but that did not mean that such barriers did not exist. "Is it really that simple a matter to you? I just slip a ring upon her finger, and all is well in the world again. I fear you will have to look to Lucerne to oblige, except she has, of course, already rejected him."

Joshua tensed. His spine went rigid, and two

blotches of high colour streaked across his cheekbones. "She has done what?"

"Did he not tell you? No matter, I'm sure he'd readily take her even now, but alas Annabella's heart resides elsewhere."

"With you?" Joshua shook his head back and forth. "I don't understand. If he offered, why would she reject him? What right-minded woman would turn down the opportunity to become a viscountess to be a mistress, even to a marquis?"

"Love is blind."

"You have ensorcelled her."

"Please, my talents are many, but they do not extend to the satanic arts. Bella was fully aware of the terms before she made her choice, and indeed, I have never prevented her from making a different one. One might say I've even encouraged it, but it is not what she desires."

"Which I am supposed to believe is you? She hated you. You were naught but a thorn in her side. Always coming between her and Lord Marlinscar."

"You are quite mistaken." Alas, Lucerne had e'er been in the middle.

Some measure of his inner thoughts must have been betrayed by his expression, for Joshua's eyes widened in an alarming way, while his nostrils flared, and he reared back onto the heels of his boots.

"My God, were you both tupping her all along?"

Vaughan almost choked on his own tongue, but he did not flinch from meeting Joshua's gaze. Truly, if such a man as Joshua Rushdale could read him so easily, he would have to construct a better mask. "I trust you don't expect me to answer," he said drawing on all his aristocratic hauteur.

"That answer is confirmation in itself. A true gentleman would deny even the notion of such a thing.

Goddamn you and Lucerne both. I should beat the pair of you black and blue."

"You are welcome to try," Vaughan remarked dryly.

Joshua promptly swung a fist at him.

Vaughan allowed the blow to connect, moving only enough to avoid a broken nose. The impact rattled his teeth and set off multiple explosions in his inner ear. Goddammit, that would probably bruise. His fist clenched, but he refrained from making a retaliatory swing. He would not be seen brawling in the streets like a peasant. In any case, a punch, if he had landed one, would likely topple Joshua over the low wall and right into the river. Annoying as he was, there was no cause to kill him. In any case, a bruise seemed a minor payment for all the sport he'd so far enjoyed and planned to continue to enjoy with Bella.

"Feel better for that?" he asked.

Joshua rubbed at his reddened knuckles. "Not in the slightest. How could you? What in heaven's name were you thinking? She's my sister, not some threepenny whore."

He and Lucerne had shared many a whore. "Indeed, such delights are a deal more costly," he retorted. "Nor was any harlot ever so enthusiastic in her willingness to pleasure two cocks at once." Whereas, Bella revelled in such perversity. It was not a wise response, but an accurate one. If they were going to trade truths, then he no longer felt obliged to curb his tongue. Let things be entirely honest between them. "I trust you are aware that neither Lucerne nor I were her first. She was already wayward and quite devoid of shame even before we met."

Joshua's lower lip jutted over the upper one as his brow wrinkled with vexation and his cheeks hollowed. "Her errors of judgement hardly negate your own despicable behaviour," he bellowed, all in a rush.

"Moreover, I have only your word on that, which it shouldn't surprise you to learn, I do not trust. Truly, I wonder that either of you can even meet my eye. But then I recall Lucerne could not. He, at least, acknowledges his depravity and knows some shame."

"While I recklessly revel in mine," Vaughan concluded. "No amount of punches will change that. My father couldn't beat it out of me. I'm damn sure you won't. Nor will you undo the past or change your sister."

"I forbid you to go near her again."

Faced with such spitting rage, Vaughan cackled. "You forbid it. Do you genuine think you can deny me anything? How will you stop me? Do you mean to keep her prisoner? She will despise you for it, and only the god-fearing idiots will congratulate you for taking her in hand. She is a person, not an animal." He backed up a little, shaking his head. "Such actions would rebound in the most caustic way. They will whisper in salons up and down the country of her folly and your actions, but it will not improve your lot."

"At least she will be free of your influence, and your reputation would not go unscathed."

"My notoriety would only increase. The thing about cultivating a reputation for debauchery and recklessness is that one conditions others to hearing such stories and accepting them as quite normal. That is why I continue to be at the top of society's invitation lists, whereas you are shunned."

"You are truly a vile cur."

Joshua swung at him again, but this time Vaughan neatly side-stepped. He grasped his assailant's arm and used his own momentum to put him off balance, and then bent him double. He kept Joshua's arm locked behind him and stretched painfully aloft.

"Unhand me."

Vaughan jerked his arm up a little higher. "It does not have to be like this between us, Joshua."

"Do not presume to such intimacy."

"If it's companionship you seek, I could easily arrange that. In London, with the right introductions, you could have the pick of the marriage mart."

"I wish nothing to do with you. A curse on you and Lucerne both. Do not call at Wyndfell again. Not unless you mean to rectify your deplorable behaviour."

Vaughan released him with a shove that sent him down onto his knees in the dirt. "Your sister and I have an agreement, and she is of age."

Joshua sprang up immediately and caught Vaughan squarely in the mid-riff with his head. The pair crashed into a puddle on the road, sending a spray of muddy ditch water into the air. Vaughan cursed, only for the air to be expelled from his lungs as Joshua straddled his chest. His hands tightened around Vaughan's throat. Squeezed.

Vaughan pried at those fingers, tears springing to his eyes, but they refused to loosen. He reached out, seeking some purchase, anything. A rock, jagged along one edge. He pried it loose from the clarts, and formed his fist tight around it. He prayed Bella would forgive him the damage to her kin. He swung his fist, only for a woman's cry to fill the air. Joshua lurched backwards so sharply that Vaughan's aim swept before his hawkish nose.

Joshua gave a wheezy gasp, and he was on his feet again, peering anxiously down the road.

Vaughan pushed himself into a sitting position. The back of his coat was soggy, and one presumed covered in mud. Rivulets of dirt trickled from his hair onto his pristine white shirt. There was a girl hurtling towards them as if a pack of hounds were on her heels. She was without shoes or bonnet, hence it was not until she streaked past him and swung to a halt, her hands fastened around Joshua's elbow that he recognised her as the chit from outside the shop – Maria Wakefield.

"What the devil?" Joshua cursed.

"Oh, Mr Rushdale – help. Please, help!"

"Gladly, but with what? Whatever has happened to distress you so?"

Maria pointed back the way she had come, where there was now another discernible figure hobbling into view, bonnet ribbons flying. Her arrival was announced by a honking cacophony.

"Geese," Vaughan helpfully deduced, rising to his feet.

"Caroline." Joshua hurried towards her at once.

Maria heaved an audible sigh and fixed her attention directly upon Vaughan. "Good day to you, sir."

"My lord," he corrected her.

"Begging your pardon." She gave a little curtsy. "Your status was not apparent. Did you fall in a puddle?"

"Do not speak to him," Joshua barked, while still running to the rescue. "He's a dire knave and a cur."

The lady's brow furrowed, but her attention remained fixed upon Vaughan's person as if she meant to read the truth of that opinion off his skin.

"It's quite true," he said helpfully.

"That I shouldn't speak to you?"

"Absolutely."

She pressed her berry-red lips together and gave a huff of irritation. "That's a shame. I'm only acquainted with one other lord."

"I know rather too many," he drawled.

That seemed to hook her interest. She tipped her head to one side, and regarded him much like matrons of the ton were inclined to. "So, did you fall into the puddle, or were you pushed?"

Vaughan took out his handkerchief and dried off his face and hands before offering her one. "Lord Pennerley," he introduced himself. "I had a hankering for a swim."

She laughed in delight. "Was not the river a better option?"

"It looked rather cold."

She wrapped her arms around herself and faked a shiver. She stopped and flicked a glance in Joshua's direction. He had almost reached her sister. "Vaughan, Marquis of Pennerley?" Her grey eyes opened quizzically wide.

He nodded.

"Why, I know you!" Colour shot through her cheeks, and she gave a nervous giggle. "Well, obviously not like that. What I meant was that you're an acquaintance of my brother and Lord M. I'm Maria Wakefield. Captain Wakefield is my brother."

"Well met." Vaughan bowed over her hand again, while she offered him another polite little head-dip.

Her expression sobered, mouth drooping at the corners. "But I believe you are no longer friends."

"It would be more accurate to say that our paths have taken us in different directions of late."

"Then we will perhaps see you at Lauwine before long for dinner."

"Perhaps." That was certainly his intention.

Joshua approached again, with Caroline in his arm. Tears streaked her oval face, and she clutched tight her bonnet ribbons. "Pennerley, if you'd be so good as to fetch my horse. Miss Wakefield has hurt her ankle."

"Badly?" Maria asked, at once reaching for her sister. "You'll still be able to attend the ball?"

Her sister gave her a wan, watery smile, and

gratefully squeezed her fingers. "I expect so, if I rest it. It... it's probably nothing at all."

"Whatever possessed you to go riling up geese?" Joshua asked. "Don't you know how dangerous they can be?"

Maria shook her head, while her sister sniffled quietly into Joshua's handkerchief. "It was entirely accidental. We took a wrong turn on our way back to Lauwine."

"I'll say."

"You did indeed, if you hoped to find it in that direction," Vaughan remarked. "Let us head back to the inn, and I'll have my carriage return you to Lauwine."

"Truly, that would be very kind." They walked a few paces, whereupon she stopped and plucked a stone from her stocking. "I wonder if it might be possible to locate my shoes." She waved off to the north where the geese were still milling.

"Let us see you safely into the village first," Joshua advised. "There is room on Jalda's back, beside your sister."

It was a relatively short walk back up hill to the coaching inn, where a gaggle of onlookers turned out to watch the lady being delivered into the Marquis of Pennerley's carriage. Joshua carried Caroline unassisted. He refused to allow Vaughan or any of his men to lift a finger. "I am perfectly able. Miss Wakefield and I have some experience of this task already, and you are rather grimy at present." He settled her carefully into the sumptuously appointed carriage. "We had better ensure there's not a third cause for me to carry you anywhere; people will declare a liaison."

"Thank you," Caroline whispered from under the brim of her bonnet. "You are very kind."

"It's my honour, Miss Wakefield. Let us return you safely home."

"Will you not join us?"

"Alas no," he backed out shaking his head. "I have business to attend."

The carriage pulled away, leaving Vaughan and Joshua looking at one another.

"I suppose I should be glad you and Lucerne are at odds, so you weren't tempted to accompany them and deprive another two respectable young women of their reputations."

"Quite." Vaughan sniped. "Forgive me, Rushdale, I need to attend to my attire. I trust our business is done."

"Not really," Joshua replied. "I ought to call you out."

"Alas, that you're not that foolish. Do give my regards to Bella." He gave a curt nod and entered the inn.

CHAPTER 14
LUCERNE

THE SYNCHRONOUS CLIP of horses' hooves brought Lucerne over to the library window. He was not expecting visitors, and though he was aware that Caroline and Maria had gone out some time ago, for he had been obliged to explain the route, they had done so on foot. Wakefield had taken himself into Richmond for the day to see old Garett Price—or perhaps it was his son these days, Lucerne struggled to tell one from the other, beyond ones hair and side-whiskers being a fraction whiter—but he would not return until after dark.

It was to his astonishment therefore that the view through the mullioned panes revealed not just a pair of horses, but a carriage hastening towards the house. Nor was it merely any carriage hurtling towards his door, but a rather specific one.

Vaughan!

Surely it could not be. Yet the coat-of-arms was unmistakable. Finally, Vaughan had come to him. He had come here, to Lauwine.

Heart in his mouth, Lucerne rushed to the entrance

hall, but he could not bring himself to stop there and wait sedately for his guest to be shown inside. After barely a moment of hesitation upon the chequered tiles, he jogged down the front steps in time to see his footmen opening the carriage door and seeing to the steps.

Lucerne forced himself into a pose of sobriety, shoulders back, head up, hands clasped in the small of his back. Through sheer force of will he held himself poised, awaiting Vaughan's descent. A figure appeared in the carriage doorway, a dark-head of hair, with ringlets at the end, but it was not Vaughan, nor even a man.

"Caro will have to be carried," Maria Wakefield announced. "Would you believe she has taken another tumble?"

Lucerne blinked, momentarily failing to grasp what was happening. Maria stood to one side, while his footmen lifted Caroline from the carriage and bore her inside between them.

"Don't you agree she's a twit, Lord M?" Maria called on the way past him into the hall.

"Pennerley?" he merely asked in return.

Underneath the façade of calm he was imitating, his emotions became turbulent. A haze seemed to separate him from his environs, as if he were somehow removed from them, and he was no longer wholly attached to his body.

Maria danced backwards to address him. "It was quite the piece of fortune that he was on hand when it happened. Lord Pennerley and Mr Rushdale were both most solicitous, even though he'd just taken a tumble of his own."

Joshua and Vaughan were abroad in Reeth together. How were the wounds between them healed while those between himself and Joshua continued to fester? How was it that Vaughan had sent his carriage, but not undertaken to come himself?

Lucerne, driven forward by a desperate need for resolution, hurried down the steps and peered into the gloomy interior of the landau. It was empty. Not even in the deepest of corners, where the shadows clung to the leather upholstery like cobwebs, could a person hide. He circled the vehicle in a desperate quest to prove to himself that Vaughan was in fact here, that he had merely slipped out of the other doorway.

Alas, he was not waiting to enact a surprise.

Lucerne fell still. Eyes closed, he drew a deep breath as his crushing disappointment spread to every cell of his being. Vaughan had not come to him, and he was a fool to imagine that he would. Shaking his head, he strode back around to the side of the carriage facing the hall entrance steps, trying desperately to shrug off the feeling of self-loathing and sadness that descended to replace his recent elation. This mess was his doing.

Lucerne had spent his whole life running from one or other thing, and a great deal of it from Vaughan, always safe in the knowledge that the other man would never let him go for long but would engineer their reunion.

This time around, the rules had changed. Vaughan had been in Yorkshire nearly a fortnight, and their paths had only crossed the once. It was intolerable. Even Charles had seen more of Vaughan.

Goddamn and bugger it! He wanted to ring somebody's neck, but now wasn't the time for it. He supposed he ought to follow the Wakefields inside and enquire as to Caroline's malady.

He plodded up the stairs, but could not quite drive himself over the threshold. "Has Doctor Garth been sent for?" he asked the footman coming out again.

"Miss Eliza Wakefield did not think it necessary, my lord."

"Not necessary?" Lucerne reared back a little. Perhaps Caroline was not so badly injured as she'd first appeared.

"If I may, my lord, she said that it would do to send young Thomas to the apothecary. I'm to hold the carriage a moment, so that he might travel there more quickly."

The lad could probably cover the distance on foot at a similar pace, but why deprive the boy of a treat? He recalled being young, and what fun it was to sit up with the driver and feel the air whistling past your face, and that had only been in an old trap his elder brothers had commandeered. Thomas would be puffed up with pleasure to be at the head of the Marquis of Pennerley's carriage.

"Where is he, then?" Lucerne looked about but could not see the lad.

"On his way, my lord."

True to the footman's word, Thomas appeared but a moment later scampering alongside Eliza, who was explaining the contents of a lengthy list to him."

"Supplies from the apothecary," she told Lucerne on seeing him. "I'm afraid your still room is rather ill stocked, though we'll be able to gather some things from the herb garden."

As Lauwine Hall had not known a lady of the house for nigh on seventy years that was not surprising. He supposed what was there was down to the efforts of his housekeeper. Herbal remedies and the like had not once entered his thoughts since he'd taken up permanent residence.

"I could see to rectifying that, if you'd like," Eliza said brightly. Her continued good cheer convinced him that Caroline's status was not a cause of undue concern.

"Could you? That would be very kind."

She smiled, and her cheeks pinked. "I do not know how you and my brother have survived so long here on your own without a lady to instruct you. I shall take stock of the situation once Caroline is tended, and provide you with a list of what is needed."

"Are you sure we shouldn't send for Doctor Garth?" Lucerne asked.

"No need. A poultice and rest will set her to rights. Tis only a twisted ankle." She waved her list at young Thomas, who tucked it under his cap, and then climbed up at the front of the carriage beside the driver.

They were about to start off again, when Lucerne waved to halt them. "I'll come along. Someone ought to properly thank Pennerley," he muttered. Naturally, no one questioned his authority when he climbed into the carriage and shut the door. By the time they had left the estate and rumbled along the lane towards the village, Lucerne began to think that it would have been rather better if they had. Wakefield would have told him outright that he was being absurd, and even Charles might have questioned his motives. He had no idea what to say to Vaughan. Thank you for sending the carriage was going to sound preposterous when he was then going to have to walk home again, and likely enough the ladies had already offered enthusiastic thanks – Maria always had an effusion of things to say.

The interior to the carriage brought back memories of happier times, of Bella singing like a lark while he licked between her thighs, and Vaughan knocking his head against the glass and almost passing out that time he and Bella had taken it into their heads to try and compete for his cock on the journey home from some wild party at Darleston House. Bella had won by default, but in actuality, Vaughan had been the victor, for both Lucerne and Bella had ended up taking turns to fellate him in order to set him to rights again.

Perhaps, he mused, looking back through somewhat clearer eyes, Vaughan hadn't been so badly addled after all, but had meant to divert their attention onto him all along. Vaughan knew well how to suck a man to completion, but he did not care to indulge in the act with an audience, not even if that audience consisted purely of Bella, and he absolutely never consented to sharing anything with her on an equal basis.

Was it possible that was the reason Vaughan had turned away from him those few days ago in the graveyard? Had his affections now shifted entirely to Bella, and now he was no longer prepared to share her with Lucerne? Would he ever again consent to share himself?

He had to know. However, barging into the coaching inn and demanding his attention was unlikely to provide him with the answers he required. Also, there would be too many eyes and ears fixed upon them there. Everyone who was anyone wanted to know the story behind their falling out. Lucerne was in no mind to satisfy their cravings for scandal. It was probably better that they kept on thinking it was all about Bella throwing him over in favour of Pennerley. At least none of them risked a rope around their necks for that. Reputations could be mended. There was no coming back from a hangman's noose.

"Stop," he hollered when they reached the next fork and applied his fist to the roof, as he'd entirely forgotten to collect his cane on the way out the door. "Change of plan."

The driver merely nodded in response. No doubt he was well accustomed to the whims of the aristocracy. Thomas paid him no heed at all. He was far too fixated on the hold he had on the horses' ribbons. Vaughan's man was certainly putting great trust in the boy to allow him the reins. Lucerne prayed he was worthy of that trust. Much as he longed for a reason to address Vaughan, he did not want to have to explain to him how his carriage had broken an axel or come off the road and overturned.

Having waited until Thomas and the driver moved onward again, Lucerne took the other fork in the road. He did not yet wish to return to Lauwine and face having to explain himself, so he settled himself on a course that would lead him down to the river in order to think. What if he sent Vaughan a note expressing a wish to meet and reconcile their differences?

It was customary in such circumstances to engage an intermediary. However, any man obliged with such a task would have to know the full details, and he could not impart those even to his closest friend. Wakefield remained wholly in the dark regarding the true depths of his relationship with Vaughan, and Lucerne meant for things to stay that way. Only a very few of their set from London had any real inclination of the nature of things between Vaughan, Bella and himself, and they had their own troubles to deal with at present. Darleston had been chased from town and was in hiding with his brother. Henry Tristan was thought to be courting Vaughan's sister, and Giles Dovecote had charged off to the Isle of Man with his new bride to visit some ailing relative.

He supposed some meeting would have to be engineered at Crakehall's ball. Surely, in amongst the festivities, they could find a moment alone to speak to one another unguardedly.

A few words of honesty, it was so little to ask, considering what they had done at other soirees.

He shook his head and crossed a stile that bore him

away from the lane and along a familiar path down into the valley. He would follow the silvery, winding path of the river to the head of a tumbling waterfall, then he would circle wide to reach the base of the falls, and rest a while. The pool at the base was wide and tranquil. Once or twice he had swum in that rocky oval, but most times he sat on the grey slabs that girdled the water and watched the foam tumble over the rocks. It helped clear his head. Leastways, whenever he left there his mind was calm, and his situation seemed less calamitous.

It was not often that he spied another person when out roaming. The area was sparsely populated, and few possessed the time or inclination to trek out to this particular spot. It was therefore with a sigh that Lucerne realised someone was already ahead. He did not see more than the shadow but heard the splash of their leap into the water from the top of the falls. The presence made him hesitant to descend, but if he wished to circle around to head back to Lauwine, he would have to carry on along his current route. To re-tread the path he had already come by would take considerably longer.

Lucerne sat on a rock. Perhaps the invader wouldn't stay very long. He was hot and sticky now. The breeze that had whistled at his back as he walked had dissipated. He took off his coat, and unfastened his cravat.

Some minutes passed, and the intruder did not leave. Impatiently, Lucerne rose and set off along the path again. It wound away from the waterfall behind some trees, making its decent via a gentler incline. He would have to share the vista, or simply carry on his course. The day was growing long, and his guests would expect him to be present for dinner. He ought to make the effort to enquire about Caroline too. He found her the easiest to communicate with, and she did not seem to intrude upon his world so much as her sisters. Or perhaps it was simply that he had become more familiar with her than the others. She was always willing to converse upon a topic of his choosing, while her sisters spoke primarily of Leesa, of bonnets, dance pumps, and embroidery.

The path turned back toward the waterfall. Lucerne dragged his feet. He could see the figure now through the trees, dipping in and out of the water. Twas a single man, dressed only in his shirt and under-breeches. He would be polite and not show his displeasure, but greet the fellow with a "good afternoon," should he raise his head in Lucerne's direction as he passed by.

The rocks were wet along the bankside, small pools having formed in the indentations. The man surfaced from the water, but Lucerne's rehearsed greeting died on his lips.

The man swimming here was Vaughan.

How could he not have realised that sooner? That physique, the athleticism, and especially the locks of dark hair that curled against his wet skin, the very person he wanted to see was right here where he needed him to be, in a neutral location usually devoid of visitors.

They could hammer this all out. He could say everything he needed to.

Lucerne's heart began to pound as his feet took him closer to the water's edge.

Vaughan emerged to the side of the fall, where a narrow outcropping of stone formed a crude walkway behind the tumbling water. Laying aside caution, Lucerne traversed that pathway. He shivered under the shadow of the rock where the sun never quite pierced and then emerged into the light again by his former lover.

"Vaughan," he began, whereupon Vaughan turned

to face him. All further eloquence deserted him. Vaughan's shirt hung heavy around his shoulders, the V of the neckline pulled low at the front, and the cloth was near transparent, so that the contours of his body were easily discernible, as too was the smattering of hairs upon his chest. Lucerne ought not to have looked, for it was too easy, once his gaze had settled upon the dark diamond of wet hair, to follow the trail of it down to where a larger shadow showed through his linen breeches. His lost lover had never favoured light colours, but today – cream. It was almost as if he'd anticipated Lucerne seeing him.

"Lucerne."

The way Vaughan said his name sent a spike of arousal through his loins. Lucerne shifted uncomfortably on the wet rock. "I hadn't thought I'd stumble upon you here." He swallowed nervously. "Thank you for helping my guests earlier – Miss Caroline and Miss Maria Wakefield. It was..."

Oh, for the love of God, he could not do this. He could not pretend that Vaughan's aiding the two women mattered to him. It did not. All that mattered was that he was practically naked within an arm's length.

He still remembered all the things he'd said, all the accusations he'd levelled and reasons he'd given for why he'd had to walk away, but looking into Vaughan's deep soulful eyes, none of them mattered any more. "I should never have left," he confessed and then crashed his lips down hard over Vaughan's mouth.

Lord, the taste of him... the scent... the sheer physicality of having him in his arms and so far at least not receiving a jab in the stomach for it. Need coiled within his loins, as he continued to ravage Vaughan's mouth. He could not help himself. He needed this too much. It was the most honest thing he'd done in eternity. With no care for comfort, he shoved Vaughan up against the rock face, startling a gasp of laughter from him before he was silenced by Lucerne's tongue questing into his open mouth.

Any resistance he might have encountered didn't materialize. Vaughan's limbs grew slack.

"I thought you'd made your choice and cast it in iron."

Lucerne swallowed hard. Their rapid breathing raised the temperature of the air between them. "I never meant our separation to be permanent. Things just had to change. Lines needed to be redrawn."

"Is that what this is?"

Lucerne's heart beat wildly as hope, fear, and desire warred within his chest. Beneath his fingertips, Vaughan's pulse drummed a rapid tattoo. "I never stopped wanting you. Tell me you've longed for this moment as much as I."

"I'm not about to sob into your shoulder. After all, you thoughtfully left Miss Rushdale behind when you departed."

"I didn't leave her. She left me. A fact I'm sure you know." Lucerne bent and licked at the beads of water clinging to the side of Vaughan's throat. "What has happened? Is this a bruise?" He drew his tongue over the red-purple mark upon Vaughan's cheek.

Vaughan pushed him off. His eyes were liquid and bright, but his emotions were locked up tight, making it difficult to read him. "Courtesy of Joshua Rushdale," he said. "He did not care for the notion we were sharing her."

"What on earth possessed you to tell him that?"

"He was most insistent that he know the truth."

"You did not tell him that we too were..." Lucerne covered Vaughan's loins with his palm.

"Were?"

If he had been uncertain until that moment, then he was no longer. Lucerne slipped the buttons of Vaughan's breeches, and began to stroke his thickening shaft. His muscles recalled the skill despite a year without practice. Vaughan's cock was as familiar to him as his own. "I've missed touching you, so much. I've missed the heat of your body, your pistol piercing me. I was a fool."

"Prove it. Show me."

Lucerne blinked, uncertain how to meet that demand. Then he stripped Vaughan's shirt from his back, and set upon exploring his chest with fingertips, lips, and tongue.

"You have no idea how many times I've replayed the last moments we spent together."

"Every day, five times over, and another twice over for every tedious explanation of our parting you've had to give Wakefield."

Precisely. Vaughan knew exactly how hot his fever for him ran. Vaughan had never hidden from it. It was he who cowered over what might result, he who had never quite committed one hundred per cent. That would change now, he swore it.

Desire for everything, all at once, burned beneath his skin, but Lucerne held himself back a little, determined to savour the moment.

"I want you."

Vaughan was impossible not to touch. He was so beautiful, so intense, and like an opium fiend starved of his addiction and then presented an abundance of it, he was incapable of doing anything besides drowning in the moment.

"I want you so much."

"I want you on your knees." Vaughan's hands landed hard upon his shoulders, and urged him downwards. Lucerne followed the path of a droplet running down Vaughan's body. He caught it with his tongue as it neared the waist of Vaughan's breeches. Very well, he would do his penance. He would open up his mouth, and allow Vaughan to fill it. He would swallow his come. All this he would do right here in the open, in broad daylight, with the fish and the rocks and the wind as witnesses, and water splashing down upon him from above. He peeled the wet fabric from Vaughan's skin, not all the way, just enough to enable him to lay his hands upon his lover's cock.

If he doubted that Vaughan wanted him, then here surely was proof. His cock already stood ramrod stiff, and wept silvery beads when he swirled his eager tongue around the cap.

The salty taste spurred him to further exploration, daring little licks into the slit, while he clasped tight Vaughan's arse with one hand, and encircled the base of his cock with the other.

"Suck, don't lick. Suck as if you mean to draw the venom from a wound."

The analogy was not lost on him.

Lucerne sucked. He could not stop doing so, heady with the knowledge that Vaughan was entirely at his mercy.

Vaughan's head lolled back against the rock face, ruby lips open around a sigh. His hips rocked to the rhythm of Lucerne's attentions. Already Lucerne's thoughts were turning to how and where they might go to fuck. He wanted to slide inside of Vaughan, drive into him with all the passion he'd fought to contain over these long, dreadful months apart. He wanted to be fucked too, hard enough that he was left tender by it. His imagination had run so wild, fantasies so fanciful of late, that he needed that physical anchor to reality to know that this wasn't merely another hallucination.

Vaughan's fingers curled against his scalp, bringing

a stinging discomfort, but also drawing them closer together. The short, shallow thrust bruised his lips. He was no longer in control of this, and no longer sucking. He was simply a willing receptacle. Vaughan's strokes lengthened, pushing deeper, pushing into the back of Lucerne's throat until he was possessing him utterly, and holding him... holding him right where he desired, his hands a cradle around the back of Lucerne's head.

"Il mio amore...That's right, take it. Take all of me."

He had little option to do anything else with Vaughan directing his movement. The assault made his jaw ache. He thought he might pass out from lack of air, but he had no mind to pull away. He wanted this too badly, wanted all of it, the good and bad, the assault on his throat, the tender stroke of Vaughan's fingertips against his jaw, even his building frustration at being unable to do a thing to ease the ache in his own prick. If he let go in order to touch himself, then he would overbalance and end up in the water, and this moment of pure bliss would come to a premature end. He deserved this. He ought not to have torn them apart.

Still, he ached.

Lucerne did not think he had ever ached so much for release, not even in all the long months of being apart.

He needed to touch himself.

His cock pressed painfully against his abdomen, fighting the constraints of the fabric that concealed it. There would be a wet patch where the head lay when he stood, possibly a rather large one. Even a small amount of friction would be enough to make him spend, as Vaughan was surely only moments away from doing.

His lover's groans grew louder. Lucerne had forgotten that low rumble, the one that became strangled and more needy the closer Vaughan got to spending. That point was almost upon him. Strings of barely coherent English and Italian flowed from his lips. "Such hell you created. Non posso vivere senza di te. Sei tutto per me. A little more, Lucerne. Just a little more." He sucked his breath in deep, then released it in a rush. "You undo me." He filled Lucerne's mouth. Coming so that he jerked and groaned with the force of the release. Only when he had stilled did Lucerne turn his lips to Vaughan's abdomen.

"And you me." He clasped Vaughan tight around the waist, holding on as though he expected the wind to rise and for him to be whipped away like a leaf from a tree. He could not persuade his fingers to uncurl, yet at the same time he wanted so badly to rise up, lift Vaughan so that he was braced against the rock wall and sink into him.

Was it too soon to demand that? He wanted them to fuck so badly. He didn't want to let go without leaving a piece of himself embedded in Vaughan's heart... Well, in his arse, if he was being entirely literal.

"Will you let me? I want you so much."

He rose to his feet, surprised to find his legs unsteady. He was still almost fully clothed, though his back and knees were damp from the cascading river. When Lucerne reached to kiss him, Vaughan jerked his head back.

Lucerne's heart plummeted. It was foolish of him to think everything would sort itself out simply because he was willing to get down on his knees. And yet, those things Vaughan had said. He did not understand entirely, his Italian was rusty, and had always been poor, but they had been statements, confessions of love – hadn't they?

He met Vaughan's gaze. His violet eyes were inky, the pupils dilated almost too wide. "Do you think I don't deserve satisfaction? Must I suffer longer for being a fool? I took what I thought was the only recourse. The three of us in constant battle—we could not continue like that. You knew it yourself. It's why you fled to Pennerley."

"I meant you to give chase."

"Are you so sure I did not?"

Vaughan blinked slowly. He shifted so that the wetted ends of his hair rearranged themselves upon his bare skin. "I'm certain of it."

"Yet you stayed away."

His look became infinitely darker, and more brooding.

"Bella," Lucerne said. "You and she... I knew it would be so. It was already apparent... So I was right."

He took a cautious step backward. "Of course, you and she are far better suited, and society will approve, even if you still baulk at legitimising your union. There will be no need for constant vigilance."

"Tis not I who ever craved their acceptance. What do I care for societies dictates?"

Of course, Vaughan had ever flaunted his deviance. He refused to live in fear, or entertain the notion that anything he did for pleasure or that they shared was wrong. He had no faith to speak of, and hence dismissed the word of God. As for rules...the laws of the realm... they were made to be broken. Bella matched him in that regard. She thrived on the knife edge of adventure. "You should make her your marchioness."

Vaughan laughed in his face. "The seasons haven't changed you at all. You are still belligerently blind to reality. She was right about you – the dowager – you are doomed to folly."

"What idiocy are you attributing me with?" Lucerne enquired. Could it truly be that Vaughan was still in denial over the depth of his feelings for Bella? Surely not.

The sound of a branch snapping from the direction

of the path caused them both to crane their necks. Stephan Crakehall was just emerging from the trees, with Charles Aubury ambling along beside him. Why was everyone here today, when usually the only intruders he saw were feathered or scaly?

Panic swirled in the pit of Lucerne's stomach. He stood mere inches from a man dressed only in near transparent under-breeches, sporting a monumental erection. Assumptions would be made. Horribly correct ones. Rumours that for years had dogged his attendance at society salons would circulate again, and a whole lexicon of words that he despised would be bandied about like curses; molly-boy, morphodite, sodomite, madge cove, backgammoner. Only one thing —well, two, if you counted Vaughan's considerable sway —had held those accusations in check before; his unofficial attachment to Bella. A man could hide a lot if he were also seen to be pursuing a suitable match. Now, Bella would have nothing to do with him. Might not that fact in itself be held up as further evidence of his unnaturalness?

They would be seen. He turned to whisper a warning to Vaughan, but he was no longer there.

Startled, Lucerne turned a full circle, but save for two wet spots upon the rocks that might have been footprints, no trace of his lover remained. Yet again, he had failed to say all that he wished to express. In fact, were it not for the slight ache in his throat, he might have convinced himself that it had all been a fanciful make-believe. It was not as if visions of Vaughan had not tormented him on numerous prior occasions.

"Marlinscar, is that you?" Crakehall was peering across the water, with his right hand raised to shield his eyes from the low sun.

Lucerne straightened out his face, and put on a smile and his coat, the skirt of which would conceal his current affliction. "It is indeed. Well met again. Crakehall, Charles." He gave them both nods of acknowledgement. "Whatever has brought you here this evening?"

"Pennerley," Charles replied. "Crakehall's looking to invite him to Stags Fell ahead of the ball, and someone said they had seen him go this way. You haven't happened upon him, have you?"

"Me? No. Not a sign of him." Apparently his ability to lie convincingly had improved. "I've only been here a moment or two myself. I'm on my way back to Lauwine. You must come along and join us for dinner, Stephen. Charles, of course, is already my guest. That is, if your new patron is not expecting your return."

"He will spare me for a few hours."

They began to walk, following the course of the river in an easterly direction. "How is your bride to be?"

"Very well, thank you."

"An agreeable match?"

Crakehall clapped him on the back and treated him to a hideously wide grin. "I would hardly say otherwise, now would I, but I think we will suit one another very well. She has some fine assets."

"Two particularly fine ones," Charles mumbled.

"What was that you said, Aubury?"

"Not a thing, just clearing my throat."

"So who is the lucky lady?" Lucerne was only vaguely interested, but the topic meant the attention of his two companions was not focussed upon him and why he'd been standing beneath the waterfall.

"Miss Hayes," Crakehall replied brightly.

Lucerne hid his surprise behind a polite cough. "The elder or younger?"

"The elder. Millicent. So, you're acquainted?"

"After a fashion," Lucerne replied.

"Wakefield—" Charles began, only for Lucerne to

jab him with an elbow. That was not a subject that needed to be discussed. He would need to warn Freddy in advance, perhaps even advise his friend not to go, just in case the likes of Charles saw fit to start a rumour regarding a past liaison. But of course, the Misses Wakefield were all in a flutter over the invitation, so perhaps Freddy would simply have to endeavour to fade into the wainscoting. It had been a stupid, stupid liaison anyway. He'd hardly liked the girl, and he'd been obsessed with Louisa at the time. Sometimes people's reason was unfathomable. Vaughan's, at present, more so than usual. He didn't know what to make of their exchange.

"I suppose it's to be expected that you'd know the family," Crakehall mused. He did not seem to have noticed Charles's buffoonery.

"I can't claim any close friendship," Lucerne replied. "We have only met a handful of times. The father is a tradesman, is he not?"

"Oh, I would not slight him with such a damning epitaph."

Lucerne winced. He had not precisely intended to. He'd simply felt obliged to say something that wouldn't lead to the subject of his doings and relationships.

"The family may have begun as simple haberdashers, but their empire has rather expanded. He has ten or so mills, now, scattered around the region, and a substantial stake in the vast steam-powered mill recently opened in York."

"Impressive," Lucerne remarked. He did not much care for the large red-brick factories that had sprung up in many of the northern towns and cities, for while they brought employment, they were also responsible for a hideous array of injuries. Not a fortnight ago the Leeds Mercury had reported an incident of a child of eight whose head had been smashed while performing the task of scavenging under one of the weaving machines. "I'm very happy for you Stephen. I'm sure it will be an excellent match."

CHAPTER 15
BELLA

I T WAS WITH considerable trepidation that Bella approached the front door of Lauwine Hall three days after Joshua told her of Caroline's accident. Lauwine had been her refuge for the duration of her childhood. It had been her playground, her fantasy home in the days before Lucerne determined to restore the property to its former glory and make it his permanent home. She still mourned the fields full of overgrown grasses, the weed riddled crooked paths, and her green cave beneath the weeping willow. She missed too, a sense of being truly welcome here. Hence, only once she was certain Lucerne was from home on estate business had she accepted the invitation from the Wakefield sisters to visit.

The interior of Lauwine had little changed, except that the scent of beeswax polish suffused the air in place of one of damp. A liveried servant showed her into the drawing room, where she found Maria settled before an easel, and Eliza and Caroline engaged in a game of cards. The latter, Bella was pleased to note, was seated upright, although her ankle appeared to be tightly strapped and elevated.

"Caroline." She went straight to her and they exchanged kisses. "How are you? Joshua told me you had taken another tumble. It's not serious, is it?"

Eliza lay down her hand of cards and scoffed. "'Tis a twist, nothing more. She'll recover well enough, providing she rests. And she would do well to watch where it is she puts her feet in the future, unless it is her intention to develop a reputation for clumsiness."

Ignoring her sister's outburst, Caroline smiled up at Bella in welcome and beckoned her to take a seat. "How good it is to see you, Bella. I am quite desperate for some spirited company from someone who is not intent upon berating me at every opportunity. They have kept me confined to quarters these last two days for Eliza insists I must keep my foot elevated, and Joanna believes it is not quite polite for me to do so in company. You don't mind, do you?"

"Of course not. You must sit however you feel comfortable."

"I pray you'll forgive my attire too, I am rather dishabille."

"There is no need."

Caroline was clothed in a simple gown, and Bella thought nothing at all of her attire.

"I'm without stockings," Caroline elaborated in response to her quizzical stare. "See." She teased up the hem of her dress. "I'm wholly outrageous. No doubt I will soon cultivate a reputation as a brazened coquette."

Bella laughed and took the offered seat. "I'm sure that is not very likely, but does this mean you won't make it to the Stags Fell affair?"

"Absolutely," Eliza insisted. She quit the game of cards and took to her feet, pacing over to the window, whereupon spying one of the house cats she scooped it off the windowsill and into her arms.

Caroline sighed and sunk a little deeper into the chaise longue. "I rather suppose it does. Pity, I was so looking forward to it, and having you introduce us to everyone hereabouts."

"Oh." How had it escaped the attention of the sisters that she was something of a pariah locally? She supposed they were not acquainted with many folks hereabouts.

"What she really means to say is that she hoped you'd help her secure a husband." Maria remarked, looking up from her watercolour. She was carefully rendering a depiction of Lauwine's courtyard garden.

"That is not true, Maria."

By now, Bella had grown accustomed to the two younger Wakefield's squabbling. It seemed mostly teasing and good-natured, unlike the quarrels she and Joshua engaged in on a far too regular basis. She did so wish she could make him happy, but she would not sacrifice Vaughan in order to achieve that. Perhaps that made her selfish, but while she loved her brother, she would not condemn herself to become an old maid, and that would be her lot if she were to sever her ties with Vaughan and remain in Yorkshire. In truth, she could not bear the thought of being parted with him on such a permanent basis. The enforced distance between them was already wholly intolerable. The ball and the opportunity to spend time with him could not come quickly enough.

"Well husband-hunting is what I intend to do," Maria announced. She put down her paintbrush and came to join them at the little card table, taking the seat Eliza had recently vacated. "Mr Crakehall dined here the other night, and knows a rather extensive cast of characters. I'm sure at least some of them are eligible bachelors of decent character and sufficient means."

"Ha! As if character has ever concerned you. I thought you were simply fixated on not being landed with a toad."

"A toad?" Bella asked, whereupon Caroline rang for tea, and then related the whole of the conversation she and Maria had previously had outside the haberdasher's store in Reeth village.

"Well, at least we already know there will be at least one such gentleman in attendance besides Lord M," Maria concluded. "Lord Pennerley."

Bella spluttered tea down her gown. "Oh, I am sorry." She stood and brushed at the stains. Eliza handily provided her with a kerchief, though she very nearly passed the cat. "It went down entirely the wrong way."

"Let me pour you another?" Maria set about the task of refilling her cup.

Bella settled in her chair again. Clearly the sisters were entirely in the dark about her history with Vaughan, too. That would not last. Such things were inevitably passed on.

"Do you suppose Lord Pennerley will attend?" Maria asked, while stirring sugar into Bella's tea, which was not how she preferred it. "I wish to dance with him, purely to irritate Freddy. Bella you should have seen his reaction when we told him that we had ridden back to Lauwine in Lord Pennerley's carriage. He was absolutely beside himself. Of course, Lord Pennerley wasn't with us, but I suppose that is just as well, or Freddy might have done something reckless in the name of our honour."

"Lord Pennerley only lent us the use of his carriage," Caroline elaborated. "Very finely appointed it is too,"

Joshua had not related that part of the incident. He had not mentioned Vaughan's involvement at all, though he had been in a frightful mood on his return.

Bella heaved a sigh. What good was it to sit here holding onto secrets? It seemed best to be honest and stomach the consequences. "I suppose you're unaware that I'm his mistress."

Three mouths dropped open at once. Eliza dropped the cat, which scampered away behind the tapestry at the far end of the room. Then Maria clapped her hands and laughed. "What a glorious jest, and you kept such a straight face."

"It is not a jest." Bella stood. "I shall go. Thank you for your hospitality, I won't trouble you again."

"Oh, do sit down, Bella." Caroline declared. She reached out and snatched at Bella's sleeve, coaxing her return to her chair. "The others may not have known it, but I did. I think I told you that I exchanged a deal of correspondence with Louisa. She spoke of you often. She was concerned by what she described as your obsession with Lord Pennerley. She feared it would undermine your future with Lord Marlinscar, and I am guessing from what you have said and what I've observed that is exactly what has occurred."

"I suppose, in a sense." Bella slowly resumed her seat, quite at a loss as to what else to say, and equally determined not to divulge anything anymore damning to her reputation or those of the two men involved.

Maria folded her arms across her bosom. "Well, I'm appalled that you kept that titbit to yourself, Caro." She huffed. "Now I suppose I shall have to cross Lord Pennerley off my list of eligible gentleman. What a nuisance. He was devilishly charming, rich, and handsome."

"But also a resolute scoundrel," Bella added. "He most certainly doesn't meet that part of your criteria.

However, I'd be happy to secure a dance with him for you if you're sure you wish to irk your brother. They never have liked one another much."

"Do you know why?" Her two companions leaned in eagerly.

She shook her head. Her notion had always been that it stemmed from jealousy. "I presume it something to do with Lucer—I mean Lord Marlinscar, but that is only a guess. I don't know for definite."

They drained the teapot and sent for more, which returned from the kitchen along with a platter of cakes.

"I'm decidedly vexed now," Caro declared, reclining against her mound of cushions with her hands upon her stomach. "I will miss out on everything, and Maria will never let me forget it."

Her sister stuck out her tongue. "Well, I don't see why we can't take you along and wheel you about in the bath chair."

"Because it would be wholly inappropriate," Eliza piped up from across the room. They had almost forgotten she was still present. She had her embroidery in her lap, and the little black housecat was curled up in her thread basket. "Of course, it means one of us ought to stay behind with you. We can't all gallivant off and leave you unattended."

"I vote for it to be Maria," Caroline levelled an expression of grim satisfaction at her youngest sibling. "It was her fault."

"Nonsense." Eliza shook her head. She did not look up, but kept her focus on her embroidery hoop. "It was an accident. Jo will stay behind. She's already said a dozen times that she'd prefer to stay here with Leesa."

Neither Caroline nor Maria argued.

"Good, it's settled then. Caro, you and Jo will stay behind and Maria and I will accompany Freddy and

Lord M. That will make travelling a good deal easier. We were rather an unwieldy party before."

"Well don't expect me to sprain an ankle whenever travel arrangements are complicated," Caroline huffed. She folded her arms, and stuck out her bottom lip.

"Bad luck," Bella squeezed her friend's fingers in an attempt to console her. "But of course we will bring back all the gossip of the event." Assuming there was any not relating to herself.

"Then you will visit again soon."

"Of course," she said lightly, but her heart grew heavy at the notion. Sooner or later, if she kept on coming here, she would inevitably run into Lucerne. She wasn't sure she was at all ready to face him again, though her reasons for not wanting to engage in another discourse were nonsensical. She was quite over him. Her heart entirely belonged to Vaughan, and that would not change. Yet she could not shake the sense of unease at the possibility of blundering into him again and discovering her heart not so closed off as she supposed.

Joanna arrived accompanying Leesa as Bella was heading for the door. "Oh, are you off already. I brought her down, as I thought you might like to see her."

"Walk out with me," Bella suggested. "I'll show you my favourite place in the garden, but it really is time I was away." If she lingered any longer the chance of Lucerne returning would grow exponentially.

The little girl happily ran ahead of them, watched over by her nursemaid, while Joanna and Bella followed at a more sedate pace.

"She really is a delight," Joanna remarked. "I'm sorry that you can't stay for longer. Perhaps you will come one afternoon and take tea in the nursery?"

"Bwella come tea," the little imp insisted.

"Yes, I will, but not today. My cave is this way. Look under here."

Her goddaughter squealed in delight, and darted in and out of the boughs. How odd it was to realise she had such a thing as a child that looked up to her. Bella shrank back from the willow cave as memories of the times she'd spent there cascaded one over the top of the other. Really, it was quite the wonder that she didn't have an imp of her own sequestered somewhere. She had not thought of such things in times past—she barely thought of them now. Obviously, she had learned one or two things during her time in London – a piece of sponge soaked in vinegar or wine, or a cap of lemon peel, and those horrid French letters that required hours upon hours of soaking to prepare – but she had not worried, for she had always felt confident that Lucerne would behave honourably if such a burdensome event occurred. Would Vaughan?

Most likely not. Any children that arose would be bastards. The notion left her unutterably sad, as if she could sob for weeks and not heal from it. In fact, tears aplenty trickled over her cheeks as she made the journey home on horseback, the wind drying the salt tracks on her face. There was no point in raising the subject with Vaughan. He would merely remind her that he made regular use of her bottom for a reason, but oh, how lovely it had felt that time at the inn when he had slid into her quim.

CHAPTER 16

BELLA

T HINGS REMAINED STRAINED between Bella and her brother, and grew more so when Vaughan failed to call at Wyndfell. It was therefore with considerable trepidation that Bella climbed into Joshua's rickety carriage to travel to Stags Fell. The movement made her woozy, and Joshua smothered the discomfiture between them by prattling on at length about high pressure steam, condensers, and puffing devils.

Bella wasn't at all sure if puffing devils were some sort of wicked sprite or the name of a specific piece of machinery. No matter. Joshua had transformed himself from looking like a country squire into a dashing beau. He had even consented to her helping him choose a new coat, breeches, and waistcoat for the occasion. Bella could only pray he would catch the eye of some lady in attendance, and they'd become hopelessly besotted with one another. Failing that, she'd have to find a broad and buxom wench to hire as a new lady's maid and nudge her in her brother's direction. Perhaps it was merely sexual frustration making him so surly, and if his bed were regularly warmed, he'd be as amiable and amenable as he'd been of old, when her previous maid, Emma, had often filled that very role.

Stags Fell was very imposing indeed. Size wise, the main house was similar to Lauwine Hall, but it was altogether grander. Its edifice gleamed white in the sunshine, while the terraces and vistas of the formal gardens sprawled around it like indolent serpents. Lord Marlinscar, Captain Wakefield, and three of the Misses Wakefield were all present from Lauwine, along with Bella's old mentor, Mrs Castleton, the Hayes sisters, Charles Aubury, and every other significant family within a twenty mile radius. There were also numerous guests from London, and a contingent of gentlemen of Sir Lartington's acquaintance who all belonged to some fellowship or other. Bella lost Joshua to them almost immediately after they had been announced and introduced to Mr Stephen Crakehall.

Crakehall seemed young and jovial enough, but with an ambitious streak that bled into his smiles and gave him a sometimes wolfish and other times hangdog air. He and Lucerne were apparently acquaintances of old, but Bella could not recall ever having met him during the three years she had spent with Lucerne and Vaughan in London, nor remember his name being mentioned. Still, they were welcomed enthusiastically, which gave her hope that they were no longer to be shunned by the families hereabouts.

Finding herself temporarily alone in the crowd, Bella made her way to where glasses of summer punch were being served, and claimed two. She then ambled amongst the guests as though she were looking for someone specific. Maria and Eliza had been announced ahead of her, so they had to be hereabouts somewhere. However, she could not find any sign of them.

"You look rather lost," a snippy voice said from behind her. Bella turned to find both Hayes sisters and an entourage of girls tittering into their fans. Millicent reached for one of the glasses in Bella's hand, but she held on to them.

"Millicent. What a delightful dress." It was a white-spotted muslin with an overskirt embroidered with tiny forget-me-knots. Pretty, but hideously modest. The neckline was gathered upon her throat so that the entirety of her bosom was covered. The Millicent of old would never have worn anything so demure.

"Likewise," she turned her gaze upon Bella's dress, and her mouth curled into a sneer. "Although, it's a little over-dramatic, don't you think?" It was the sort of dress she had worn all the time in London, where it would never have been considered anything out of the ordinary. She had promised Joshua she would not draw undue attention to herself, but apparently country styles remained stuck in the previous century. "But I suppose old maids must do all they can to entice an offer."

"I have no cause to entice anyone."

"That's not what I heard," Millicent stated, to a chorus of laughter. "Didn't you elope and return home unwed because the man in question realised you'd be unsuitable as a wife?" Her gaze, along with those of her entourage, swivelled in the direction of Lord Marlinscar. As neither of the Hayes sisters were wed, and Millicent was of an age with Bella, neither had anything to crow about. They were no better than her. More importantly the Rushdales weren't tarnished by the stigma of trade. "I do hope you didn't part with your most prized asset too eagerly. A wife should be demure and dainty, Bella. No man wants a whore in his bed."

Bella snorted. "On the contrary, I believe it's what every man desires."

"Then you mustn't have been a very good harlot either." Miranda, the younger sister, peevishly stuck her nose in the air, while Millicent gawped at her momentarily lost for words.

"She's evidently good enough for Lord Pennerley."

Bella did not know who among the onlookers had contributed that remark, but she could both have kissed and cursed them for it. It set the Hayes sisters further off kilter, but also started a wave of muttering.

"That's nothing more than hearsay," Miranda snapped. Not one among the little clique apparently possessed the nerve to ask Bella directly. "No matter." Millicent thrust her bosom forward. "I'm soon to be respectably married to a member of parliament."

Millicent Hayes was to be Stephan Crakehall's wife! Bella could hardly contain her astonishment. It made sense of why anyone of any standing from hereabout had been invited though. There was no way Millicent would miss out on crowing about her accomplishment. Not that Bella supposed she had anything to do with the match. It had clearly been negotiated between her father and Sir Thomas Lartington.

"My congratulations to you, Millicent. You must be unutterably proud of yourself."

"Why wouldn't I be? You're all here because of me. Just imagine how grand our wedding will be. Accept it. I've outdone you Bella. No one is going to take you after Lord Marlinscar has cast you over, and even if that silly rumour about you and Pennerley is true, it'd make you a mere mistress, nothing more, and everybody knows a mistress has no status whatsoever. You'll remain a nobody, exactly as you are now."

"I fear for Crakehall's ambitions if this is the sort of tact his future wife is given to displaying."

Vaughan!

"Lord Pennerley." Two bright crimson spots flared

upon Millicent's cheeks. She hastily dropped him a curtsy. The rest of her circle of maidens did likewise.

Bella blinked. He was exquisite, every blessed inch of him. His dark hair curled over his perfectly tailored coat, which was slate grey, and beneath which he wore a rich ruby-red brocade waistcoat. Breeches and shoes too, in place of his customary boots. Somehow Vaughan always endeavoured to look as if he'd just stepped out of a painting. It was effortless elegance he possessed, and she had never been more enamoured of it.

He ignored the fawning of the women around him, and looked directly at her. "Miss Rushdale, I believe luncheon is about to be served. Can I offer you an arm to walk in upon?"

Vengeful joy filled Bella's chest. She could not have been more delighted, or hoped to elicit such a reaction if she had stuck two fingers up at the gaggle of offensive twits. "That would be delightful. Thank you, my lord." Jaw set, she took a breath and lifted her head high. Let them think whatever they wished. If that meant people tattled about her behind her back, then she would just have to learn to tune them out. There'd been gossip aplenty about her and Lucerne, and her and Vaughan, and indeed, Vaughan and Lucerne while they were in London, but doors had remained open to them. Besides, she was happiest at his side. If sacrifices had to be made in order for that to be possible, then she'd make them.

She slipped her arm around his, and he guided her away from the group.

"I didn't hear you announced," she said to Vaughan once they were away from the toxic huddle. "How long have you been here?"

"Long enough that your need to be rescued was apparent. I can't believe you let that country gillflirt

Millicent Hayes get the better of you. You've handled grand dames of the ton with more panache."

"I was rather surer of my circumstances, then."

"Just because I do not reside upon your doorstep, does not mean you are not in my thoughts. I saw you just over a sennight ago, and I've been here since yestereve. That is not so very long."

"It's been more like a fortnight." And it felt like eternity. Still, she summoned a smile, pleased to know she'd been in his thoughts. It was too easy to believe he didn't think of her at all when she wasn't in sight. "Is it Crakehall you know or Sir Lartington?"

"I'm tenuously acquainted with both. I believe Lartington and I may even have an ancestor or two in common a generation or two back. Crakehall called on me in person to extend me an invitation, not that I was around to personally accept it, but it wouldn't do at all to have a marquis idling at the inn when everyone of import from hereabouts is celebrating an announcement."

"It's only a betrothal," Bella remarked. "The amount of fuss being made seems vastly out of proportion. Was a family dinner not sufficient?"

"Not when you're as ambitious as Crakehall. Grandeur attracts people, and contacts are the one thing he lacks. That will change soon enough, no doubt."

"I don't wish to discuss politics."

"Me neither. In fact, I don't mean for us to do much talking at all."

"Oh?" Bella looked around and realised they were now some way from the others. Nor were they on the approach to the house but to the right of it, heading into something resembling a thicket.

"Where are you taking me? I thought you said luncheon had been announced."

"It has. To be served at half past two, which—" he consulted his timepiece. "—will not be for another forty-four minutes."

"How precise you are."

"It often pays to be so."

Yes, she supposed it did. "And in the meantime, I suppose we are to stroll around Sir Lartington's gardens."

Vaughan shot her the sort of look that could only be interpreted as not a chance.

"Meanwhile," he elaborated. "Your brother is engaged with Lartington and his cronies in the engine sheds over yonder." He waved in the opposite direction to the way they were walking. "And I mean to enjoy the opportunity that has afforded us to explore your garden."

Bella's stomach fluttered at the notion. She turned her head and gazed longingly at him, and was rewarded with a kiss. It felt so right when his mouth was on hers. "It won't do to turn up to luncheon with leaves in my hair and a green gown."

"Quite right, though I might enjoy the spectacle of it."

As would everybody else, except perhaps Joshua. And herself. She was not feeling so brazen anymore. "Vaughan, if we're caught..."

Things were vastly different here in Yorkshire, with her brother to think of and other people's sensibilities to take into consideration. In London, she had hardly cared what they got up to

"There are too many guests." A scandal here, today, would scare off the only friends she could currently claim to possess. It would also ensure that Joshua never married. He did so definitely need someone to love him.

"But none among them," he said, drawing a brass

key from his waistcoat pocket, "who are in possession of a key to this paradise."

It was evidently a paradise only he could see.

"I see you doubt me, but there is in fact a delightful spot just right about this corner that will serve our purposes admirably."

Right then the twisted pathway of rhododendrons opened out into a circular vista, at the centre of which sat what appeared to Bella to be a kind of miniature fort. It was comprised of red-brick, only a single storey in height, but with curved towers on each of the corners.

"What is it?" Bella asked. "A folly, of course, but..."

"Lartington uses it as an observatory. Leastways, he uses the roof for that purpose, although his delightful wife, Mary, informs me that he has rather lost his zeal for the stars since he's been introduced to dirty, puffing, steam engines. Apparently he prefers coal dust to celestial objects these days."

"And do you happen to have that key because she asked you to observe some celestial bodies with her, perhaps?"

"Miss Rushdale, what sort of reprehensible nonsense are you implying."

Bella poked her tongue firmly into her cheek. He might not be quite the notorious rakehell he had once been, but his reputation for acquiring access to ladies' quarters remained legendary. "Your reputation precedes you."

"Alas, my heart is already claimed these days."

Her smile faded. "By Lucerne," she whispered. Although, had that not ever been the case?

He softly brushed his curled fingers against her cheek. "All these doubts do not suit you, my nightingale. Clearly there's a pressing need to drive them out."

Bella smiled up at him, but it was through a veil of tears that she refused to spill. Her emotions were all desperately jumbled these days. She had always been quick to anger, but she was no leaky water bucket.

Vaughan swept his thumb down across her lips, parting them slightly. Then he kissed her and pulled her tight to his body.

Bella curled her fingers into the back of his coat and held on tight. Then not a second later, she struggled equally hard to be free of his embrace.

"What the devil is the matter with you?"

"I don't know that I can do this anymore. I don't know how to feel, or even what I should allow myself to feel." Agitated, she paced away from him, only to return and face him again. "What game is it you're playing with me?"

"There's no game, Bella. Only desire." His hands snaked into her hair again. "Is this not what you want? Is it not what you've longed and begged for since that very first time I happened upon you with your groom at Lauwine?"

"It was... is."

"Then let us not waste what time we have." He clasped her hand and led her to the building, where she skipped from one foot to the other and could not stop herself from constantly peering over her shoulder as he unlocked the door.

The interior was gloomy, except for a space in the middle where the sun left an outline of the windows reflected upon the stone floor. Various pieces of stargazing equipment she had no hope of naming occupied various shelves and tables. There were two telescopes supported on stands, but the only view through them would be of the walls or ceiling. A spiral metal staircase lead up to what she presumed was a flat roof.

"Frustration ill suits you, Bella."

The observation startled a laugh from her. She turned her head so that she could see his face. "If it so ill suits me, why do you deliberately vex me so?"

"Oh, the one and the other are not same. The one leaves you in this curious state of flighty panic that is most peculiar to witness, and the other..."

"Go on."

"It turns you into an incorrigible minx. I like your fire, Miss Rushdale. You have always been willing to match me, word for word, action for action. Do not change that now."

"It is this place. It stifles... it sobers me."

"I assume you mean Yorkshire, and not Stags Fell or this building itself, not that any of them make sense."

"Very little makes sense to me right now."

Vaughan ignored the remark. "Was it not in this wilderness that Lucerne happened upon a wretchedly wanton maid who so enchanted him that he actually contemplated casting me off for her?"

"I don't believe you actually had him at that point, so it would be me being the one cast off. That's how it feels right now."

"Who's casting you off, Bella? Certainly not I, and from what you have said, and my own observation, Lucerne's only too eager to entice you into his arms again."

"Pfft." She waved away the mere notion of that. She and Lucerne were done. There was not a thing that could bring them together again. Perhaps not a thing, but a certain individual might. The one right before her, whose expression, as ever, was unreadable, but whose gaze burned with a zealot's fanaticism. He captured her gaze and cocked his head to one side. His lips thinned and curved upwards at one corner. "I'm going to eat you up little bird. Better run before I pluck you of your feathers."

He lurched quickly towards her, and Bella squealed and ran. The way to thwart him would be to stand quite still and passively allow herself to be come upon, but that was not the game. Total surrender did not excite him. He tired and lost interest of anything that didn't prove a challenge. Besides, it felt good to run, to dance about freely, and let loose her voice in any manner she chose.

"When I catch you, I'm going to bend you over and stripe your behind for getting me out of breath. Then I'm going to make tender use of your prettily striped derriere. What do you think of that, Miss Rushdale?"

She loudly cackled, and shrieked as he almost set his hands upon her. It was only at the last moment she managed to dart out of the way and circle behind the wing-backed chair. "Devil. You'll never take me willingly."

"Fie, woman. You're always willing. You like nothing better than a hard prick up your arse."

Bella coughed in mock outrage, still jiggling on the spot and wondering which way to run. To the right sat a table overloaded with specimen jars, stuffed animals, to the left, a lectern with an assortment of maps and charts upon it. The table would offer better protection, but he would expect her to go that way, and she didn't want to end up bent over it with that stuffed weasel judging her on her disorderly conduct with its dead eyes. Nor was she too eager to determine the contents of any of the stopped jars.

"Your language is pure filth, my lord. And there are, in fact, several things I like better."

Skirts held high to avoid tripping, Bella decided upon the table, but darted beneath it rather than around it, and then scampered across the central carpet to where the telescope stood.

"I challenge you to name but three."

Three: a mere three? She would have no trouble naming dozens upon dozens, although he would henceforth use the knowledge so that he might dangle such favourites before her like a driver might tempt his mule with a carrot.

"Well?"

Damn him for his foils and agility. He nearly had her once again. Well, she had feints of her own she could make.

"Two pricks inside of me together."

Sure enough, that brought him to a standstill.

"Your mouth upon my cunny."

She wasn't certain he heard the second; he still seemed rattled by the first. No doubt he was reading far more into the admission than he ought. Admitting to liking the feel of two cocks at once was simply that, and not an admission of anything else, like a desire for their former arrangement with Lucerne.

Vaughan leapt into motion again, causing her to become quite out of breath. That damnable new maid had tied her stays impossibly tight. She ought not to feel so squashed.

"That is but two, Miss Rushdale."

She barely had the breath to holler a third.

Bella dipped beneath the body of the telescope, then around behind the astrolabe, where she found a moment's respite leaning against the side of the grandfather clock. "Watching you fuck Lucerne as he fucks me." She spoke the latter part all in a rush as if she did not quite want to acknowledge what she was saying.

Vaughan clapped his hands together, and slowed to an amble. "And there we have it. So, the idea of Lucerne pricking you is still what keeps you up at night."

Although very tempted to say otherwise, Bella deigned to keep her silence and concentrate on recuperating her breath. In truth, her liking of such intercourse had little to do with her physical gratification, what truly excited her about it was the opportunity to see the two men together and share in their intimacy with one another. She would have liked to see Lucerne swiving Vaughan, but Vaughan would never agree to that. She was not certain that was something that ever happened. In any case, speculating about what might have been, served no good purpose. She did not wish to rekindle those times.

Sexual gratification was one thing but not everything. At some point, one had to step out of the bedroom and engage with reality. One had to attempt to make a decent life of the kind that provided some measure of security for one's self and one's family. She was doing a terribly dismal job of it so far, but it was as if she'd lived in a drunken daze for four years, and only now was she almost sober and could see the wreckage such a lengthy absence had caused. Then again, maybe that glimpse was no more than a speck of something that she ought to rinse from her eye.

Staid normality would never suit her.

Vaughan caught her around the waist, making her squawk. "Were you asleep?" he remarked. "I have you." He spun her around so that her back was pressed to the wainscoting and her fore to his body. He leaned close and Bella watched his mouth descend, eager for his kiss, but he stopped short of granting it. "So, Lucerne's still the master of quim. I ought not to be surprised. It was always about him for you." His words were playful, but his expression was most assuredly darker.

"You don't believe that, and if you do you're a fool. How many times must I tell you that he is nothing to me anymore? I only want you."

"You say it, but is it truly what's in here?" He placed one hand over her heart.

Bella tangled her hands in his hair, and held him so that he faced her. His dark eyes shone like black diamonds in the dim light. "I liked watching you together. I liked being part of the intimacy that existed between you. Just for a few moments, I could be part of what you felt for each other and not feel like an interloper. You only accepted me at Lucerne's insistence, and Lucerne... he only wanted me around so that the world didn't recognise him for what he truly is."

"Which is?"

She shook her head. "You do not need me to say it. Society condemns you. You may not give a damn for their viewpoint, but he does. Lucerne craves approval, and society, alas, approves all the things he is not."

"Ah, my nightingale." He kissed her. "You are far too philosophical for this time in the day. It's not evening yet."

"I don't want him to fuck me, Vaughan. I want you. He's not the master of anything. Leastways, he's not my master."

"Your pussy doesn't weep for the kiss of his cock?"

Somehow, even though his words were crude and ridiculous, the seriousness behind them kept her mirth in check. It seemed Vaughan required as many assurances from her as she did from him. Not that he was providing any, other than with his presence. That was something. He was here, locked away in this odd little structure, and not fluttering around Lucerne, flattering him and cajoling him into bed.

"My cunny would very much like to feel the kiss of yours."

He arched a brow. "Aye, but I believe you said you liked my mouth there best."

Beast! She knew he would turn that admission against her.

Vaughan dropped elegantly onto his knees. He bunched her skirts, and stuck his head beneath them. His tongue struck true to her sweet spot. Oh, how he tortured her emotions. She could not fathom the possibility of pushing him away, for his touch played exquisite havoc with her senses, but simultaneously, she wanted to beat him around the head until he turned into the man she wanted him to be—one who loved her exclusively, and whose heart didn't belong to another.

"Do you bugger me because you've been unable to have him?"

He gave a snort, which was largely muffled by her skirts. "No, primarily because it enrages you so."

Oh! Now she was tempted to knee him on the chin.

"Calm yourself. This is one of your favourites, remember. You did not list me fucking you as every other man fucks his harlot." His grip tightened upon her thighs, pushing them outwards. Soon, only the tips of her toes remained upon the ground, while his mouth encompassed her puss and his tongue rode along the split.

It took all of her effort to keep upright and breathe, and not burn away like a candle with too long a wick. Every touch of his tongue heightened her pleasure. He was ruthlessly demanding, bringing her right to the edge of release and then leaving her dangling there.

Bella pulled his hair, which only prompted him to further torment her.

"You'll thank me for the delay."

"I'll thank you to let me come."

"I've not yet tired of the taste of you. Nor is your pearl as hard as it can get."

It felt to her like it could not possibly swell any further, nor could she take so much direct attention.

Then, right on the cliff edge of pain, his tactics changed, his touch softened and became whisper light. The tremor started low down, then leapt between every sensitive point on her body, until she was engulfed by violent shakes and pleasure poured from her in the form of cries and sobs, sweat and tears.

He stood once her fingers unclenched from where they were locked tight within his dark hair, and grinned lopsidedly at her. "You can return the favour later. We ought to get to luncheon. It wouldn't be right to steal all the attention for ourselves by arriving late and advertising our misdemeanour, when the day assuredly should belong to Crakehall and Miss Hayes."

Bella shook out her skirts. "As if you give a damn about Miss Hayes or Crakehall."

"He did fag for Lucerne. He warrants close attention."

"They were boys," she cried, giving his shoulder a gentle shove. However, when he continued to regard her with a twisted smile upon his lips, she gave a sigh. "Really, you're just impossible."

CHAPTER 17
VAUGHAN

VAUGHAN WAS TOO little of a glutton to take any great delight in dining, although amusements could be fashioned from even the most tedious affairs. This particular occasion had only two things cast in its favour. The first, that due to the archaic seating plan, he was seated directly opposite Lucerne – a position that afforded him every opportunity to goad the man without seeming to pay him any attention whatsoever. And secondly, that a quiet word with the hostess meant that Bella was placed in the chair beside him to his right. That was done entirely to irritate her brother. He had not forgiven, nor would he, the bruises Joshua had delivered with his fists. He was the Marquis of Pennerley. He did not brawl in the dirt like a commoner.

"If he casts another forlorn glance in your direction, I believe I shall be sick," Bella remarked, socco votte. "It really is too much. It reminds me of Fortuna Dovecote—Allenthorpe, as she was—that time at Pennerley. Do you remember? She was half out of her dress while we were still on the chicken course."

"That is not my foremost recollection of that dinner."

"Is it not?" Bella opened her eyes wide feigning surprise. "Whatever could have topped her display?"

He credited her with the lewd smile she was seeking. She had unfastened his breeches that night and taken him in hand while the rest of his guests ate, but in truth, nor was that his major recollection either. His heart...his soul... had been in turmoil. Lucerne had been absent. Bella only too eager to please. Things had begun unravelling before him, and he'd been powerless to prevent it. Whereas tonight, he meant to truly begin piecing things back together again. That was, if Lucerne were genuinely as willing as their encounter at the waterfall had led him to believe.

Bella slipped her hand onto his thigh. "If the fish isn't to your liking, I could—"

He slapped her hand away. "Do try to behave yourself."

The remark prompted her to laugh, drawing stares from both Lucerne and her brother.

Another time, another location, he might have swept the dishes from before them and spread her across the table to feast upon instead. Tonight, his plans required more subtlety.

"Whatever it is you're planning, I shan't be part of it, Vaughan."

"Do pass me some of that trout," he said.

She handed him the eels in aspic instead. "I know you are planning something. I know you. I know how you think, and all your expressions. The way you're aware of him, but seem absolutely not to be. I won't be part of it."

"You're already part of it."

She responded with an angry shake of her head. "I've told you, it's over. I can't endure a repeat."

Vaughan stabbed his fork into two buttered potatoes, which he deposited on her plate. "Two at once. You said it yourself, only a little while ago, and that's without making any mention of your desire to peep at two particular gentlemen engaged in certain gentlemanly pursuits."

"Don't," she muttered so quietly that even he barely heard her.

"Bella, I have to."

Her gaze settled upon her hands holding her cutlery over her plate. He saw them tremble. Watched her snatch up her napkin and hide her despair within its folds.

"That's not true." The linen muffled her words, but he heard them clearly enough. "It's only what you're choosing to do. Why can't I be enough?"

"Truly, you wish to discuss this here and now?"

She gave another sad little shake of her head.

"Good, for there is surely to God nothing new to say. You know why. You want the same thing. You just choose not to admit it because you cannot let go of past slights."

Her gaze flew to his face. "He..." She bit her lip, and her gaze drooped towards her plate again. "As you say, it's best we go over this some other time." She turned to her right, and engaged the gentleman sitting there on the subject of steam powered pistons.

Lucerne eyed him from across the table, his eyebrows betraying his wary interest. Somehow, he was going to have to reconcile this pair of fools to one another, but first, he had to ensure he had Lucerne properly ensnared. He didn't want them to simply fall into one another's arms and slake their lust. Not that getting physically intimate wasn't a large part of what he desired, but this time around, there had to be firmer foundations. He wanted permanence. A union that would last into old age. So that when they were too geriatric and impotent enough to even contemplate getting it up for one another, the bonds of love between them would still remain as strong and fierce as ever.

Love was what he wanted. Love had always been what he wanted.

Lucerne's and Bella's.

Somehow, he had to find a way to tie them all together again.

He met Lucerne's agitated gape and held it until the other man blushed. Though, he was pleased to see that even scarlet cheeked, Lucerne did not turn away.

Vaughan had never been an easy man to read, and tonight proved no exception. The dinner groaned on interminably long. The company was quarrelsome, and the food too rich and over-salted. Lucerne craved an empty parlour where he and Vaughan could be alone. They needed to talk to one another; the few brief sentences they'd exchanged since Vaughan's arrival in Yorkshire weren't enough for him to determine the course of the future.

It was as the ladies were rising, and the gentlemen rearranging themselves around the table to partake of brandy and cigars, that he seized the opportunity to discreetly lean into Vaughan.

"May we speak privately?"

They could not continue dancing around one another. They needed to determine what exactly they both wanted, and if whatever that was were even possible. Wholeheartedly, he wished them all back together and at peace with one another, but feared it would never be. Indeed, it never had been, but at least in the past there had been some unity. Now, Vaughan confused him with every action, and Bella hated him. She studiously avoided him. They had not even exchanged greetings.

"To what purpose?" Vaughan replied, prompting Lucerne to study his face, his eyes. He looked quickly down, unable to hold the other man's gaze. It terrified him, what he saw there... what Vaughan allowed him to see there. If someone were to see them looking at one another like that all hell would break loose. Yet, wasn't this exactly how he desired Vaughan to look at him? A lump of desire stuck in his throat. He pulled back his shoulders stiffly.

"Do not pretend you don't know."

Vaughan laconically inclined his head a fraction. "When and where?"

Oh, Lord! His heart hammered fit to burst. Lucerne looked swiftly away. "The billiards room," he remarked out of the side of his mouth, while his body was already reacting to all the possibilities a meeting with Vaughan might bring about. "You make your excuses first, and I'll find a reason to follow."

In a desperate attempt to curb his impatience, Lucerne forced himself to remain in his seat a full five minutes after Vaughan left. Alas, the only way to manage it involved the consumption of copious amounts of brandy. He drank three...four fingers of the stuff in half as many minutes. The resultant buzz in his brain only made his agitation more pronounced. Thankfully, a lively discourse had ensnared the party, and they were all too deep into the political ramifications posed by the news of the Earl of Dartmouth's recent death to pay his exit any real heed. Only Charles got in his way, pouncing on him in the doorway.

"Lucerne, just the fellow. Have you heard? There's a girl gone amiss. Tis said, she's from your parish."

Lucerne attempted not entirely successfully to edge around him. "You don't say, Charles. How unfortunate."

"I thought maybe we gents could form a search."

"A search," bellowed one of Crakehall's parliamentary cronies. "What the devil would we do that for? Chit's probably taken off with some disreputable rogue or another. There's nothing to be achieved by us galloping about the countryside and risking laming good horses. No, no, that won't do. Tis likely enough they're well away by now."

"Wayward. Wayward, the peasantry are." Mr Hayes corralled. "Ain't no preaching to them. I see them all the time hereabouts. Sunday sermons go in one ear and right out of the other, and nary a seed takes root."

"Something taking root is probably why she's scarpered. Afraid of her old dad finding out, I should think, and boxing her ears."

"That is no way to treat a woman," Charles lamented. Lucerne, ignoring the tug of guilt at leaving Charles to challenge the misogyny in the room, slipped out. In all likelihood, they were right, and the girl had run before she ripened, or else got forced into some loveless union. Still, he'd try to remember to make some enquiries once he was back at Lauwine, see if there was anything to be done. And just in case there happened to be an actual villain on the loose. He would hate for one of Wakefield's sisters to be set upon or carried off while a guest under his roof. Although, in some regards, he wouldn't exactly mind that. He turned his head about smartly, just to ensure he wasn't about to be waylaid by one of them. They did have a habit of springing out of the woodwork at the most inopportune moments. Of course, Caroline, the worst offender, was safely back at Lauwine convalescing.

He breathed a heavy sigh of relief, and then to cement the notion that he was in actual search of his timepiece, went up to his room, and spent a minute or two rifling through drawers. Ivo would resoundingly curse him for the creases later.

Lucerne's impatience had grown to tempestuous levels by the time he reached the billiards room, where he found Vaughan lingering in the doorway.

Lucerne grasped him by the shoulders and bundled him into the room before they were seen. Alas, he had not been in here before to realise the aspect was wholly unsuitable for their conversation. Windows on three sides of the room left them exposed to anyone who might be passing by outside, and an additional door evidently adjoined the drawing room. He could hear the ladies quite clearly.

"This way," he insisted, and propelled them both into the cupboard where the cues and such like were kept, and shut the door firmly behind them.

"Is it discourse you're looking for, Lucerne, or a fuck?"

Vaughan's words hit him like a smack, bringing heat to his collar. He faced the other man but could barely discern his outline in the dingy closet. Since their encounter at the waterfall, he'd been planning and rehearsing what it was he wanted to say. Now, every line of it flew from his head and left him gaping like an imbecile.

Somehow, even in the dark, he suspected Vaughan could recognise what a fool he was.

"You have to admit, one might wonder, considering our location."

He hadn't planned for things to be quite so dark and intimate, but those bloody windows with the shutters thrown back, and Lartington's engine enthusiasts milling about all over the place. Only a pair of them had appeared at dinner, the others one presumed were in the sheds tinkering with machinery, but they might return at any point, and what impression would it leave if they were to spy he and Vaughan intimately embroiled. Even a simple discourse might be misconstrued. Add in the possibility of a stray touch being observed, or hell, something that left no question about anything, and it would add up to an almighty disaster.

"Talk," he blurted. "We have to. I need to. I need to know." He squashed a craven impulse to heartily agree that his actual purpose was as Vaughan suggested and drop his breeches. "I'd just prefer we weren't seen or overheard. This business is between us, not us and the rest of the county."

Vaughan gave a nod. At least, Lucerne supposed he did, considering how little he could discern of the fellow.

"Say what it is you need to get off your chest, Lucerne."

Lucerne coughed to clear his throat. "It's been weeks since you arrived, and we've spoken hardly at all. I need to know where we stand. I hate existing in limbo, not knowing what it's safe to wish for, and fearing that we'll be forever at odds, or that I'm to be dandied along on the end of a string until I go mad from it."

"If you wished to see me, Lucerne, you had only to issue an invitation."

"But would you have come?" he asked hurriedly. That was the question that had riddled his mind for months. If he called out to Vaughan, admitted he was a fool, would he be forgiven? The Marquis of Pennerley was not known to be the forgiving sort.

"That depends entirely upon why it is you were issuing the summons."

Lucerne drew a not entirely steady breath. He could feel the heat of Vaughan's body less than a foot away. "I thought I'd made my feelings abundantly clear at the waterfall."

"Ah, Lucerne." He stiffened in response to Vaughan's chuckle, even as a stream of pure excitement ran from his jaw to his chest to his breeches, as Vaughan's curled fingers brushed his cheek. "All I know is that you crave cock, but I'm not a whore that you can summon to oblige you on a whim."

"It's not that sort of intimacy I crave."

"Is it not?"

"Well, of course n—That is to say, yes, I want you and I want that, but not exclusively." Goddammit, why was it so deuced difficult to express himself plainly?

"What then?"

"You know," he whispered.

"But say it," Vaughan prompted him. "I'm not sure you ever have before."

"I..." He couldn't. He couldn't say it. That was assuming the it he thought Vaughan meant was the actual it in question. He felt it, obviously. This man turned him inside out in every possible way. However, if he said it aloud, then there was no withdrawing it. Forever after, it would be dangling between them. Was it worth the risk? For all he knew, this was merely a means of exacting revenge upon him. Bella hated him. How certain was he that Vaughan didn't feel the same way? He might open his heart, only to have Vaughan laugh in his face, or else screw him senseless and then do so. He had spent three long years as a pawn in their games; for all he craved their company, he did not want to return to that position.

The soft swish of Vaughan's hair against the fabric of his coat told Lucerne that Vaughan was shaking his head. "How easily those words have slipped from your mouth in reference to Bella. Are you even aware how often you expressed the depth of your feelings for her? But never once did anything remotely similar pass your lips in reference to me. You are right, Lucerne, all was not equal between us in the past, and nor is it now. You have never treated or regarded us equally. Is it any wonder that we fought? Life has been simpler without you in it."

His heart lurched into his throat. His fingers curled into claws. "Then you truly mean us to go our separate ways?"

"That is up to you, Lucerne. I will not simply hand over Bella and be content with what is merely implied anymore. You accuse me of toying with your affections, yet you have toyed with mine from the day we met. You have always known what I desired of you, and it was not your body. Excuse me if I tire of doggedly pursuing something clearly unattainable." Vaughan turned and reached for the door knob.

"Wait! Please." Lucerne slapped his hand down over the top of Vaughan's, and laced their fingers together. The heat of the touch seared his skin, but he did not want to let go. This all sounded horrifically final. If he allowed Vaughan to walk away now, he feared it would truly be forever over. "If I could do it all again—"

"Then you would do the same thing again. You left me, Lucerne. I'll not lie, there's space in my heart for you even now, and I won't pretend otherwise, but I will no longer chase after you."

"I've not your stomach for scandal," he admitted

softly, keen to dissipate the tension. "Society will never accept us. I can't abide their condemnation."

"We faced it for years."

"Not truly. Bella was an acknowledged part of it. No one thought over hard about whether we touched one another."

A cruel laugh rent the air between them. Vaughan shook off Lucerne's hold upon his hand. "Tear off the blindfold, Lucerne. We were discussed in every society drawing room and gentleman's club London boasts and in many farther afield. So long as we are merely a source of speculation and neither confirm or deny a thing, then there is no issue. People do so love to gossip. In any case, I am not asking you to speak before witnesses."

It was Vaughan who was blinkered. "Darleston is currently hiding out in the wilds in fear of his life due to rumours of such conduct."

Again he was battered by that cruel laugh. "Lucerne, he is nursing a broken heart because the man he loved rejected him." Vaughan cast wide the door, leaving Lucerne blinking at him as the light flooded. "He is in the countryside because he is unable to brazenly face down such rumours while the pain of his loss is so raw. Some things are not so easy to hide. I should know, having spent the last nine months at Pennerley. But I suppose you thought I was making merry hell with Bella."

God's truth, he could not deny it. "Were you not?" Whene'er he'd thought of them ensconced together in Vaughan's castle he'd envisaged them engaged in ribald, rambunctious entertainments. "I have been ensconced in the countryside too," he said. In case it wasn't apparent that he also had been hiding himself away, in order to nurse his hurts.

"Yes," Vaughan replied simply. "I'm sure you and

Wakefield have been thoroughly enjoying one another's company. I suggest you get back to him now. I'm sure he has one of his sisters lined up for you. He's not man enough to admit to wanting you for himself."

"Wakefield isn't—" Lucerne stopped. Vaughan was already gone. The door to the billiards room slammed behind him, rattling the collection of oriental vases in the cabinet beside it. Such arguments were pointless. Vaughan knew perfectly well that his relationship with Wakefield was not of that nature. It had simply been a jab intended to provoke him.

"Goddammit!" Lucerne kicked the base of the billiards table, leaving himself wincing as pain curled his toes and sent a streamer of fire up his shin and into his groin. They were no further forward than they had been before. If anything, they were two steps back.

"I daren't love you, Vaughan," he hissed between his teeth. It would be madness to do so.

Mad, of course, was exactly what he was. He'd been besotted with the man for the longest time. Why else was he proposing they meet in cupboards to thrash things out? Confessing it aloud though – it just wasn't that easy to do. His parents, and grandparents, and his elder brothers would turn in their graves. One might be permitted to discreetly liaise with another man if one were so inclined, but one did not admit as much, and one always took a wife to ensure the dynasty.

They were all dead, his whole family. The burden of ensuring the succession of the Marlinscar line sat squarely on his shoulders. Moreover, he wanted children. It had shocked him to learn how deeply it affected him to have his goddaughter reach out to him and snuggle her tiny body into his. He loved the baby scent of her skin, her antics and laughter. And most especially, her unfiltered honesty.

And there it was, stark before him, the reason he

kept ruining things by holding back. He wanted Vaughan, but he wanted a family too, and whichever way one looked at it, there didn't seem to be a way of reconciling the two.

He'd believed, once, that he could settle down happily ever after with Bella, and maintain his relationship with Vaughan, too. In fact, all these months he'd still been hoping that were the case. But it had been a fool's dream. Bella wouldn't even speak to him, and Vaughan was asking for more than he could give without reassurances.

Let's face it. You missed your chance, sapskull. He'd allowed the tides to sweep them apart, and no matter how hard he fought the current, they were drifting further away.

After enduring forty minutes of Millicent's hideous crowing over her engagement, Bella almost squealed with relief when the gentlemen joined them in the drawing room. Her respite was short lived when a swift perusal of the faces entering revealed neither Vaughan's nor Lucerne's. Her heart immediately dropped into her stomach.

'Twas only a matter of time... Even knowing that, it still felt like a scourge upon her back knowing that they were off somewhere reconciling their differences.

Three years of intimacy between them had left her with a vast array of pictures with which she might illustrate the scene. She knew vividly how Lucerne looked with his normally starched-into-submission cravat rendered askew, his shirt pulled free of his breeches, and his waistcoat missing a button or two.

Vaughan in turn would be all wild-haired, wild-eyed, red-lipped savagery.

All would be focussed on their hands, their mouths, and the way their loins could be made to fit together.

They fit together so very well. She knew it.

Why? She took herself over to the window to rage quietly within her own head.

I don't want you to fuck him. I don't want you to get lost in that wasteland again. I know you love him, Vaughan, but what good does it do any of us to express it? He won't give you what you want... what you need. I cannot abide the thought of losing you, or having to share your heart with him again. It will only lead to more heartache and disaster.

She would never share herself with Lucerne in that way again. She had shut down all thoughts of such a possibility the night he'd split all their hearts in two.

Can you not see that he will break you all to pieces again?

The reflection in the French doors was hers, but it was Vaughan she imagined facing her. He will lead you into darkness again.

Only she had stayed at Pennerley and borne witness to the despair. Only she had stood by him, held him, been there for him through the fits of anger, and interminable bouts of indolence. She'd accepted his curses, even as she rallied against them. And she'd let him fuck her until his rage was burned to ashes, while her own tears had run into the strands of her hair.

It was not fair that Lucerne could now snatch Vaughan away from her again. It made her so mad. Hadn't she given them both all she could? First Lucerne and now Vaughan would cast her aside.

"Tis not like you to be lingering in the shadows, Bella."

"Wakefield." She summoned a smile for him,

though it riddled her with cramps to do so. "The shadows are where this crowd expect me to dwell. As you know, I'm not altogether respectable, and while no one will breathe a word against me while my protector resides under this roof, that does not mean they are obliged to welcome me when he is not about."

"They were your friends of old."

"All the more reason for them to distance themselves now." She pressed a hand to his arm, seeing the concern erase the smile-lines from his face. "Not to worry, Captain. I do not crave their company or approval. I'm content."

He placed his hand over the top of hers and tapped it lightly. "You seem distracted to me."

"Speculative," she corrected him. "But you have sought me out for a reason, I think. Go ahead, what is it?"

Wakefield stiffened. "You read me remarkably well. I did wish to engage your aid upon a matter. Or rather, an opinion, I suppose."

"Oh," she turned to present him with her undivided attention. "On what topic could you possibly be seeking my advice?"

"That of the happiness of two people most dear to me."

Oh, dear God! She clamped her lips together tight, only just stopping the exclamation from escaping her mouth. Her nerves were already frazzled—now they were scrambled even worse. He could not truly mean to engage her opinion on what she thought he meant to. But his stance, the uneasy set of his shoulders confirmed it. He meant to address her regarding Lucerne, and the breakdown of their affections for one another.

"I've seen that Caroline has become quite..."

Bella took a step back from him. He paused, and his eyes narrowed.

"That is to say, I'm sure you must have noticed it too; this growing affection of hers for a person of our mutual acquaintance. You've always been attuned to such things. Womanly instinct, I suppose."

Truly, he was obtuse enough to address her on the affections of another woman for the man to whom she'd practically been engaged.

"She is not here."

"I know. It was unfortunate about her ankle, but that is by the by. The thing is, Bella, if there is some truth to it; damn me, but I can't find a single reason to object to such a match. He's my oldest, dearest friend. I should be overjoyed to consider him my brother."

Christ! He truly meant to marry his sister to Lucerne, and he was brazenly putting it to her as if she were possessed of authoritative wisdom on the subject. Her mind had been howling in outrage before, now every bone in her jaw ached from the strain of holding her indignation inside. Was the injustice of Lucerne seizing Vaughan from her not enough for one evening, but now she must be consulted on betrothal plans between a lady she considered a friend and the man she'd waited for long years to offer for her.

She could only gawp at him in disbelief. Only after he had prompted her with a cough did she find any words at all. "I'm sorry, Captain Wakefield. I can't fathom what it is you wish me to say. Truly, if a tendresse exists between them, I can't claim to have witnessed it. I thought Maria merely teasing her older sister as siblings often do."

"But if it were more than that, you wouldn't have any objections?"

Bella drew a deep breath. Objections? Of course she had objections. They could run a mile long. And not one of them made any sense. Not a smidgen of it. She didn't want Lucerne anymore. Didn't she say so to herself at least a hundred times a day? But that didn't mean she wanted to see him married off. Naturally, Vaughan would have a deal to say on the matter too. He'd sabotaged Lucerne's previous betrothal plans; no way would he stand for this. Wait until she told him. He hated Wakefield at the best of times, this would intensify matters.

"You don't approve. I can see it."

Bella watched Wakefield's jaw tighten, his eyes become flint-like in their coldness.

"It's not as if you have a claim upon him anymore," he snarled. "It's my understanding that it's all quite over between you, and has been for the best part of a year."

Yet here he was, consulting her on the matter.

"Do we appear to you as two people who have a claim upon one another?" Her voice emerged so waspish and sharp, that he ought to have been cowed by it. For definite he tensed, but like a dog with a bone he refused to let go of the matter.

"I don't know, Bella. I have heard Lucerne's side of this story, and there are more holes in it than in a vagabond's sock. I know he has omitted things; things I presume he feels reflect badly upon him, or you. I do not know. He tells me it is over, but then I see how he looks at you, and you at him."

Swallowing, she held her head high, and met his gaze. "I do not look at him in any such way."

"Bella, I only wish my sister and my friend happy, and neither of them are happy alone. Why should I not bring them together and inject some joy into their lives; give them both the family they each wish for?"

She kept her chin high, her eyes unblinking, while tears gathered at the backs of them. He'd unwittingly crowbarred open a locked trunk in her brain and was now rummaging about in the contents with no regard for her feelings. Every muddled emotion she had for Lucerne escaped at once, they swirled around her in the air, so many ghosts whispering endearments; so many poisoned memories and possibilities. Right now he was upstairs, or out by the lake, or someplace, she didn't know where, snatching the man she loved from her. She did not need the premier thought in her head to be one of him wrapping his arms tightly about her, kissing her, and telling her that everything would be all right. Things were not all right, they were hellish beyond all imagining.

"Bella?" Wakefield prompted her softly. "If there's something I need to know, pray tell me."

"I do not know why you are speaking to me of this," she snapped. Unconsciously, she fished a kerchief from her pocket and covered her mouth and nose.

"And I do not understand, if it is over between you, why this is upsetting you so."

"Because," she hissed. "It quite evidently isn't."

His eyes narrowed to slate-grey splinters. A long, breathless minute passed, while he studied her face. Then he nodded once and stepped back, like inspection were over and he was falling back into formation. All outward appearances of friendship were stripped away.

He snarled into her face; "Then damnation, Bella, explain to me why you're flaunting your relationship with that detestable rogue Pennerley in his face?"

How dare he confront her like this, and imply she was the villainess.

Her heels drummed hard against the floor.

"Did it never enter your thoughts to question where they both are at this minute?"

Wakefield's head immediately turned, and he made

a quick cast of the room. It confirmed that neither man was present. "Where are they?"

"Not with me," she snarled, vibrating with anger. "Open your eyes, Wakefield, and consider if Lucerne is really the man you want for your sister."

Whatever veil he had erected over his suspicions was suddenly torn away. He blanched a sickly hue, save for two livid scarlet spots on his cheeks. "He is... he is the most exemplary, the kindest, the most loyal and decent ... the very best of men," he blustered.

"Who just happens to enjoy the intimate company of other men," she sniped in return. Let him chew over that fact and then tell her that Lucerne was such a paragon. He was not, and never had been. He was foolish, spineless, callous, and all too easily swayed. And after all she'd endured, there was no logical reason why she should feel any damn thing for him, but she did.

Goddammit, she didn't want to... But she did.

CHAPTER 18
BELLA

FURY STILL POUNDED inside Bella's skull when she entered her room. She had abruptly excused herself before Wakefield could make any sort of response.

God help him, he had to have known. No one could be so blinkered.

However, it wasn't done to speak of such things.

Still, he'd asked for that gunshot of truth to be fired at him. He ought not to have riled her so.

Lucerne marry Caroline – of all the preposterous notions! He belonged to Vaughan, body and soul. Even she had not been able to sever that bond, and Caroline was a guileless mouse in comparison. She hadn't the slightest clue how to entrance a man like Lucerne.

Bella swiped at the door so that it slammed behind her causing all the pictures frames to rattle, then cast herself across the bed. A moment later, she was up again, tangled up in her skirts, but propelled towards the window nevertheless. She wrenched the sash open wide and stuck her head outside. The sun was just edging over the horizon, throwing a last few golden streamers across the lake. A lone white peacock stood upon the lawn proudly displaying its tail feathers. It stared imperiously up at her.

"Preening popinjay!" she cursed it, but it paid her no heed.

Bella took a deep breath and exhaled a sigh. She ought not to have said what she had to Wakefield, but, nor should he have addressed her in the way he had. How could Wakefield claim such a close friendship with Lucerne and not be aware of what was plain as day? By rights, she ought to be frightened he might react in some fearful way, but she remained more tormented by his proposal than concerned for Lucerne and Vaughan's safety. It was no new knowledge she had imparted to him. How could it be? He had lived with Lucerne these past nine months. Rather, she believed, the captain chose not to acknowledge what was obvious, in the same way that near everyone else did.

Well she could not ignore it, nor pretend it wasn't real. Hellfire! She was glad that it was real.

Or at least once she had been.

Now?

Now, she was stuck here, relying on the evening breeze to cool her temper, and they were off somewhere together doing who knew what.

Fornicating... Fucking.

She excised the word from her head, but a multitude of pictures dazzled her nonetheless. Knowing how well, how neatly they fit together under these circumstances was far from a good thing.

Curse them, if they were actually... if they were actually doing that, then by rights she ought to be with them and part of it.

Damn Wakefield and his ridiculousness.

Damn Lucerne for his stupidity and contrition.

And damn Vaughan most of all, for being unable to

resist the thought of spreading Lucerne's lily white cheeks and embedding his prick there.

Bella pulled her head indoors, and sagged to the floor with her back to the wall below the window. A lock had been turned inside her head. A dusty trunk opened, and now all the pleasant memories she'd ruthlessly scourged from her thoughts were free again. She hadn't meant them to get out. She hadn't ever intended to allow Lucerne the means of hurting her so catastrophically again. Bad enough that he would steal Vaughan from her, but as long as she did not love him, then he could not unravel her in the way he had done last October.

"I hate you," she cursed him, while in her mind she was reliving the euphoria of their first kiss, their first illicit tumble, that first time the three of them had all made love together.

Love had had nothing to do with it. She could tell herself that, repeat it as often as she wished, and maybe that first time it had merely been about scratching an itch, but all else had developed from that moment. It was only because she'd loved him that he'd had the power to hurt her so much, and it was only because she loved Vaughan so savagely that she was willing to tolerate this whole horrid mess.

"You abandoned us," she growled bitterly imagining Lucerne before her. "You gave up on us. Why should I allow you the opportunity to destroy us all over again?"

She could make the saints' ears bleed shouting him down, but it was for nothing. If she wanted to hang on to Vaughan, then she would have to reconcile herself to the inevitable.

Vaughan took himself out into the fresh air after his departure from the billiards room. The pacing helped him to contain the violence he wanted to enact. Woe betide anyone who crossed his path at the moment. Returning to the assembled company, to sip tea and pretend all was right with the world, was out of the question. Pretentious drawing room twaddle left him livid at the best of times. He ought not to have pressed Lucerne. Asking him to make a definitive declaration was always going to be a risk – the man was a living embodiment of indecisiveness – but he hadn't been asking for an opinion on the state of the union, or whether mustard or peppercorns made the best sauce for steak. He'd asked for confirmation that he was wanted for more than a quick illicit thrill.

Evidently, he was not.

While, once upon a time, it had been enough just to hold Lucerne, to have that physicality between them, that was no longer the case. He wanted so much more than that, and he was certain that deep down, so too did Lucerne.

He had to want this as Vaughan did. He had to love him. For if that love didn't exist, then what? He put a stopper on those thoughts, for that way lay only despair and desperation. He would not have his lasting epitaph be one of pity. Here lies the 6th Marquis of Pennerley, who pined away over a love unrequited.

Shameful affair. Shameful affair. He could imagine all the mourners shaking their heads and inwardly sneering at his weakness; bad enough to fall in love with another man, but to pine away because he didn't feel the same way—that was womanly behaviour.

Vaughan absentmindedly stormed through a puddle. He could not in his heart believe that physicality was all Lucerne sought. If that were so, then he would surely have found a means of relieving that itch by now. Lucerne might live in the arse-end of the countryside, but there were more civilised places within a day's ride; Ripon, Harrogate, even York if one wanted to venture a little further from ones doorstep in the quest for a particular kind of company. To his knowledge, Lucerne had done none of those things, which tended to suggest that what he craved was Vaughan alone. So, perhaps his unwillingness to speak was due to something other than a lack of feeling. Fear, perhaps? Or, as this was Lucerne, out of some jumbled sense of honour. He took some of the strangest actions under the pretext of upholding Aristotle's virtues. Personally, Vaughan wished he'd concentrate on championing magnificence and wit. Honour inevitably landed one in deep water.

On which subject, the further he ventured around this blasted lake, the more sodden the pathway became. There was a good chance he'd end up wading before too long. Lartington ought to put one of his infernal engines to use to drain it.

But what to do about Lucerne? There was no engine yet invented that would drain him of his folly. We're meant to be, Lucerne. Surely after all this time you've figured that out.

Vaughan stopped and rested against a tree trunk, while he watched the breeze make ripples across the lake. As far as he could see it, there were two options open to him. One, he waited and prayed that eventually Lucerne would seek him out and declare what was surely what he'd felt all along, or two, he went ahead and fucked the bugger in the hope that in the heat of passion, Lucerne wouldn't be so reserved.

He'd said that he wouldn't give chase again, but sitting on his hands waiting wasn't in his nature. Besides, there was a limit on how long anyone could wait around for one man. He'd been hanging around since last October—longer if you fathomed in all the years of pursuit before they had settled in London with Bella.

No, he was as done with inactivity as he was with chasing. What was needed here was something different altogether. A sharp shock, if you would, to remind Lucerne what it was he was missing out on. And what better way of providing that than by flaunting how well he and Bella were getting along.

A grimly determined smile plastered across his face, he turned abruptly and squelched back around the lake to the house.

The entrance hall was lit like a beacon, with the front door stood open to the night air. Several of the gentlemen were taking snuff upon the steps. Within, various other guests were making their way to their rooms and alternative entertainments. It seemed several of the older folks had deemed it time to retire. Country bumpkins! Unless you were a farmhand or a labourer, you had no business rising with the larks and retiring at sunset. All of life's most vital functions took place during the hours of darkness. And all the most successful enchantments were wrought by the light of the moon.

He strode back towards the billiards room, thinking he might still find Lucerne there knocking a few balls about the table. He'd once claimed it helped focus his mind. Alas, the room was empty of the company he sought.

"You haven't seen Marlinscar anywhere, have you, Pennerley?" Charles appeared at his elbow as he made to duck out of the door again.

"What?"

He was not about to announce that he also was looking for Lucerne.

A port-wine blush infused Charles's plump cheeks and jowls. "Lucerne, you've not seen him?"

Vaughan brushed a speck of lint from his coat cuff, and stared down his nose at Charles, fighting to avoid the sort of nervous agitation that would give him up. "He was opposite me at dinner."

Boldly, for Charles, he waved away the response. "I meant since then. He went looking for his timepiece over an hour ago and hasn't reappeared since. I was going to propose some billiards, and I just wondered if—"

Vaughan scowled.

"Well, evidently you didn't cross paths, so I won't trouble you any longer, Pennerley." He propelled his robust body a few feet, before turning his head to address Vaughan again from over his shoulder. "Then again, I don't suppose you'd be interested in a game or two?"

"Alas, Charles, I've other torments in mind for tonight."

All the hot colour drained from the man's face. He tugged uncomfortably at his collar. "Of course. Right then, I'll make sure to leave you to it. Perhaps I'll try Marlinscar's room. Yes, that's the ticket. Say, I don't suppose anyone can tell me where that is?"

"I haven't the faintest idea," Vaughan declared. It was the actual truth. He did not know who had been housed in which room, and until now, had possessed no inclination to find out as there were no windows through which he was inclined to climb.

"Of course, I forgot," Charles blustered. He smoothed his waistcoat down over his stomach paunch. "Scatterbrain." He tapped his head. "You're not so closely acquainted as the pair of you once were. I say, why is that?"

"None of your goddamned business, Charles."

"Right. Yes. Well..." He bowed to Vaughan, then scuttled off after Wakefield, who was heading up the stairs with two of his three sisters. "Wakefield. Hey, yes. You don't happen to know which is Marlinscar's room, do you?"

Vaughan made a point of eavesdropping.

Wakefield turned his head, but wrinkled his nose. "Heavens, man. If he wanted to play billiards, he'd be in the billiards room. Please do stop hanging on my coattails and let me get to bed."

Charles sagged, only for the youngest Wakefield girl, who was following the others up at a slight distance, to pause beside him and remark, "I believe it is the next along from Miss Rushdale's, at the end of the hall. I noted it, for it is horrible planning on the part of the hostess, don't you think?"

"Oh, yes," Charles agreed, eyes bulging and jowls aquiver. "Terrible. I'm sure it was quite an accident, not deliberate at all to put them side by side. That would be quite wrong when they're known to have an attachment, and doubly so, when they're now estranged," he finished dubiously. Somehow, his gaze had strayed back to Vaughan again. He gave him a thoughtful glance, blinked, and returned his attention to Maria. "I expect it was done to discourage anything untoward."

Maria gasped and lifted her hand to her mouth. "Mr Aubury, I really don't know what you could mean. Are you implying that Miss Rushdale would do something illicit with Lord Marlin—"

"Heaven's no, not with him." Charles cut her off.

Vaughan rolled his eyes. Yes—Lucerne was such a saint.

Charles rested his hand upon her arm and drew her conspiratorially close, earning him another vicious glare from Wakefield. "You're young, and I think not all that worldly, Miss Wakefield. I'm sure your friend, Miss Rushdale, would never engage in such deplorable activities as visiting a man in his bedchamber—"

Oh, that was a good one. Time past she'd have done whatever she thought she could get away with. Nonsensically, Joshua kept a far closer eye on her these days.

"—but there are those here who are considerably less scrupulous; Lord Pennerley, for example. He would think nothing of entering a lady's room, with or without her permission. He's a reputation for it, you know. Devil of a man. You should keep your distance. Hopelessly charming but thoroughly treacherous. Do you know he once chased me across a hillside with a sword in his hand meaning to run me through? And all over the trifling sum of sixty guineas."

"Oh, my! That must have been very alarming for you." Bright, dancing laughter shone in Maria Wakefield's eyes, unmistakeable even from across the room.

"Oh, it was. It was."

"He climbs in windows, you say?" She caught Vaughan watching them and winked at him.

Minx. If she was hoping he'd pay her a visit, she was going to wind up disappointed. She was of no interest to him. Well, other than as a way of irritating her sap of a brother.

Charles coughed. "He has a reputation for it, and worse."

Enthralled, Maria seemed keen for further details. Her eyes were like saucers, and glittered with morbid curiosity, but Charles wasn't drawn by her subtle cues. He'd never been able to read women. He possessed some blessed strange notion that the way to their hearts was with ribald poetry and ogling their tits.

"Well, I thank you for the warning, Mr. Aubury. I'll

be certain to lock my window tonight, and keep my distance from him. Although," she paused to consider, and to remove Charles's hand from her arm. "He was very kind to my sister, Caroline, you'll recall, when we were beset by those geese on the outskirts of Reeth. So perhaps, he is not altogether bad, or has turned over a new leaf. Mayhap, I should converse with him in order to find out. It would be unfair to condemn him for past deeds if he's reformed."

Charles stared at her aghast. "Pennerley reformed. Oh, no, my dear. I must dispel you of that notion. He is very bad, very bad. Quite the most deplorable rogue you are ever likely to meet. Your brother would be horrified if you were to be seen talking to that man. Keep your distance, please. He'll never reform, not even on his death bed."

How gratifying to know that without doing a damn thing in forever, he remained infamous. Vaughan snorted. Time was he might have crawled through her window—a lock was no foil for him—just to teach her a lesson about offering an invitation to a notorious rakehell, but he had wickedness of another variety in mind. So, Lucerne was next door to Bella, was he? Good, he couldn't have planned it more perfectly.

CHAPTER 19
BELLA

WHEN HER DOOR flew open, Bella scrambled at once to her feet. Vaughan hadn't bothered to knock, nor did he bother to utter any sort of apology for his intrusion. Angry as she was, it was impossible not to fixate on how glorious he looked. He literally stole her breath as her gaze slid over the snug fit of his charcoal-grey coat, and the glorious wine damask of the waistcoat beneath. How perfectly they shaped his body, and emphasized his shoulders and height.

The wind, or something, had ruffled his dark hair so that the ends fell in loose curls upon his lapels, and the upper part framed his narrow face. Something inside her tightened. He'd come to her, when she'd not expected to see him this night.

In some far corner of her brain, she was distantly aware of demanding, "What? Why are you here?"

He didn't reply, and indeed, she hadn't expected him to.

Instead, she watched him shrug off his coat and loosen his cravat. The former, he dropped on the stool before the oval looking glass, making it easy enough to deduce the purpose of his presence. He meant to use her for his pleasure.

Bella shuffled warily from foot to foot.

Stripped of his outer garments, Vaughan proceeded to the fireplace and tended the blaze, heaping it with coals and setting to with the bellows. He had the flames crackling away merrily within moments.

"I was warm enough already. It is summer." She had on three...four layers.

"I don't want you shivering."

"I'm not cold." But she was trembling. "Why are you here? Is it to regale me with your exploits?" A rough tangle with Lucerne would explain the blush across his cheekbones, and the sapphire-gleam in his eyes. "No doubt you have tumbled him and now mean to trouble me with the details. Well you may save your story; I do not wish to hear it."

"Of course not," he agreed, far too amiably. "You'd be frightfully disappointed. It wasn't at all satisfactory."

Bella circled around behind him warily. How well the stuff of his shirt clung to his shoulders and the grey back of his waistcoat framed his body. She crossed to the door, and closed it, so as to maintain at least some vestige of dignity. The entire household did not need to be privy to their business, and she most especially didn't want her brother suddenly appearing to add his tuppence worth.

Vaughan resumed an upright stance as Bella reached the hearth. He turned and reached for her, but she back-stepped away from his arms. She knew how easily he could draw her in to one of his games.

"Don't imagine that barging your way in here will lead to anything. You can wash those thoughts right out of your head. You can't flit between his arms and mine as you did in the past. I won't have it, Vaughan. It's abhorrent that you even presume it would be fine. We are not the three of us embroiled anymore."

"Bella..."

The way he drawled her name, was as if he'd wrapped a cord around her heart and now tugged upon it. It physically hurt to resist him, but it did not matter how much she craved his touch, she would not be used to slake his thirst for somebody else, and neither would she be the trophy he raised for his success in getting what he wanted.

Clearly, Lucerne was his again.

Vaughan leaned in to her, and she watched his mouth descend. "No," she squeaked right before their lips brushed. She did not push him away, but instead parted her mouth, eager to feel the dance of his tongue with hers.

Stupid. So stupid.

With one hand, he encircled the back of her neck, held her exactly as he wanted her. Then broke off the kiss, but kept her close so that only their foreheads were pressed together.

"You have it all wrong, Bella. We didn't fuck. I've spoken to him this evening, but that is all. His lips haven't even touched mine."

Was that true? His eyes were as black and fathomless as ever. For certain, she detected no hint of Lucerne upon him.

"Should I therefore conclude that you're here expecting me to act as surrogate? I won't do it, Vaughan. It is not fair of you to treat me like this—as if my feelings do not matter. Touch me; come to me because you want me, not because he will not give in to you."

"That is not how it is."

"Is it not? Your heart is full to the brim of him."

"And of you also."

"Lies."

Vaughan weathered the retort with an imperious arching of one brow. "There are no lies between us."

Bella cast him the sort of glare that she hoped stated very clearly her thoughts on that subject.

"Very well, sometimes I confess, I have omitted certain details or been lax in informing you of them, but I have never said a thing to you that I did not mean." His hand cupped her cheek, long fingers stroked across her lips and chin. "He's desperate for every morsel of affection I'm willing to throw him, Bella. Even the smallest touch excites him. His breath quickens whenever I lean close. He would, I think, risk compromising himself for the fleeting joy of having me fuck him."

Unconsciously, Bella opened her mouth to allow Vaughan's thumb to sweep around her lips and caress the tip of her tongue. There was no taste of Lucerne upon his hand either.

"Then why not give him what he wants? Why come to me?"

"Mayhap I think he deserves his agony to be prolonged."

He surprised a cough of dry laughter from her. "No." She pushed him away. "Do you imagine me so unaware? So enthralled by your touch that I can't figure out what you are doing? I know that his room is the next along. This is no more than a way of shouting 'See what you are missing.' You don't desire me. You only mean to provoke him."

"Provoke!" The lulling caresses ceased, and his grip tightened suddenly around her throat. "No, Bella. I plan to give him a raging cockstand."

Damn him, he moved so quickly. Within a heartbeat he was forcing his mouth back down upon hers, stealing her breath and determination and raising her skirts so that he had all the access he might desire to her quim. His arms cocooned her, the scent of his skin inflamed her as he bore her backward first into the wall, where he held her while he savaged her lips, and then towards the bed.

"No, Vaughan. No. Let go of me."

To her genuine surprise, he did so abruptly, so that she dropped stone-like onto the mattress on her back. Bella stared up at him. A tic fired along the side of his tense jaw. "Earlier, you wanted nothing more than for me to touch you forever, now you have that, you're hollering for release. Just which is it that you actually desire, Bella?

"I want you, but I won't be used as a means of you getting him."

He gave a coarse huff of laughter. "You've always been that."

She pushed up onto her elbows. "I know. I accept that we all used one another, but no more. I was your means into his bed, and he my way of crawling into yours, but all it made for was knots and riddles and heartache."

Vaughan's eyes narrowed to slits, and his lips squashed into a tight moue. "So what do you propose? Are we to go separate ways and all live unhappily ever after?"

She pushed the strands of her hair that had come loose from her coif back from her face. "Oh, of course not. You know I will not choose to give you up, but nor am I choosing to take him back. I don't wish him in my life anymore. I cannot just forgive him as you seem able."

She was lying to herself, at least a little. She could hear the deceit in her voice, meaning Vaughan would likely recognised that shrill tremor for what it was too. Lord dammit; why could everything not be simple?

Loving two men at once was too complicated. Not that she was admitting to that level of affection for Lucerne. Yes, she did still feel something, but he had hurt her deeply. He'd hurt Vaughan too, even if he seemed able to brush such things aside as if they were nothing.

"I don't care for the anxiety having him back in our lives is causing. It would content me greatly if we were to return to Pennerley and forget him altogether."

"That, Miss Rushdale, will never happen." Vaughan retreated to the window, and perched on the sill with one leg crooked. He regarded his fingernails contemplatively.

"It's not as if you've rushed to reclaim him."

"A little time apart seemed prudent."

"A little! You call eight months a little?"

He threw a shrewd glance in her direction, one that made her distinctly uncomfortable. "One had to wait until the appropriate time." Why did he make it sound as if he'd been waiting for her compliance? He'd been the one that was hurt, distraught, not her... She'd not fallen into inactivity... Her brow crumpled. Memories sprang up of him stood before the fireplace at Pennerley, while she paced back and forth. Memories of sitting alone in bed staring into the dark unable to sleep.

Well, she'd been angry, of course that had upset certain rhythms.

Bella shuffled to the edge of the bed and untangled her skirts, so that they fell once again in smooth lines to her ankles. "Don't you ever get tired of having your affections pulled in multiple directions?"

Vaughan glanced up. "I do not comprehend what is so difficult about caring for more than one person."

Bella sprung lightly to her feet and made a pace or two toward the hearth. "You mean besides having to constantly split ones heart and time in two, the spars, the jealousy, and the endless, endless nights where you lie awake wondering if today will be the day when you wake entirely alone because your two lovers have agreed they would prefer to simply be with one another." His head lifted, but Bella jumped in before he could make a response. "Pray do not tell me you never felt any of those things, for I will know you are lying. You feared Lucerne and I would marry and that you would be left out."

"I still do." He closed his hands as if in prayer, and tapped his steepled fingers against his lips. "There's still a part of me that rebels at the very notion. That sees you as the enemy to be thwarted at whatever cost."

Bella whipped her head around to glare at him, a frown gouging creases in her brow. "As if there was any likelihood of that." She rolled her eyes. Then, pushed her hand into her pocket, and traced the cold, hard surface of the ring Lucerne had given her. "You are the one intent upon having him again, not I."

His shoulders slumped a little, and they lapsed into an uneasy silence. Almost, she wished they were still yelling at one another and exchanging poisonous kisses. At least then she did not have to endure the feeling of being wounded to the point of hysteria.

"Say something," she demanded after the silence grew prolonged. She disliked the stoicism of his pose, and the way he seemed to have closed off his emotions. Vaughan blinked before tilting his head a fraction, regarding her with an expression borne of sadness.

"It seems you and I have a problem."

Bella crossed to where he maintained his perch, and rested her fingers upon his knee. "That is hardly a new thing. There's barely been a moment since we met when we have not been at odds with one another over something or other."

"But this regards Lucerne."

"It has always been about Lucerne. He's been at the centre of everything."

"Yes," he agreed. The word was softly spoken, but inside she knew he was wound as tightly as a clock spring. "But while you maintain you no longer want him, I still do."

That simply spoken phrase was no great revelation to her; it was the manner of its delivery that shook her to the core. It came straight from the heart.

"I've given him plenty of time to ruminate. Nine months ought to be enough for a man to know what he wants. I'm done idling. I can't stand back and watch him falling over his own feet while hoping he'll eventually fall the right way and land in my arms. I want him in my life... in my bed. I want his love."

"And what of me?" She enquired, equally quietly.

"I wish to love you also."

Bella gasped, and pulled her hand away from his thigh as if she had just been scalded. "Do not throw that word around lightly."

"When have I ever. I am not given to saying things I do not mean."

"You love me?" She stared at him, eyes wide.

Vaughan slipped from the sill and reached for her. The clasp upon her shoulder was firm but non-aggressive. "Why is that so very hard for you to accept?"

Fearfully, she met his gaze. His violet eyes were two small rings around his dilated pupils.

"I don't know," she decided at length. "It's...That is, it complicates things." Oh, it most definitely did that. Nervously, she wetted her lips, then turned her back on him and paced. Even in her soft pumps, the floor of the old house creaked with every movement. When she was by the door, she turned and faced him once again. He had not moved at all. "If that is the truth, then why am

I not enough? Why must you have him also? If you are in love with me, then I should be enough."

He crooked one eyebrow quizzically. "That is not how love functions, Bella."

"For everyone else, it is."

He shook his head. Bella watched him chew over several thoughts. For a wonder, he actually seemed to be considering his reply and choosing it with some measure of care. Not that Vaughan's responses weren't always calculated for the best effect, however this contemplation felt different.

"Everyone else lies to themselves, but I refuse to. They bind themselves to one person, claim they are the centre of their universe, and then take lovers and mistresses and fuck the groomsmen on the side. I would rather be honest with myself and those I care for. Love is complex. It doesn't adhere to rules, and it knows no bounds. No mother ever only loved one of her offspring."

Bella's eyes began to prickle. She sucked at her upper lip.

"Bella, you wish me to be forthright, and so I will be. It does not matter how much I love you. I will always love him too. I always have, you see, since the very first moment I saw him. What I feel for him—specifically him, and not any other man—it isn't rational. I have no command over it. And if any other person ought to understand that, it is you. That is, after all, why you are sitting here listening to me proclaim my feelings for someone else. It's because there is no alternative for you, because you feel that way about me."

"I hated you the first moment I saw you," she snarled.

A thin smile crept across his lips. "You desired me. You only hated me because I would not give you what you wanted, and in the end, is hate not just the flip side of love? It requires the same intensity."

"I believed I was in love with Lucerne," she said wistfully. In those first days at Lauwine, she had been convinced of it. Lucerne had entered her little world from outside of its normal boundaries and seemed magical as a result of it. Vaughan though, he had been intoxication itself. She'd craved his attention, even as she'd recognised the futility of trying to acquire it. But of course, she had not recognised all those things at the time. Not until much later had she realised her heart belonged to Vaughan, and that it was him she wanted above all else, she'd only been fooling herself thinking she was in love with Lucerne.

Vaughan swung his legs up, and sat upon the bed, his back against the headboard. He patted the eiderdown, signalling her to join him. "Now is it clear why I cannot let him go?"

"All too," she sighed, while climbing up beside him. She rested on her knees, facing him with her skirts fanned around her. "But, I still maintain you ask too much if you simply expect me to capitulate. I don't desire him in that same way."

"Good." He closed his eyes and a broad grin turned his mouth up at the corners. "Then I shan't have to worry about you running off with him."

"Vaughan," she aimed a backhanded slap at his thigh, but he caught her hand before she struck her target. He turned her hand palm up and traced the long line that traversed its centre. She felt the touch as if he'd stroked directly between her thighs. Eyes wide and dancing again, he laced their fingers. Then, nose to nose, he regarded her.

"I'm not going to give you up, my nightingale, but you must allow me the freedom to mend things with Lucerne."

Bella blinked. Her head and heart were both all of a muddle. Two fat tears rolled down her cheeks. Whereupon, two gentle sweeps of his thumb saw them off. "These are not necessary." He cupped her face and kissed the salt tracks. The rings on his right hand were cold, or maybe it was her skin that burned.

"I don't know that I have faith enough to believe what you say."

"You're mine, Annabella Rushdale. Did I not steal you from under another man's nose? From under two different men's noses? Why would I do that, if I meant to let you go?"

He had taken her from Raffe Devonshire's bed, a place she had never truly belonged, but he'd also, perhaps unintentionally, purloined her from Lucerne.

"Nothing you do ever makes any sense." She gave a sad little shake of her head.

Vaughan lifted her chin. His jewel-like eyes sought her gaze, and he smiled in a way that lit the depths of his pupils. "You're the only person to whom my actions make sense. No one else understands."

She looked into his face, at the angular set of his cheekbones, and the faintest brush of stubble poking through his skin forming a shadow around his jaw. The light from the blaze licked his skin with bronze and golden hues. "I think it is more truthful to say you do not wish them to."

"Why would I only let you in, Bella?"

Her heart skipped.

The answer was surely plain enough. She held a sacred position in his life.

Was it true, then?

She had hoped so long, and so desperately for his love, that she'd convinced herself it was futile. But he was looking at her in a way that left no doubt, assuming that his words hadn't already made it clear.

He loved her.

Lord, she was trembling. Tears streamed down her face, that she brushed away with the back of her hand, as comprehension gave way to glee.

Vaughan Peredur Forvasham, 6th Marquis of Pennerley loved her, and every inch of her seemed to have realised that fact at once.

"You're shivering," he observed.

She was also grinning like a lunatic if the ache in her cheeks was anything to go on.

The next moment saw her reaching up, pushing her hands through his dark hair, and locking them around the back of his neck. She sought his lips, and gasped into his mouth when he delivered.

Vaughan drew her closer, up to straddle his lap, as they hungrily explored one another. He slid her forward, cupping her rear, until she was pressed tight into the V formed by his thighs and hips. She stole a few giddy breaths, and their mouths locked once more. Lord, she could drown in the taste of him. Always, there was that rush of vertigo. Their tongues tangled, flicked coaxingly against one another, until she was wrapped in a cocoon of heat and desire. Blood pumped torrent-like through her veins. Of her own volition, she drew them closer still, wanted for them to be bound as only a man and a woman could be.

In times past, Lucerne could always be relied on to be tender with her, but with Vaughan, passions flared white-hot and brutal. Pleasure and pain were twinned. His caresses stoked her to fever-pitch, but he was equally likely to bite, pinch, or leave her a hair's breadth from satisfaction as he was to deliver ecstasy. That or he'd fly her to the pinnacle of bliss, but with his hands around her throat. This time that frightening knife edge simply didn't exist. They were too lost in one another, and in the joys of sensual wonder, to fight what had been so obvious for so long.

He loved her.

It would take some time to reconcile that knowledge with her reality.

Was this how he was when he was alone with Lucerne? She had often wondered. Or was it all savage beauty between them too? Alone, did Vaughan open up his heart? Was he only rough with Lucerne when she was around to witness it? Was he only brutish with her in order to keep her at a distance, and if that were so, did this mean the walls were finally tumbling and as he insisted, she had found a way into his heart?

"If you continue to tug on my buttons like that you will give my man an apoplexy."

She was quite unaware that she was doing so. Why did men insist on so many fastenings, and fiddly ones at that? It was impossible to find any sort of purchase on the fabric. She had tried, and was more than ready to damage the work of art that was his attire in order to get them to the point of being skin upon skin.

Vaughan pushed her hands away after the fifth button. He quickly dealt with the rest, while she reached for the less taxing fastenings of his pantaloons. He was eager for her; already she was aware of the solid press of his shaft between them, and her own readiness for him.

If life never gave her anything else, then she would still be blessed to have been given this beautiful man with his ramrod of an erection.

"I want to remove every stitch of clothing from you. Lick you. Kiss you. Draw dirty pictures on your skin with the seed I've caused you to spill."

He laughed. "I was banking on spending somewhere hot and moist."

She released her grip on him to draw her fingers across her parted lips.

"No, I don't mean your mouth."

Her breath hitched.

"Nor your derriere, either. Didn't we establish that you're mine, Bella? You don't belong to Lucerne any more. Your cunny is wholly in my possession."

"Yes." Her gasp loosed from her lips, shockingly raw, to be met by another heart-melting kiss. "Do not move." She rifled through the trinkets on the dressing table until she came upon the item she needed. Shamelessly, she hitched her skirts to set it in place, before swiftly returning to Vaughan.

Nimble fingers set to work, and Vaughan's cravat slithered from around his neck like a long albino snake. Bella parted the edges of his shirt, exposing his throat, and set upon exploring the pulse point at its base. Meanwhile, Vaughan relieved her of a multitude of pins. All the ones holding her hair in place, and those keeping the edges of her gown sat just right. He flicked each of them across the room, tiny slivers of silver that flashed bright and then vanished in the dark. After the last one shimmered and disappeared, he expertly divested her of her dress, and she of his shirt, boots and other accoutrements.

The rush of pleasure as bare skin met bare skin left Bella tingling all over. Their thighs met. Her breasts pressed tight to his chest, and the diamond of crisp dark hairs that lay between his disc-like nipples. Her hand found his cock, while she tongued around one of his nipples, and then bent to trace the scar that snaked like a silver river across his ribs.

"Always straight for the target, Miss Rushdale."

"Would you prefer me coy? I like the feel of you in my hand, so hard, so supple. I want you, Vaughan."

"Then you should definitely take me."

He held her, aided her balance as she lifted herself over him. They slid and shifted, the head of his cock rubbing rude circles around the entrance to her pussy, taunting her with a promise of what was to come, until she could stand it no more and fit them together like the pieces of a puzzle. Their bodies clove to one another. Met and melded, like hand and glove.

Bella revelled in the newness of having him beneath her. She sought his mouth again, and seized from him urgent kisses.

"Yes," he encouraged. "Take what you need. Show me how much you want it."

"I want it." She roughly shoved him so that his back hit the mattress, and he was spread for her pleasure, gazing up at her astride his cock. "I want all of this." Her hands traversed his body, squeezing and caressing, lingering where hard muscle covered bone. "All of it."

Her hands locked around his upper arms, pinning him in place against the mattress, while she tossed her head and rode him at the gallop.

Everything fell away until their motions were borne purely out of instinct. Bella bent her head and licked the sweat from the hollow of his throat. The sharp tang of salt exploded on her tongue. "Let go, Vaughan," she whispered into his neck. "I don't want you to hold back. I know you're reining yourself in."

He freed himself of the grip she had upon his arms and attempted to pull her to him. Bella rose up again, out of his reach.

"Bella, what sort of lover am I if I revel in purely selfish pursuits?"

"The one I've chosen."

The muscles across his torso bunched. His neck tendons grew pronounced as he strained to catch her. "Ever consider that I might enjoy making you climax?"

"This time, I want to watch you come."

"Of course you do."

He took hold of her hips, lifted her, adjusting their position, and thrust up as he urged her to bear down. Again and again, he impaled her upon his staff, until her head buzzed and her limbs were jelly. It was by no means a given who was deriving the most pleasure from the motion, particularly when he shifted his hand so his thumb was catching against her clit, dragging over it as she lifted, and pressing down as she descended.

Teeth bared, deep moans of satisfaction burst from her lips at the culmination of every thrust. Vaughan filled her completely. They fit so perfectly together, and that infuriating scrape upon her senses sent shivers of delight right up her spine to tingle in her scalp, and across her skin and nipples.

"Harder. More," she encouraged.

Vaughan drove up; bouncing her so that each time their bodies met it was with a powerful slap. He fucked her hard, sparing nothing. Holding back nothing. The world started to spin out of control. Bella's senses exploded. She threw her head back and luxuriated in the unfiltered, naked decadence of the moment, before the pleasure fragmented, and she toppled headlong over the precipice into bliss.

Vaughan followed her barely a heartbeat later.

Spent, she rolled onto the eiderdown, and Vaughan spooned against her back.

"Promise to fuck me at least once a week like that, and I'll be yours forever."

His breath puffed hot against her ear, and she felt the graze of his teeth. "You're mine anyway. And only once a week? It would seem your appetite for me isn't as robust as it once was. Am I boring you, Miss Rushdale?"

She turned her head and kissed his nose. "Never, but there has to be time for all the other ways we might enjoy one another, and even you must know that sex alone cannot sustain a relationship. We'll have to be seen, and eat, and rest." She deliberately avoided any mention of Lucerne's inevitable pull upon his time and stamina. "Ah!" She yawned, eyelids fluttering. "I am quite exhausted by you and the thought of it all."

"Then rest." He wormed his way down the bed a little so that his head rested upon the pillow beside hers, their hair spread around them, the strands all intertwined. Then he tucked her back against his body. It was not long before his muscles relaxed and his breaths grew soft. Cocooned within the warmth of his embrace, Bella's eyelids drooped, and she fell contentedly into sleep.

CHAPTER 20
LUCERNE

AFTER VAUGHAN LEFT, Lucerne lingered in the billiards room a while, taking pot-shots with a couple of balls. He failed miserably to bag anything as his limbs were trembling so much. Vaughan had always possessed the ability to unnerve him and reel him in at the same time. Part of him wanted desperately to run after Vaughan, catch him, fall on his knees, and utter the sort of mad proposal one might offer a woman.

It wouldn't do. It seriously wouldn't do.

That sort of behaviour would endanger both their lives. Being hung for ones appetites did not sound like an appealing prospect. Dying for love had always struck him as hideously impractical. Still, it was only the billiards cue that prevented him from succumbing to such a rash action. For a wonder, he did not snap it in two with his iron grip.

It was only after the other gentlemen had re-joined the ladies that Lucerne quietly lowered his anchor to the baize and sallied upstairs to his room. He could not be around company. His thoughts were too addled, and he feared the sort of smile he might fix in place would induce fainting fits among the ladies.

His valet was thankfully absent, the unfamiliar room dark and quiet. He stood with his back pressed to the inside of the door, eyes closed, and breathed. If he had remained downstairs, he would inevitably have been found. Then, Wakefield would have pried into his absence and state of mind, Crakehall also, and Charles would have made some not-so-innocuous remark that would have him reddening to his hair roots while trying to spin his actions in a favourable light when there was nothing goodly about them.

He sighed, and that was all before he considered the practical realities of being considered prime marriage material in a room filled with husband-hunting ladies. The coy glances alone were enough to turn a fellow into a shrivelled wretch.

Actually, maybe he ought to have gone down, because being in that dingy, confined space with Vaughan had left him more than a little spritely in a certain department.

Lucerne idly dragged his hand down over the bulge in his breeches. No—considering how highly his waistcoat was cut, parading anywhere at all was madness. They'd be whispering behind his back again, concocting tails of his blackguardly antics, as if he stole away young women on a regular basis and debauched them.

Bella had been the exception, not the rule. And actually, it wasn't he who had persuaded her to leave home and Yorkshire all those years ago. He'd proposed it, but Vaughan had been instrumental. He ought to have recognised that as a toll-bridge on the horizon then and there. The pair of them were made for each other. If he'd not allowed himself to be dazzled by their words, and focussed on their actions, then just think of all the time he'd have saved juggling the pair of them.

Dammit, if he wasn't still juggling them now, just in a slightly different way.

His relationship with one was completely bound up in the other. He could not negotiate with them as individual entities any more.

He'd wager Vaughan never had to prompt Bella into making a declaration. No doubt she expressed her wholehearted commitment to him on a daily basis, and without ever demanding the same in return.

Sometimes he really did despair over his own actions in not defying Vaughan and offering for her in the manner he'd originally intended. If he'd made the proposal that night in Ned Darleston's sitting room he wouldn't be the one shivering in the dark on his own now. He could not even swear with any certainty that proposing to Bella would have lost him Vaughan, and in any case, he had lost him anyway.

It was some minutes later that a repetitive thumping noise drew him to raise his head from his knees. He had slumped into a sitting position, still with his back to door, when his legs had seemed ready to buckle.

Aw, shit!

No worldly man alive could mistake that particular noise for anything other than the percussion of intense coitus.

So he was to be punished.

Bella's blissful mewls penetrated the plaster and echoed in his ears, soon accompanied by all too familiar grunts.

Dammit! Satan's angels could not have concocted a better torture to lacerate his soul with—Vaughan and Bella making love. He could not sit in the dark and listen to this, not without altogether coming apart. It was too much. Nor did he doubt that one or both of them considered it just punishment for him being a self-centred twit.

Maybe he was, but he had not acted wholly in self-interest. If it wasn't for him, would Bella and Vaughan truly have ever found one another? Confessed what they felt for one another? He'd had to leave for that to happen.

Lucerne did not want to encounter company, so he strayed only as far as the end of the corridor, where a set of double doors led out onto a balcony overlooking the wooded vista to the right of the lake. It was in this location that Charles discovered him with a cry of alacrity only a short while later.

"Marlinscar—here you are. I have been all over this confounded house seeking you."

Lucerne straightened his back, but did not turn around, better his expression remained shadowed and outward facing. "Is something amiss, Charles?"

"Aye, plenty, as there always is when folks are housed altogether. I had hoped we could wager a coin or two on a round or two of billiards. But, I rather suppose it too late now. Near everyone has turned in."

Lucerne bowed his head in agreement. Even if the hour had not been so late, he had no wish to emerge from the shadows and socialise. "I'll have to beg our hostess for forgiveness for my absence tomorrow."

"Oh, she barely stayed a minute after the announcement. I doubt she missed you. Where was it you got to? Surely you weren't searching out your timepiece this whole time? I say, you have found it, haven't you? There's not a thief about?"

"Eh? Oh, yes." It had slipped his mind that he had supposedly mislaid it. "I have it." He turned to show Charles that it hung from his waistcoat, but did not offer an explanation as to its, or rather his, previous whereabouts. Charles smiled mindlessly at him. He was nursing a bottle of port, his lips already heavily red-stained from it. Also, there was a deal of snuff clinging to his monstrous cravat. A country soiree did not warrant that much froth at one's throat. In fact, no occasion warranted it.

Regardless, Lucerne held his tongue, and instead concentrated on sinking back into the shadows, with his forearms resting on the balustrade.

Charles had never been good with silences. It was therefore inevitable that he would endeavour to launch another topic of discourse within a few moments. "Crossed paths with Pennerley, did you?" he asked.

Lucerne stifled a fictitious yawn. "Only briefly." There seemed little point in denying it.

"So, have you settled things?"

Lucerne made to shake his head, but stopped himself and only tilted it towards one shoulder instead. "What is it you think there is to settle, Charles?"

His friend attempted to snort and ended up blowing port bubbles through his nose. Once he had made loud use of his handkerchief, he gesticulated with his hand. "You know; all that business about Bella Rushdale, and how he pilfered her from under your nose. I suppose he's with her now, is he? And that's why you're out here. Can't bear to listen to him drilling her, eh?" He nudged Lucerne's elbow in a chummy sort of way. "It always sets my teeth on edge to hear another man winding the clock. It's like they're rubbing it in your face that you're not as blessed. And then there's the fact that most of them are ungrateful wretches. They take a dip in the well, and then they're off making eyes at some other pretty young thing. A gentleman ought to be more respectful."

"I'd rather not speak of it, Charles."

The other man went so far as to cup Lucerne's

elbow, and give it a squeeze. "Too painful, what? I imagine it's tiresome, dreadfully tiresome and vexing losing out to him, you pair having been so close. 'tain't right what he's done. Everyone was rooting for the two of you, I mean for you and Miss Rushdale, not you and Pennerley. We were all on absolute tenterhooks in anticipation of you sallying down the aisle together. I, like many others, took a bet on the date."

"Charles. Please."

"Hey. Oh, quite. I am sorry. I didn't mean to... I'll quieten now."

"Please do."

How long had it been? Would they have worn themselves out yet? Any other couple surely would have done so by now, but Vaughan was capable of presiding over torment after torment. Their antics could go on all night. One of the household servants would find him frozen out here at first light.

Charles slapped him between the shoulder blades. "Rouse yourself, Marlinscar. They're done. It's now safe to go to bed."

"Huh?" Lucerne about turned. It was on the tip of his tongue to enquire how Charles could be so certain—they could not be heard from here—only for his heart to lurch wildly as he recognised Vaughan coming towards them, all smiles and outward contentment. Well he might look smug given he'd just fucked Bella to the moon and back.

He also happened to look more handsome than any devil had a right to—dark hair shimmering in the candlelight, eyes ablaze. Lucerne's teeth ached—he ground them together, trying not to notice the disarray of Vaughan's attire. He was carrying his cravat in his hand. Neither waistcoat nor shirt was fastened, so that a sliver of his torso was on display. And only one side of his breeches was done up.

Moreover, the Graces themselves could not have moved in a more fluid and sensuous way—the muscles of his torso sliding and tightening under his shirtsleeves as he prowled towards them. He was entirely without a coat. Lucerne curled his fingers into his palms, forming tight fists. He wanted to grab Vaughan by the open edges of his shirt and shake him until his teeth rattled loose. Or rather, he wanted to dig his fingers into all that fine flesh and demand treatment of equal parity to that which Bella had received. He'd never wanted to be screwed so much in his life.

"Pennerley," Charles began.

Vaughan strode straight past him without so much as a glance in his direction, and right up to Lucerne. Anticipation jerked Lucerne to attention. He knew what was coming. Knew he ought to do something, react in some manner other than standing still and welcoming it. Vaughan's hand caught him around the front of his throat. Lucerne was a fraction taller, but that didn't seem to matter. Their lips met. Lightning crackled between them. Flames ignited across his skin. God! It was perfect—the perfect kiss, exactly the right angle, the right pressure. Their tongues tangled in a fiercely erotic way, resulting, not unexpectedly, in him being bone-hard in a heartbeat.

To his right, he heard Charles's jaggered gasp.

That should have put an end to it, but it didn't. It had been too long a wait. His need was too great. This was magical, mind-scourging. Exaltation worthy. He reached out to Vaughan, but the moment his fingertips brushed the other man's clothing, it was over.

Lucerne groaned. He stood statue-like, refusing to blink, too afraid that if he did so, he'd realise his imagination had got the better of him, and he'd fantasised the whole thing. It was Charles's continued spluttering as much as Vaughan's continued hold upon his person and the heat burning his lips that assured him that it was, in fact, real.

Rationally, that ought not to have been assuring. This—this madness was a very bad thing, a very bad thing indeed. What was Vaughan thinking, coming up to him like this, kissing him like this, when there was a witness not a foot away? He didn't wait around long enough for Lucerne to find his voice and ask. Nope, he was off, swaggering down the corridor as if not a thing had happened.

"Marlinscar," Charles croaked.

Lucerne blinked as if waking from a daze. Indeed, he had been spectacularly dazzled. "Yes, Charles?"

The man's chin was butting his chest, he was flushed a deep crimson and perspiration peppered his brow. "What the devil?" He took out his handkerchief again and mopped his brow

"I don't know what to say, Charles."

"I should think not. Kissing a fellow... Of all things! And, on the lips too. Shocking. Also, I note, not so much as a how'd you do, just struck like a snake," He gesticulated a strike. "Then he goes and walks off still without saying a word. What in heaven's name does he mean by it?" He downed a large swig of port.

Lucerne grabbed the bottle off him and did the same.

"I don't know."

"Is he likely to do it again? Are any of us safe? Imagine if he were to do it in front of the ladies."

Lucerne shook his head. His wits remained fragmented. The concept of ladies and shame were rather diffuse at present. They'd rather lost any sort of solid meaning that he usually attached to them. He only prayed that Vaughan would kiss him again, and a whole lot more besides. Whether there was an audience, at this moment, was irrelevant.

"Lucerne?" Charles enquired. He reclaimed his bottle. "What will you do if he does?"

"Fuck." Lucerne swore.

Aghast, Charles dropped the bottle, which shattered over the floor tiles. His jowls trembled as he stared at Lucerne in horror.

Some measure of reality began to seep in to Lucerne's consciousness. "No—good heavens, I didn't mean... It was an expletive, Charles. I only meant that— Bugger!" Damn it, that too was an ill-choice of expression. Attempting to explain himself was just landing him in deeper water. "Well, how would you react if he kissed you?" he blurted.

Charles's watery blue-grey eyes were near protruding from their sockets. He'd turned puce from the neck up. His gaze darted between Lucerne and the burgundy river now snaking across the floor towards the balustrade. He shook his head in that slow way one might after having seven bells knocked out of you. "You..." He dramatically swallowed. "You and him. It's all true what they say." He seemed to find his wind. "I mean, we knew. We all knew. That is, we suspected, but there was always the niggling suspicion that it was a finely crafted ruse the two of you concocted for a giggle, and that you laughed about in private, over how easily you made us question everything we knew. Not that such beastliness ought to be a laughing matter, but Pennerley's sense of humour can be somewhat perverse.

He paused and squinted quizzically at Lucerne. "Mayhap this is more of the same. Some deception you and he planned in order to make me appear foolish. Do you know; I'm tired of being the butt of everyone's jokes?"

"Charles—"

"Hisht" He swished his hand before Lucerne's face

to quieten him. "I won't fall for it. You'll not make a fool of me. My lips are sealed on the subject."

Thank Christ and all the saints for that!

"I'm not some young greenhorn, you know."

"I've never thought you so."

"Hm," Charles's shoulders relaxed, and he gazed forlornly at the puddle of port and glass at his feet. "I must say, it was in very poor taste. Very poor taste. One could get into all sorts of trouble... Darleston's seeing the sharp end of that stick at the moment."

Lucerne put his hand upon his friend's shoulder. "Pennerley is a law unto himself, you know that."

Charles nodded. "Aye, I do, but you...you normally have more sense."

"Do I?" Lucerne mocked himself, eyebrows raised.

"Of course. Mostly. Well, sometimes..."

Lucerne clapped his hands. "We should find someone to clear up this mess," He stepped over the mess "I'll ring for a maid to come and deal with it. Come," Hand back on Charles's shoulder, he guided him away from the balcony. "You should retire, I think, after your shock. I'll tell Vaughan it was too much. Here, this one is your room, is it not?"

"It's mine, yes. Mine and the captain's. And do. Do talk to him. Someone most definitely needs to have words with him." He peeped cautiously at Lucerne, as if ascertaining whether he considered him up to the task. Charles would never consider standing up to Vaughan, verbally or otherwise.

"I'm sorry, Charles. Goodnight."

"Goodnight, Marlinscar. I don't know what game it is the two of you are playing with Miss Rushdale, but you might want to reconsider your role in it."

Lucerne nodded his head using only the tiniest of motions. "Sound advice, friend. I'll do that."

It just wouldn't be in quite the fashion Charles

intended. The moment Charles's door closed, Lucerne pressed his back to the wainscoting. Dear God—that kiss! He was still ablaze from it.

What in hell was Vaughan thinking?

What did it mean?

Was it a taunt, and invitation?

He clasped one hand over the other and pressed his knuckle between his teeth. He needed to think this through somewhere quiet. Luckily, he could have that in just a few paces.

A loud sigh eased past Lucerne's lips when he finally closed the door of his room. He pressed his head to the wood as he fastened the latch. All was now quiet next door, the drama and hammering of earlier no more than an echo in his head. He closed his eyes and relived the shocking brush of Vaughan's lips. It had been an utterly reckless thing to do. Any one of the other guests might have witnessed them, and not all were so easy to manipulate as Charles, who would hold his tongue out of fear of making himself appear an even greater buffoon than normal. That said, Lucerne suspected that in his heart, Charles knew the truth. And maybe that, more than fear, was the reason he would remain silent.

It was as Lucerne sat on the bed removing his shoes that the note appeared under the door. He stared at the neatly folded white square for several moments, before snatching it up and breaking the wax seal.

Should you still wish to talk, I'll be in the observatory. Come and find me.

CHAPTER 21
LUCERNE

LUCERNE DID NOT know where Lartington's observatory lay, but he set out to find it without a moment's hesitation. Nor, when he located it, with the aid of a rather helpful plan of the grounds he found among some papers in Lartington's vast library, was it the sort of building he expected it to be. He'd been anticipating a tall, narrow tower that reached up into the heavens, not a relatively squat building; clearly built with no consideration to practicality in mind. He guessed it the work of a prior family member, perhaps one who intended it as a banqueting house or gentleman's retreat. Perhaps said gentlemen had also been a scholar of the days of chivalry and crusader knights.

The door swung inwards on well-oiled hinges. A few well-positioned lanterns illuminated the interior. It was a single room, housing a vast array of odd materials. Lucerne edged between some of the more esoteric artefacts, seeking some evidence that it was Vaughan who had summoned him, and not another, intent upon blackmailing him.

The groan of metal caused him to turn his head, whereupon he spied an iron staircase towards the back of the room, just a little across from where he'd entered, which lead upwards in a winding spiral. A slender, booted figure appeared at the top—Vaughan!

Lucerne still had the note clasped within his hand, which he lifted as an explanation to his presence. "You said you wanted to talk."

Vaughan's eyes flashed in the lantern-light. "I lied." He disappeared from the top of the stairs, forcing Lucerne to climb the twisted iron pathway in pursuit. The stair emerged onto the roof of the structure. It was flat, and reminiscent of the roof at the top of Pennerley's south tower. Where this building differed was primarily in terms of height and shape. From the top of the Pennerley's octagonal keep, one could see for miles. Here, the view was obscured by the surrounding woodland; only the heavens above were observable with any clarity. There was naught on the roof, no flag pole enclosure, no scientific instruments besides a mount for a telescope. Vaughan rested against the crenulations on the western wall. He was still sans coat, and his white pantaloons were now fastened, only two of the buttons of his waistcoat were, while the neck of his shirt hung open displaying the flesh beneath.

He was breath-taking in his magnificence, black hair blowing in the breeze, a sliver of silver at his ear, and the stars behind him, illuminating the heavens in a vast streamer of light.

Lucerne edged his way closer cautiously. "If we are not here to talk, then why summon me?"

Vaughan beckoned him closer still with an idle tilt of his wrist. "Is it not obvious?"

"I can't in all honesty say that it is. I had half a thought that it would not be you, but someone with rather more ignoble ends in mind."

"Oh, let me assure you, mine are pretty ignoble." Vaughan reached up towards Lucerne's face. Where his fingers made contact with the skin, sparks sizzled.

"Truly?"

"Exceptionally." His lips turned upwards into a smile. "Is that not what you wanted to hear?" He tilted his head, aligning them perfectly for a kiss, while at the same time, his thumb traced the surface of Lucerne's lips.

It was everything Lucerne prayed for, but still he balked at placing all his faith in the moment. Instead, he stood trembling at the touch, unable to act, unable to construct even the simplest of phrases to explain even a fraction of what he felt.

They were so close, and so alone out here. Far more alone than they had been in that wretched closet, or even in the graveyard, or at the waterfall. His heart was pumping wildly again. He hardly dared breathe. What if this was just another tease, Vaughan's way of proving yet again that he had the upper hand and that his will was the only one that mattered?

He recalled that they had danced around one another like this before, back when he'd strove so desperately to deny that nothing deeper than friendship existed between them. How things had changed. Years had passed. They'd both grown, changed. Yet, standing here, now, all that time seemed compacted into mere moments.

In his mind's eye, he watched himself skid across the dusty floors in the unopened rooms at Lauwine, Vaughan right on his heels. He'd been terrified, feverishly excited, so desperate to be caught, and just as ardently afraid of it. Love between men—it was not something someone lightly embraced. Yet when Vaughan had tugged him into his arms, he'd not only wanted what was offered, his need for the other man had overwhelmed him. He craved Vaughan in exactly that way now, but the situation was hardly straightforward. Their parting had been angry and acrimonious, and while it seemed a white flag of truce was waving, Vaughan could be mercurial in the extreme. He had only to look back on the previous few hours to see that.

"You had better tell me what it is that…" His words trailed off and he swallowed hard, as Vaughan dragged his thumb down over Lucerne's bottom lip.

"Talking is over-rated. What say we forgo words and rely upon actions to spell out what we want from one another?"

As the right words, or in fact, any words were presently beyond him, Lucerne nodded. They both moved at once, leading to them bashing heads and releasing startled breaths right into each other's mouths.

"God, Vaughan, I've missed you every bloody day."

"So you claimed before."

"Believe me; it's the truth."

Lucerne pushed his hand through Vaughan's hair and curled his fingers around the back of Vaughan's head. When he pulled, Vaughan came. They kissed like kissing was something just invented, like the clash of tongues, teeth and lips would never be enough, and stopping was impossible. They kissed until Lucerne was lightheaded from it, and his body was being buffeted all over by angry butterflies.

"Why now? What's changed to make this possible?"

"Always with the questions," Vaughan sighed into his mouth. "Why not let it ride and enjoy the fact that it is occurring?"

"I'm just concerned it's going to be over before it's begun. Nine months – I never for a moment believed you'd stay away so long. At Christmastide, I was sure you would arrive, and then again, at Easter, but nothing... not even a letter."

"Nothing we have to say to one another can be expressed in such a way."

"Then tell me now."

"If I'd been alone, then maybe I would have come then." Vaughan blinked. There was a watery sheen across his dark eyes. "However, Bella was not ready to see you."

"Bella? She left me. I begged her to come north, but she would not leave you."

Vaughan gave a nod. "I know. I do not think she believed you would go and not return almost immediately. You broke her heart, Lucerne. Even now she's struggling to admit it. It suits her narrative more to believe that I was the one lost to despair."

"I have been," Lucerne confessed. "But I could not go back, not without knowing—"

"If I'd welcome you or not."

"The rejection would have killed me. It is killing me."

"Shh!" Vaughan's teeth and lips grazed the line of his jaw. "All is well now. Just tell me what it is you want."

Lucerne's hands settled upon Vaughan's rear. "Must I spell it out? Is it not apparent? I want you. I need you in my life. It's been wretched without you, save for a very few small mercies."

Vaughan snorted. "Stick to the big picture, Lucerne. You were doing so well. I don't need to hear how good a friend Wakefield has been, or how delightful you find his sisters."

"It's his daughter who is a delight. I've no designs upon his sisters. All I want is in my hands right now."

"My arse. Pray what are you going to do with that?"

"What I also pray you're going to do with mine in the next few minutes."

He didn't allow Vaughan a response, but insisted upon another taste of him. Their tongues tangled within Vaughan's mouth. Vaughan tasted of salt and brandy, a delicious combination that reminded Lucerne that not so long ago, his lover had been entwined with another. He felt no pang of jealousy though, more a dull ache of longing that he wasn't in a position to also warm her bed. And concern; concern that this might make mending things even more difficult. He could not stop, though, could not let go of what he finally had. He simply had to have faith in Vaughan.

Eager to bring them closer, he grasped Vaughan's hips. The feel of the unmistakable bulge of his lover's cock pressed fast to his own loins, caused him to release a groan into the hot cavern of Vaughan's mouth. When those of a religious bent described rapture, this was surely what they had meant. He had to get them closer, more tongue, more cock... skin on skin contact.

Vaughan was already half undressed. It would take little to divest him of his waistcoat and shirt. Lucerne set to work releasing the buttons, then tugging the whole lot over his head. He was even more perfect, lit by moonlight, than Lucerne remembered. Immediately, he tore at his own clothing, Vaughan's nimble fingers aided him when he fumbled with the seed pearl buttons of his waistcoat. The moment the last slipped free of its tether, he cast off the layer and hoisted his shirt. Vaughan's hands were at his breeches, releasing the front placket in order to form a fist around his cock while he was still blinded by fabric. He froze, stood gasping, as with quick, sure strokes, Vaughan masturbated his shaft.

He'd come by his own hand so many times in the

last months that he'd lost count, but having another man stroke him did things that touching himself didn't. It was as if the sensitivity were cranked up a hundredfold. His balls began to draw up, even as his cock thickened.

Giving voice to still more groans, he reached out to Vaughan and dragged him close once again. Even though the breeze was slightly chill, Lucerne experienced only heat. Vaughan always seemed to run a little hot, as if some of Hell's fires flowed through his veins. He dragged his tongue up the front of the other man's neck, bit his chin, before Vaughan captured his tongue and drew him into another kiss.

Panting, they parted briefly for air. What had possessed him to ever think he could do without this, that walking away was the best option? Hell, to ever think of seeking pleasure elsewhere besides in Vaughan and Bella's bed, that was pure insanity.

"I need more than just your hands and lips on me," he gasped.

"Poor Lucerne, you really are gagging for a fuck, aren't you?"

He was. Absolutely.

Still, Vaughan's words sent him reeling. He tensed, convinced that this moment was about to end. Vaughan would step back, fasten his pantaloons, and walk away. If he did that, it would undo Lucerne completely. What was it he had to do to prove that he was sorry for the heartache he'd caused, sorry for leaving, sorry for wanting more than the less than perfect arrangement they'd fallen into without thought for practicalities? That they would find a way to all happily and seamlessly co-exist together was his utmost desire.

Lucerne willed his pulse to slow a little. The pounding of it was like a marching drum in his ear, so loud he was afraid he would miss whatever words

Vaughan might choose to utter next. When none came, he raised his head and met the other man's gaze. There, mirrored in his eyes, was the same frantic need, the same urgency that he felt. There was no hint of rejection. "Vaughan," he gasped, simultaneously clawing his fingers into the hard muscles of Vaughan's back and shanks. "Won't you fuck me? Please."

The mere thought of being taken thus was the surest method he had found to ensure he spilled in moments when he was alone. He'd always enjoyed it – the fullness, the stretch, the fineness of the line it rode between pleasure and pain, but until he'd lived without it he'd never truly admitted to himself how much it turned him on to be ridden. It did not, as he'd once felt, make him any less of a man. Not that he'd ever invited, or been tempted to invite, any man other than Vaughan to possess him in that way, but if he had, it still wouldn't have unmanned him.

They made quick work of the rest of their clothes. It was a simple matter of gravity once the buttons of their breeches were undone to let them fall.

"Turn around."

"Why not face to face?" Lucerne asked.

Vaughan was already tugging upon his hips, positioning him just so between two of the crenulations. "Because of the practicalities of our position, and you, my lord, have not done this in a while. I think a little exploratory warm up in order."

Lucerne allowed himself to be turned. It was no hardship to brace himself against the wall, or to have Vaughan's hands upon his arse, kneading and squeezing the firm cheeks. Nor to have him sink his teeth into the flesh where it was softest, then soothe the bite with soft licks and kisses. His thoughts all but leaked out his ear when the wet point of Vaughan's tongue flicked against his hole. A more exquisite torture had not been invented, unless it was to have one lover on their knees rimming his arse, and another fellating his cock. In the absence of Bella, Lucerne took his cock in his own hand, and massaged the length with faltering strokes, needful of the touch, but determined not to spill too soon.

He stilled when Vaughan's lips left him. His ears strained for some clue that this would continue, and he was soon rewarded by the rustle of fabric and the pop of a cork being released from a bottle. The scent of marzipan filled the air. Then a slick finger circled his hole, the tip dipped inside, only a little way at first, then deeper, and deeper still. And following that two fingers speared into him and nudged that nub inside of him so that his cock rose like he'd been caught in a hangman's noose.

He could never work his own fingers deep enough, and while he'd entertained the notion of purchasing some sculpted device or other, he'd shied at actually doing so. Vaughan though... Vaughan stroked him expertly, with exactly the right pressure, and in exactly the right way. It left him clawing, clinging to the battlements, while his cock wept with need. A few slow strokes was all he dared give it.

"Vaughan, please." He was already teetering so close to the edge.

The digits pulled free of his body, whereupon Lucerne felt their loss and leased a keening wail. A trickle of warm oil flowed between his crack. Then strong hands grabbed his hips and spread his legs wider.

"If you've changed your mind, now would be the time to mention it."

"I've not. I won't... ever. Please."

"You always did plead so prettily. Say it again; tell

me how badly you want this. I want to hear the desperation in your voice."

Part of him might hate the games and the word play, but part of him revelled in it. "Fuck me right down to the root of your prick," he responded without hesitation. "Fuck me like it's the first time, and the last. Do it like you mean it."

"Oh, I mean it, and you definitely deserve it. Just let me enjoy this a moment—Viscount Marlinscar, arse bared to the wind, pleading to be sodomized. It's not something I've been privy to in a while, and I'm finding myself quite overcome."

"If you're teasing me, I swear I'll— Oh, God!"

Only the very tip of Vaughan's cock had penetrated him, but even it was enough of a shock. Why did he think he wanted this? It was too much. Vaughan was too big. Too hard. He'd split him in two.

"You'll what, Lucerne?"

A cry whooshed from his throat, not quite a shriek, but too thin and reedy to be mistaken as encouragement.

"Fuck, Lucerne, you really have been closeted like a monk. You're as tight as a bloody virgin."

"I've never been with anyone but you."

Vaughan eased back a little, then slid forward again. "I know," he whispered, voice soothing and soft. "And I pray you never will allow any other man this privilege. That's it." He repeated the short shallow movement again, and again. Slowly, he sunk a little deeper, brought their bodies a little closer together. "Better?"

"Yes."

"You're relaxing. Good. That means less dancing on the edge." Lucerne pressed back a little as Vaughan sunk forward, and his cock sunk in to the hilt.

Damnation! "You're huge."

A light rumble of laughter filled the air. "You're such a flatterer."

Actually, he was struggling to catch his breath. "No, I mean it. You feel enormous!" The exclamation rushed up from his lungs and sounded like a rumble of thunder directly overhead, not to mention strained and a tad demented.

"Need me to ease off a little."

"Don't you fucking dare."

Vaughan's laughter washed over them unrestrained this time. "I see. Then I'll take that as a plea for more." Sure and swift, Vaughan pushed into him, filled him with leisurely, confident strokes. Each drag backwards rasped at the edges of his nerves as if it were a little too rough, each slide forward set him blaspheming. It was as if when Vaughan filled him, his cock were sliding right through him and into his own cock, filling it up from the inside. Lucerne palmed his length again, and clung to it. He did not stroke its length, for anything beyond the rigid grip he had would surely send him spiralling over the edge.

Tension of one sort ebbed out of Lucerne's body, even as tension of another sort built. The strokes of Vaughan's cock became longer, easier, the melding of their flesh, fluid. This was how it had been in the past between them, all sliding, aching, persistent joy. The tide of it rising, tugging at the pleasure centre of the body and mind until the charge towards release was all consuming.

"Stop. Let me turn around," Lucerne begged.

He hated the loss of Vaughan's cock from his arse. It was awkward face to face, although a low ledge in the wall aided a little in providing him a perch that allowed them to balance, and Vaughan to settle between his thighs and enter him again.

Gratitude spilled from his lips, as Vaughan's cock

filled him. Their upper bodies were jammed together, lips locked in a series of biting, gasping kisses. Lucerne whimpered as his staff, trapped between their abdomens, was rubbed from both sides.

"Shit! It's coming. I can't hold it back."

"And, indeed, why would you want to?" Higher and higher, Vaughan's thrusts pushed him, until they were both slick with sweat, and it was hard even to keep a proper hold upon one another, but the gut-knotting sensation wound tighter still, forcing him towards climax with unremitting ease.

Lucerne twisted his head and cursed into Vaughan's shoulder as his seed forced its way from his body. Warm jets of it shot over them both. Vaughan continued to hold him steady, his pace even more brutal in his pounding determination to also cross the finish line.

It was almost too much, but Lucerne held off on crying for mercy. He wanted Vaughan's come inside of him. He wanted that mark. So he curled his fingers into the other man's flesh and held on.

"Almost there...a moment more..." Vaughan's plea would have convinced him that the grate across his over tired nerves was worth it, even if he hadn't already determined to hold out already. "Lucerne..." The last cry was ripped from his throat as his spine arched. He came in five or six hard spurts, and Lucerne felt every moment.

Spent, Vaughan rested his head upon Lucerne's shoulder. It took a good few minutes before either of them moved more than that. Then they slowly peeled apart, fingers uncurling from the death grips upon one another's bodies first, then torsos and hips. Vaughan's cock slid free of Lucerne's body, making them synchronously sigh. They sagged down onto the rooftop, movements languorous and slipshod. It was impossible to heal everything with one good fuck, but it sure knocked the edges off the trauma.

It was not long before they were comfortably cocooned against the chill, wrapped in a layer of clothing, Lucerne seated between Vaughan's legs with his head upon his lover's chest. Agile fingers twisted and twirled the longer strands of his blond hair. Finally, things were falling back into place, although not everything was resolved.

"It can't be like it was before," Lucerne whispered, uncertain he wanted to be heard. Looking back might destroy the moment.

"It won't be. It will be better."

"I can't face the constant tug o' war."

"Things are different now," Vaughan insisted.

He wanted to believe in the spell Vaughan was weaving around him with his words, and his caresses, but in his chest, his heart beat with a definite heaviness.

"What about Bella?" he sighed.

"Shh!" Vaughan covered Lucerne's lips with his fingers. "Don't. Not yet. Not now. There's time. We can figure it out. Please, for the moment, let's concentrate on what we have. Then we may figure out how Bella fits."

He lifted his fingers one at a time, freeing Lucerne to speak again if he wished. There were so many questions, so many hurdles on the horizon, but he did as Vaughan insisted and held them in his mind. Instead, he reached up and pulled Vaughan to him so that they could kiss. "I just want to idle here forever."

Vaughan touched his face. "Me too."

CHAPTER 22

BELLA

B ELLA STARED AT the snowy pillow beside her. Vaughan's dark ringlets were spread across its surface. He so very rarely slept beside her, and even when he did, he nearly always rose well before her, so it was a novelty to wake beside him. "Vaughan," she murmured, snuggling against his back. She was chilled, and no wonder, the eiderdown clung to the edge of the bed at the bottom left corner having clearly been tossed off at some earlier point. His blood ran hot. The top sheet too was in disarray, wound around Vaughan's middle in a series of folds that covered just enough for her fingers to twitch over the thought of pulling it away from him. She might have done, if he had not been so contentedly asleep; eyes closed, cherry-red lips parted, his brow pressed fast to the crown of Lucerne's blond head...

Wait. How could that be?

Something tugged at the back of her mind. Like she was viewing the scene refracted through a poorly ground lens.

She shook it off. They were all together. They were

always together, that's how it had been ever since they'd arrived in London. It was how it was between the three of them. They all loved and made love to one another, and she was at ease with that. They all were.

At least, mostly.

Her pulse beat an uneasy tattoo at the sight of Vaughan's arm—and one leg—draped possessively around Lucerne's body. They had their backs to her. No one was holding on to her. Neither man had even noticed that she'd stirred.

The fact was they'd only ever had eyes for one another. She was merely the means by which they preserved their positions.

Ned Darleston had said it best. Admittedly, he'd been trying to bed her at the time, so his motives had been suspect. Still, that did not detract from the truth of his eulogy to the Free Lovers Society: Women Lend Legitimacy to the Love Between Men. The short version being that as long as there was a woman in the bed too, then a man might do anything he pleased with another of his gender, and no one would think any less of him for it, or suggest any kind of unnaturalness. "It is only two men alone that the world balks at, and that, primarily, Miss Rushdale, because they cannot sire heirs."

A cold trickle of fear made the hairs on the back of her neck rise. It was not true that she was simply the foil they employed to make their bond palatable to the world. It was a true partnership between the three of them.

Well, more or less. Vaughan was rather difficult. It was hard to tell sometimes if he did more than tolerate her, but Lucerne more than made up for that. He treated her as though she were royalty.

She stared again at their two bodies entwined upon the bed. There was a small gap between them. Not exactly large enough for a person, but with a little wriggling...

A clang and a scuffle startled Bella awake. She sat abruptly and blinked at her surroundings. Her maid from Wyndfell lifted something from the floor and dropped it into her apron front. "I'm very sorry, Miss."

Bella shook her head, allowing reality to slowly form around her. She was at Stags Fell in Yorkshire, not London, and the sheets beside her bore only the impression of her body. A pillow was plumped and placed vertically in the bed where Vaughan had been when she'd fallen asleep. There was no sign of him in the room. No indication that he had ever been present.

"Shall I ask for a tray, Miss, or are you going down to eat?"

"Down." Bella swung her legs out of the bed. The sun was bright outside. Hot rays spilled through the sash window. For definite, the hour was no longer early. If she hurried, she might still come upon Vaughan at the table. She was not at all sure he understood how against renewing their relationship with Lucerne she was. She did not want to fight with him, but she did want some further reassurance that he was taking her opinions seriously, and that he would entertain the notion of a compromise. Not that she had any idea what that might entail, but surely after last night – he had told her that he loved her – they were on the right footing, and could manage to discuss things sensibly. Surely, he would not so easily cast her aside for the possibility of something with Lucerne that might not amount to anything or survive beyond a fortnight. Had not that man already proven himself fickle and disloyal?

Lucerne had left Vaughan before. She never would. She would get dressed. She would find Vaughan.

They would talk this through. "Find me some clothes," she demanded. "I'll dress and go down."

Tilly curtseyed. "Very well, miss. Which dress would you like, the green or the blue?"

Bella shook her head. "You choose, just do hurry about it."

Charles and Joshua were at the table when Bella descended. Eliza arrived on her heels. There was no sign of Vaughan, which left an uneasy feeling in Bella's stomach.

Her only comfort was the recollection that Lucerne typically rose later than her. In the past, he'd kept London hours even in the countryside.

"Time was, you weren't such a stay-a-bed," Joshua remarked, as he stirred sugar into what appeared to be a second or third cup of tea. Bella scowled. There was no need for him to rub it in. She was perfectly aware of her own tardiness.

"Did you miss my company, brother?" He was back in his old buff and tan clothing that made him look so much like a sparrow. Really, if he wanted to attract a wife he needed to put in a little more effort. Even Charles made an effort to look as if he belonged to this century and not the last. "In any case, you can hardly have risen much earlier than me, if you're still at breakfast at this hour."

"Ha. That Bella is where you're mistaken. I've been abroad with the Puffing Devils since a quarter to five." He flicked his forefinger against the rim of his cup, making the china sing. "Lartington's engine is the most beautiful thing. It's going to make an enormous difference to the way in which we mine and travel in the future, make no mistake. And that is before its potential is applied to a host of other industries and services quite unknown to us yet."

Bella yawned. "I suppose you endeavour to become a member of these Belching Imps."

Her brother scowled, while Charles chuckled into his neck cloth. He was engaged in eating something that looked suspiciously like steak and pigeon pie, which he was washing down with a great deal of claret. There was no evidence of pie being dished up to anyone else.

Joshua ignored her derogatory remarks. "It would be a great honour to be accepted among them. They are all skilled and scholarly gentlemen. My understanding is positively rudimentary next to theirs. Lartington himself has written a treatise on the subject, and Mr. Whistler has spent a deal of time down in Cornwall helping to develop a locomotive device. Heavens Bella, even Stephen Crakehall has a better understanding of it all than I. It's all quite extraordinary. Do you realise, they have devised a system that drives the internal pressure of the engine up to one hundred and thirty pounds per inch?" His eyes widened.

Bella shook her head. It was no use; the numbers were meaningless to her. She did not share his love of mechanical pumping devices or what application might be one day made of them for things other than efficiently draining mines of water.

"That is high, one presumes," remarked Eliza, who had been dithering over which chair she should settle into. She decided upon the one beside Joshua's. Whereupon, he hopped up to assist and then to aid her in pouring some tea.

Bella, relieved to be excused from the conversation, helped herself to a large slice of seed cake and smothered it with lemon curd. She had a strong hankering for something both tart and sweet this morning, perhaps as a result of her dream of waking beside Vaughan and Lucerne. In the days following Lucerne's initial departure from Pennerley, she had experienced such nightmares often, but it had easily been six months since the last one. It was fear over what was to come, no doubt. She wasn't going to dwell on it. She'd locate Vaughan and insist they discuss this sensibly. She wouldn't be able to stop him liaising with Lucerne, but she could make it plain she wasn't going to be part of it, nor used as any sort of bait to entice him.

Her hand slipped as she tipped the milk jug, leaving a puddle in her saucer.

Curiously, none of the liveried servants who had constantly been on hand yestereve were around now to attend to it. Bella dabbed it up with a napkin. It rather seemed that now the betrothal of Crakehall and Miss Hayes was formalized, Lartington had returned to his foremost pleasure – that of well-oiled machinery. No doubt, abandoned to their own devices, most of the guests would depart tomorrow after the celebratory ball. One or two—those involved with the Belching Imps—would stay longer, perhaps a week or two. She did hope Joshua wasn't planning on them staying that long. Much as there were definite advantages in staying here, such as the time she had eked out with Vaughan, most of the company made her feel distinctly unwelcome.

"And is there not a deal of danger in creating such a system?" Eliza asked.

Joshua nodded sagely. "There are dangers associated with every new development, but it would be foolish not to press forward with such innovation."

Heaven help her, Joshua would become her doting lapdog if Eliza continued indulging his passions in this way. Bella was half-tempted to give her a friendly nudge under the table, except that would only mean Joshua would return to addressing her instead. Puffing Devils, indeed. She inwardly rolled her eyes. What was so enthralling about some dirty, noisy machine?

The conversation rumbled on around her for several more minutes as Bella consumed what was before her and added a piece of turtulong to her plate. It was rather hard on the jaw, but washed down well with the dregs from the teapot. "What is everyone else about today?" she asked, when Joshua's raptures over Lartington's engine finally ceased.

"Maria and I are to make up a party consisting of the Misses Hayes, our brother, Mr Crakehall, Mr Rushdale, and Mr Aubury that Mrs Lartington has kindly organised. We are to take a picnic out onto Askrigg Common. Are you not to join us? But perhaps you aren't aware of it yet."

Bella rather supposed she'd be deliberately excluded. Millicent's doing, no doubt.

"What of the other guests?"

Eliza tilted her head to one side. "Well, I believe Mr Hayes is attending to business, and Mr Whistler is heading into Hawes to procure some piece of metalwork from the blacksmith there. I saw him right before I stepped into breakfast."

"Lord Pennerley? Lord Marlinscar?" She tried hard to keep her voice and expression neutral.

Joshua set down his teacup with enough force to upset the sugar bowl, so clearly, she'd failed. He righted the china, but a devil of a frown had transmuted his expression from one of quiet joviality to that of barely concealed rage. For a wonder he didn't burst some vessel or other.

"They've both tootled off," Charles muttered. None of them had been paying him much attention, but their combined focus settled upon him now, prompting him to wipe his jowls with his napkin.

"What?"

Her brother's pinched lips took on a rather self-satisfied moue. "They're no longer here is what he said."

Bella set down her knife. "You mean to say that they have left?" The Lucerne she knew rarely, if ever, rose before ten, and Vaughan... He had no business rushing off anywhere without even penning her a note to that effect. "But the ball is tonight. Perhaps you're mistaken, Mr Aubury, and they've just stepped out for some air and a bracing walk."

Charles waggled his soiled napkin at her. "I ain't. There's both of them come down with some dastardly infection or other. Thought it best to leave and avoid passing it along to the rest of us. Considerate, don't you think?"

Perhaps, if she'd thought for even a minute that either of them was actually ill. Neither man had shown any signs of it last night. No, Vaughan was not sick, and neither was Lucerne. This was a ruse. Hellfire and damnation! She hardly dared ask it, but had to know. "Surely, they have not departed together?"

Bella noted that her brother's shoulders were winched up beside his ears. He had a death grip around a teaspoon.

Meanwhile, Charles shrugged. "Lucerne tore off at first light. I couldn't rightly tell you when Pennerley left. I suppose it's possible, and it would make sense of sorts, as both Lauwine and Reeth lie in the same direction."

Hands braced upon the table, Bella stood. This could not be. For them to leave without breathing a word of anything to her. Lucerne she expected as much from, but Vaughan... Goddamn him! He'd sworn only last night that he loved her, and that she was more than second best. But he hadn't really meant a word of it.

He'd just seen a means by which he could placate her. And she'd fallen for it. She'd behaved exactly as he'd wanted, and had no doubt aided him in going about the business of seducing Lucerne. Curse him for his manipulative, self-centred thoughtlessness. He must have waited until she was asleep, left her room, and gone straight to some already arranged rendezvous with Lucerne.

"Say, you're looking a little peaky, Miss Rushdale, are you all right?"

"They are not ill," she swore, hammering her cup down on the table.

Charles sat upright, and puffed and blustered.

"They can't be. They were both perfectly well at dinner last night."

"Well, well... actually, if you'll recall, they did both excuse themselves early."

Bella swayed. She was too hot, and a tick seemed to have found its way into her ear, where it was making a horrid, horrid noise. She wiped her clammy hands against her dress.

"Bella?" Joshua enquired, on the way out of his seat.

She opened her mouth to respond, but gagged instead. Then she disgorged her breakfast over the tablecloth.

"Bella!" Both Joshua and Eliza were by her immediately. The one clasping her about the shoulders, and the other throwing a napkin over the mess, before finding her some wine to drink.

Charles ambled over to the sideboard and rang the bell. "Seems it's too late to contain the contagion. You'll be away home now as well, Miss Rushdale, and the rest of us will be giving Reeth parish a wide berth for a while. Sickness and disappearances, that's quite enough to warn a fellow to stay clear." When the footman arrived, he added. "Do get her out of here, clean up this mess, see that Mr Rushdale's carriage is prepared, and their things are packed. They'll be leaving before the hour's out."

It was the most efficient Bella had ever seen him. She did not recall much of what happened next, only that soon enough she was seated in Joshua's rickety carriage being driven back to Wyndfell, the motion of the carriage making her feel twice as bad. Damn, why couldn't someone invent a better way to travel that didn't make ones insides lurch in response to every rut in the road?

"We'll get Garth to come and take a look at you, once we're home," Joshua remarked. "It's a pity he and his wife didn't stay over at Stags Fell last night. It'd have been rather convenient. I suppose now we'll be waiting on him to see Pennerley and Marlinscar first."

"I don't need to see him," Bella mumbled. "Garth is a hopeless quack. He'll feel me in inappropriate places, then prescribe opium tincture and bleeding, and tell me it's just that my humours are misaligned. I'd rather have cook see to the settling of my stomach."

"Garth's a gentleman. You might not wish to see him, but I'm summoning him regardless. You just cast your repast up over the dining table, if you don't recall, and you appear on the verge of disgorging whatever remains of that meal now."

"Carriages always make me ill," she protested. She refused to be ill. She had Vaughan to relocate. If she was out of sorts, then it was his and Lucerne's doing.

Damn and blast them. Would it really have been so hard to leave a note, a token, something?

Bella took to her bed at once when they reached Wyndfell, and made a concerted effort to sleep through the entirety of Doctor Garth's visit, thus he didn't trouble her with an examination. Joshua, rather noticeably, didn't leave him alone in her presence. He nevertheless proclaimed a diagnosis of virulent vomiting sickness, for which he prescribed bedrest along with some noxious potion and an ointment to smear over her belly that smelled like chicken dung. Bella disposed of both out of the window immediately after he left. The only illness from which she was suffering was one of the heart.

In the early evening, Joshua brought her a bowl of cook's special chicken broth. "I didn't know if you were hungry, but if you can manage some of this it might help."

"I'm famished." She snatched the bowl and spoon from him before he got any idea of feeding her.

"Garth says he hasn't seen Pennerley or Marlinscar."

"They've more sense than to have him waste their time and to pay him for the privilege. Lucerne is at Lauwine, then?"

"Apparently so."

"And Vaughan?"

"There's no sign or word of him. He's not returned to the Dog and Basin, so one has to assume he's gone home."

"Oh! No. He won't have done that. He wouldn't leave without me." Bella was halfway out of the bed before Joshua quietly pushed her down.

"Here." He plumped her pillows, and urged her to settle. "This might come as a shock, Bella, but he has a reputation, even among those whose notoriety is well documented. Pennerley does as he pleases, and if it pleased him to return to his estate he would do so without consulting you or anyone else. Sometimes I think you forget what a precarious position you have placed yourself in. You are nothing more than a toy to him. If you do not think he will discard you without a twang of remorse, then you are being wilfully blind to reality. The man's a monster."

"Says the man who has spent the last month insisting that said monster should marry his sister."

"I'm just trying to do what's best for you. At least if you were wed to him you'd have some guarantees. That said, I'd prefer you entirely rid yourself of the association, but you are so deluded by whatever spell he has woven around you that I know there is no point in even wishing for that."

"I am not ensorcelled, Joshua. I love him. And he loves me."

"Is that why he has vanished without a trace, and why you are now taken to your bed, sick with worry? That's the truth of your malaise. You're afraid that he is gone, and you will have nothing. You have dismissed Lucerne, scourged your reputation for that man, and what has he given you in return? Nothing, that is what. You are not the first of his conquests, sister, and I fear you won't be the last either."

"He has not abandoned me. If he is not at Reeth, then he has gone someplace else to recuperate. Charles Aubury was the one who said he was ill, not me. He has no reason to lie. Vaughan may well have gone to his place in Middleham. It's not so far."

"Not far," Joshua echoed. "Only far-fetched. You don't believe he is there, any more than I do."

They avoided one another's gazes for several minutes before Bella insisted, "In a few days, he will be well again, and I'll hear from him."

Her brother shook his head. "I ought to have

consulted Garth over the brain fever you possess, not the minor malaise of your stomach." He peered at the empty bowl she had put aside on the nightstand. "Since it, and not stomach troubles seem to be what ails you, but then you were always possessed of a fevered imagination."

Bella treated him to an angry scowl. There was nothing wrong with her mind or having a fevered imagination. Such a thing was valued among certain circles. In London, her appetite for the macabre and love of gothic novels had been appreciated, but not here in Yorkshire. Here, anything that didn't involve mining, sheep, or harvesting was regarded with suspicion. A person could expire from sheer lack of stimulation. "There is nothing wrong with my mind, and I'm feeling much better. The sickness was probably down to something I ate. Maybe the eggs were off."

Joshua made pooh-pooh noises. "I ate them. In any case, only someone soft in the head would imagine Pennerley possessed of an affection for them, ergo you are distinctly addle-brained."

Bella opened her mouth to protest, but Joshua shushed her and insisted quiet and rest were required, or to be endured—either would work. Also, she should shut up and take her medicine. Naturally, her gaze strayed over to the window as he said it, which lead to a long lecture about obeying orders.

"You do worry me so, Bella. It is clear that you have not been taking proper care of yourself. And clearly I have done an atrocious job of it too, what with all this mess between you, Marlinscar, and Pennerley. It has to stop. It's really not right at all."

Wearied that they were to go over this again, Bella groaned. "Our neighbours will be too busy relating the story of me casting up my assets to give much thought to my attachments these coming days."

"I should have beaten you more as a child, or something," he remarked earnestly. "Then maybe I wouldn't be counting it a blessing that you fell ill in front of witnesses."

"More? Joshua, you never raised a hand to me once, and I thank you for it." She raised a hand and affectionately touched his stubble-roughened cheek. "I don't care what they say or that they mock at me. I'd rather endure that than live without him." There was no need to qualify who it was she referred to. "But I am truly sorry for the pain I've caused you. It's not fair that you're alone. We'll work on that. Vaughan will help. He can make introductions."

"I am never accepting that man's help. Heavens, Bella, I can't imagine why I would want an introduction to any woman of Pennerley's acquaintance. They are surely all frightfully tarnished."

"That's not true. They're all very handsome and well-bred." Well, they were, even if some of them possessed rather bohemian notions.

"Yes, dear, and both those things could also be said of you. No, it won't do, nor will this nonsense between you and him. It has to end, Bella."

"He loves me, brother."

"If that were true, he would offer for you."

"It's not that simple."

"Gracious, Bella, it's the simplest thing in the world. If he were a decent fellow and genuinely cared about you, he'd have done so already."

"It's not possible."

Her brother's eyes opened wide, and he reared back on his heels. "I swear, if you say he has a wife locked away in an attic, I will summon Garth back here at once. You are not the heroine of some gothic romance, Bella, and even if you were, Pennerley would not be the hero set upon your rescue. He'd be the villain that casts himself from the roof after being assailed with remorse for his hideous deeds.

"He hasn't performed any hideous deeds."

Now he was staring at her with his mouth hanging open. "He has thoroughly debauched you and makes no attempt to conceal the matter. If anything, he flaunts it. He has stolen you from another, and... and..."

"And?" Bella prompted. That was the thing. Vaughan had this diabolical reputation, but when it came down to it, few could precisely say what he'd done to earn it.

"And..." Joshua said.

Bella couldn't help it. She started to laugh. Nor was it a chuckle she let loose, but a wild braying laugh. "Surely, you mean to say he has deflowered a thousand virgins and sacrificed them on an altar to the devil on his estate. Oh, and that he has duelled and killed and stolen and acted as a spy and passed sensitive information to the French and that he steals babies and eats them."

Whatever sermon Joshua had planned, completely dried up.

"What? Does that not about cover it, or did I miss something? Oh, hold up—unnaturalness! When he doesn't have a convenient young miss on hand to ravish, he likes to fornicate with domestic animals."

Perhaps that last part had been a step too far. Joshua was puce from the neck up—and possibly below, she couldn't tell. He actually staggered and clutched the footboard in order to steady himself. "I never thought to hear such things from you."

Shaking her head at him was her primary answer. "I'm sorry. Truly." She rolled her head upward. "Only, you are being ridiculous. Utterly ridiculous."

"I won't listen to any more of this. You're ill. Clearly

very ill." He blew out her candle, then made an abrupt turn and left.

"Pig," Bella yelled after him. "There was no need to leave me in the dark." She threw the spoon, which hit the back of the door and fell onto the wooden boards with a clatter. "You're so wrong about everything, Joshua. Vaughan does love me. That's real, not imagined, which you'd know if you knew anything at all about him and hadn't let parish gossip sway your opinions. You liked both him and Lucerne when they first arrived. You took part in their japes. I know, he's told me."

She expected the door to swing back open and Joshua to storm back into to resume their fight, but evidently, he wasn't going to be baited and had determined to have the upper hand. Gah! Bella threw her pillow, and was then forced to retrieve it on unsteady legs. Perhaps she wasn't entirely ready to be up and about yet. A good night's rest would fix it though. Then she could enquire herself as to Vaughan's whereabouts.

Back beneath the quilt, she pouted at her reflection in the cheval mirror that sat facing the base of the bed. In the dark, her image was largely comprised of shadows, save for the white of her nightshift. In truth, she already knew where he was, and it was not Middleham, but much closer. Vaughan was almost certainly less than a dozen fields away currently rolled within the sheets of Viscount Marlinscar's bed, and if either of them were actually sick, she'd... well, she'd consent to swallowing one of Doctor Garth's noxious potions. Matter of fact, the only real sin that Vaughan engaged in was that of loving someone society decreed he should feel no more than brotherly towards.

For a moment, she almost hoped he was buggering Lucerne senseless, just because it was a way of sticking two fingers up at preachy moralizing of people who wouldn't recognise real love if it bit them on the nose.

Love and happiness ought to count for more than money and securing one's property and family line.

CHAPTER 23

BELLA

B ELLA FELT MORE or less herself the very next morning. She wasn't sick again, but a sense of weary lethargy settled over her, that made it hard to climb out of bed. Luckily, whatever malady it was she'd brought back from Stags Fell did not strike any of the other members of the household, and so with cook's chicken broth as a restorative and a huge batch of her famous parkin, she was soon ready to face the world again.

However, a whole five days passed before Joshua deemed it appropriate for her to leave the house and then only to venture as far as Lauwine to see Caroline Wakefield.

"Visiting one's neighbours is the mark of civilization," she remarked before climbing astride her mare, and heading off at a gallop, keen to blow the cobwebs from her mind and off her person.

Lauwine's imposing edifice and countless windows gleamed in the sunlight as she approached. The rhododendrons lining the driveway were darkly verdant. The gates were closed, so she was forced to dismount in order to make her way inside. They were freshly painted, but otherwise unchanged from how they had been years ago when she had slipped past their boundary to frolic within her own private paradise. It seemed such a long time ago. How simple everything had once been. But she did not truly long for the return of those times. She had not known love, then, and while it brought such heartache, it brought so much pleasure too.

A liveried footman greeted her and saw to her mount, while another escorted her into Caroline's presence.

Miss Wakefield sat playing the pianoforte in the music room, dressed in a pink-spotted muslin, with embroidered primroses around the hem that Bella guessed to be the work of Eliza Wakefield. Caroline stopped playing the moment Bella was announced and near bounced off the stool to hurry to her friend.

"Bella Rushdale, thank the Lord and all his angels. Dear, it is so very, very good to see you. Ha, another living soul." She pushed Bella to arm's length so that she could take in the whole of her, then turned her about before pulling her into a warm embrace. "I am positively overwrought from lack of company, if you haven't guessed it. The tedium of this place is immense when there is no one here to share a word with. Do you know, there are thirty-seven clocks in the main wing of this ridiculously overlarge house? And they are quite enough to drive even the sanest person quite mad. You should hear them all, chirping and chiming and donging away together on the hour, every hour of the day and night. For certain, something needs to fracture the wretched silence of the place, but that cacophony is hardly a worthy substitute for another human voice."

Bella hugged her back warmly. "But surely you are not here alone. Joanna—"

"Pfft! Joanna spends all of her time with Leesa, and they have not left the nursery since Lord Marlinscar's return. No sense putting the wee one at risk. It's sensible, of course. Leastways, it would be if Lord Marlinscar had even been seen."

"You've not seen him?" Bella asked, as Caroline drew her towards the salon, where a table was set for a fine tête-à-tête. If he was sick, then she supposed it not unusual that he was abed, only a little odd that the Wakefield sisters had not taken upon themselves the role of nursing him.

"Nary a glimpse." Caroline confirmed. "If it wasn't for his man, Ivo, informing everyone that the master was home and indisposed, I'm not at all sure I or any of the servants would believe it. He's most insistent."

"Ivo is a dependable sort." Not that she believed Lucerne was lying ill upstairs, herself. Why it had been days since he'd left Stags Fell, and her sickness has passed within four-and-twenty hours. If it wasn't that she had her own suspicions as to his whereabouts and doings, she would have suspected foul play. Still, she had not come here to speak of Lucerne.

"And your other sisters, I suppose they are still at Stags Fell?"

"With Freddy and Mr Aubury. Yes. They are having the most delightful time, if Maria's letters are to be taken at face value. The ball was divine, and she writes me that Eliza has turned the head of one Mr Whistler, but I suspect it is a lie, or else a vast exaggeration. Eliza has never hooked the attention of any gentlemen in her entire life. I cannot think what would be so different about Stags Fell that would in any way change that."

"Belching imps," said Bella, causing Caroline to screw up her pretty nose in confusion.

"I beg your pardon, but whatever does that mean?

Is it some London cant you have learned from the underclasses?"

"Puffing devils," Bella corrected herself. "Mr Whistler is a member of their fellowship, as now, too, is my brother Joshua. They are devoted to all things steam-driven, and Eliza shows an apparently genuine interest in their baffling mathematics and oil-slicked pistons."

"Heavens," Caroline drew her hand to her mouth. "That sounds frightfully dangerous." She giggled. "Not to mention rather rude."

Bella chuckled. "It's all dreadfully scientific, but I suppose Eliza is of a practical bent. Say, I do wonder what they will make of her though, if she offers to roll up her sleeves and away to the engine sheds with them to tinker. I can't decide if they will be more besotted or mortified. In any case, I believe there is likely some truth to Maria's letters—she did write to me the once too—although there are likely some embellishments."

"Well," Caroline declared, thoughtfully picking up the teapot, in order to pour them each a cup. "I rather wish she would make the embellishments more fanciful. A good yarn might keep me from sliding into total stupor. Prior to visiting here, I did not believe I would ever pray for some industry to busy myself with. There is simply nothing for me to do. Every task is already assigned a dozen souls."

"And I suppose you are only just recovered, and not well enough acquainted with those hereabouts to go calling upon people."

"That is the meat of it."

"Then we ought to rectify that. Do something that will allow you to meet people."

"Oh, Bella. It hardly seems worth it at this point. We shall all be returning home to Bluebell Lane before very long. We've already imposed upon Lord M for far longer than we intended, and we cannot go on doing so indefinitely. So, there is hardly time to become acquainted with anyone."

"Dash it. That is sorry news. I have so enjoyed having you all as neighbours."

Caroline grasped both of her hands. "And us you. You must come and visit us in the Dales. Our cottage is not big, but it suits us all well. I confess; I'm quite excited to see it again, though I will miss this grand old edifice, with its drafty, winding hallways and plethora of reading material. Even after this last week I have barely reached halfway along one shelf."

"I suppose it will be quiet, when you get home, too," Bella said.

"Quiet? Heavens no, it's never that, and there will be jobs aplenty to keep us all occupied—that is, presuming we can convince Joanna to actually leave. She may have to be hogtied, or rolled into a carpet and carried out, she's so besotted with the babe."

Little Louisa was a darling, but Bella could not conceive of wanting to spend one's every waking hour with an infant.

"Also, Bella, I am rather afraid that the lad we employed to take care of our garden was not entirely up to the task. It would not surprise me at all to find the flowerbeds overrun with brambles and bindweed, and the clematis mulched up in the compost heap. We will have our hands full with the harvest too, and the making of preserves for the Michaelmas fayre."

It sounded jolly and busy, full of bustle and love. Envisaging the sisters expertly weaving around one another in their cosy kitchen took no effort at all, though it did leave Bella feeling rather wistful. There had always been such a large age difference between herself and Joshua, and while there had existed an easy sort of camaraderie between them in the past, it was no longer.

Caroline, perhaps mistaking her reflection for sorrow, gave Bella's fingers a solid squeeze. "I will miss you, and I will write. One should definitely keep at least one scandalous friend."

With a little effort, Bella summoned a weak smile. "I expect I'll be leaving Yorkshire too, before long."

"Of course, you will return to Pennerley, I suppose. Or did you mean to winter in the Capital?"

Bella sucked her teeth and then took a long sip of her tea. "Mayhaps farther afield. I did think to maybe see Switzerland or Bavaria."

Her friend snatched up the teapot again, and cradled it to her chest. "Surely you don't mean that. Are you sure it is safe? Surely Lord Pennerley can't mean to travel abroad when things are so uncertain."

Bella made some vague noises. She hadn't consulted Vaughan, nor sought anyone else's opinion on the matter. It had only occurred to her as a possibility while she had been abed these last few days.

"It sounds a very dicey prospect to me. Not at all safe. Your brother won't approve."

Joshua didn't approve of any of it. She still couldn't be certain that he would even allow her to leave. At least, not without causing a considerable stir. If only everything would settle down and stop being so turbulent. It wasn't at all helpful having him create additional barriers to her being with Vaughan, when things were so uneasy between them already. Where was he? Not at Middleham. She had written and had her letter returned. Nor had he returned to his lodgings at the Inn in Reeth. A letter to his sister had received a speedy reply, but had been of no use. Niamh's response—I thought he was in Yorkshire, with you.

Therefore, she was left considering alternative

possibilities, one of which was almost too frightful to contemplate, and hence the most likely truth.

Caroline continued to chatter on about the dangers of travelling on the continent, so Bella sipped her tea, nibbled a piece of gingerbread, and listened. Leastways, the words flowed and she recalled some vague details of them. Apparently, some young women travellers had been assaulted and carried off by either soldiers or pirates or rebels and then sold to brothels, where they were forced to carry out unspeakable tasks involving monks and wax candles and a great deal of rope. When pressed, Caroline couldn't say how their story had come to be known. "Why, they must have been rescued." Nor did she have any fresh news regarding the young woman, Annie, who had vanished from Reeth. Though she did speculate a good deal about the possibility of her having also been carried off by soldiers, rebels, or marauding Vikings who had sailed across the North Sea, landed in Scarborough and trudged all the way inland to seize a decidedly average girl of no position from a family who barely scraped enough money together in a week to feed and clothe themselves.

"Surely," Bella pointed out. "Such effort warranted a bigger prize. Someone for whom they could demand a ransom."

"Then perhaps she simply decided to join them."

Bella came to an entirely different conclusion. "I think you definitely require some company," she declared. "Now, what can we do about it?" It did not take long to devise a solution in the form of a farewell party that would take place at Lauwine, where the Misses Wakefields—or more specifically, Caroline—could meet the other well-to-do folks from hereabouts before they headed back to Bluebell Lane.

"It should be in the form of a grand picnic, with

lawn games to play and treasures to hunt around the grounds."

Caroline got to her feet and clapped her hands. "That's a delightful idea. You'll help plan it, won't you, Bella?"

She gave an enthusiastic nod.

Caroline skipped around their chairs in delight, only to freeze a moment later, the glee wiped from her face. "But we cannot. Lord M is ill."

It was on the tip of Bella's tongue to remark that the only illness he suffered was one of unnaturalness, but that was out of disgruntlement. She had no proof that Lucerne was faking his malaise, nor did she believe love between men was unnatural.

"Yes, but he surely won't be so for much longer. What does the doctor say?"

Her friend resumed her seat, now quietly solemn with her hands clasped in her lap. "I'm not altogether sure one has visited."

That confirmed it. Lucerne would not lie ill in bed for the better part of a week without summoning a doctor, even if he then disregarded everything the fellow said. His indisposition definitely had a different cause.

"I am absolutely convinced it will be fine. Why don't we find Ivo and have him consult his master right away?"

"Later," Caroline insisted. "I do not like to disturb him unnecessarily." Bella would happily have Ivo carry messages back and forth all day. Not that she meant to create extra work for Lucerne's valet; she simply relished the opportunity to interrupt his repose.

He was not ill. He was up there with Vaughan performing unspeakable acts. Knowledge she did her utmost best to keep from her expression, least Caroline suspect something.

This was not the first time the two men had closeted themselves away from the world in order to indulge their passions for one another. Admittedly, when they had done so in the past, the duration of the retreat had not been so lengthy. Then again, in the past, she had been present to rattle the doorknob and remind them they had other duties to perform in addition to servicing one another. And then, they had not been apart for three quarters of a year.

The remainder of her visit passed uncomfortably. Bella, agitated by her supposition, forced herself to sit primly while she imagined storming upstairs, breaking open Lucerne's door, and pelting the pair of them with whatever came to hand. It was only the possibility of such actions endangering them that kept her seated. After all, they'd clearly gone to some lengths to keep Vaughan's presence a secret. Therefore, if he were to suddenly appear in Lucerne's private rooms rampant speculation would result.

"Lawn billiards," Caroline suggested, drawing Bella back into the here and now. "There is a set of balls and mallets in the hallway cupboard. We could play that." She raised a finger to her lips. "Although, I don't exactly know the rules. Do you, Bella?"

She shook her head. "Do you mean now?"

"At the party."

"Of course. Then I expect one of the gentlemen will know how one plays. Mr Aubury, perhaps, if Lord Marlinscar doesn't. I dare say they might know of some other games you might put on too, and that they, in turn, might wager upon. Wagers are what best keeps them entertained in my experience."

"I'm sure by rights us fillies in our Grecian dresses, ought to be enough."

"Alas, we never are," Bella muttered. "No matter

how much effort we put into presenting ourselves. We never are."

After she bid Caroline farewell, Bella did not leave directly, but instead took a detour to the coach house. It was wrong of her to snoop, but the suspicions that had been gnawing about at her innards while she'd been cooped up at Wyndfell Grange had ballooned into a whole set of rampant imaginings. They had not been allayed by Caroline's lack of sightings of Lucerne, but amplified. Thus, coupled with the evidence that only his valet was permitted to attend him, and yet no doctor had been summoned, she sought confirmation of Vaughan's presence at Lauwine in a practical fashion. The coach house was rather more easily accessible than Lucerne's private quarters. The servant's, once she was outside of the house, paid her no heed.

It took only the most cursory of glances to confirm everything. Vaughan's carriage, complete with the Pennerley crest, sat right beside Lucerne's brougham. Bella pinched her pursed lips. There was no point in spilling tears over it, but her vexation was difficult to curtail. Stiffly, she walked to where one of the stable hands was holding her horse and mounted up.

Damn, and curse them both.

She had known from the first that neither of them was sick. When they did re-emerge into society, she had no doubt the evidence of their exploits would translate into sore-throats, and all manner of bites and bruises that could be explained away with talk of leeches and other quackery. However, she would know the truth.

If she were able to set her hands upon them right now, she would throttle them both.

Perhaps, it was just as well that wasn't so. Although, a part of her did consider storming back inside and creating a grand kerfuffle. It was not as if she needed an escort to know where Lucerne's rooms lay. Oh, to catch them mid-act. To see their wretched faces.

They would have excuses, explanations, but she would hear none of them. They had done nothing but lie to her from day one.

That they had flown from Stags Fell not due to the virulent vomiting bug, but in order to rendezvous here, where they might attend to shagging one another senseless in complete privacy was just... it was just despicable... the most contemptable, horrible...

Oh, what was the point? All her cursing made no difference to anything, and while she was angered by their actions, she could hardly claim to be surprised by them.

Vaughan loved Lucerne. He always had and he always would. Nothing ever changed in that regard. Lucerne had presumably realised what an idiot he had been and how much he in turn loved Vaughan, hence he was making amends.

It has no bearing on how they feel about you.

She could tell herself that until she turned blue in the face, but her head still doubted, and her heart remained crushed.

"You told me you loved me," she huffed, under her breath, seeing Vaughan's brilliant eyes shining in the darkness. "But he had only to smile at you and present his arse for inspection, and I've been all but forgotten."

"What's that, miss?"

"Nothing," she growled at the squat youth, who was still holding her reins. She claimed them and turned her mare in the direction of home. Only when the groom was out of earshot did she add, "Just that your master is a stinking turd and his lover an even greater one." Hadn't Lucerne sworn to her that he did not mean to steal Vaughan from her? Yet that was precisely what he had done. Ensnared him, ensorcelled him, and carried him off to his manse to enjoy at his leisure. And as for Vaughan, he had clearly gone straight from her bed to Lucerne's, exactly as he had countless times before. Sometimes it seemed the world hardly changed at all.

Bella shook her fist back at the house, her gaze honing in on the dark windows of the upper storey of the east wing. Surely there was something to be done. Whatever it was, it was beyond her fathoming.

Ned Darleston's warning words echoed in her head yet again. The wild roar of the wind as she kicked her mare into a gallop and hurtled across the fields was quite unable to drown them out.

Why indeed would the two men love her, when they could love each other just as well? She was nothing in the grand scheme of things. Just a plain miss from a once respectable family, while they were both aristocrats who could trace their lineages back to the Norman conquest.

Your only option is to tolerate it or walk away, the same as it has always been. You haven't done it yet, so don't fool yourself that you're about to do so now. And even if you were capable of cutting yourself free, what then?

If there were anything worse than being a kept woman, it was most assuredly being a formerly kept woman.

CHAPTER 24

BELLA

LTHOUGH BELLA RODE hard, circling around Wyndfell several times before returning to the grange, her rage still hadn't blown itself out. When she stormed through the front door, Joshua took one look at her, and his congenial expression transformed into a hawkish sneer.

"What now?" he barked.

Bella swept passed him and headed for the stairs, meaning to go straight to her room, but her brother caught hold of her arm.

"Annabella."

Her glare was met with an equally cold one of his own.

"Vaughan is at Lauwine."

Joshua blinked once, and then released her. "I see. So their friendship is renewed, and now you are wondering how you fit into this new arrangement, for you are surely a continuing bone of contention between them. How could you not be, when you have given yourself so freely to them both? Does Pennerley tire of you now? Is Lucerne considering taking you back?"

She stomped her foot. "You are hateful. I don't wish to take him back, and my relationship with Vaughan is unchanged." She continued to clomp her way up the stairs.

Joshua did not follow, but he did call after her. "If you were so certain of that, you would not be in so foul a mood. The truth is, you fear he will cast you aside, as many a man has done when he has grown bored of his mistress—"

"He is not bored of me." Her voice echoed so loudly it was a wonder every person in the house didn't come running. Instead, they were probably lined up by the kitchen door with their ears to the keyhole.

"Can you not see now why you should have held out for a marriage proposal, or why embroiling yourself in a triangular affair was exceptionally dim-witted?" Something about his tone caused her to pause and look back. Joshua peered up at her, his fine dark hair shot with silver upon the top. His face now twisted in revulsion. "I hardly recognise you as my sister. Yes, Bella, I am aware of exactly how little regard you have for your own virtue. If it were not bad enough that you should embroil yourself in one tawdry affair with a peer of the realm, you deign to go one better and share yourself with two of them. One doesn't dare to speculate as to what level of intimacy needs to exist between two fellows for that sort of arrangement to even become a possibility. For certain, it is not a godly one."

"Perhaps not godly, but beautiful," she snarled back.

Joshua goggled at her, and the skin around his collar turned the all-too familiar shade of puce. Time was that would have been enough for her to swallow some of her worst retorts and simmer down her temper, but what use would that serve her now? Why not simply be honest and speak the absolute truth for once?

"I may be a wanton and fool, brother, but better that than what you would have me be."

"Virtuous? Respectable?"

"Miserable," she yelled.

Joshua slapped his hand hard against the bannister, making the whole thing shake. The tremors ran straight up Bella's arm and into her shoulder. "Yes, because you are so deliriously joyful at present. You claim, he...they have made you happy, but I see little evidence of it. It strikes me that they are perhaps hoping that I will finally take you in hand, leaving them free to be merry together. No doubt they have a new conquest in mind. Perhaps one of Wakefield's sisters, or even all four of them."

"You are vile." Why was it he could so easily hone in upon all her silly anxieties? She stomped back down several steps, her heels clacking against the wood. "Hateful and vile. Take that back, Joshua Rushdale. Take. It. Back." She swung at him with the fichu which she tore from around her neck.

Arms raised to ward off her attack, Joshua shortened the distance between them. He caught the end of her fichu, and with one deft tug, the lace scarf slithered free of her grip. "I'll tell you what I am, sister dear, I'm the voice inside your head. The one preaching all the things that you yourself have already thought. Tell me honestly that isn't so, that you didn't churn such thoughts and worse all the ride home. You may once have been happy, but that is no longer the case, and you can't predict what the next move will be, but there is a high likelihood that it will result in your abandonment."

"No," she huffed quietly, all the fight suddenly whooshing right out of her, so that she sagged into a heap upon the stairs like a crumpled shirt without a body to lend it shape. "Vaughan will not leave me."

He was giving voice to all her worst fears; the ones that had tormented her these past four nights, howling in her head like some wild spirit trapped in a gibbet. Vaughan did love her, she reminded herself. He had said so, and he didn't lie to her. He had promised her honesty in that regard, and to the best of her knowledge had always given it. That he also loved Lucerne did not alter what they had. That he loved Lucerne was nothing new, and she ought not to fear it, but to accept it. Everyone had to make sacrifices for love; that was the nature of it. Furthermore, she had to remember that nothing had really changed. Lucerne may not have been in their lives during their time at Pennerley, but he had certainly never left their thoughts.

Really, there was no cause for alarm or fear.

"You have heard naught from him in a week."

"I've been ill. He's been ill. I'll hear from him soon enough."

Joshua slotted into the space between her and the balustrade. "Why must you insist on deluding yourself? He abandoned you at Stags Fell, Bella, without a word. Now we find out that he is a mere two miles away. Is that not a clear sign that he has washed his hands of you?"

"No."

"Try to think logically."

"I am." A loud sniff rid her of the urge to sob. Nevertheless, her shoulders shook, and her nose prickled too.

"I am not your enemy, Bella. I have never been that. I could have dragged you home a long time ago, and maybe I should have done so. So often I often regret the decision to give you the rule of yourself." His tone was much softer now, though there remained a slight shake to his words, as if he were holding back a vast tide of emotion. Well that made the both of them.

Bella lifted her head and considered him. He looked less mawkish, and more brooding than a moment ago. Nor was his colour quite so high.

"My life would have been much simpler had I done so. It'd have been less ridiculed. I'd have had my pick of the women hereabouts to take as wife."

"I do so hate that expression," she mumbled, following it with another almighty sniffle. "As if none of the women should be afforded any say in the matter, and you could just pluck one, as you might a rosy apple off a tree."

"Of course they'd have a say," he rebuked her, although they both knew that wasn't entirely truthful. "Nevertheless, what I'm trying to say is that I want your happiness, obviously I do, but you really can't go on fooling yourself that Pennerley is anything but a dastardly rakehell who obviously places his friendship with a fellow peer more highly than he does the virtue of some country miss with whom he's enjoyed a bit of fun."

Bella irritably rubbed her nose. She was hardly a simple country miss anymore. Also, dastardly? Wherever did he find these descriptions? If she hadn't known better, she'd have said he'd been devouring her favourite novels.

"A few days of silence is nothing," she said. "Vaughan and I have occupied the same abode and gone longer than that without exchanging a word. He told me that he loved me, and I have faith that is still the case. He would let me know if it were not. Vaughan is no coward to cast me off without saying a word." Rather, it would be with the sort of brutal finality that would leave her in no doubt that their association was done, never to be renewed.

"Then you are storming about why, precisely?"

She shook her head, then bowed it gain. "Tis better you don't hear it. You would only find it distasteful, and it will raise your ire." He sat alongside her now with his hands enfolded in his lap. To her surprise, Joshua grasped her hand and gave it a squeeze.

"I'm a poor brother if you cannot confide."

Expecting her to confide after all the constant beratings he'd given her these last weeks rather stretched credulity, but somehow she found herself opening her mouth to explain regardless. "Primarily, I fear temptation, Joshua. If Vaughan and Lucerne are united again, then what is to say I won't be persuaded to forgive and forget too? Then, we will all be back where we were before, all in a muddle, emotions constantly strained to the point of snapping. I don't know that I can face it again."

It was really rather predictable, that his shoulders would creep up towards his earlobes, and he'd let go of her hand. "You mean to resume a..." Whatever word he was looking for eluded him, leaving him humming and harrumphing.

It would be utter folly to return to how things were before without first addressing the many issues that had arisen, and even if they all spoke their hearts and proposed solutions, it was still likely the stupidest of stupid ideas. In any case, she no longer loved Lucerne, nor had any wish to be with him. She had told him so too, and if Vaughan hadn't understood that yet, then he was bloody well going to have to learn it soon.

Joshua peeled himself off the stairs again and took a step or two. "I swear this whole thing is utterly ridiculous. You're ridiculous."

"Well, it so happens that I think you're being ridiculous too, not only in that you expect to bully a marquis into marrying me to appease your sensibilities, but that you imagine everything can be set to rights over a saucer of tea. If it were that simple, do you not think we would have drunk ourselves sick by now?"

"Not a single thing about this whole matter makes sense to me, Bella. Not a single thing. But I suppose if I'm not going to lock you in your room, this overblown drama must be endured until it reaches some reasonable conclusion. For my part, I dearly hope it is soon, and since we are being so direct with one another, I pray it results in them departing Yorkshire for good so that you might be left to make an altogether more agreeable match. Although heavens knows if any man will ever show an interest in you when your reputation is so tarnished, and your virtue entirely errant."

While his tone was brusque, it was not unkind. "You are so old-fashioned, assuming that only pious priggish sorts contemplate marriage. I've had several offers from men who were perfectly aware of my attachment to Lord Pennerley."

Joshua shook his head in despair.

Perhaps she oughtn't to have brought that up.

"They won't have been serious offers," he said. "They'd have shrivelled into nothing the moment you were ready to bite. It'll have been a game of one-upmanship, that's all; a means for them to increase their own notoriety by getting one over on Pennerley. Much as Pennerley enticing you away from Marlinscar probably was."

"It most definitely was not," she said crossly. "How little value you give me, Joshua. Did you consider that perhaps, unlike you, they see value in something Vaughan obviously treasures, or that they might find a woman with some...?" She paused, seeking an appropriately tactful word, and failed to secure any that was delicate enough for her brother's ears. "What I'm saying is that some men value experience. They want a wife they're going to enjoy being with. It must be dreadfully tiresome attempting to prick someone who barely tolerates your presence at the breakfast table, let alone in the bedroom."

There, she'd thoroughly shocked him now. A fine web of lines had etched themselves around his eyes, and sweat beaded along his upper lip. "It's what you liked about Emma," she couldn't resist adding, thinking of her former maid.

"I should wash your mouth out with soap and water. The things you imply."

"I'm not implying anything. I know exactly what you used to do in the parlour when the rest of the household was tucked into bed."

"It was when I wound the clock."

"I know what that means, Joshua. You are acquainted with the company I keep. And you may as well face it, I'm an unrepentant romp. You're not going to turn me into a saint, or even a respectable sort, no matter how hard you try. Maybe it'd be best if you just disowned me."

He paced up and down the hallway. "Bella, you're my only kin."

She did not want to lose him either, but if an estrangement would make them both happier in the long term, then wasn't it sensible to at least consider it? "I'm tired of fighting with you." Suddenly, she felt hopelessly weary. "I have enough to contemplate already. It is quite difficult enough navigating the intricacies of a complicated relationship without constantly waging a battle on a separate front, too."

He considered her with a clerk-like composure. "No," he concluded with a vehemence that actually surprised her. "I won't give you up, but there must be some resolution to this nonsense, Bella. You cannot stay in Yorkshire and continue to be his mistress. If he won't marry you, then you must both leave the county and return to his estate or London."

"I quite agree," she said, nodding her head and going to him. They stood facing one another in the centre of the hall. "I half wish that we had never come north, but I cannot simply decide to leave. Can't you see, Joshua? I'm subject to Vaughan's whim, and right now, his whim is to hole up with Lucerne at Lauwine."

"Then you must insist on seeing him, or you should write him a letter, or something..." He flapped his hands, as their housekeeper often did when she was herding the hens out of the kitchen garden and back to their coop.

"I can hardly arrive at Lauwine and demand an audience with someone who isn't officially there." Writing Vaughan a letter was entirely out of the question too. Imagine if such a missive were to fall into the wrong hands! The result could be catastrophic.

No, she would content herself with imagining breaking into Lucerne's quarters with a brace of pistols and putting a couple of holes in his headboard. Anything more than that would have to wait until the Marquis of Pennerley was Lord Marlinscar's official guest. Truly, she had to question again, what had possessed her to come north. Fulfilling Louisa's wishes had caused nothing but heartache and trouble.

"I suppose I will simply have to wait and see what Vaughan pleases to do next," she murmured.

Joshua responded with the sort of baying yawn that implied he'd tired of the subject. "You mean you intend to spend a deal more time mooning over him, and crashing about like a miniature thunderstorm."

Sauciness returned, Bella planted one hand on her hip. "Yes. Precisely that. If I focus on one asset at a time, it should take me a good long while." He and Lucerne could not stay locked up together forever; eventually one of them would get tired or sore. After five days of having his arsehole stretched, Lucerne would definitely require some respite. God, she hoped it left his ring on fire and that he couldn't sit.

On the subject of rings, his still lay in her pocket. She slipped it onto the end of her finger as she made her way up the stairs.

"Bella," Joshua called after her.

She leaned over the bannister to see him.

"Just so that it is clear. I still greatly disapprove of all this, and if he does show his face, I will continue to insist that he marries you."

She rolled her eyes. "The more you insist, the less likely it will ever come about. He does not like being told what to do."

"Well that is one thing you both have in common. I always supposed there had to be something besides a talent for mischief and irritating me."

Bella crashed into her room, and closed the door with her rear, whereupon she heaved a deep sigh. Everything was still awry, and numerous anxious hours, if not days, stood ahead of her. It was rather imperative that she spoke to Vaughan, but as she'd said to Joshua, she could hardly go to Lauwine and insist upon it, when Lucerne was officially ill, and Vaughan's presence likely a secret. In any case, he would be with Lucerne, and she didn't want to speak to him with Lucerne present.

A mere moment after she pushed away from the door, her maid came in.

"I suppose you heard all of that?" Bella huffed dryly, having narrowly missed being hit by the door.

Tilly peered sheepishly at her from beneath her mop cap. "You were being rather loud, Miss. I wasn't deliberately listening in."

"No, of course not," Bella responded waspishly. "You were going about your proper business, just as everyone else was. It's mere coincidence that you were all required to be cleaning doorknobs at that particular point in time."

Bella kicked off her boots, leaving them in the middle of the floor for Tilly to collect. She sat with a disgruntled huff at the dressing table, and stared at her reflection. How worn she looked. Anger and anxiety warred within her eyes, and her lips were pulled into a thin moue.

She removed her riding hat, whereupon Tilly approached her from behind, and began the task of unpinning and brushing her hair.

"Everything is in a right pickle, so it sounds, Miss. I'm right sorry that you're going to be leaving us again so soon after you came back."

"Who said I'm leaving?"

"I thought that's what Mr. Rushdale said, and you agreed it would be best."

Bella met the maid's enquiring glances in the cheval glass. "I'm not going anywhere while Lord Pennerley remains at Lauwine." Much as it was vaguely amusing to imagine riding off and having Vaughan chase after her, she wasn't foolish enough to believe that would actually happen, should she take it into her head to leave. Would he even notice she'd gone while he was preoccupied with Lucerne's finer attributes?

"I'm glad if they've mended their differences," Tilly said, when Bella showed no more signs of elaborating on the subject. "We used to hear stories about them in the past, all sorts of wild things, but then it was said they'd fallen out, and all the stories dried up. When Lord Marlinscar came home last November, I didn't think it could possibly be the same man that all those tales had been about. He wasn't anything like what they said."

"And Lord Pennerley, is he like the tales?"

"He's a devil, Miss. I'm sure of it. Can't be any other explanation for him being so handsome, charming, and rich. I just pray for your sakes that he's not all wickedness but that there's some kindness in him too."

She did not care for the direction the conversation had turned. Things were intolerable enough without her own maid weighing in with an opinion. "I'd like you to leave me now, Tilly. I can do the rest myself."

"Very good." The little maid gave a stiff curtsey. "Shall I come back in a while to ready you for dinner, or shall I tell cook that you'll take it up here?"

"I'll ring if I require anything." Truthfully, she was ready to climb into her bed and shut out the world for a while. If it was daylight and a new day when she emerged, then all the better.

"There were a couple of things, Miss."

Bella sighed. Truly, there was no peace to be had in this house. "What is it Tilly?"

"I did wonder if you'll be requiring me to come with you when you leave? If it is, I should like time to let my family know."

Bella turned her head to give the shrewd little maid a penetrating stare. "As I said, Tilly, I don't know that there are even any plans to depart. I could be here in Yorkshire for weeks or months yet."

"Surely not months, Miss. You'd—. I expect the Marquis will want you to leave before then." She swallowed. "I mean, he always used to move around a lot in the stories that were told. He never stayed anyplace too long."

Bella gave a nod. It was true, Vaughan did have a reputation as something of a wanderer. "And the other thing? You did say there were a couple." Tilly backed up. Her hand rested on her apron pocket, then tentatively pushed inside it. "There's this," she said striding forward once more. She placed an item on the dressing table before Bella. "I don't know the meaning of it, but I did think you might want it." Words said, she immediately scuttled towards the door.

"Wait!" Bella gawped at the gold chain and locket gleaming against the dressers dark wood. The item was not hers, though she was as familiar with its surface and contours as she was her own skin. The locket belonged to Vaughan. "Where in heavens did you get that?"

The maid peeped sheepishly from beneath her mobcap. "At Stags Fell, miss. I found it on the pillow when I was packing up your stuff. It and a note. They'd got jumbled in the covers."

Vaughan had left it there deliberately, so that she would know she wasn't forgotten and that he meant to return. He would not idly have cast the locket aside, nor forgotten it. It meant too much, was far too precious.

Bella opened the clasp that held the two sides together. Within, behind a small pane of glass, lay a golden lock of Lucerne's hair. Her breath caught, seeing there was now also a dark brown strand of her own shade entwined around it, and two dates engraved in the metal where before there had only been one.

"The note? You said there was a note."

Cowed, Tilly stared down at her own chest. "There was, miss."

"Well, where is it? And why did you not give me these things before?"

The maid sadly shook her head. "I couldn't. I

shouldn't have probably done so now." Her voice trilled thin and reedy.

Bella got to her feet. "Tilly, you're not making any sense. What the devil is going on?"

"Oh, miss! Mr Rushdale took them for safekeeping, but I think he must have burned the note. He put the locket in the fire too. Lally found it when she was doing the fires this morning. When she showed us in the kitchens, I knew it was yours, but you'd gone out by then, and then when I heard you arguing with Mr Rushdale..."

Bella covered her mouth with her icy fingers. Her heart was pounding. Her head too, as she struggled to make a coherent whole out of fractured slice of reality.

Joshua. Over and again he'd pointed to the fact Vaughan had left her with no word, yet all along he'd known that wasn't true. He'd just wanted her to believe that. He'd wanted to drive a wedge between them. She was on the verge of stomping down the stairs and crashing a pan over his head, but she stopped herself when she saw the maid's anxious face.

"I won't lose my position over this, will I?" Tilly scrunched her apron front into a knot. "It's only if he took it bad, my brother, my da, and the young 'uns they're all in the employ of the mine. If he was to—"

"He won't," Bella insisted, cutting her short. "Thank you for bringing this, Tilly. We'll say no more about it. If Mr Rushdale enquires after it, then you must let me know."

Bella sank onto the bed after Tilly had gone, the locket clasped tight within her palm. Without the note, she couldn't be certain of what Vaughan had meant to say, whether he had explained his actions, or even invited her to join them. What she was certain of, was that he had left his most precious object behind so that she would know that she remained in his thoughts, and as an indication that he would not be gone forever.

CHAPTER 25

VAUGHAN

VAUGHAN RECLINED ALONG the length of the sofa before the fireplace in Lucerne's quarters at Lauwine, swaddled only in a burgundy silk dressing gown. The once near derelict east wing of the house had been lovingly restored, but access to it remained restricted, and all the rooms save the four that made up Lucerne's private suite were swaddled in dust sheets. He could not have come up with a more suitable location for them to sequester themselves in if they had travelled all the way to Shropshire.

While the farthest corner of the east wing had always struck Vaughan as an odd choice for the location of the master's suite, he was glad of it now. No one knew they were here, discounting Lucerne's valet, the occasional mouse, some intrepid spiders, and two frogs—a pair they'd caught fornicating in Lucerne's dressing room earlier.

Lucerne was presently absent from the room. He had made some remark about requiring actual sustenance. Apparently, man could not live on love alone. Vaughan had lost track of whether they had been here three days or six. Time had rather lost all relevance. He was not especially hungry, other than for Lucerne.

"More port," he yelled. He could dimly hear Lucerne's voice drifting in from the next room, where he was dictating his list of requests to his long-suffering valet.

"Is he bringing more port?" Vaughan enquired, when Lucerne eventually returned.

"Yes." Lucerne closed the door behind him and turned the key in the lock. Just in case. Ivo was the height of discretion, but he didn't need the sight of them caudle-making burned into his brain, even if he knew perfectly well what was going on.

"Did you order us a banquet?" One eye only half open, Vaughan followed Lucerne's movement across the room. He was achingly beautiful. Tall, lean...dishevelled. Every piece of clothing he had on—there weren't actually many—was hopelessly crumpled, and his blond hair stuck up at sixes and sevens from the top of his head. A golden shadow outlined and softened his rather angular jaw. Lucerne came to a rest behind the sofa upon which Vaughan lay, and curled his palms around its gracefully carved back.

"Yes. I'm hungry, even if you're not."

"Oh, I'm hungry." Vaughan reached up with one hand and curled his fingers around the lapel of Lucerne's dressing gown so he could tug him down for a kiss. His lips were soft and a little puffy from overuse. He tasted of liquorice root. Having claimed what he wanted, Vaughan pushed his lover back a little and eyed him curiously. "What's wrong?"

Something had knocked the easy smile from his lover's face.

"Bella was here," Lucerne said, straightening to his full height again.

Vaughan pushed himself up a little, supported on his elbows. He was not overly shocked by the revelation; in fact, he had more or less expected her appearance. Once his lodgings in Reeth had been ruled out, this was the obvious place to seek him—leastways, it would be obvious to Bella. She knew him much better than most and far better than he sometimes wished. Also, he'd left her a note, be it a rather cryptic one. "Looking for me?"

The swift shake of Lucerne's head suggested otherwise. "Officially, to see Caroline, but unofficially...? I'm sure she has her suspicions."

A pang of guilt twanged inside his stomach. What if he'd been too cryptic? Still, it wasn't as if he could have been less so. Writing: with Lucerne would have been far too incriminating. In any case, it had been paramount that she didn't come tearing after them right away. That would have undone everything. He and Lucerne had needed time alone to heal the wounds they'd inflicted upon one another and to confess exactly what it was they both wanted and felt. Bella was another step forward again from there. You couldn't glue this sort of relationship back together with flour paste. It required something stronger, applied in layers if they wanted it to endure, and Vaughan wanted more than anything for this to endure.

"She knows I'm here, Lucerne."

His lover pursed his lips, but nodded. "There's more. Caroline sent up a note."

Ah, Miss Wakefield. She'd been sending missives with increasing frequency. Gentle enquiries about Lucerne's health, offers to attend his needs or to mix restoratives. "Does she offer to bathe your fevered brow and read you a book, or something more risqué?"

Following an irritated sniff, Lucerne slipped the folded rectangle of paper from the pocket inside his voluminous sleeve. He handed it to Vaughan, who squinted at the flowery script. "You'll observe there's only the briefest mention of my health. She requests permission to hold a gathering here—a farewell party."

"So she has abandoned hope, and decided to leave you but demands a final occasion on which to persuade you of her true devotion."

Lucerne sighed and took back the note. "You realise, you only show your wretched propensity for jealousy with such remarks. Miss Wakefield merely wishes that she and her sisters might say farewell to the friends and acquaintances they have made before they return to Bluebell Lane. It is not a dastardly attempt to flirt with me."

Vaughan nodded, but with his eyes open wide to show he didn't believe a word of it. Whether consciously or not, Caroline Wakefield had developed something of a tendresse for Lucerne. One only had to hear her speak of him to be aware of it. That was, unless you were Lucerne, who was apparently oblivious or wilfully deaf to it. Vaughan suspected it was a third of one and two-thirds the other.

"'Tis a pity they're not taking their oaf of a brother along with them when they go."

"Vaughan," Lucerne snapped, ire flashing in his eyes, that he immediately tempered. He took a breath, made a show of quashing his anger. "Would you please cut him a break? He's endured a difficult year, having lost his wife and sacrificed his commission in order to be a parent to his daughter."

Ah, yes. He had bred another of his ilk, though it was said the child favoured her mother – thank Christ! It disturbed Vaughan a little that Lucerne seemed to have a soft spot for the babe. Certainly, he would not hear a word said against her and had dismissed out of hand any suggestion that she and Wakefield move elsewhere. They had talked through a lot of topics these last few days, and little Louisa Wakefield had cropped up rather often. He could not, prior to this, claim little girls had ever featured in any of his conversations. Vaughan could say, with all honesty, that he had no desire for them to do so again. In no way could he fathom their appeal.

"What should I tell her?" Lucerne prompted, forcing him to return to the tedious topic of the Wakefields.

"I have no opinion on the subject. Do you want people tramping all over the place? If so, let her organise it. You needn't involve yourself in the minutiae."

Miss Wakefield likely had other ideas about that.

"I suppose that is true, and it may keep her occupied until the rest of them return. As the virulent vomiting bug has spread no further than us and Miss Rushdale, there's no reason for them to stay any longer at Stags Fell."

"Then get her to hold this luncheon, or whatever it is, on Saturday. Then you can be rid of them by early next week. Wait—" Vaughan pushed himself up into a seated position "—Bella has been ill?" This was news to him.

"Apparently she returned to Wyndfell a few hours after we arrived here, according to the kitchen staff. She was laid up until yesterday. However, Ivo reports she seems in robust health now."

Vaughan sucked his teeth, concerned her malaise a response to their impromptu departure from Stags Fell.

"So, I guess I'll tell Caroline to go ahead." Lucerne walked around the sofa and cast the note into the fire. It caught and curled into ashes. "I suppose the only difficulty will be over the Rushdales. Bella has befriended the Misses Wakefield, and they are my closest neighbours. It's going to be deuced uncomfortable having them here. Not only has Joshua not forgiven me for failing to make Bella my viscountess, but Bella, as you know, will barely acknowledge me. I suppose this" —he drew a hand through the air to indicate them both—"won't have helped matters."

"This?" Vaughan enquired, raising one brow. He was feeling comfortably lethargic and didn't want to be roused from his indolence with thoughts of a taxing nature. He settled his head back on the sofa arm again.

"You and I. And the fact I did precisely what I promised I absolutely wouldn't do—that is, steal you away."

Vaughan clacked his tongue against his teeth. "You've stolen nothing. My being here is entirely my own doing. Nor have I taken up with you at her expense. I told her as much myself." Leastways, he'd left her a coded message to that effect.

Lucerne stared down his nose in a hideously autocratic way. "I highly doubt she sees it like that." There was a hint of disappointment in his tone too. Really though, there was no cause for him to be so snippy. Admittedly, Bella would require some careful handling. While Lucerne hadn't carried him off, Vaughan had left her bed in the dead of night. However, the thing he needed both her and Lucerne to understand was that they were not rivals for his affections. There was no need for them to compete. He was perfectly capable of keeping them both contented, if they'd only let him.

"Think of it this way, Lucerne. If you play host to a party, then it at least provides an opportunity for us all to run into one another without having to go to the bother of attempting to orchestrate some impromptu rendezvous."

"I suppose that is true." Lucerne sounded neither comforted nor convinced, prompting Vaughan to take hold of his hand.

"You do realise that she hates me."

As a matter of fact, he did not believe that to be true. Admittedly, he had heard Bella express such a sentiment more than once, but her hate was only reserved for those who inspired great emotion in her. It was truly the flip side of her love. She still purported to hate him on a regular basis too, which was quite frankly ludicrous, even given the fact he'd provided her with more than ample reasons to do so. This affair with Lucerne being only the latest in a very long list.

"She's still angry with you. That doesn't mean she won't forgive you in time."

Lucerne sucked his upper lip. "I don't even know how to begin to make amends. I'm fairly certain I've made a frightful hash of it so far."

Vaughan swung his legs down onto the floor so Lucerne could occupy the sofa alongside him. "But you do wish to, Lucerne?"

"Of course I do. I know I made some stupid choices, and there are things I really ought not to have done, and others that I should have done and didn't, but no amount of apologising will change them. And, I am not even sure that they are why she is mad at me."

Vaughan raised their hands and kissed Lucerne's knuckles. "I think maybe she's working on figuring that out herself. You and she were close in ways that she and I were not. You were friends as well as lovers. You betrayed that as much as anything else."

"I tried Vaughan, when you left; I tried so hard to make it work between us. Lord, I wanted it so much, but the spark was gone. She had no interest in me. She was consumed by your absence."

"Well, that is because she could see what you apparently couldn't, that we are all better off together."

Lucerne bowed his head, then rested it upon Vaughan's shoulder. Their hands remained tightly clasped, and not a hair's breadth separated their shoulders. "I was being torn apart by it. I could no longer stand the subterfuge and the deceits, all the lies we told ourselves and one another. She would not admit that she loved you. And you were no better. I did leave for selfish reasons, but I also hoped it would give you both the space you needed to be honest with one another."

"And it did." He further mused Lucerne's hair. "There is a way for us all to be together and happy, Lucerne. I don't know precisely what it is yet, but I'm determined that through patience and perseverance we will find it."

Lucerne placed a kiss in the centre of his palm, then let him go. "I don't possess your talent for either of those things."

"Yet here we are. Did you not coax your way back into my affections?"

He refused to let Lucerne sink into despair over this. That wouldn't serve any of them very well. His lover tugged on the edge of his dressing gown, where it had split apart at the front to reveal his chest beneath. "Leave it. I like looking at you." He knocked Lucerne's hand away, whereupon the other man sagged against the sofa back. "I'm not fool enough to believe that. We're here because you chose to capitulate. I'm not going to take any credit for the timing. I just assumed you'd decided I'd done enough suffering."

"Because I'm that much of a beast?"

"You are."

He was. "If it were as simple as that we would both

be still at Stags Fell. It would be more accurate to say that I succumbed to my own passions."

Lucerne cocked an eyebrow.

"The urge to screw you senseless became too strong."

"Then I trust your desire for me is now well satisfied."

They had done a great deal of screwing.

"Temporarily abated," Vaughan drawled, a darkling smile playing upon his lips. He slipped off the sofa and onto his knees. A tug on Lucerne's hem pulled the edges of his dressing gown apart, exposing a pale line of flesh from shin to chest. His cock was slumbering in its nest of golden curls, but one idle brush of Vaughan's thumb along Lucerne's inner thigh awakened it.

Lucerne peeped down the length of his body at Vaughan. "Dare I ask what you are about?"

He settled himself between Lucerne's splayed knees, and smoothed his palms up his lover's shins to the soft skin of his thighs. "Proving to you yet again that you have nothing to worry about. If you let it, all will come right."

"I'm not worried."

"Of course you are. You're convinced that Bella will never forgive you, and will do her very best to split us apart so that she might claim me absolutely. Failing that, you're scared she'll take a horse whip to your hide. Perhaps both. She tried that on me once, you know." He stroked his thumb across his lower lip as the memory reformed. "It was rather delicious."

Lucerne visibly flinched. "Yes, well I'm not so keen on being lashed."

"No. I know," Vaughan stretched upwards, between his thighs. "You prefer to be pampered." He landed kisses on his lover's upper thighs, then one on each hip, and repeated the action, but inching inward towards Lucerne's now stiff cock with each successive kiss.

"Are you going to—"

He liked that rush of breath that told him Lucerne was eager for this.

"Yes." They'd done quite enough soul-searching for one afternoon, particularly when there were other far more enjoyable ways to spend their time together than worrying over the future. Sometimes, it paid to live in the here and now.

Vaughan liked to explore and took his time traversing Lucerne's lower body with his fingertips. Too often it was all about one's prick. Not that he was in any way intending to leave that off his itinerary, but a little build up, stretching out the moment between the promise of something and actually delivering the prize could make all the difference to how satisfying the experience was.

"You're going to kill me. Touch me, goddamn you."

Once upon a time, Lucerne had been a patient man.

"I am touching you."

"I want to feel your mouth around me."

"I know," he crooned. "Soon, my impatient one. Don't you want to know what it feels like to have your ballocks tickled first?"

Lucerne's breath ratcheted inside his throat, as Vaughan dragged a slow lick upward from the underside of his ballocks. He shoved his knuckles between his teeth. "That is way too sensitive," he claimed, his voice high, sweet and extremely needy. Notably, he didn't say stop. Instead, he sucked in great gasps of air, as if that could counteract the mauling of his senses. "Please."

"Oh, very well then." Vaughan relinquished. "Is this more to your liking?" He swirled his tongue around the tip of Lucerne's cock, then enclosed it within his mouth. Judging from the noises leaking from his lover's mouth, that met with very definite approval. Lucerne did always strive so hard to contain his appreciation of things but never did quite manage it. One always knew if you were mixing things correctly, and how far you could push him before he reached his limit.

Naturally, it helped immensely that Vaughan liked sucking him. His own cock was already stirring in anticipation of that thrill.

Having encircled the shaft with one hand, Vaughan slid his mouth over more of the head. Salty bitterness tingled on his tongue; Lucerne's unique taste, mixed with the musk of their earlier couplings. A handkerchief could only wipe away so much. They ought to get Ivo to fill a tub and sit in it together. It'd make an interesting alternative to the bed, or the carpet, and indeed, most of the suite's other furnishings. All of which had seen a fair share of intercourse. It'd make cleaning up afterwards easy too.

He released Lucerne's cock with a pop, and kissed down the length of his shaft to the springy, velvety blond hair at the base. The scent of him got his own cock speedily thickening. God, he'd missed this man. He had not lacked for intimacy during their time apart, but there was something about the bond between them that got him in a entirely visceral way.

After kissing around the base, he licked up the shaft again, and returned to sucking.

Vaughan couldn't deny he'd always loved the power implicit in this act. One had a surprising degree of control, for a being on one's knees, especially if one were a good enough student to know what merely served, and what heightened, pleasure. He pushed his hands between Lucerne's bottom and the sofa, and raised him off the seat. In turn, that got Lucerne's cock a deal deeper into his mouth. He relaxed, and swallowed, and didn't get in a panic when Lucerne's hips bucked and pushed his cock deeper still.

This wasn't something one could do for a long time, but it was rarely necessary. Normally the sensations involved, and the visuals of it, brought things to a rapid close.

Predictably enough, Lucerne's muscles pulled taut as his cries grew louder. The strain showed all along his thighs and in his stomach. "God, Vaughan! How are you doing that?"

His lover's hands clawed and dug so deep into the fabric of the sofa; there'd henceforth be two permanent grooves in the cushions. And, as for the cries winding their way free of his throat, if he'd heard them independently of knowing their cause, he'd have sworn it was a wounded animal baying in pain, not a man driven mad with pleasure.

"I need to come, Vaughan. Shit! Let me come."

As if he was doing anything to prevent it.

Very well, he might have been putting pressure on a particular point that tended to shut down the mechanics of things.

"Please."

Sweat beaded across Lucerne's brow, the tendons in his neck stood out, and his eyes, which had snapped open, were as two brilliant sapphires, glittering in the candlelight.

"Not yet." He was a cruel bastard, he really was, but a little torment always did put a smile on his face. Grinning, he sat back on his haunches, and wiped his lips clean.

"Vaughan." Lucerne sat forward, his plea one of ultimate outrage, but simultaneously, pleading and confused. "Please."

He shrugged. "A few touches should set you off.

Take a good hold of yourself, and work your wrist. I want to watch you spend."

Perhaps not as eagerly as Lucerne wished him to swallow, but all Lucerne said was, "You're such a pig."

"I'll see if I can't catch it on my tongue," he remarked in response, which absolutely did the trick of getting Lucerne's wrist working furiously. So intently, and with such zeal, that he almost lost a grip on himself.

Almost, but not quite, as Vaughan was there to steady his hand, and brush his palm over the top of Lucerne's glans.

It set him off at once. Jets of his seed hitting their hands, and indeed Vaughan's tongue. He pulled Lucerne in for a kiss, once he was fully spent, and allowed him to slump. Meanwhile, Vaughan stretched out, cat-like on the carpet before the hearth.

Lucerne rolled his head to one side, following his movement. "You bastard, I should pin you down and bugger you for that."

Vaughan turned over onto his stomach. "I'm all yours," he drawled silkily. "Assuming you can get it up."

He had his face turned towards the fireplace, but he still heard Lucerne swallow. Unable to help himself, he snatched another glance at him. Lucerne was staring at him, an expression of what could only be described as astonishment writ into his features. Never had those blue eyes looked so luminous, or his jaw been so slack. As for his chest, it rose and fell at twice the normal rate. "Just like that you toss that out there." His tongue swept over his kiss-sore lips.

"If you're able," Vaughan reiterated, ignoring how tremulous Lucerne sounded. A sly glance up at Lucerne's body suggested that maybe given a minute or three, he might be. What's more, that wasn't a problem. It wasn't as if he'd never taken Lucerne's cock up the arse before.

But only in anger, said a little voice inside his head. It was true that in the past, Lucerne had only fucked him at the culmination of a fight, be that during or after the argument. "Am I to assume you want to?"

"Want to?" Lucerne's wonderment was so pronounced it almost seemed exaggerated. "You have no idea. Yes, of course, I want to."

"Then do it."

"But what's changed?"

Everything.

And nothing.

"If it pleases you to fuck me, why should I deny it, Lucerne?"

"Dammit, Vaughan. Don't play with me. You've never been submissive in your life. What is this going to cost me?"

He couldn't recall them ever making any sort of decree about who was allowed to do what to whom; such discourse had been more about when. His relationship with Lucerne had been rather more equal in its infancy. Bella's inclusion had changed the dynamics. He'd been cast into a particular role that required him to be a very specific someone. He and Bella had been rivals, and one never showed weakness to the enemy. No—it was not weakness, but rather the lack of control he'd recoiled from displaying.

Bella was not present. Besides, the relationship he shared with her had metamorphosed too.

Lucerne left the sofa, and crawled over to where Vaughan lay on his front. His shadow fell over the hearth. "Vaughan."

A warm hand brushed the back of his thigh and slid upwards under the hem of the robe. "Take this thing off."

Wordlessly, he complied and returned to his

previous position of repose, now utterly naked. Why resist what he craved with all his soul?

CHAPTER 26
LUCERNE

LUCERNE COULD HARDLY comprehend what was being presented...nay, offered to him. Vaughan's body intoxicated him. He was currently spent, his cock drained of its vigour, but he could not let this opportunity pass by.

Yet, even as he traced the contours of his lover's body, he maintained a degree of caution. Any moment, he half-expected Vaughan to shift abruptly. Then to find his head inches from the fire, coal dust in his nostril and either Vaughan's cock inside him or the door slamming behind him.

Yet, he had no reason to doubt the man's word.

Encouraged by that thought, Lucerne trailed a second caress up the back of Vaughan's thigh, this time traversing the skin all the way to his buttocks. This passivity, it reminded him of the very first time they had genuinely fucked. It had been here, in this house, in this very wing, though not this room. He closed his eyes, falling into the memories: dextrous fingers massaging him, the slide of a tongue teasingly dragged along the length of his spine to the tip of his tailbone, and then lower. How wildly it had excited him. How easily it had made pushing his fears aside and giving in to what his body had craved for countless years.

He opened his eyes again, and followed that same approach now, teasing each vertebrae, following the curve of Vaughan's spine to his arse, and then delving into the groove there with his tongue. His reward—only the quietest of sighs.

Encouraged and eager to produce a more substantial reaction, he trailed his tongue in circles across Vaughan's cheeks, leaving behind a wet trail, before delving into the valley between those firm globes again and exploring the hidden pucker.

That touch earned him another faint gasp of approval. At least, he chose to interpret it as such. Certainly it was not a rebuff. Hence, he continued, still keenly aware of Vaughan's indolent compliance, and his own now thickening arousal.

Petting Vaughan was akin to caressing a fearsome beast. One was simultaneously enchanted by its beauty, and the harnessed power within such sinews, tendons, and muscles, while remaining keenly aware that such daring might cost one a limb.

Still, he couldn't persuade himself to stop, didn't even half-heartedly try.

It felt good to have Vaughan under him. Considering how recently he'd come, and how explosively, his cock ought to still be slumbering. Evidently, the right sort of stimulation could make almost anything possible.

"What are you about?" Vaughan enquired, half opening one eye.

Lucene chuckled, for was it not obvious. "I'm kissing your arse." Again he skimmed his lips over the curve of Vaughan's pale cheeks. "Does it not please you?"

Vaughan responded with a bemused snort. "I pray you don't actually require a sensible response. In any case, what you're doing can hardly be called kissing."

"Then what, pray, would you call it?"

"Licking."

There was the declaration; the assertion that he was still in charge. Lucerne allowed the jibe to roll off him. "Very good, I'm arse licking, then. And do you have opinion to share upon my talent for it?"

"Passable, if not wholly accomplished."

Lucerne cracked his palm down on Vaughan's left cheek. "Fuck you, Pennerley."

"You do keep promising."

He made another swipe at Vaughan's arse, this one more playful. "Someone's sounding awfully eager."

He pressed the pad of his thumb to the little puckered opening, which all too readily accepted the intrusion. Vaughan squirmed in a theatrical fashion. Encouraged, Lucerne straddled his legs, and tried his cock against the hole.

The visuals alone were almost enough to undo him. Coupled with the actual sensation of soft skin against the head of his prick, well, he had to take a hold of himself to get his excitement under control.

"Is there a problem, Lucerne?"

"I don't want to hurt you."

"You won't. It's not as if we haven't done this before."

"It was different then. I was angry. You were angry."

His lover acknowledged that with a tilt of his head, which set his hair tumbling over his shoulders. "Lucerne, I'm not going to break, but if you treat me like glass, I might break you. Use some oil. Give me a chance to adjust to the feel of you."

"Yes," he agreed.

The sweet smell of almonds infused the air as he dribbled warm oil between Vaughan's cheeks and applied it liberally to his cock. Back and forth, he slid himself along the groove between Vaughan's cheeks, teasing out the moment of penetration until he was weeping silvered beads and Vaughan was making chirp-like groans whenever he tapped against his hole.

"Now you know what it's like to be teased, to be held on edge until you almost go mad from it."

"I've been poised there a long time, Lucerne. Longer than you can possibly fathom."

"Italy," he guessed, only to correct himself immediately. "Eton."

Vaughan gave a choked cry, and gasped. Lucerne tangled his hand within the sable ringlets of his hair. "I know I chose to remain blinkered for years, but don't imagine I'm wholly unaware of how long ago you got it into your head to seduce me."

"It seemed only fair, considering how completely you'd enthralled me."

Lucerne's grip tightened. "And now? Now, are you still enthralled?"

"Never doubt it."

His heart was beating wildly, and Vaughan's drummed right alongside it, matching its pace and rhythm, like they were two parts of a whole.

"Now, fuck me, Lucerne."

This time, he didn't hesitate. Forgoing any more preamble, he struck his target, and pushed past the resistance. That was... Well, it was heaven and hell twinned. So tight. So hot. Lucerne pulled back and pushed in again, this time burrowing a little deeper.

That slide was damn addictive.

"So tight, my lord," Lucerne breathed against Vaughan's ear.

"Are you mocking me, Lucerne?"

"Never. If I'm mocking anyone, it's myself. When you enter me like this, hold yourself right on the cusp, ready to drive in deep, it makes me burn for you. Does it make you burn for me? Do you long for me to drive deep? Fill you with my strokes? I want to fill you with my strokes. I want to thrust every inch of my cock inside of you, until my ballocks smack your arse."

"I want everything you're prepared to give."

That was enough of a yes to content him. Lucerne brushed Vaughan's dark hair aside, stretched over him, and sucked at the skin of Vaughan's throat, where the rapid tick of his pulse rode just beneath the skin, but only for a brief moment. Then he gave himself up to driving himself repeatedly between Vaughan's cheeks until they were both red in the face and lathered. His muscles yelled at the exertion, but there was a rhythm to their joining that held him tight in its relentless grip.

A fluttering sensation centred around Lucerne's groin; it spread through his torso and out to his fingers and toes. He wanted to come, but he didn't want it to end.

"Lift up." It shocked him when Vaughan pushed himself up off the carpet and onto all fours, although it was simple enough to move with him. Vaughan reached behind him and clasped his arse. His position would not allow for more than a fleeting touch, but it communicated what he needed it to.

"Stay with me. I just need." He was on his knees, body upright now, his hard cock pressed taut to his abdomen, and his back against Lucerne's stomach. "Hold me and fuck me."

Kneeling behind him, Lucerne moved from the hips. Vaughan's sinewy, graceful body arched against his own. He grasped Vaughan's hair, turned his head, so that their mouths could meet.

"If I stroke you how long are you going to last?" He formed his fist around Vaughan's shaft.

Vaughan tightened his hand over the top of Lucerne's. "Longer than you will."

"You think?" He thumbed the crown of Vaughan's cock, circling around and around, where he knew it was sensitive. The shivers that rode right through Vaughan's body immediately proved his point. "Because I think, if I just keep doing this, and press upwards like this, that you're going to hit yourself in the face."

"Hm," Vaughan purred. "Maybe so, but you'll still come first. You always do."

Vaughan, bastard that he was, took control of their motion and set about sliding himself back and forth on Lucerne's prick. It was too much all at once, particularly coupled with Vaughan's murmured words of endearment.

Lucerne came in one deliciously long explosion and then held his lover tight as he did the same.

CHAPTER 27

BELLA

"MISS…MISS…"

Bella resisted the pull on her conscious. Lucerne's strong body arched before her, his head tilted back in the throes of passion. Vaughan reared behind him, holding him, while her legs were splayed wide around his hips, as he spent.

Such dreams, of the three of them together loving as one, had been disturbing her every night since her last visit to Lauwine. Each night the colours and sensations were a little more vivid, and it became a little harder on waking to remind herself why such a reality couldn't exist.

Tilly gave her another, more determined shake. "Miss? You're giving me ever such a fright screaming out like that. Miss Annabella, are you well?"

The warm cosy vision dissolved into near total darkness. Bella blinked myopically at the figure hunched over her, with a candlestick clenched in one fist. "Tilly? I'm fine…" She waved the petite maid away. "Just a dream."

"A night terror, Miss? Tomorrow, I'll get some salt from cook and make sure we ward the windows."

"Nay," Bella sighed. "They're good dreams. I don't wish to keep them out."

Tilly tutted and fussed with her covers, bringing the knotted tangle of blankets and bedspread up over Bella's body. "Tis a peculiar sort of pleasant to make you cry out like that. It sounded as if a wild beast were ravaging you."

"Two – it was two wild beasts."

Tilly's brows furrowed into even deeper grooves. "Well that's very peculiar. I'm sure I wouldn't find it enjoyable to be savaged by any number of beasts." Tilly checked the window, which was shut up tight, exactly as expected.

"I'll wager there was a demon here tormenting you," Tilly insisted, in her quiet but forceful way. She shook her head some more, and clucked her tongue. "Don't fret though, hinny, I'll make sure it doesn't come back."

Bella lay still and made a point of neither agreeing nor disagreeing. Even intoxicated with drowsiness, she knew any sort of answer would see her subjected to a range of local remedies, and then, if all else failed, an exorcism by a priest. She preferred to keep her two demons close to her chest, thank you. And she wasn't swallowing any noxious substances or being splashed with holy water and sitting still to have incantations spoken over her. Better to just let Tilly sprinkle salt and hang up corn dollies.

"I'm going to try to get back to sleep now, Tilly. Go on back to your own bed."

The woman hesitated. "Perhaps I should stay." Bella was thankful the maid couldn't read more than a couple of lines, or she might have taken it upon herself to sit in a chair and drone parables in her ear.

"I'm certain. I'm perfectly all right now."

Bella closed her eyes tight, and tried to slide back into the fantasy that all was perfect, but the ashes were cold in the hearth of Lucerne's bedchamber, and the only occupant was a lone mouse nibbling at the corner of the Persian rug.

CHAPTER 28
BELLA

S ATURDAY, THE DAY of the Wakefield's farewell luncheon, arrived surprisingly swiftly. Bella rose to a world of hazy sunshine, fragrant with the smell of dew-sodden grass. The earthy scent made her feel oddly disheartened as she strolled around Wyndfell's gardens waiting for Joshua to ready himself. There was a melancholy in her soul that she couldn't shake, brought on, according to Tilly, by her nightly visitations. Yet, it was only in her dreams that Bella found contentment. It was all so easy then, so perfect, whereas the reality was a torrid mess.

In her dreams, it was so easy for the three of them to be together. They were as one, each secure in the knowledge that they were loved by the other two. There existed no rivalry, and no resentment. If only that were true of the here and now.

What was official was that Vaughan was definitely Lucerne's guest at Lauwine. The Misses Wakefield – including Joanna – had confirmed it two days ago when they had visited in order to deliver an invitation to their farewell luncheon, and to plead with Joshua to attend.

"Please, for one afternoon, will you not put past slights asunder?" Caroline had begged.

"I'm afraid, Miss Wakefield, that some things are not so easy to forgive and forget," he'd replied stiffly.

"And we do not ask you to do either, only to box them up for an afternoon, so that we might wish you a proper farewell."

"There will be cake," Maria added. "And lawn billiards."

He'd agreed, in the end, down to Eliza's charm and willingness to converse at length on the subject of puffing devils. It did seem to be a genuine interest she held, too, and not merely an enticement. Perhaps in time, a tendresse might grow between Eliza and Joshua, so that Bella's brother could finally find some happiness for himself. Bella would not mind having practical and efficient Eliza Wakefield as a sister. Also, then he would not be so sour and pouty and determined to thwart her happiness.

She had held back from challenging him over the locket and the letter. It seemed senseless to stir up additional trouble, when trouble already dogged her every step. She would see Vaughan today and set everything to rights between them.

With Joshua still not arrived, Bella clipped a rose from one of the bushes, and idled on the old swing with its petals pressed to her nose. Why was he taking so long? Had he suddenly realised he would be unable to hold his resentment in check? It was a fear she held herself −reassurances aside – and waiting around only left her with additional time to ponder how she would react when faced with the possibility of seeing Vaughan and Lucerne side by side, knowing that their love was restored.

Was it even right to be angry at Lucerne? She couldn't seem to summon up any anger towards

Vaughan, for he had only done what he had always intended and reclaimed his errant lover. Should she not instead be thanking Lucerne? It was directly down to his actions that had allowed her and Vaughan to see one another clearly. They were no longer enemies, but freely admitted their feelings for one another without fear of opening themselves up to persecution. Such a thing had been near unthinkable a year ago. Then, she had barely allowed herself to dream that one day Vaughan might confess his love for her.

She had been holding fast to that thought this past week. Vaughan did not say things he did not mean. He did not lie to her. He would never have entrusted the locket to her if he didn't mean to reclaim her as his. Therefore, his silence was not indicative of her having lost him, only absentmindedness, or perhaps a determination not to cause a stir while he was mending things with Lucerne. Or perhaps, even now he was wondering why she had not responded to his letter. He could well have asked her to follow, to join them as she did in her dreams.

Was that what she wanted?

If there was no option to keep Vaughan all to herself, then didn't it make sense to attempt some measure of reconciliation with Lucerne? It wasn't as if she could claim to feel no pull towards him, not when he was there every night alongside Vaughan haunting her sleep.

"Are you coming?" Joshua demanded, startling her so that she jumped and pricked her finger. He stomped past her towards the carriage. The rose fell underfoot, as Bella sucked the bead of blood from the tip of her thumb. "Don't tell me you have changed your mind."

"I have been ready to leave these past twenty minutes. It is you that has been tardy. Whatever has taken you so long?"

It was quite obvious, facing him in the carriage. Joshua had polished himself up spectacularly well. Clearly, he was seeking to impress. Nevertheless, they had barely turned into the lane before he was grumbling and shaking his head.

"I'm still damned ill at ease with this," he muttered. "You know there is still too much bad blood between us all to be engaged in such a social call."

"Pfft. If I can muddle through you can." Thank heavens it was only a short journey if he was to be like this, but gracious, the carriage suspension needed work. It was like being tossed around inside a butter churn. "I'm the one folks will be whispering about. 'Oh, the horror! You wouldn't think she'd dare. Isn't she the one that Lord Marlinscar jilted? I heard he caught her canoodling with the Marquis of Pennerley, and lo, he is here too. Gosh, I can see why she might though; isn't he something? Do you suppose Marlinscar and Pennerley have made amends? Why, I shouldn't forgive anyone for doing such a thing to me.'"

"You've made your point," Joshua huffed.

"You see, I'm the one in danger of being a pariah, not you. You're just the fool that accepted the invitation because a certain young lady smiled at you and offered to tinker with your piston."

"She did no such thing," he bellowed, opening his mouth wide in his outrage. "I'll have you know that Eliza Wakefield is a—"

"Perfectly respectable lady, and not a thing like me." Bella patted his knee and laughed at him. "I know, Joshua. I know. She would suit you perfectly—"

"I'm not casting about for a wife."

"—and once you are wed, I'm sure she'll oblige and happily tinker with your piston."

"You are the crudest romp ever to have lived."

Bella snorted, "If you believe that, then you are

truly sheltered. Besides, it's only rude because you interpret it so."

"And you mean it to be so." He scowled at her, but settled himself into the squabs again. He was only still for a moment, before he hunched forward over his knees again. "You know it would probably be wise if you refrained from reminding me that you turned Marlinscar down. It still sours me to the marrow to know he offered and you refused. Honestly, Bella, it was preposterously short-sighted of you."

Bella folded her arms across her chest. "Please, let us not rehash this again. I no longer loved him, Joshua. It would not have been right to accept."

"You most likely would have done again, if you'd given it a chance, but no, you had to throw your lot in with that rakeshame, Pennerley."

"Whom I never have to even consider my love for, as it's absolute." She glared at him, challenging him to even dare to suggest otherwise.

"Is that why he has left you to stew over a week without a single word?"

"I daresay there were more than a few he left me in the letter you burned."

He goggled at her, but didn't deny it.

"Did you read it?"

"Of course not."

"Pig," she snarled, but her anger was cold.

Joshua turned away to look out of the window. They were not far off their destination now. The chimneys of Lauwine were just dotting in and out of view behind the treeline.

"This is insane. This is the last place I wish to spend time."

Bella gave a sniff. The carriage turned off the lane and onto the estate through the old wrought iron gateway, and the rhododendron path. "Swallow your resentment, brother, as I am doing, and remember that we're here to see the Wakefields."

"It's still Lucerne's house."

She nodded, for yes, it was. "But it's large enough that none of us need spend a single minute in the same room together, or even the same suite of rooms, if we do not wish it. I pray you will not spend a moment with me."

He raised his brows. Then, sat back again, lips thoughtfully pursed. "I've no aching wish to clash with Lucerne again, and I'd rather not be forced into exchanging pleasantries with that feckless rogue you are inexplicably besotted with. I thought not hearing from him might awaken you to his faults. If it were anyone else, you would be ready to hang, draw and quarter them."

"The temptation to do so to you is rather strong. And while you claim you have no desire to argue with Lucerne, you are certainly determined to have one with me. I am not here seeking conflict, brother. I confess to having been resoundingly angry several days ago when I first learned of your deception, but I've since had time to reflect. The fact is, I can do nothing about it. There may be a very good reason for his actions, one I might have known about if it weren't for yours."

"And when you learn that their renewed friendship comes at the price of your head? Did you consider that maybe I was doing you a favour?"

Irritated, Bella rubbed at her nose. It always grew itchy and tingled whenever she was becoming vexed. Why did Joshua have to make this more of a torment than it was already? She was striving so hard to keep her temper in check, but here he was, nettling her in the way most likely to cause upset. Bella clenched her forearms more tightly, and shook her head. "It won't," she said firmly, relieved to find she sounded more convincing than she felt. "And now stop pointlessly baiting me."

"About the two rogues? Never."

She rolled her eyes up towards the carriage roof, then squashed herself into a corner. This was getting desperately tiresome.

"I note that you are back to referring to Lord Marlinscar by name," he said with a slimy grin.

Why, he had done so himself only a few moments ago.

"It is only the two of us here. Be assured, if I should have the misfortune of having to address him, I'll be entirely appropriate."

"That will be a first." He smiled in response to her scowl. Bella forced herself to relax her jaw, determined to hold onto her hard-won sense of calm for once.

"Pray stop it, Joshua, and don't take it on yourself to bait Vaughan either. I wish to speak to him in a civilized manner, which will be impossible if you have set upon him with your ridiculous demands."

"I don't care to see him treating my only sister like chattel."

"He doesn't. He cares for me, and I for him."

"I ought to call him out."

"No! Heavens, Joshua, swear it to me that you won't ever think of doing something so ridiculous. He would be ruthless... merciless." Not to mention it would entirely wreck the Wakefield sister's farewell party.

Joshua looked down his nose at her, then examined his fingernails. "He's just a man, and like ordinary men, he still bleeds. I suppose it escaped my mind to mention that I punched him in the face a fortnight ago."

"You did what?" She stared at him agog. If the old carriage had not been rocking so alarmingly over the ruts in the road, she would have also been up out of her seat. "And you declare me insane. Tis a miracle you're still breathing. For certain, it is only because you are my brother. What in heaven's name possessed you?"

"It's testament to your own blindness that you even need to ask that question. God's blood, Bella, the man is tupping you. It's more than any brother should have to endure."

"And yet, endure it you will. I'm not giving him up, and nothing you say or do will influence him in any way, so please just avoid him and make no mention of marriage today, you will only cause a scene and spoil everything."

"I will spoil things? I will make a scene?"

"Yes. Please Joshua, let me handle this my own way. I will never forgive you if you destroy what little I have, and I am already exceedingly vexed with you. Much more, and I will leave here, and you will never see me again."

He glowered sullenly, arms folded across his chest in a mirror of her own defensive posture. "Then may I suggest you perfect the art of disappearing into the wainscoting, and avoid continually making a spectacle of yourself?"

"And may I suggest you spend the day talking about greased axles and snuffling pistons with Eliza? That way, we might both arrive home again this evening. Agreed? Good. And never steal my mail from me again." The carriage slowed to a jerky stop. Bella was out of her seat before Lucerne's footman had even opened the carriage door. She shot Joshua a venomous look before plastering on what she hoped was a pleasing expression and descended onto Lauwine's gravel drive.

While it might suit Joshua for her to become some nondescript part of the furnishings, it did not suit her one bit. She was never going to be a wallflower. As it was, she'd been holding back her instincts rather too much of late. While there were reasons for that, she had begun to suspect it had not been the right course of action.

Standing by while the man you loved courted someone else's attention was no sort of action at all. It was a passive surrender.

Well, Lucerne could not have Vaughan—not all to himself. He'd had him nine days, and that was quite enough. She still regretted not battering down the doors to Lucerne's room and making her presence felt earlier, but a fight with Vaughan was not what she was looking for, and dictating to him never worked. Any negotiation would have to be handled most carefully.

Bella hugged herself. Alas, Lucerne wasn't the only topic they needed to discuss.

CHAPTER 29

BELLA

"DID YOU HAVE an issue with your barber, Pennerley?"

A small crowd was gathered upon the lawn at what Bella always considered the rear of Lauwine. It was where the old stonework of the original building melded into the red brick of the later expansion. At one end lay the music room and yellow morning room, and the other deserted rooms she'd only ever glimpsed by peeping through the windows. It was the central room – the grand hall, with its cartwheel candelabrum and minstrel's gallery – that was open to guests today, though few were currently indoors. The late summer sun had drawn everyone outside to partake in the lawn games and idle upon picnic blankets. It was from near one such chequered cloth that the echo of laughter rose.

"Does Marlinscar have mice that savaged you in your sleep?"

"Did you shave using a butter knife?"

It had not been Bella's intention to make a direct beeline towards Vaughan, but rather that they should just naturally happen upon one another at some point during the afternoon, however, the laughter could not help but draw her, as it was drawing others.

She could not see Vaughan at first, for he was at the centre of the little huddle. Bella squeezed between Mr Crakehall and the Garths in order that she might discover the reason for the good-natured jibes. At first glance, he appeared perfectly presented. A snow-white shirt and cravat was topped with a grey brocade waistcoat and a darker charcoal-coloured coat. Silver filigree lent him an air of eccentricity, as did the addition of a slice of lace upon the ends of his cravat. It was around his eyes and jawline that the differences were apparent. His skin was scratched and tender-looking. No amount of white cravat could hide that fact. Also, there were deep shadows below his eyes, which, when combined with their violet luminosity, gave the impression of bruises. She herself had suffered a similar affliction a time or two—the abrasions were the indisputable physical evidence of what her heart already knew. He'd spent days swiving Lucerne. He had severe stubble burn.

"I'm not sure your man even used anything as sharp as a butter knife. Mayhap, he mistook it for a spoon."

More laughter rippled around her, and several of the gentlemen nudged one another. Bella's heart throbbed so hard the pain of it rooted her to the spot. It was unlike Vaughan to weather such mirth at his expense without returning some withering retort, but all he did was smile good naturedly, clearly too filled with happiness for negativity to penetrate the glow of love. Love, not for her, but for Lucerne.

Even when his gaze came to rest upon her, then met hers, there was no change of his expression. No acknowledgement that she might not share his gladness.

"Miss Rushdale. Good morning, if it is still so."

Somebody confirmed it was, by a minute or two.

Vaughan bowed over her hand and kissed her fingertips, while offering her a smile devoid of any deviance or subterfuge. It left her cold inside.

"Is it?" she snapped, all her plans for civility and composure flying from her mind. She'd deluded herself thinking that all would still be well between them, that despite him holing up with Lucerne, his affections for her would remain very much intact.

The truth was that he'd forgotten her entirely.

Without instruction, the crowd that had separated them seemed to melt away. One or two of the menfolk lingered, but after a moment, even they seemed to get the hint and wandered off to join other conversations and occupy different picnic blankets.

"I suppose one need not ask what you have been about," Bella remarked. "As it is written on your face, and several other places besides, I imagine."

Prompted by her words, Vaughan raised a hand to his scuffed jaw, and for a moment an expression of whimsy transformed his features into something near unrecognisable – the man he might have been if he'd been born into a different world, with a different family and different values. "I suppose it is true that my recent indisposition has left me tender in certain places."

Bella scratched a nail through his oddity. "Then you should be grateful that we are in public, my lord, else some of them might hurt rather more." For two particular tender parts might have accidentally collided with her shin.

At once, he was her Vaughan again, eyes ablaze and his lips stretched thin. "Is that so?" He closed the gap between them in one stride, and took hold of her arm just above the elbow. She winced as his fingers bit into the tender flesh. "Walk with me, Bella. It seems there are things on your mind. Things you perhaps might wish to spit out."

Allowing her no option to refuse, he transported her away from the house to where the rolling slope of the lawn gave way to a steeper decline, at the bottom of which rushed the beck, shaded on both banks by a copse of trees. In times past, Bella would have happily tumbled downslope to stroll under the green canopy. A little further along, there was a spot where it was possible to paddle and where dabbled light illuminated all the motes in the air making them sparkle. Presently though, she knew that if they were to stray away from the other guests, Joshua would come after them and the resulting scene would not be pretty. He was glowering at them even now from across the lawn. Hence, she dug in her heels. "Take your hands off me. We can speak perfectly well here."

The remark earned her a huff of disgust. Vaughan released her, making an exaggerated show of it. "Normally you're begging for my touch."

"It's not your touch that's the problem, but what you've been handling."

"Oh, indeed. Is this true vexation, Bella, or are you merely mindful that we are being scrutinized? One must be seen to be conducting oneself as expected. I assume your brother still feels the need to stomp his foot, while all these others merely hope to be at the front row of spectacle."

Bella had not noticed anyone else was paying them heed, but it was obvious now that he had pointed it out. Too many raised fans and cups, too many sly glances cast in their direction, and bodies turned towards them, even though conversations were taking place between neighbours. She turned her back to them. "What manner of spectacle did you have in mind? Me kicking you in the river?"

Lilac flashes licked across Vaughan's irises. His lips curled upwards at the corners. "And it is not apparent to people why I find you so enrapturing. If I take a dip, then you will be swimming with me. I daresay a good dunking might rid you of some of the excess of yellow bile you're exhibiting. "

"If I'm angry, then who is to blame? I thought we did not lie to one another, Vaughan, but you used me. Coaxed me with pretty words, then left my bed, and went straight to his."

"Where is the deception in that? I spelled it all out plainly enough in advance. I told you my intention was to give him a raging cockstand. One assumed it was blatantly apparent one intended to make good use of it."

"And I told you I would not help."

"Ah, Bella," he reached out and drew a finger down the side of her burning cheek. "Is it my fault that you deceive yourself?"

Bella batted his hand away, and took a step back for good measure. "Don't put this on me. You left in the dead of night, with barely a word. I've not heard a thing from you since. What am I expected to think, Vaughan? Am I supposed to believe that those heartfelt whispers you crooned into my ears in the heat of passion were genuine?"

"You should. They were."

"In the way that you've genuinely been ill? I know what sort of indisposition you've suffered."

A smile flashed across his lips. "And is that not an illness, according to the great and good of our society?"

Somehow he could always find a means of twisting things to suit his narrative.

"There was no need to send additional word, for

you knew exactly where to find me, and what I was about."

"Ten days, Vaughan," she growled between teeth clenched so hard her jaw ached. "Ten days. Truly, you were so busy fucking him that you couldn't spend even a moment's thought for me?"

"For pity's sakes woman, keep your voice down. There is far too much attention turned in our direction." He caught hold of her arm again, and this time refused to release his grip until they had reached the bottom of the slope level with the beck. The river idled along beside them grown somnambulant by the lazy summer sun, entirely out of synchronization with Bella's mood. It ought to be raging, swift and fierce as it did when the autumn rains swelled its waters and threatened to burst its banks.

Vaughan spun her to face him. There was heat in his eyes now, but not so much that the radiant glow he'd sported when she'd first come upon him was dimmed. "If you'd wanted us, you'd have come, Bella. I thought maybe you'd come."

Was he truly so dim-witted. "Us! Therein lies the problem. Tis you I want, not him."

Vaughan snorted. "And you brand me a liar."

"I..." She began, but could not force out the words to refute him. Some part of her did want Lucerne – the Lucerne she'd first fallen for, not the man he'd become in London. He'd warned her how it would be before she'd ever set foot there. "London has a strange effect on people. It makes sensible young men do irrational things." After a year away from the place, perhaps he was the man she'd once known again. He'd still stolen her lover away from her, though, and she didn't suppose he meant to hand him back.

Vaughan held her, both hands tight upon her arms

now. "Tell me, my nightingale, did you frig yourself last night imagining the three of us fucking one another?"

How could he know?

"Fever dreams," she spat, exactly as Tilly had said. "Meaningless. It's not like I have any control over my nightmares."

He leaned close, and her heart leapt, craved even as she recoiled. Vaughan raised her hand and brushed his lips against the inside of her wrist. His smile twisted – oh, that smile, and every wicked insinuation it encompassed – it didn't waver, no matter how caustic her scowl. "You do over the waking ones. Say the word, Miss Rushdale, and we'll slip away right now and do everything you imagined. We'll fulfil every, little, dirty, fantastical, fantasy." He punctuated each word with a kiss, moving along her arm to her shoulder, the last one landing to the right of her ear.

Vaughan didn't hold back. He would indeed agree to every sordid fantasy. He'd take her dreams and magnify them, perfect each and every one. But afterwards, when the shadows drew close and the passion burned down to embers, what then? All the troubles that had tormented them in the past would remain, exactly as they did now. She could not brush them aside and pretend they weren't real. She was done treating in passing pleasures. It was imperative she thought long term now, for herself and for...

"We could take you both together. Or hell, just perform for your pleasure."

"No." She shoved him away, and backed up so that the treeline swallowed her. "It's a fantasy. We can't exist inside a dream. I don't want him. I don't forgive him. I can't even fathom why you think it is a good idea. Do you not remember before? We fought Vaughan. All of the time, we fought. Bitterly. Constantly."

Vaughan followed her under the canopy, backed

her against aged oak. "You and I, over Lucerne, yes, but it would not be that way now. By your own confession, you do not love him, or was that another lie? Either way, he's no longer the lynchpin."

She raised her hands. It was a feeble guard against the draw of his body and the fantasies he was spinning. How easy it would be to slip back into that land of make-believe. But, things had changed. She was no longer the same woman who had blithely climbed into a carriage casting reputation and virtue to the wind in order to participate in some grand adventure.

"Instead, Lucerne and I would be forever at odds over you. And while I'm sure that notion delights you, I don't find it the least bit comforting. Curse me for it, but I want more stability than that. I need it. I don't want to live my life forever at war, unsure every time I wake whether you'll still be in my bed or if you've finally grown sick of pretending and admitted to yourself that Lucerne is still your one and only love."

"If he were that, why would I even bother to tempt you? Why would I be here arguing with you now? Why would I have bothered to make sure you knew I'd return? I'm not going to leave you, Bella. I'm not going to wake up and wonder what the hell you are doing in my bed, because I know...I already know exactly why you are there."

It was her turn to laugh. The bitter dry rattle leapt from her throat. "Listen to yourself. Can you not hear the lies? Vaughan, you already did. You already left me. And it was down to Charles Aubury to tell me that you were gone."

"What?"

"I didn't get your note. Joshua burned it."

Anxiety flared within his eyes.

"I have the locket; you need not fret over that." She took it from her pocket and pressed it into his hand.

"Bella, I left Stags Fell. I did not leave you."

"You ensnared that which had been running free, and you forgot me. I'm not interested in being second choice, Vaughan. I want you to love me."

"Which I do." He shook his head so that his dark ringlets stirred against the lapels of his jacket. "Have we not been over this?"

"Me and only me. Not him as well."

He reared away from her, his eyes two dark pools, turbulent with emotions, and his cheekbones drawn into sharp relief by the way in which he sucked in his next breath. "I can't promise you that, Bella. Do not ask it. Do not make me choose between you."

Bella pulled her spencer more tightly around her body. "It seems you have already made that choice."

"I most definitely have not. I desire you both. Bella, you have had me as your own for months. Is it really so unforgiveable that I've given myself to him for ten days? There were things we needed to say, to express that could not be done in front of another, just as there are things between you and I that are not for anyone else's ears. And things that you and he ought to say to one another too."

She heard him, every syllable, but those words were like the beats of a butterfly's wings useless against the iron barricade she'd erected to protect her heart.

In his agitation, Vaughan began to pace. Normally, he was not so easy to unnerve.

"I know that he hurt you," he said, voice softening. "I do understand that. I am not blind to reality. And no matter how ardently you claim to the contrary, I am not the only one who was wounded by his departure.

"It's so much easier to deal with someone else's pain than your own.

"You have felt everything that I have felt during

these months apart, perhaps so more, since I never lost sight of our reconciliation."

"That is not how it was," she insisted.

"Why lie to yourself now, when there is no longer any cause? We can mend this? Bella, if Lucerne had not gone, then my eyes might never have been opened to how much you mean to me. Can we at least agree that in that respect he did us both a service?"

She gave a grudging nod.

"Will you not talk to him? For me, will you not do that?"

"We have spoken. What more is there to say?"

"You say you don't love him, but that is not the truth. He, at least, is willing to admit that his affections for you have never waned. He wants what I want, Bella. Tis only you who is determined to keep us apart. And why? Can you not find some forgiveness in that great heart of yours, instead of perpetuating the pain?"

"It is not fair that you place all the burden of this upon me. I am not the one who left or sought affections elsewhere."

"Georgiana – is that the sticking point?"

She shrugged.

"Hellfire, Bella! It was a mistake, one he owns and has paid dearly for. Lord, you might as well curse me too for swiving de Maresi."

"That was meaningless, and we both know it."

"So the fact that in his case it wasn't makes it unforgiveable?"

She shook her head and pushed Vaughan away. "I don't care one whit about Georgiana St John, or whatever it is about her that made Lucerne act like a spectacular twit. I care about us, and what he will do to us. What he is already doing to us."

Vaughan raised his hand to his brow; fingers spread wide, and sighed in a way that shook his whole body. "You realise he never meant his departure to be permanent? He left so that we could find one another. And we did, hence we came north. That was the entire purpose of us coming here – that we might mend things and start afresh."

"I came north for the christening." Tempting Lucerne back into her bed had never been part of her plan, nor assisting Vaughan in tempting Lucerne into his bed. Not that any tempting had really been required. Lucerne had proved only too willing to prostrate himself. Although, truly, this wasn't anything to do with Lucerne. She simply needed the confirmation that she still resided in Vaughan's heart. Needed it now, when things were changed, needed it, as she had never done before. "Did you even realise that I was genuinely sick?"

Vaughan ceased his pacing, and turned his head to regard her. The scrutiny made her want to raise her hands in order to place a barrier between them. When he looked at her in that way, he always seemed to see into the very heart of her, so that he could pluck out the truth of things, her wants, her needs, her fears. "I'm truly sorry to hear that, Bella. I confess I was not aware of it until after your recovery. Then it did explain much."

"What did it explain?"

He shook his head. "I was surprised when you didn't arrive armed with a pistol and a battering ram. I surmised that you couldn't decide which of us to turn the thing upon first."

"All I am is a source of amusement for you."

"Now you are being absurd." A dark look threaded through his expression. "Stop this, Bella. It is pointless. If you will not speak to Lucerne and at least attempt to resolve your differences, then at least be honest with me and with yourself. You want what I am offering. I know you do, for I know you, just as you know me. It's only fear that's holding you back. You're afraid, but there's no need to be."

"Afraid. Lord... I'm not certain I even know what it is you're offering."

"Myself. Obviously."

A cackle of hysterical laughter forced its way free of her throat. "'Tis more like a ticket for a fixed lottery that you're offering me. You're not giving yourself, only a share."

"You already have me. Haven't I already told you? Must I say it again? I love you, Annabella Rushdale."

Bella raised her hands covering her ears. "Pretty words, but that's all they are. I don't have you, Vaughan. Is there a ring upon my finger? Are we wed? Pledged to one another before God and our families? I'm not even truly your whore, for we have no formal contract, and you discard me from your thoughts as easily as one when it suits. Look at you. Look at us. I am screaming, pleading with you, and you are still smiling inside because you carry him in your heart. You ask me to be honest, well, I say, be honest with yourself. All you ever wanted was Lucerne, and now you have him again. I'm not angry, Vaughan. I'm beside myself. The man I love is standing before me the happiest I have ever seen him, and that happiness has nothing to do with me."

"I am hardly joyous at this moment, and nor am I likely to be if you continue this charade. If we spend just a single night together, I know that we can fix this."

Bella dug her heels into the hard earth. "I... I cannot."

"Bella, please." He scraped his hair back off his face and gripped it tightly, while the heel of his other hand drummed against his furrowed brow. Only once before had she seen him this anguished, when he had cried out to Lucerne and his lover had turned his back and walked away. She was not running, but standing steadfast.

"I can't be with both of you."

"Why?" Vaughan came to her again. For all the world, she wanted nothing more than to swaddle him in her embrace and give in to his every whim, but the last few days had taught her that sometimes you had to step outside the moment and look at things objectively. Situations changed. Things that made sense before could alter and become impossibilities.

"I have told you." She tried to turn away from his gaze. It was too intense; the vestiges of civility stripped away leaving only raw emotion behind.

"No, you have spat bold claims and demands, but you haven't given me a valid reason why you are so determined to reject all that you want, that I want, that Lucerne wants. Why is my love suddenly required to be so absolute? You may have wanted it before, but you've been wise enough never to insist upon it. You know it is not something I can give. Love cannot be curtailed on a whim."

She blinked, her eyes filling up. Her throat was choked up and dry. "I need you to love me."

"Bella, I'm trying to understand. What is behind this? What has been said? Is this even about Lucerne?"

"It's about us. What we are. What we are to become."

"Estranged," suggested a tart feminine voice. Millicent Hayes sashayed her way along the path trailed by her usual entourage of fawning ninnies. "Things not so golden between you anymore? What a pity."

"Go to hell, and help your mother make bitch pie!" Had she been within arm's reach Bella would have struck her simply to wipe the smug grin from her face. As it was, Vaughan pre-empted her instincts and his hand closed fast around her wrist staying any possibility of her lashing out. He inserted himself between her and Millicent. Bella bent his fingers away from her skin, freeing herself. She swept a fierce, angry glance towards Millicent, then up at Vaughan, before turning her back on them both and leaving the copse. Only once free of the trees and part way up the bank did Bella pause to look back. The view was obscured, but sounds travelled, and Millicent's pale dress stood out clear enough between the sprays of foliage. She had her head of pretty curls tossed back, and was baying in a most unbecoming fashion, but then she had always possessed a horrifically horsey laugh. "Seems we've rid you of the trouble of her," she dropped Vaughan a curtsy.

In turn, Vaughan looked down his nose at her. "In the words of the indomitable Miss Rushdale: go to hell."

CHAPTER 30
LUCERNE

L UCERNE COULD NOT settle himself to his duties as host. Usually, it was a role he fell into with little effort, but today, he was far too aware of certain undercurrents and most particularly the ones pertaining to himself and likely to ignite like a barrel of gunpowder. Both Bella and Joshua Rushdale were here, having somehow inveigled their way into his home without being formally announced to him. As such, they had been spared an awkward greeting, but now he was afraid to step outside and join the revellers on the grass for fear of running into either of them.

Joshua would never forgive him his role in Bella's fall from grace – for stealing her away and then abandoning her unto a man who would never marry her. As for Bella, he was certain she had a whole tome full of complaints, the most primary at the moment, undoubtedly his inability to keep his word. He had promised not to break her heart again, and certainly, that was not his intention. However, he could not pretend that stealing Vaughan away from her this last week would be interpreted as anything other than a direct strike against her.

It did not matter that his intention was not to sever her relationship with Vaughan.

The reality was that he wanted her relationship with Vaughan to endure. How else would they fix things between them so that they could genuinely find a means of living harmoniously? His optimism, sadly, didn't extend as far as his lover's—that it would all be fine— but then Vaughan hadn't witnessed the one real encounter Lucerne had had with Bella in recent times. She was not going to magically forgive him his trespasses against her. Rather, he anticipated her skewering him with them every time they were forced to interact.

Lucerne's heart dropped into his stomach, as he spied her from the window. He reached out a hand to the pane as if he might touch her from afar. He missed everything about her: the way she skipped so lightly on her feet; the scent of her hair and the way it tickled his bare skin when their bodies were entwined; also the way she would pluck in frustration at his clothing, despairing over the multitudes of buttons and other fastenings, and most especially the stitches Ivo sometimes placed in his breeches so they sat extra snugly around his backside and hips.

Damn! The path back into Vaughan's affections had been torturous enough, getting Bella to even admit that a spark still existed between them would be like griddling one's arse in hell. He wasn't even sure that Vaughan's normally astute instincts could be relied on in this instance. Mayhap he was too blinded by his own desires, that he couldn't admit the truth that Bella was done with being pulled in two directions at once, and absolutely meant it when she claimed Vaughan was the only man she needed or wanted in her life. Certainly,

Lucerne couldn't construct a valid argument to the contrary. He was no Vaughan. He lacked his wit, his wealth, his beauty, his mesmeric charm, and his finesse in the bedroom. Matter of fact, he was hard pressed to understand what it was Bella had ever found so endearing about him. Of another woman, he might have said his title, but Bella had never really been swayed by such things. He supposed he'd initially been a novelty in a world comprised of people she'd known from birth, but once she'd left that place and glimpsed all the diversions that London had to offer, then he was nothing special any more.

"You were the light to his darkness, the balm with which to weather his rapier wit," her voice seemed to echo to him from the past. "You are not Vaughan, and I never wanted you to be. The contrast between you is a necessity. I love him, but without you to temper his actions... Lucerne, I don't know that I'd survive his excesses without you. Let us not pretend he is perfect. Sometimes his actions are driven by cruelty and nothing else."

"And yet you stayed with him when I was gone."

"I can't be without him. I crave him with my whole being, like some men crave an opium pipe."

Was it any wonder that he'd fallen short of her expectations? In the end, her love for Vaughan had grown so big, she had nothing left to spare for him anymore. He wasn't sure, despite Vaughan's assurances otherwise, that the past ten months had changed that. Being honest, he had nothing new to offer her. Where in the past he'd been her security, now he was merely another blockade to overcome if she was ever to secure a position of permanency in Vaughan's heart.

Maybe what he ought to be doing was petitioning Vaughan to make an honest woman of her.

Too bad his damn heart fell out of his bottom at the

thought. Lucerne glanced down at his feet, almost expecting to see the grisly mass thumping away on the floor. He'd meant to put a ring on her finger.

"Did your man fail to put an adequate shine on them?"

Lucerne raised his head to find Wakefield squinting at him from the other side of the glass.

"What are you doing indoors? Why are you not out here among the guests?" As the upper sash was open, it was easy to hear one another.

Lucerne plastered on a smile. "I was just on my way out to do so." He made a move towards the nearby open door, only for Wakefield to wave him back to the window. "Actually, I was hoping to catch you alone for a moment. That's if you can spare a minute?"

He had no reason to hurry, and every reason to avoid mingling. A shrug therefore seemed the best answer.

"I'll come in to you." Wakefield made a hand gesture towards the doorway Lucerne had been about to use.

Lucerne's gaze strayed across the lawn again as he waited for Wakefield to join him. The huddle that had minutes ago surrounded Vaughan had dispersed and now, his lover was engaged with a single figure. Tension immediately caused his fingers to curl. He watched as the pair headed down slope together towards the beck. It was interesting how people's perceptions had changed. Ever since the christening, he'd noticed there was a certain degree of sympathy being cast in his direction. Instead of being the villain who had debauched a formerly respectable member of the parish, he'd been transformed into a wronged party. The shame and the majority of the ill words were now being cast in Bella's direction.

"What an outrageous madam to jilt him!"

"Well, she always was a wild one."

"The poor lamb–" him "–must have been distraught."

"I expect it's for the best. It's obvious she wasn't a suitable choice. She'd have made him a very poor viscountess."

"Very poor..."

What followed was inevitably a soliloquy about the virtues of the speaker's own daughter or niece, and their suitability to be his betrothed. There was rarely any acknowledgement of Vaughan's part in the proceedings. Somehow being a notorious scoundrel precluded one from everyone's wroth, or perhaps it was simply his title and reputation for retaliation that stilled the wagging tongues. None of them fancied making an enemy of him, leastways, not while he was young, wealthy, and free of matrimonial shackles. Any one of them would sell their daughters to him at the drop of a hat.

"She married a marquis, you know."

A claim such as that could bolster ones family's reputation for generations.

Wakefield finally arrived at his side, and Lucerne was forced to turn away from the window.

"Heavens, you look frightfully serious. What is it? Is there some issue with your daughter?" A nervous twitch was playing in the side of his friend's jaw.

A brief expression of panic swept Wakefield's face, before he shrugged it off. "No, my daughter's fine. She's with the nursemaid, and her aunt Joanna."

"Of course."

"If I look serious, I guess it's down to what I wish to discuss."

"I see. Well, go ahead, what is it?"

"There are two things, actually."

Lucerne had been anticipating this particular

outburst from the moment Wakefield had returned from Stags Fell and found Vaughan present at Lauwine. This was the first opportunity that had presented itself for his friend to address the topic.

"I cannot believe you have let him into your life again so easily. Lucerne, after all that he has done – tis madness."

"Perhaps," he replied as softly as he was able. "You may brand me a fool for it, but I did miss his company."

That perhaps was not as tactful a statement as he might have made, for Wakefield drew back his shoulders and puffed out his chest as if he'd been dealt a personal affront. Vaughan was required to provide stimulation, as he, Frederick Wakefield, had failed in the task.

"Also, what point is there in holding a grudge? He and Bella—"

Wakefield grasped his forearm. "He stole her from under your nose."

Lucerne shook his head, and brushed off Wakefield's hold upon his coat sleeve.

"That is neither accurate nor fair. Perhaps I have been overly circumspect with the details. Bella had more than justifiable reasons for leaving me. There was another woman."

"What?" Wakefield's brows near hit the ceiling. Charles, who had entered the room at the far end, shot an interested glance in their direction. "And to think of all the lectures you gave me on such idiocy. Such foolishness almost cost me Louisa. Do you not recall? And, Bella, she is not... she is not the meek, forgiving sort."

"Then you can understand why she might go about finding a means of punishing me."

"Tis still a savage blow to throw you over for that

bastard Pennerley. And also, no justification for his forgiveness."

"Perhaps not," Lucerne mused. This was familiar territory. Wakefield had long turned a particularly steadfast blind eye to the intricacies of Lucerne's relationship with Vaughan, and he was not about to alienate an old and much valued friend by forcing him to acknowledge the truth.

"What you're failing to recognise is that what started out as nothing has grown into something between them. It would be quite wrong of me not to wish them happiness together."

"Hm! Well, it's a funny sort of something if you ask me. He's taken her as his mistress – the man has had many – and not to wife. Unless you are suggesting such a proposal is imminent?"

He was not. Vaughan had long held the opinion that marriage was not for him. His sister's sons would inherit. Also, Vaughan had had far fewer mistresses than most presumed. Indeed, far fewer relationships of any kind.

"I thought not. It seems plain enough that Pennerley is simply taking advantage of her, which if you still care about her, begs the question why you would renew your association with him."

There was no way to win the argument without disabusing Wakefield of his blindness. Luckily, Charles stepped in.

"I think there's been liberties taken on both parts. They are well made for one another, and Lucerne must choose for himself whom it is best he associates with. You may not like Pennerley, Captain, but only an outright fool would counsel maintaining a grudge with such a powerful man."

Wakefield cast Charles the sort of venomous look that generally preceded a blow to the jaw. Lucerne inserted himself between them, but with his head turned in Wakefield's direction. "Perhaps, Freddy, we had each best keep our own counsel on the subject. You may consider me an idiot if you please, even a particularly profound one, but your words are not going to sway my opinion. We should therefore let this matter drop." He waited a few moments, before adding, "Agreed?"

The question garnered him a glower, but eventually also a nod of the head.

"What was the second matter?" Lucerne asked. Hopefully, it could be dealt with as swiftly as the first. He did not want to hang back and leave Bella and Vaughan alone too long. While Vaughan had hopefully paved the way to a discussion between the three of them about future arrangements, Lucerne realised the true bridge building would only occur through he and Bella interacting on a personal basis. He would grovel on hands and knees before her, if he had to, in order to secure a second chance.

"Tis a private concern." Wakefield made shooing motions towards Charles, who parted with a huff, but went only as far as the drinks cabinet.

Wakefield threw a sour look at his back, but he could hardly order Charles from the room, and Lucerne felt no inclination to do so. Perhaps it was a sort of premonition, but he suspected having the other man within earshot might prove beneficial somehow.

"Go ahead, Freddy. There's obviously something weighing on you."

"You're right. It has been on my mind a lot of late, and particularly now that my sisters are on the verge of departing."

"How quiet it will be without them," Lucerne remarked absently, his attention drawn back to the world outside the window by Bella's reappearance on the lawn. She paused at the breast of the hill and glanced swiftly back before setting off again towards the front of the building. A deep frown etched her oval face.

Clearly all was not well.

"What it got me wondering in particular, was how long you thought to make that absence."

"What's that?" Lucerne glanced at Freddy. Had Wakefield some notion of inviting them back here again, maybe at Christmastide? He had no overt objections to the idea. Although, he had his fingers crossed that he would be someplace cosy with Vaughan and Bella, doing wicked things involving holly and mistletoe and figgy-pudding and brandy cream.

"What I'm saying is that it's been wholly marvellous watching you emerge from your hermitage, and I think we both know the cause. It's been quite impossible not to notice how changed you are. How much happier you are."

Had they not just agreed to their differences of opinion regarding this matter?

"I know I should bite my tongue until you find your nerve and all, but we're old friends, Lucerne. I thought as she's away so soon, now was the moment to—"

Lucerne held up his hand. "I'm sorry, you've lost me. What—who is it we're talking about?"

"Why Caroline, of course."

"Of course," Lucerne echoed, still utterly confounded. "No. Actually, not of course. I feel I have most definitely missed something."

Now Wakefield appeared deuced confounded too. "I've seen you together. It's been quite apparent how well you get along, and I understand this last week she has been nursing you. It's quite wrong, of course, that you should have ended up unchaperoned here together, but—"

"What in the blazes are you accusing me of?"

"I'm not."

Agitated, Lucerne reared onto his heels. "I see." Only, he didn't. "You're entirely mistaken about her nursing me." The closest she had come to his bedside was the doorway to his suite, when on two occasions she had thought to enquire after his well-being. Eliza had spoon fed him some medicine the last couple of days. She'd been mightily concerned about the croak in his throat, much to Vaughan's endless amusement. But then that rapscallion knew exactly how the soreness had come about. "Also, we were never here alone."

Why did he feel so cornered? It took a glance over his shoulder to assure him that he wasn't hemmed in.

"Caroline is so immensely fond of you, and naturally I couldn't be happier at the thought of joining our families."

Wakefield wasn't hearing him and this was now getting altogether out of hand. "Freddy. Your sister...! She's delightful, bu—"

"There we go." His friend beamed at him from ear to ear, and patted him in much the way one might a clever dog. "You absolutely have my consent to speak to her."

Oh God! "Now hold on a moment," he countered. "What I was in fact saying was that as lovely a woman as your sister is, I'm not in the market for a wife. I don't know what impression has led you to believe I have designs upon Caroline, but let me disabuse you of the notion. There is no affection, no attachment there. None."

It was Wakefield's turn to sway off balance. "Oh!" He pulled his chin back towards his body, causing the surrounding skin to concertina. "But I've seen the change in you since her arrival."

"It ain't her presence that's perked him up," Charles remarked from across the room. The sound easily carried. Damned, he had known Charles's befuddlement over the kiss he'd witnessed wouldn't last. Clearly he'd put two and two together and made sex... six... whatever. Lucerne glared at him, hoping that would be enough to deliver his silence. What it in fact accomplished was to draw Charles back over to them. "Can't you damned see? It's mine. He's been singing like a lark ever since I arrived." He clapped Lucerne soundly upon the back. "It's the billiards and brandy that's done it." He added a wink and an elbow bump as if the first slap hadn't been signal enough for Lucerne to play along.

"Indeed, both have been truly cathartic."

He wasn't convinced that Wakefield believed a word of it.

"Although, it's not all been down to Charles. It's as you've said many, many times. I needed to get out more, engage with people, and that's exactly what I've been doing."

"I have been saying that for the longest time," Wakefield admitted. "You've been deuced stubborn about it. I was saying it as far back as last Christmas, do you recall?"

"Absolutely, and you were right. So, you see, it's not some tendresse for your sister that's changed me, it's—"

"Everything else," Charles finished for him. "Behold, the Marlinscar butterfly emerged from its cocoon."

"I hardly think the transformation has been that dramatic," he remarked caustically. Charles was prone to take things to extremes. He was frightfully glad of his assistance though. "Anyway, I'm dreadfully sorry about the mix up, Freddy. I do think all of your sisters are delightful, and I'm certain they will find their matches, but I can't pretend that Caroline and I are a perfect fit. She deserves a man who loves her, don't you think?"

"Love could grow. It could happen," Wakefield huffed. He was struggling to keep the dejection off his face.

"It wouldn't be fair to ask such a thing. Imagine if it never came to pass. That would be..." It would be most society marriages. "It would be a resounding shame. No, you must find a man for her who is besotted by her very person."

"As I suppose you mean to tell me you still are with someone else."

Lucerne bowed his head and ran his fingers along the window ledge. "I'd be lying if I claimed my feelings for a certain lady were shrivelled."

"Yet minutes ago you were telling me that you see no sense in holding a grudge because Miss Rushdale and Lord Pennerley clearly share a heartfelt bond."

"I was, and I stand by it. However, it doesn't mean my feelings towards her are changed. If anything, it means that I appreciate more keenly what it is they have found together, and that it should be celebrated, not held against them."

"You're turning down my sister in order to moon over a woman you know you cannot have? Have you lost your mind? I thought you hoped for a family of your own."

He nodded almost imperceptibly. "It's lunacy, I realise, but it is what it is. Now, if you'll both excuse me, gentlemen, there's something to which I should attend."

CHAPTER 31

VAUGHAN

WHAT IN THE devil had got into her?

Vaughan pursued Bella out of the woodland and across the lawn. She led him on a very merry dance, through the formal gardens to the front of the hall, passing in and out of the maze. He had thought briefly that she meant to take refuge in the little oriental-styled building at the centre, but the leafy pathways were proving too great an attraction for Lucerne's other guests. Then, he had lost sight of her for a minute or two before he spied her sneaking into the drawing room through the door that opened onto the courtyard.

Naturally, he'd expected some measure of vexation. Bella, like him, was a creature of passions. Her anger, however, normally flared hot and then died back just as quickly, particularly when she knew that what was offered was truly a thing she desired.

He accepted that perhaps her passion for Lucerne was not as acute as his, but she still craved what the three of them had once shared. She dreamed of their bodies entwined. Her mind wove images of her watching him with Lucerne. The interactions between them had always fascinated her, and of course, she took tremendous pleasure in being filled by both of them at once. Something though, was causing her to resist that which ought to be pulling them together. What was it though, he couldn't quite determine. Not, he believed, her brother's scowling disapproval, which had existed for so long now it was barely worthy of note. Rather, there was some new concern behind this reluctance.

The drawing room stood empty. Vaughan passed through to Lucerne's grand chamber. He stood in the centre of the space and turned a slow circle. Now where had she skipped off to? He was about to head in the direction of the yellow morning room, when a noise caused him to about turn and pass into the guard room instead. No doubt the room had a more formal name, but sported twin sets of mediaeval mail and plate armour, hence his designation. It was also where Lucerne's hounds could often be found lounging before the impressive stone hearth. No fire burned there today. Instead, candles lit the dingy space, which appeared to have been fashioned into a sort of retiring room. The far end of the space had been sectioned off with the aid of several carved wooden screens.

"Bella?"

A scrape accompanied a swish of fabric across wooden boards. "Vaughan? Damn, you should not be in here."

When had that ever kept him from anywhere?

"Do not come round, I'm—"

Too late, he was already in motion.

"—indisposed." She swore furiously at him, before rising from her squat position over the chamber pot to launch a nearby ornament at his head. Thankfully, he had wits and speed enough to move out of its trajectory. It whistled past his ear and struck one of the suit of arms with a clang like a dinner gong. "Can't a lady get any privacy anymore? What is so urgent that it necessitates you barging in on me while I'm—"

"Pissing," he helpfully suggested.

"—about my toilette," she retorted, voice shrill with overstated hauteur.

The two things were one and the same, so her tone was unnecessary. Also, he didn't know why she was making such a fuss. It was perfectly usual for folks to relieve themselves just out of sight, while maintaining the conversation they were engaged with at the dinner table. As a matter of fact, he'd also seen her relieving herself before. What stopped him from reminding her of those facts were the fresh tear streaks drying upon her cheeks. They stood out like silvery rivers as she turned her head to stare at him. Bella rubbed defiantly at them with the back of her hand when she realised upon what his gaze had fastened.

"What the devil do you want? Stop gawping at me like I'm a morsel you're about to chew."

Too many times, he'd chosen not to delve into the emotions of their relationship. Tensions between them inevitably played out the same way – snarled insults and breathless sex. He reserved the deep emotional connections for when he was alone with Lucerne.

"Our conversation was interrupted. It was not done."

She sniffed dismissively. "It was done. There is nothing more to say. You wish me to accept your lover as my lover, and I don't wish to. Nor do I care to be cajoled or persuaded to do so."

"I believe it was the why of the matter that we were stuck upon."

"And I believe I was perfectly clear upon that point. Not that the reason should matter, only that I have one. I won't be forced into this, Vaughan." She took a shuddering breath. "If you wish to excite yourself with Lucerne, then that is your prerogative. I cannot, and will not attempt to stop you, but I cannot be part of it, and I do not know that I can be part of your life either, if that is your choice."

Heavens above, she had worked herself into a tremendous state. "What madness are you speaking?" He moved towards her, only for Bella to hastily put the chamber pot between them. "Are you saying you will leave me, if I continue to associate myself with Lucerne?"

She turned away from him, refusing to make eye contact. Her shoulders lifted into a shrug.

"I can't stay in Yorkshire any longer, Vaughan. There are too many complications. It's all too awkward and infuriating."

There was more, he was sure, but not that she was willing to give voice to. In truth, what she'd just outlined was enough. Her brother had stifled both her freedom and fancy, while the local gentry poked at her soft underbelly in ways the harridans of London society never managed.

"So, it is Yorkshire you proposed to leave, and not I?" He stepped over the china potty in order to close the gap between them. "Where is it you intend to go?"

The question was met only with silence. "Bella?" He wrapped his arms around her from behind, and pulled her against his body.

"Pennerley?" she murmured, voice laced with tremulous hope.

"And if I were to invite Lucerne to join us there?"

She stiffened at once, then rested her head against his shoulder and sighed. "Why must you love him so much?"

He bent to her, tracing his lips across her cheek and then the side of her throat. "Why does it matter that I do? It doesn't alter how I feel about you. Have I not explicitly told you that I love you just as much?"

Her eyelids fluttered closed. "Tis hard to have faith, in light of your actions."

Only because she was so determined to close herself off from Lucerne. "I am here with you now. What do you need from me, Bella? I cannot carve him out of my life, but I will split myself into two parts if that's what it will take."

She turned in his arms. "Engaging in two separate love affairs is not what you want."

He could not agree more. "Life rarely gives us what we want. One simply has to make the best of what one can get, and always strive towards obtaining something better."

Her body quivered as she gently nodded her head.

"Why not let me worry about how I will organise myself in order to keep the pair of you happy?"

She nodded, but the lingering air of sadness clinging to her didn't disperse.

"Vaughan, I am so dreadfully unhappy. I wish I were not. I wish we were at the beginning of this again, and not at the end."

"What riddles you weave today." He pressed a kiss to her brow. "We are not at the end of anything. You are here in my arms, and I'm not letting you go. I don't know what fear it is that has you so deep in its thrall, but whatever it is won't change us."

"I think perhaps it already has." Fresh tears welled in her eyes. "I won't ask you to give him up. I won't ever ask it. I know... I know how deep your love for him is. But, I don't know that it's possible for us to be as we were anymore. Things are changed, Vaughan."

"For the better," he insisted. "We all understand one another better now. Our motives are clearer, to ourselves and to one another." Leastways, that was true of himself, and Lucerne. Clearly there was much still on Bella's mind that required unravelling. "I'm not letting you go." He kissed her brow, and her eyelids. Then the tracks of her tears as they rolled in heavy droplets over her cheeks and towards her mouth. Gently, he teased her lips apart with his tongue.

Bella clove to his body, feeding upon his mouth with increasing ferocity. It was as if she had forgotten his taste, or meant to commit it to memory, as if she envisaged this moment as one of farewell. "Make love to me, Vaughan."

"Here and now, where anyone might stumble upon us?" He wasn't concerned for himself, but if they were seen there would be no question of her remaining in Yorkshire, not unless he bowed down on one knee. He had to wonder if that wasn't her plan; if her brother wouldn't promptly arrive and demand satisfaction of one sort or another.

"Everyone is outside, and if by some happenstance someone was to venture indoors, then we would hear them coming long before they arrived."

"We could just as easily go upstairs." There were rooms aplenty they might make use of.

She shook her head. "This is far more us, don't you think?"

He couldn't disagree. Their early relationship had been composed entirely of such illicit moments.

"Please, Vaughan. I do so need your touch. I've burned for you, this past week. It has been an effort not to think of you and touch myself." She knew just how to reel him. Hence, he edged her deeper into the corner.

"I think you were perhaps enjoying denying yourself what you knew you could have had if you were only willing to cross a few fields in order to claim it."

The colour that licked across her cheeks seemed to confirm as much.

"The thrill is so much sweeter, when one denies oneself?"

He could not help wondering if that's what she was doing, in denying that she felt anything for Lucerne. He himself had initially held Lucerne at bay for much the same reason. A little suffering made the eventual capitulation so much sweeter. Perverse, perhaps, but he knew his tastes ran counter to normality.

"If I had come upon you and Lucerne, what would you have done?" she asked.

Vaughan responded with a smile. "Why squeezed you in between us, of course, so that we might all tumble together? And we would not have worried who touched who, for all things would have been equal."

"I wish I could believe that with the same conviction you claim it."

As did he. "You should, for it could be like that, Bella. It was never Lucerne who struggled with sharing himself, only we two with sharing him. And—" He cupped the side of her face. "—with admitting how much we desired one another."

"I believe I was more honest than you on that score." She shot him a glance out of the corner of her eye that reminded him of what a glorious romp she could be. Her mouth had curved upwards at the corners again too, but a melancholy shadow remained within her eyes.

"So, about that fuck you were offering me," he said in order to provoke a reaction.

"Oh, you!" she huffed, and shoved him with both hands. "Does any other thought ever pass through your head?"

"Not often." Vaughan captured her hands and pulled her with him. They staggered together, narrowly missing upsetting the chamber pot, hands and mouths upon one another, until his back thumped against one wooden screen, and threatened to topple it. They reversed their position, so that they were braced against the wall. Then, all that mattered was how fast they could claw the clothing from one another's backs.

Off came her spencer and his coat and cravat. Her hands were inside his waistcoat trying to find a way underneath his shirt, while he plucked the pins from the bib-front of her dress. Each sliver of metal, he flicked into the air, where they spun amidst the dust motes before pinging against the stone floor.

"They'll be impossible to find again."

"I'm certain you're not short of pin money."

"That won't help me out when I have to venture out from behind this screen."

"I don't mind holding you in place," he teased, scooping her breasts into his hands and pushing them together so that they were perfectly framed. If they could keep this light-hearted banter up, maybe it could keep all the demons at bay. "Mmm, in the words of our dear friend, Mr Aubury, "You have the most glorious tits in existence."

"Vaughan," she screeched, only to hush herself while he buried his head in her cleavage and then groaned deliriously as he teased her nipples.

"You know what needs to happen now, don't you," he said, after a moment or two of rapturous exploration.

Bella stuck her chin in the air. "I'm sure I can't imagine."

He was quite certain she could.

"Chair." He pointed her towards a broad, gilt-edged monstrosity, with golden clawed feet, covered in rose-coloured floral patterned damask. It was no wonder it was lurking in a corner; it was hideous beyond reckoning. Whoever was responsible ought to be made to suffer for it. It was, however, of an incredibly convenient height. "Skirts up, legs wide, sit."

"And if I don't want to?" she remarked archly.

"Then I'll save this for Lucerne." He got his cock out, at which point her eyes lit, and all trace of contrariness vanished from her face. Instead, her tongue peeped out and wet her plump lower lip. Damn, if she didn't render him grotesquely horny with her lascivious display of flesh and eagerness.

"I don't think I should let him have all the fun."

"Quite," he agreed, pleased to see that she'd obeyed his instructions to the letter, and that she was at least contemplating the notion of allowing Lucerne some of the fun. Damn! If she wasn't driving all the contention from her own mind, then she was certainly driving it from his.

A pearl-like bead of precome already glistened at the tip of his cock as he angled it towards her body. Then, taking one breast in each hand, he moulded her cleavage around his shaft. Heaven could definitely be found wedged between the mounds of a generous bosom.

"When I said make love to me, this is not what I envisaged."

"No?" he sighed, innocently. "But you weren't very particular with your request. You know, you rarely, if ever, are."

"Beast," she cursed as he shifted back and forth within the pillowy prison. He tried to slow things down, stretch out the torment, but it was just too good. Before very long he was painting her a pearlescent necklace.

Bella snarled and ground her teeth as Vaughan stood back to admire his work. Of all the vexatious things he liked to do, purely to torment her, this numbered among those she found most infuriating. Not that she ever stopped him. Not once.

It was almost as if she took pleasure in bemoaning his barbarity.

"Are you furious now?"

Her eyes narrowed, and she scowled at him. "I'd have every right to be. It's such a horrid thing to do."

"Curious," he lifted his brows. "I find it utterly delightful." He held her challenging stare a moment.

"You would, but it hardly affords me pleasure having you rut against me like that. You may as well grind yourself against a pillow."

"Ah, but then you would miss out on your reward for your patience."

She considered, with a smart tilt of her head. "What manner of reward?"

"The best kind. One you've striven for. That you've had to work hard for... One that makes you sing like a nightingale, and then caw as if you're about to breath your last. And you know, Miss Rushdale, when it is that you experience this most desirous of states?"

She met his gaze and held it but didn't interrupt him with a reply, choosing to allow him to enlighten her instead.

"It's not when I drive between your thighs. It's when I bow down and worship you with lips and tongue."

The tiniest trace of a smile illuminated her face, which she vanquished immediately. "I can't see that there's much in the way of worship occurring here presently."

That was his prompt, and he was ready.

Her cry lengthened into a string of gasps.

"That's right, my sweet. Sing for me."

She shook her head, as if she wished to deny him the knowledge that he was pleasing her. Alas for her, he knew her well. Knew exactly how to make her rage and spit, but also how to make her heart race as though there were a little bird trapped within her chest and desperate to escape.

He'd known many lovers over the years, but none other than Lucerne with whom he'd ever formed so painfully delightful a connection as he had with her. Somehow, from their first interactions, they'd forged the sort of bond that many would claim was pre-ordained. The fact they'd both fought it for so long was what had made it most excruciating. "But love is blind, and lovers cannot see the pretty follies that themselves commit."

He found a curious sense of harmony wash over him as her thighs began to quiver, and her breathing became more raw. It grew more pronounced as he exalted in the sensations of her release. Bella's body pulsed and became liquid against his tongue. That taste – it was a miracle he wasn't permanently on his knees. Although, moving forward, with both her and Lucerne to keep content, perhaps he often would be.

Spent, Bella reclined on her gaudy throne, skirts and limbs akimbo, thoroughly dishevelled. Although momentarily sated, he knew he'd not given her enough. Past times, this was where Lucerne stepped in. He glanced around, thinking it a pity he wasn't around to do so. The pair of them needed to admit that they still felt deeply for one another, and that it wasn't a problem. It didn't detract from how they felt about him.

"Vaughan?"

Right now it seemed she needed the reassurance that he belonged to her in the way he claimed he did. That he had not wholly given himself up to Lucerne, but had all the heart he needed to satisfy them both.

"Vaughan," she hummed. This time reaching for him.

"Hold that thought," he said, rising in order to fetch something. He returned momentarily, holding a candle. He did not explain the acquisition, merely watched her gaze follow the flame, as he once again knelt before her. The scent of beeswax grew thick in the air between them.

"Why can you never just give yourself?"

"That's not who we are, Bella. If all we had ever done these years was fuck one another as others do, then we would have tired of one another long ago. You know as well as I that is the truth."

"Perhaps," she mouthed after a moment's thought.

One brow cocked, he murmured, "Indulge me."

"If you'll do the same."

"Does watching me stroke my cock excite you?"

"It gets you hard. That excites me." There was an implication behind her words that she didn't expect to experience such things again, which almost convinced him to button up. However, she reached for the candle.

Puff—he extinguished the flame, whereupon, her pupils grew huge, as he placed the still warm shaft firmly into her hands. It wasn't as if he needed to say anything. They both knew what came next, and how much pleasure he'd get from watching her frig herself, and how much pleasure she'd derive from giving in to the dirtiest of deeds.

Giving in was exactly what she was doing. He just wasn't certain what exactly he was giving in to.

Fate?

The opinions of what that might mean had never seemed so divergent.

This wasn't going to be the last time. If she had learned nothing else about him over this last year together, surely she had learned that he did not let go of those he valued, he only allowed them to stretch the leash from time to time.

He watched her closely, noting the way she didn't shy from watching him, or from pleasuring herself fully.

He'd known professional whores who were less willing to debauch themselves than her. But wasn't the fact that she didn't shy from the perverse one of the reasons he admired her so? They'd engaged in the sort of lewdity together that others would have fainted at the mere suggestion of. And, of course, the best of times were had when Lucerne was around to torment together.

In no time at all, he wanted to rut like a ram with her. One of these days... one of these days he was going to completely lose his head in her presence. Meanwhile, he regretted extinguishing the candle flame, and the lost opportunity to introduce her to the sensations of hot wax dripped upon sensitive places. That at least would have bought him some time.

Time for what?

To rail himself in, so that she couldn't see how ardently she affected him? Weren't they past that?

He could pretend his delaying tactics were geared towards extending her pleasure, but he preferred to avoid lying to himself.

"I'm afraid I've rendered this candle quite unusable," she remarked. "I'm sure our host will be frightfully appalled."

"His housekeeper, maybe. The only thing Lucerne is likely to be appalled at is that he was not here to witness the act that rendered it so bent."

She dug her teeth into her lower lip, but the motion of her hand didn't stop.

"He still wants you as I want you, Bella. Isn't there part of you that longs for him to walk in right now? To see us? To join us?"

She gave a grunt in response, then added, "Don't be absurd." But her words did not match her expression. He witnessed the flick of her gaze, seeking the other man out. He heard the disappointed catch of her breath, too, on failing to find him.

Vaughan left off stroking himself and leaned in to suck upon the tender flesh of her inner thigh. "You wouldn't be reduced to bending candles out of shape if he were present. You know Lucerne has never shied from providing."

"Unlike you. You're as stiff as a poker, so why don't you poke me?" She cast the misshapen candle aside. Then, peeped at him from under her eyelashes and in a syrupy voice added, "I know you want to."

Vaughan sucked harder, distracting himself from the sort of madness she infected him with, but there was no distancing himself from the cry she made as he marked her. The bruise rose livid immediately. He drew his tongue across it, leaving her skin wet, and turned to her other thigh. Lord, how it made her squirm. It didn't, alas, stop her from making demands upon him, only succeeded in making her pleas more fervent.

"Vaughan... If I'm yours... If you genuinely love me as you do him... Fuck me. Fuck me as you fuck him."

"Your brother would wash your mouth out if he could hear you."

"Fuck me," she demanded again, this time louder. Loud enough that anyone passing through the grand chamber would surely have heard her, and definitely loud enough for the shadow he'd spied upon the stairs to have heard. "Fuck me, Vaughan. Prove that you're not just wild about Lucerne."

Goddammit! She'd have every damn guest running in this direction if she became any shriller. He put his hand over her mouth, but she bent back his fingers. Really, there was only one solution, to do as she bid.

Vaughan grasped her around the waist and flipped her over, so that she was bent near double before him, head down towards the chair, then filled her with one satisfying thrust.

"Yes!" She moved against him, ensuring he got deeper... and deeper. It was going to be fast. Sod finesse. This was about satisfying an itch that just wouldn't ever go away. One that had been burning in his brain since the first moment Lucerne's head had turned in her direction. He'd known she was different, that she spelled trouble, but all his efforts to direct them along a different pathway had failed. Maybe he'd always known it would come to this.

He shook his head, refusing to capitulate.

Ha—there he was lying to himself. Capitulating, was exactly what he'd done. He was screwing her bare, exactly as she'd begged him to, and goddammit, he was going to spend like an artillery blast inside her and worry about it afterwards.

Bella was clinging to the chair now, her fingers curled into the damask, while her nose was pushed into the cushion.

"Vaughan. Oh, God! Oh, God! Vaughan." she continued to blaspheme and cry out his name as they both snarled and sobbed their way to concurrent crises. He came as her muscles fluttered around him, milking him like a succubus until he had nothing left. Barely even the capacity to stand. He flopped over her bent form, cradling her body close. "I love you," he whispered, while easing himself gently from her body. "Goddamn me, but I love you."

That shadow was now regarding them from the bottom of the stairs. Vaughan buttoned himself up. He helped Bella to stand. He knew the moment she registered their observer, even though the only contact between them was where their palms touched.

"Lucerne!"

And there it was, the moment of contentment shattered all to pieces by a single name.

CHAPTER 32
VAUGHAN

B ELLA REARED BACK, head high despite her state of undress. "Can't you see this was a private moment?"

He wasn't fooled by her frigid tone, recognising it as the mask it was to protect her bruised and battered heart. Why couldn't she see that forgiving Lucerne, and forgiving herself was the only way in which things would heal?

"I think you've forgotten where you are," Lucerne retorted. "You are on my property."

Obviously, he referred to Lauwine. Only, the catch in his voice gave the impression otherwise. Shit! What he didn't need was them both getting possessive and spitting fury. That was entirely the wrong way to negotiate a reconciliation.

Bella fumbled with her dress front, which refused to stay in place without the multitude of pins that lay scattered across the floor. Irritably, she bent to collect them. "I've not forgotten anything. Not. A. Thing."

"Curious, I find your memory is rather selective. It's only the bad you recall, none of the good. I admit I made mistakes, but one bad call should not annihilate years of pleasures shared."

No, Lucerne, he wanted to say. You need to allow Bella her rage; give her the opportunity to vent all the resentment she's clinging to. However, it'd be self-defeating to say it aloud. Instead, he knelt to help collect up her pins.

"I can manage," she snapped at him. "It's your fault that they're scattered everywhere."

"That is why I'm helping to pick them up."

"My comfort isn't generally your concern. If it was, you wouldn't..." her gaze flicked to Lucerne. "... with him."

Damn, now she was on the offensive with both of them, and her irritation was riling him. Her comfort had loomed rather large in his life these last few months.

"I suppose you knew he was there watching us."

"Not exactly."

"Damnation!" She pounded her fist against the floor, which bounced the pins in all directions.

Lucerne joined them on hands and knees. He gathered several of the pins in his palm and held them out to her.

Head bowed, Bella studiously ignored the offer, instead excavating one that had fallen into a crevice.

"You were looking for him yourself in the moment."

That, at least, she didn't refute.

"Bella, please," Lucerne sighed. "This is ridiculous. I'm sorry I intruded on your moment. It is purely by chance that I was coming down the stairs. I had to change my shirt. Leesa knocked into me, and I spilled claret down it."

Leesa – Wakefield's brat. What the devil was she even doing at large while there were guests about?

Bella studiously ignored the explanation, forcing

Lucerne to pass the gathered pins to him, so that he could pass them on. "Thank you... Thank you..." She accepted them one by one, taking the time to jab the ruthless little spikes through her dress front, until she was once more perfectly attired.

They stood, more or less, in time with one another. He and Lucerne opposite one another and Bella forming the third tip of their triangle.

"I never intended to take him away from you, Bella." Lucerne began, voice noticeably wavering. "Our leaving Stags Fell was entirely un—"

She cut him off with the swift slash of her hand through the air. Smack! Her palm struck his cheek. "I don't have anything to say to you. I don't even want to look at you, or listen to you. I'm only here because of the Wakefields. Every promise you've ever made me, you've reneged upon. 'I won't take him from you, Bella,' but you did at the first opportunity. 'I'll stay with you always.' Do you recall making that promise too? Let's see, 'I'll always be here for you.' That's another, and don't even think to tell me that you love me. You don't love me at all. I'm not even sure you love Vaughan, only yourself. If it were otherwise, then we would not be in this position now. Once, we had something unique and special, but it is lost because of you."

"I know, and I am deeply sorry for it." Lucerne took a step towards her, but that only made her back towards Vaughan.

"Bella, it doesn't have to be this way. We can forge things anew," Vaughan insisted. "You know it yourself, why the devil will you not just admit it? At least half of what you're cross for now is that he stood back and didn't join in, not that he saw us. The rest is down to old wounds that will not heal because you refuse to let them. You hate him because he left, and now you hate him because he wishes to return. It's nonsensical. You want him to care for you, and he does."

"I do," Lucerne insisted.

"Admit there's part of your heart that still belongs to him." Vaughan rested a hand upon her arm. "It's all right for you to do that, Bella. I know that it does not mean you love me any less."

For a moment, he thought that she would succumb to his plea. He stood poised ready to catch her between them when her body crumpled with the relief of admission, but she buttoned her mouth up tight and folded her arms across her bosom.

Damn her pig-headed obstinacy.

"We'll give you a moment," he said, startling both her and Lucerne. "It's obvious you need a minute or two to think it over."

Her mouth dropped open. The words "I don't" sat ripe upon her lips but remained unspoken.

"Lucerne?" He guided the other fellow around the screen, one arm comfortably slung around his back, pausing only long enough to reassure her they'd be waiting before herding him in the direction of the nearby billiards room.

The moment they were through the door, Vaughan closed all the shutters so there was no possibility of them being observed by the guests milling about the grounds. Only then did he allow a little of his frustration out.

"You missed your cue, Lucerne. You ought to have joined us, not stood gawping like a parlour maid. Why in heaven's name didn't you?"

"Joined you! Only a madman, or one with armoured ballocks, would lay a hand on her without her permission. I'm neither."

"Who said anything about touching her? You ought to have fucked me."

"I ought to have..." Lucerne regarded him, a slack-jawed expression of astonishment eating up his face. "You would have had me fuck you while you were inside of her? Christ and bejesus! You've changed your tune. Whatever happened to never performing for her pleasure?"

"Exactly what you hoped," he snarled through gritted teeth. "I fell in love with her."

Silence so deep it hurt his ears swelled between them, and stretched like the void of the heavens.

Was I not supposed to fall so deeply?

Lucerne's mouth formed an O. He exhaled sharply. "Fuck! You really are in love with her. I mean I knew you were, but..." He huffed an uneasy laugh. "You realise that makes me an even bigger cad than she already believes me? Here I am, trying to push my way into something I ought to leave well alone." He began to back away, one arm outstretched as if to hold Vaughan at a distance.

"Lucerne," Vaughan's sharp tone thankfully stilled him. "That sort of nonsensical anguish doesn't help anyone. I love you both. I desire you both. That should be the beginning and the end of it. I will not choose one of you over the other, and as far as I can tell it is only the lack of faith you both have in me that has us in this unenviable position. Do not make things worse."

Lucerne shook his head. "I won't. You'll have us both, Vaughan. I'll help in whatever way I can. Do you really think us waiting here is the best thing to do? Will it not just convince her all over again that I've stolen you from under her nose?"

"She's ready to capitulate, Lucerne. She just needs a moment to reconcile her head and her heart upon that matter."

"You know that wanting something doesn't make it

real. Did you ever consider that maybe you are all she wants? And that it's you who is in denial?"

He shook his head. "I thought you knew her better than that."

Lucerne's brows furrowed. "I've barely exchanged a handful of words with her in the last ten months."

"It's not a conversation that's going to fix this. You need to stop being so damned polite."

"You mean force the issue." He shook his head. "Not my way, Vaughan. It's never been…"

Vaughan pulled him closer. He jammed Lucerne up against the billiards table and ground their loins together as he seized a kiss. "Pity. You do so shine when you're riled and aggressive, and Bella thrives on excitement. Perhaps you've forgotten how many linen closets I've had to extract you from due to her whim."

"I prefer to leave the teeth snapping and snarling to you."

"Then she'll continue to fight what I know for a fact she feels."

"Then what?"

"Then this… If you won't pin down Bella, then I'm just going to have to pin down you."

"What? That doesn't even make any—" his breath caught. "—sense. Oh, you sodding git."

CHAPTER 33

BELLA

B ELLA STOOD STARING at the gap between the edge of
the screen and the wainscoting. The effrontery
of the man never ceased to amaze her. She
obviously needed a moment... They'd be waiting... How
many times over did she have to express herself before
it sunk in? She didn't want Lu—

Turdmongers!

She scowled. That was an outright lie and she knew
it. The problem with Vaughan was that he'd always had
rather more clarity regarding her wants than she did,
perhaps because he didn't knot everything up in an
excess of emotions. While he was unforgiving and
capable of twisting everyone's will this way and that, he
was always honest with himself.

He loved her. He had room in his heart for both her
and Lucerne.

Wasn't it time she was honest with herself too, and
admitted she felt the same way? That she'd always felt
that way. It had only hurt so much when Lucerne had
left because she was still in love with him.

Goddammit! What were they doing now? Not just

standing around waiting. Vaughan didn't stand around. Were they discussing her? What were they saying? What were they doing? Was Vaughan reassuring Lucerne all would be well, that in a moment she'd be along and they could get back to being the perfect equilateral triangle again?

Lord help her, Joshua's mathematical tripotage was rubbing off on her. And, no, Vaughan wouldn't say that, rather he'd say, "We're definitely obtuse Bella, and your legs are the ones spread the farthest."

She clamped her hands fast over her mouth to cover the way her lips tugged into a smile, while tears beaded in the corners of her eyes.

What the devil was she waiting for?

Despite the bright sun outside, the interior of Lauwine remained draped in shadows. Bella left the guard room and crossed the chequered tiles of the grand salon, pausing briefly in the centre of that wide space to determine which way to turn; a subtle crack from up ahead, led to the upturning of her lips; the billiards room was where she'd find them.

True to her deduction, the billiards room door sat half open, and a warm orange glow spilled across its threshold. Bella paused, knowing what she would find even before she peered around the door's edge. The bright afternoon sun would have been blocked out by the shutters creating an illusion of privacy. A fire would be roaring in the hearth, making the room snug enough that one might comfortably idle in just shirtsleeves. A scattering of cushions would litter the floor before the fire. Two glasses would be discarded thereabouts. As for the room's occupants, she might find them in any of a myriad of poses and postures – stretched out upon the cushions, at the table with cues in hand, sitting, standing, or intimately entwined.

Bella took an expectant breath and leaned forward

to take a look, still hesitant despite all rationality. The cues lay discarded upon the baize, along with a long snake of white cravat. Twin brandy glasses sat upon the table edge. Lucerne had his back to her and the table. His blond hair was mussed at the back, as if someone had clenched a fist around it moments before. She could not see his expression, but it was not necessary to determine his state of being. That was apparent from the set of his shoulders and how his hands were planted either side of him, fingers curled around the table lip. There were auditory clues too – the shake that accompanied each intake of breath, and the ever so soft lapping one might associate with kitten licking up milk.

There were no cats in the room – unless one counted a panther in human form.

Bella knew, even before she took the two paces necessary in order to see the other side of the billiards table, what had Lucerne in such a state of disarray. Knew it and revelled in it despite the jelly it made of her insides.

There he was, on his knees – Vaughan, Marquis of Pennerley, bowed before a man of lesser rank. His coat had been discarded, and only two buttons of his waistcoat remained pushed through the button holes. He was peering up through his eyelashes wearing an expression of silky adoration. One hand was clasped possessively around Lucerne's arse, the other—it was being used to guide that which was upstanding towards his mouth.

The head of Lucerne's cock was already shiny with pearls of semen and saliva.

They didn't speak, but it seemed to her that a conversation was nevertheless taking place.

"Is this what you desire?"

"It's everything I desire."

"My lips? My tongue?"

"Your mouth. The whole of it. Suck me right down to the root."

"I suppose you mean to spend in my throat."

"Goddammit, Vaughan. I'll spend anywhere you see fit to allow it. It's been so long. I swear I'm barely holding it together."

"Had I then best use a super light touch?" Vaughan stuck out his tongue and teased the point of it over the slit in Lucerne's cock.

Lucerne inhaled a juddering breath. "Fuck. Don't tease. I need this too much to tolerate you being such a merciless sod."

"Au contraire, mon ami. It's the very fact that I know exactly how to touch you to give you the maximum amount of pleasure that makes your need so all-consuming and urgent. It'll do you good to teeter a while."

"It will not," Lucerne complained, but the rasp in his voice rather implied otherwise.

Bella could not quite tell what it was that Vaughan was doing, something with his fingers, she thought. Lucerne meanwhile, continued to drown in pleasure without succumbing to his body's need to spend. It was as he leaned back, spine arching, mouth opening around a groan that he spied her. Immediately his head turned and fastened upon her figure.

"Bella. You came." He smiled warmly at her in a way that went right to the heart of his cornflower-blue eyes.

"Of course she did." Vaughan remarked, barely breaking pace and without turning his attention in her direction, instead remaining wholly focussed upon Lucerne's pleasure.

Bella tugged at the puffed sleeves of her gown. "You led me to think— Is my presence unwelcome?"

"The very opposite. Come closer, and see what this

fiend is doing to me. He is capable of the most exquisite torments, as I am sure you are aware." At that very moment, as if to prove the point, Vaughan's ministrations caused Lucerne to arch and writhe. He gripped tight the top of Vaughan's head. "Stop toying, you devil, and finish me."

Almost predictably – Vaughan rarely complied with demands – his lover pulled away, releasing Lucerne's cock. He cast Bella a sly look as he rose to his feet. He was sleek as a panther in his black breeches, even with his clothing in utter disarray. As she watched, he unwound the cravat from around his throat and cast it aside. "What say we put this glorious asset," —he traced a single digit up the length of Lucerne's staff— "to better use? Miss Rushdale has come to us, should we not reward such effort? She's going to be very disappointed if your prick is as limp as a month-old celery stick. I'm sure she'd prefer it firm and shoved in her cunny."

"Must you be so coarse?" Lucerne protested, though it was noticeable that he did not dispute the substance of Vaughan's words. Indeed, Lucerne beckoned her closer with a tilt of his dimpled chin. It was all so familiar; the heat, the smouldering resentment in the dark of Vaughan's eyes as Lucerne traced his thumb across her lips and leaned in to kiss her, even the way her heart flipped and nerves sang at the press of his lips. He tasted of cognac with a little hint of something musky thrown in. It was not so difficult to envisage what that musk was. Not when a mere two paces taken in the direction of the door had Lucerne breaking off the kiss.

"Don't leave," both she and Lucerne said as one.

Vaughan closed the door and secured the latch. "I have no intention of going anywhere, but since we are all three here together again, let us avoid unnecessary intrusions. No doubt Master Aubury is still prowling, and we wouldn't want to offend any of the Wakefields' sensibilities."

"I'm surprised you care," Lucerne remarked. He had pulled Bella close and was again gently caressing the side of her neck. She had quite forgotten how skilled he was at that and how it made tremors run through her body.

Vaughan gave a shrug of his broad shoulders. "I don't, but one is expected to attend to ladies when they faint, rather than just leaving them there. I don't find such disturbances at all conducive to my entertainment. I suppose some men might enjoy having a maiden limp in their arms, but I prefer something warm and vital."

Like a cock, Bella was tempted to say, but that was being unfair.

"I've missed you," Lucerne whispered into Bella's ear, drawing her attention back to himself. The sweet press of his lips continued to trace the side of her neck and the top of her shoulder. Bella tugged free the pins at the front of her dress again so that the sleeves fell off her shoulder.

"Is that an invitation to delve deeper?"

Her simple nod elicited smiles. His hands formed either side of her breasts. "Lord I've missed these." Then his head was buried in her bosom, while his hands worked her chemise downwards in order to expose more creamy flesh. Bella gave a squeak, when his mouth fastened around one nipple and sucked.

"Lie back," he urged, lifting her so that she was seated on the table, then sprawled backwards across it. Her breasts spilled from her stays, which somehow he had inveigled a way to loosen. "Gorgeous. Doesn't she look gorgeous, Vaughan?"

"Ravishing," the marquis agreed in a tone that gave

nothing away. Only his continued presence suggested his approval, though his stillness unsettled her. Vaughan was not the sort of man who stood back, unless he was disengaged. She didn't want him here merely as a witness. He had to be part of this union. He had to want this as much as she and Lucerne obviously did.

"Lord, Bella, are you ready for me?" Lucerne massaged her breasts as if he couldn't get enough of the sight and feel of them within his hands. "This fiend has me all upstanding, and my prick's desperate to be reacquainted with your quim. Tell me you're just as eager."

"You'll never be a poet," Vaughan mocked. "Even Aubury can manage something with a little more zest."

"My quim is equally desperate to be reacquainted with your prick."

"Dear God! Please, for the sake of my sanity, the pair of you, forgo further endearments and get to the main act. I mean there's little point in all this preamble. You're about to blow, and Miss Rushdale is forever begging for a nice hard poking."

"Only because a certain person takes unnatural delight in denying me such things." It was good-natured ribbing of one another, not the prelude to a fight. Curious that she could feel the difference, even though their spoken words to one another hadn't really changed.

"I deny you nothing. I gave you everything you wanted, not ten minutes hence. And have I ever failed to bring you to completion?" Vaughan answered himself. "Not once. Every time, raptures."

"You insist on defiling me."

"He does that to me also," Lucerne confessed. A swatch of pink rose across his cheekbones. "I admit though,"—he said between drags upon her nipples—, "that I rather like it. Do you not take pleasure in the wrongness of it, too, Bella?"

She did, but she was damned if she'd say so. Instead she said to Lucerne, "I'd like to take pleasure in the rightness of you." Then, having seized hold of her skirts, she bunched the hem to her knees, treating him to a tantalizing display of finely embroidered stocking. Lucerne helped lift her skirts higher, running his warm palms up her legs to the bare skin above her garters. He bent and kissed where his fingers first traced. Bella clung to the fabric, as he teased ever more sensitive parts.

"You're sure you wouldn't rather I worshipped you on my knees?" His tongue teased across the lips of her split. Oh, she would never object to such a thing, but...

"I want you inside of me," she whispered. It had been so long since they'd all been together, since Lucerne had been hers to hold, since he'd been all stiff and eager, and so desperately ready to please. So long since she'd been able to admit to herself that she craved his touch. "Please, I want you to fuck me."

"You're sure it's not Vaughan that you want?"

"I want you both."

There it was; the truth she'd been fighting against for so long. The admission left her giddy, heart soaring, while she smiled so hard her cheeks ached.

"Greedy," Vaughan chastised. He was on the move again, sliding in and out of view, while his shadow made leering shapes upon the wall. Suddenly, he seized her wrists from across the table, and held her down. His head appeared over her, dark hair falling like a curtain around them. He was so close, but he did not kiss her. Only his breath buffeted her lips. His eyes were dilated, the pupils two huge inky pools she could fall into and become lost forever. "Don't hold back now, Bella. Spell it out to him what it is you want. I can hold you down here, if that's what you wish, to make it easier."

"But then you won't be able to do what it is I wish."

He arched both brows. "And pray tell, what is that?"

With her eyes and her chin she beckoned him closer, so that his ear was pressed close to her lips, and she spilled her vision of what ought to happen. Vaughan reared up, shaking his head, but smiling nonetheless. In times past, he would have refused her. What a heady pleasure to realize he might actually not only oblige but facilitate in providing for her wants.

Vaughan released his hold upon her wrists. "She's all yours to enjoy, Lucerne. Here, let me come and part her curls and help you slip on in."

He was around the table and by Lucerne in the space of a heartbeat, while he made a V of his fingers and parted the lips of her pussy, he also wrapped a hand around the back of Lucerne's neck and pulled him close for an aggressive kiss. "Take her now, and mind you give her satisfaction."

"Please, Lucerne." He was poised at her entrance, and so erotic in his state of rude dishevelment it was difficult not to strain to bring him closer. Also, the press of Vaughan's fingers either side of her nub was driving her to distraction. Her womb ached. Her breasts were aching and heavy too. Experimentally, she squeezed her own nipples and grinned in delight when two sets of eyes immediately turned in that direction. "God's blood, I'd forgotten how lascivious you were."

"Fuck me, Lucerne," she said, holding his gaze. "Fuck me so that this table shakes... So that the whole house shakes."

"Yes...yes." He sank in, and they both paused, breaths frozen for a moment, savouring the sensations. Then it was all about the pace and motion; how deeply connected they could be to one another and how quickly.

Vaughan didn't move his hand. He was an infuriating prickle on her senses, too good to bark over, but not sublime enough to detract attention away from what she was sharing with Lucerne. He let them bask in their moment, savouring the delights of their joining. Only when they were showing all too obvious signs of reaching completion did he make his move.

The feathering dance of Vaughan's fingers against her nubbin abruptly ceased. Instead, he moved to Lucerne's rear, but off to one side where Bella was still able to see him. He stripped off his shirt, and stepped free of his breeches. Entranced, she watched the light dance over his pale skin, creating hollows that emphasized the planes of his abdomen and chest. Lower, his cock stood proud, long, hard, and curved, a little like a sabre. It jutted accusingly at her. Bella licked her lips. She might be instrumental in his condition, but it wasn't to her she intended him to look for satisfaction, but rather, as she'd pleaded, Lucerne.

She would give him Lucerne, as he had given Lucerne to her.

"You'll have to still yourself a moment." Vaughan's soft red lips brushed against Lucerne's shoulder. His strong hands settled upon Lucerne's hips, and pulled their bodies tightly together. "I want in on this, and Bella longs to see how inspiring you find the kiss of my prick."

Lucerne made a sort of choked laugh. "You're both impossible. Know this, I'm going to spend the moment you enter me if you do this while I am coupled with Bella."

"No." Bella assured him.

"You won't," Vaughan agreed, his voice low and sweetly abrasive. "Don't worry. I can take care of that.

I've learned a thing or two on my travels. Sometimes, it pays to stave off the urge to surrender; it can make the final release that much more intense."

He did something. She wasn't sure what, only that Lucerne's eyes briefly slid shut, and all his muscles seemed to tighten. "Relax, Lucerne. We have you. We're going to take care of you. You only need to relax and give yourself freely, and the flight will be the best you've ever experienced."

"Vaughan, I don't think I can... Oh, God!" He pushed forward, deep into Bella. On the backstroke, she knew he was impaling himself more thoroughly upon Vaughan's cock. The resulting pleasure, writ into every one of his features, was intense. Hot colour flooded his fair skin. His lips were pulled wide into a magical smile, and his eyes, when they flicked open, blazed with intense joy and love.

This was how it was meant to be between them, and how she always wanted them to be from this moment forward – the three of them acting together to make things work for all of them, not constantly sabotaging their own best interests.

It didn't have to be a competition.

The realisation filled her with an intense glow. It was obvious really, and yet had proved so difficult to put into practice.

It required trust – trust that had only been built over time. And understanding of one another's wants and needs. In the past, it had been too easy to react to what was presented on the surface, without ever taking the time to stop and consider what lay beneath. They had never taken the time to really chip away at the facades they all presented, and hence be truly open and honest with one another. But this – this was surely the first step.

"It's too much," Lucerne rasped. His breath was

short, sharp, and riddled with ecstasy. "It's too good. No trick is going to hold the tide at bay." His hips continued to jerk, even as he spoke, like he was a man possessed. "I can't stop. I can feel it coming, and I can't stop myself."

"We don't want you to stop." Bella reached out and stroked what she could reach of his body.

"You're not going to disappoint anyone by letting go, Lucerne. Enjoy it. We are. Our purpose here is to provide you with pleasure."

"And in so doing, gain it for ourselves," Bella added. "We want you to take everything you need."

"Yes," he gasped, in what Bella assumed was agreement. "Yes, it's so good. It's... so... good!" An involuntary cry streaked past his lips as his whole body succumbed to his release.

CHAPTER 34

VAUGHAN

I T WAS IN the quiet afterwards, when they were no longer tangled or warmed by one another's heat, but were once again dressed and more or less presentable that Vaughan got the first inkling that not everything was quite resolved. Bella straightened herself out and took herself off towards the shuttered window. It was only a moment or two before her breaths became ragged, and he knew she was weeping, and not with joy or relief. He left Lucerne and came to her.

"Bella?" He gently touched her shoulder, imagining she would turn and burrow herself against his shoulder. Instead, her spine took on an iron-like rigidity.

"I'm sorry, Vaughan." She sniffed. "This has all been so right... so wonderful, but I know it can't last."

"What the devil are you saying Bella? Don't be nonsensical." He tried to pull her closer, but she was immovable.

Instead, she looked at him through a waterfall of tears. "You don't understand," she said, and she was damned well right on that score. "I've failed you. And it hurts so much. I know you're already lost to me, that this is mere fantasy that cannot be. I want it. I do want it, Vaughan. So much. I wish it was possible. And that the three of us could live as you want us to, but we can't..."

She reached out her hand and he took hold of it, squeezed her icy fingers in his warm ones. "You're not making sense. Bella, there's nothing in the way of this, nothing that anyone can say or do to prevent the three of us being together." He held out his free hand to Lucerne, who came readily towards them, only for Bella to shake off his hold the moment the other man drew close.

There were things the two of them still needed to say to one another. One couldn't fix the world with a single remarkable fuck. However, that didn't add up to this reaction.

"Bella, you haven't failed me." The only way she could do that was by refusing to acknowledge the fact that the three of them were bloody perfect together.

"But I have," she insisted. "That's how I know you're already lost to me." She took Lucerne's hand and put it into his. "Just... just love him and be happy."

With an anguished cry, she fled.

He and Lucerne were left staring at in bewilderment at one another. After a moment's silence, Lucerne spoke, "Will you go after her? Or should I? And what the devil does she mean, she's failed you?"

Vaughan steepled his long fingers and tapped them against his lips. Those words disturbed him too. "I have no idea. However, I think perhaps we ought to give her a moment or two. I guess this has all been rather much, and tearing straight after her will achieve nothing besides a drama for your illustrious guests to feast upon like the wake of vultures they are."

Lucerne wasn't precisely listening. "It seems

almost as if some other thing or person is influencing her. Her brother, I suppose." He seemed about to say more, but instead stooped and plucked Vaughan's cravat from the table.

"If I had the answer..." Vaughan stared distractedly at the doorway through which she'd fled, and not at Lucerne's face as his lover retied his cravat for him.

"But some notion is playing within your thoughts, some inkling. Tell me." Lucerne leaned in to him, and touched his hair where it curled upon Vaughan's shoulder.

"You're mistaken. I'm as lost as you are. There is no insight I can offer to explain her remarks." All he possessed was a determination to figure it out.

Lucerne closed his eyes and sighed through his nose. He nodded. "We knew it would be difficult. What we've shared, it's irregular, even before the matter of our recent pasts are factored in. Whatever has Bella within its grips, it will surely come to light soon enough. Meanwhile, we will not give up on her." He pressed their brows together, and wove his fingers through the back of Vaughan's hair. "Let me kiss you, and remind you that not all is lost."

A kiss would in no way aid the matter, especially if Bella were to return. Seeing them together would only reinforce her belief that they could live without her. God in heaven, what did she mean, she'd failed him? In what way could she have failed him? Only in the matter of her failure to love Lucerne, and she had just admitted her love for the ridiculous fool before him still existed. "You realise we're not behind locked doors anymore," he said, as Lucerne tilted his head. "Anyone may walk in at any point."

"You didn't worry about that a few minutes ago when you were set upon enticing her, or while you were crouched behind that screen."

"The hullabaloo if we're seen together will be infinitely louder than any ruckus over me being caught canoodling with Bella. But if it pleases you."

"It very much pleases me." Lucerne's fists clawed at his back and in his hair as their lips met. He kissed savagely, roughly invading Vaughan's mouth when Vaughan wished him to be soft. Bella's words had struck a deep knell of discord within his chest. Aggression wouldn't deliver him from this madness. He didn't believe Lucerne thought it either, but rather that he was seeking solace.

When they parted, it was Lucerne's turn to stiffen and sigh. "Before we go about seeking out Bella, there's something else you ought to be made aware of, and you'd better hear it from me, for inevitably it has passed around the grounds thrice already. Wakefield – he proposed that I marry his sister not ten minutes hence."

Vaughan fought to keep his expression neutral, but there was no doing it. "Twat-scourer! I trust you told him what to do with his proposal? Such as shoving it up his arse so far he's at risk of choking on it."

"As I have nothing but admiration for his sisters, I did not. I did, however, make it plain that my heart is tied up elsewhere, and a marriage of convenience would satisfy no one."

"Dare I ask which of the delightful spinsters he offered, or were you to take your pick?"

A tired sigh wheezed its way past Lucerne's lips. "What does it matter?"

"Humour me, Lucerne. I prefer to acknowledge my competition rather than cower from it." That was what he feared Bella was doing.

"She isn't. And it was Caroline."

"The clumsy goose maiden."

"There's really no call to resort to name calling."

As if on cue, a shrill voice rang out only metres away, "Lord M? Lord Marlinscar? Are you here?"

Dear God, have mercy. "It would seem Wakefield is fielding his queen already."

"Oh, where are you? You must come quickly." Caroline gave a sigh of exasperation, which drew Lucerne out of the billiards room. "Blessed be. I did not think I would ever find you."

Curiosity got the better of him. Vaughan also emerged and made his presence known. Caroline's bright gaze swept back and forth between them, and a quizzical furrow split the centre of her brow. However, whatever thought crossed her mind did not cause her to pause for breath. "Lord Pennerley." She dipped him a curtsy, before returning her attention to Lucerne. "It's Leesa. She's missing. Freddy asks if you will come. He's quite frantic. Please, you'll help, won't you?"

"Of course," Lucerne readily agreed. "But surely she is with her nurse."

"She was, and Joanna was with them too. I don't really know what happened, only that one moment she was present and playing happily and the next she was gone."

"Gracious." Lucerne took her hand and gave her fingers a reassuring squeeze. "We'll come. We both will. Lead the way."

Miss Wakefield happily curled her fingers around Lucerne's coat sleeve, and they trotted off together, leaving Vaughan to follow. He wondered, unkindly, if the tot was actually missing, and not tucked up snug and well in the nursery, ready to be produced when Wakefield determined his concocted drama had served its actual purpose of compromising Lucerne. Did the man actually have the wits for that? Just in case he actually did, Vaughan quickened his step.

CHAPTER 35
VAUGHAN

THEY FOUND WAKEFIELD, head bowed and necktie askew, pacing back and forth over the gravel by the fountain. Quite clearly his daughter was not going to be found in the few square yards of his search area, but his expression divested Vaughan of any supposition that this was a hoax. The man looked as if he'd been skewered with a pike, and his guts were about to unravel from his abdominal cavity.

"Lucerne." He reached out to his friend, whereupon Lucerne swaddled him in an embrace.

"Freddy. Tell me what I can do."

The captain shook his head. His eyes were glazed with the sheen of one caught in a waking nightmare. "Crakehall has sent out those willing to stay and search. I'm afraid your other guests have left."

"That is of no consequence, save to expose them as the venal, self-seeking vultures they are for not lending their aid." He clasped Wakefield's hand. "We will find her. Where am I best used? Do you need me here, or should I join the search?"

"Find her," Wakefield's voice cracked as he begged for aid. "She is all I have."

"I will. We will," Lucerne insisted.

"Where was she last seen?" Vaughan asked. If the child was to be found, time was surely of the essence, and inactivity would not reward them.

It was as if Wakefield noticed him for the first time. His gaze narrowed, and his mouth puckered as if about to unleash some accusation, or a hail of insults, or to protest Vaughan's presence, but what came out instead was, "You – you would help me?"

Vaughan passed on the opportunity for a bonding moment in which they might finally set aside their differences and reach an accord. He and Wakefield would never be friends, and a crisis wasn't going to change that. However, nor did it mean he was going to stand idly by while the bantling was lost. Children, while incomprehensible, alien things, were, he admitted, precious, and a necessity if the race were to survive. "Your daughter, she was with her nurse, was she not? Whereabouts were they when the child was last seen?"

A look of profound incomprehension crossed Wakefield's already clouded features. "I'm not precisely sure. Where is that dratted woman, or my sister? Where is Joanna?"

"Freddy." Caroline interposed herself between them. She clasped her brother's arm, as if by doing so she might lend him her strength. "Allow me." She about turned to face Vaughan. "My lord, if you'll follow me, I can show you."

It was testament to just how shaken Wakefield was that he didn't even mount a protest, where under normal circumstances he would have baulked at one of his sisters even communicating with Vaughan. Hell, he normally guarded them like they were the Pleiades, and needed to be cast into the heavens as doves, so that he – wicked, villainous Orion – would not capture and seduce them.

"Gentlemen?" he enquired.

Lucerne shook his head. "You go. We'll cover more ground if we search independently, and you know this land almost as well as I do."

Vaughan warily agreed.

They had turned the corner of the house before Miss Wakefield remarked, "How terribly disappointing you are, Lord Pennerley. You've been at Lauwine for some days now, and no scandal has erupted. I was led to believe you were wicked to the core, but here you are, helping to find my missing niece."

Interestingly, she was nowhere near as frantic as her brother over the child's disappearance, but then she also seemed rather more resilient than her brother. Vaughan had always found Wakefield rather fatalistic, curiously so, given he was a soldier; a career that surely required some degree of optimism.

"You know, one should always take what one hears with a pinch of salt, Miss Wakefield, especially that which is passed between tattlemongers."

"You should call me Caroline, or else everything becomes frightfully confusing and long winded when both I and my sisters are present. As to what I've heard, I should say that most of what's attributed to you is accurate. Why else would my brother dislike you so?"

It didn't surprise him that Wakefield hadn't gone into the details. "Have you never disliked anyone?" he asked.

"Not without cause," she shot back immediately.

He gave a nod, which prompted her to squint at him like one might peer at a wild, but ultimately savage beast.

"So there is cause. Care to enlighten me as to what

it is that set a Captain of the 33rd Regiment of Foot against a peer of the realm?"

"Jealousy," he suggested amiably, prompting her to snort and shake her head.

"Freddy is not jealous of you. Why there is nothing to be jealous of. " She stopped and dug her teeth into her lip. "We should concentrate on finding Leesa. It's this way. Straight ahead."

He continued to follow her, but he was not going to allow her to harry him without delivering some sort of response. "It seems to me you assume rather much about my person, while knowing very little. If you bothered to take the time to know me, you might find the truth of me is very different to the picture others have painted."

"Perhaps I might," she acknowledged, rather too agreeably.

Damn her, couldn't she endeavour to be a little less pleasant? He scowled until his jaw ached to remind himself she was out to poach Lucerne.

They paced nearly the entire east-facing elevation before Caroline spoke again.

"It is interesting that no one ever mentions your compassion and willingness to aid in a crisis when they speak of you."

"A propensity for heroics would hardly fit their narrative or purpose in bad-mouthing me. It might drive goodly folks into my circle of influence, and then who knows what manner of madness might ensue."

"You might fill them with radical notions," she suggested.

"Or inspire them to take part in satanic rituals and orgies."

Intriguingly, she dismissed the notion at once. "I don't think you've much time for organized religion. There isn't that zeal about you."

Good God, she actually prompted a laugh from him. It did appear that mousy Caroline Wakefield might not be as witless as her brother after all. "Orgies only, then." He sighed dramatically. That made her giggle.

"I suppose it's titillating for people to imagine, but I don't think you're actually that depraved either. Not if you're friends with Lord M. He wouldn't associate with a ne'er-do-well."

Marlinscar, he almost corrected her. There was just a fraction too much intimacy implicit in that shortening of Lucerne's title. "How little you know," he murmured instead, as if to himself. "Blond, beautiful, angelic, Lucerne – why he's one of Lucifer's own. Fell down from the heavens with him."

She laughed again. "Yes, I think you'd like me to believe that. But I've seen nothing but good in him."

She stopped where the vast rhododendron hedge formed a semi-circular grotto, and eyed him warily. "This is it. Where Leesa was last seen." They were now on the opposite side of the house to where Wakefield had established his command post. The shady grotto sported a marble bench on which Vaughan assumed the nurse had been sitting while watching the child play upon the blanket that still sat spread over the dried patch of lawn. It was easy to see the appeal of the spot, for it provided a vantage point over the entire east side of the gardens, save for the point where the lawn sloped sharply towards the copse of trees he and Bella had wandered into earlier.

"Joanna was here with Leesa and the nurse. They searched this area before even sending word that the child was missing."

"And where are they now?"

"Inside, I believe. Nurse went back to the nursery. Joanna is with Maria. They are searching out all the cubbyholes Leesa might have strayed into within the hall." Numerous doorways stood open onto the grass, so it was not an unreasonable assumption to suppose she might have gone indoors.

"I find it hard to imagine how a child could slip past quite so many people entirely unnoticed to enter the hall." There were no refuge points upon the lawn. No ornaments, walls or planted borders like those that existed within the more formal garden on the opposite side of the Lauwine; nothing that a child might hide behind or within. Only one route existed from here that would allow her to pass unobserved. His attention turned to the woodland. Long grasses bordered the pathway into the trees, where the lawn dropped in a steep incline towards the river.

"You cannot mean to suggest..." Caroline's gaze settled upon the bubbling beck, then drew swiftly back to his.

Vaughan's intention had not been to alarm her, only to point out the painfully obvious.

"Surely we would have heard the splash, if she had fallen in the water?"

"Would you? Perhaps if you were close by, but if you were not watching, you might attribute the noise to a bird swooping to catch a fish, or some other form of wildlife."

Skin bleached to a notably ashen hue, Caroline started off at once downhill, passing as swiftly as her long skirts would allow her.

Coarse grass boarded the river's edge. She darted along the bank, one hand clamping her ribbon infested bonnet to her head. "It's too muddy. I cannot see into the water." Nor could she easily get down to the very water's edge; the bank being steep and uneven, and the very edge difficult to accurately determine due to the profusion of plants.

"Careful," he caught her arm, when she risked tumbling head first into the water, a result of leaning over too far.

"But I think I can see something." Again she strained forward. This time the wind snatched off her hat, and set it down in the river.

"Damn and blast!"

"It's no loss," he assured her. "It was quite unbecoming."

"As a matter of fact that was my best bonnet," she huffed.

"Then I beg you not to appear before me in your worst."

"I see you've determined I'm not worthy of your legendary charm," she huffed in return. Two bright pink spots sprung up on her cheeks. Caroline tapped her foot. "Did I do something to offend?"

She was trying to steal Lucerne out from under him. That was a crime above all others.

"I'm terrified you might ask to attend one of my orgies in an eyesore of a hat," he drawled.

She peeped at him a moment, then laughed. "Oh, you are wicked. Leastways your tongue is." Her face paled. "Look. I told you I had seen something." A little way out into the water, a small clump of rock, mud and grasses formed a tiny island. "There is something caught amidst the foliage."

Vaughan's waistcoat buttons were already undone, and he had unwound his cravat, before he'd even formally determined to wade into the river.

"Take these." He thrust both items as well as his coat into her hands.

Though the water was not particularly deep at this juncture, merely thigh-high, the current still tugged at his breeches with icy fingers, while underfoot, the shingle bedrock slipped and slid, making it difficult to stride purposefully towards his goal. At least from the water, it was easier to see his target. Eventually, he reached it, and wrenched the white cloth from its mooring amid a clump of ramsoms and gout weed.

"It's her bonnet." She made the sign of the cross. "Lord have mercy. It's Leesa's bonnet." A great sob erupted from her throat, while her attention returned once more to the water, as if she expected to see the girl's tiny body floating by.

Vaughan scrambled up the bank. "Hers it might be, but it's not conclusive of anything. There are many reasons why it might have ended up in the river." The wind having taken it being the most obvious, just as it had snatched her bonnet. He pointed out her hat, now some way downstream.

"You're right, of course. I mustn't jump to conclusions." She took a deep breath and pulled herself up tall. "We ought to follow the river, and see what we can find downstream." Not waiting for him, she set off along the bank, oblivious to the fact he was now soaked through. Vaughan's feet squelched inside his boots. Like her, he couldn't bring himself to believe the brat was in the river. They'd have found her by now if that were the case. But just to be absolutely sure, he dove back in and put his head underwater.

❦

"Why were you arguing with Miss Rushdale?" Caroline asked, sometime later. Vaughan was still in the river. He'd retrieved her atrocious bonnet, and searched up and down both banks. He'd now progressed to sweeping the area of reeds that had waylaid her bonnet. He was quite certain the child wasn't in the river, but to satisfy Caroline's whim that a body might become entangled among the plants, he remained at the task. Poking and prodding with an overlarge stick she had found.

"I beg your pardon?" Vaughan paused in his search to look up at her standing on the bank still clutching the crocheted baby's bonnet, and her own soggy, beribboned affair.

"You were arguing with her earlier."

"If I was, what concern is it of yours?" He didn't recall her being among Millicent's followers, but it was quite possible he had merely overlooked her. She was frightfully easy to overlook. She would never do for Lucerne, even if the world was quite different and Lucerne wasn't already taken.

"Only that she is my friend, and I believe you have made her unhappy."

"Is that so?" Head down, he resumed his sweep of the reeds and river detritus. In some sense he accepted that responsibility, but most of Bella's current woes were of her own creating. She seemed determined to act in her own worst interests.

"Do you plan to cast her off? She's your mistress, is she not?"

Irritation raised a shiver along his spine. They'd been engaged in this wary skirmish a while now, but this was taking things a step too far. "You're exceedingly impertinent," he remarked.

Her mouth formed a challenging moue, while her hands landed squarely upon her hips. "You're the one who said I should make my own determination as to your character rather than take as gospel the opinion of others."

True enough. He had said that. He just hadn't anticipated her taking heed. "I don't recall saying anything about blatant effrontery."

"I couldn't see a polite way of asking," she said.

He again hefted and probed with the pole. "That's because there isn't one."

"Exactly," she agreed amiably. "I'm glad you agree. So what is your answer?"

Bella had anger and acceptance issues, neither of which would be overcome with the snap of his fingers. Nor did she readily forgive crimes against her, particularly where the perpetrator committed a crime of passion. None of which he was about to explain to Caroline, no matter how impatiently she tapped her foot.

"I actually believe you ought to free her, particularly if you don't mean to honour her." Caroline remarked. Evidently silence was not going to thwart her attempt to dig up answers.

"Honour her?"

"With marriage. Don't you think she'd make a grand marchioness? How stately you would both look." Her gaze swept over his soggy, dishevelled form. "Withstanding your current circumstances."

Good God, the audacity of the woman. Telling him he should wed, and looking him over like he was the local vagabond. "Do you have any concept of what you speak?" The cold was getting to him, or he would never have allowed her to rile him.

"Of course, she'd make an even better viscountess. I suppose you realise she's still enamoured of Lord Marlinscar. I think that's why she's so deeply unhappy. However, if you let her go, then they could be together, and all would be well again."

"Is that so?" Her grasp of the topic was staggeringly naïve. Yes, Bella was still in love with Lucerne, but it was her unwillingness to admit it that was causing the problems. She claimed her love was directed solely at him, and that there was nothing left over to give to

Lucerne. As to the nonsensical notion of marriages – that was out of the question for any of them unless a day came when it was permissible to openly conduct ones selves as a ménage a trois. "Did you ever consider that maybe she loves me?"

She gave him a look that was identical to the one her brother deployed when struck with disbelief. "She loves Lord M more. She loved him first. Freddy says you seduced Bella away from Lord Marlinscar. So now, instead of being happily wed, they are both hideously miserable, and a horrid feud has developed between Lord Marlinscar and Mr Rushdale. We had to all go and beg Mr Rushdale to get him to agree to himself and Bella attending today."

"Twat-scouring, beetle-headed, tuft hunter," Vaughan muttered.

"What's that you said? You're speaking too softly for me to hear."

"I said he ought to keep his opinions to himself instead of spreading scurrilous rumours."

Caroline took two steps closer to the water's edge. Her attention fixed so steadfastly upon him, he'd have feared for his shirt catching alight if it hadn't been soaked through.

"I don't think that's what you said at all. You were being exceedingly rude about Freddy I believe."

"I'm not going to apologise for my use of plain English, Miss Wakefield, if that's what you expect. Your poisonous turd of a brother deserves all those epithets. It's also well past time he stopped meddling in my affairs. Any more, and he will regret it."

Her mouth drew into a tight, yet amused, pucker. "I suppose you mean me to interpret that as a threat to call him out?"

She could interpret it any way she damn well wished.

"What a glorious contradiction you are. You detest him, and yet you're still searching in icy water for my niece."

Vaughan responded with a sniff. "There must be some reason for it. I knew the chit's mother."

Ho, that wiped the smirk from her face. She gawped at him, mouth wide, utterly aghast. "How dare you? You liar. Louisa was—"

"—such a sweet unsullied innocent." He rolled his eyes heavenward. "Did you even meet her? She was a tender parnell. Goodly. Sweet. Forgiving, but then she'd have to be, considering your brother is a rampant meat-monger who couldn't resist sampling every bit of quim on offer, and all while courting her. Go ahead, curse me again and call me a rakeshame. At least I do not pretend to be something I'm not."

Caroline continued to scowl at him. He was content for her to do so all she liked. Not a word of what he'd said was fabricated, whereas Wakefield's entire persona was built around falsehoods.

"You are not simply a rakeshame, you're a contemptible beast to sully a dead woman's name. I hope Bella casts you off and marries Lord M instead."

Vaughan threw away the stick and waded back to the bank. "I'm the beast!" he growled, making her brows shoot up her forehead. "I'm the one attempting to orchestrate reconciliation between Bella and Lucerne, while your brother was so busy trying to pair you off with Lucerne this afternoon that he managed to mislay his own daughter."

"Wa—it! What?"

The wind whipped right through Vaughan's shirt, filling it like a sail as he hoisted himself onto dry land. Caroline continued to gawp at him, failing to avert her gaze, even though his linens were soaked enough to be near transparent. In fact, she damned well drank her fill of him.

Vaughan retrieved his coat from a tree branch. "We're done here. I'm frozen to the core, and the child is not in there. She's probably swaddled before the fire, and nobody thought to inform us. And, I'm frankly tired of your sauce. It's really not done to stare at a beau when his ballocks are encrusted with ice."

"I wasn't staring at them."

"Much."

"One moment." Caroline darted in front of him blocking the path back to the house. "What do you mean Freddy was pairing me off?"

Vaughan struggled into his coat and turned the collar up. "You mean you didn't whisper a few words in his ear to prompt him to it?"

Her frown deepened. "I don't know what you're talking about. I haven't whispered or prompted him to do anything."

The coat did little to warm his skin. "You wish me to believe you are unaware that he proposed a match between you and Lucerne?"

"No. You're making it up."

"Oh, am I?"

"But it's blessedly obvious he's still doe-eyed for Bella." She huffed a lengthy sigh. "I do wish Freddy wouldn't take everything Maria says so literally."

Whereas, he wished Wakefield into a dank rat-filled pit somewhere. "Would you get out of the way, please?" He had lost all patience with this infernal tribe of idiots.

Caroline grasped his forearm, only to let go immediately in response to his glare. "Please, do you know what Lord Marlinscar said?"

"Buggering hell, no!" he suggested. Clearly, they were unlikely to have been Lucerne's actual words, but to his mind, they were close enough, and would hopefully get the point across that the proposal was a lost cause and ought to be abandoned forthwith.

Lips drawn into a narrow line, Caroline focussed on a point part way down his chest. He looked down and realised she was staring at his locket, the clasp of which had come open so the two curls of hair within were clearly visible. He shut it up tight.

The snap of the catch seemed to jolt her from her ruminations. "Mayhap he thinks my bonnets are hideous too."

"A fair assumption." Vaughan rubbed his nose. "He does endeavour to cut a dash."

She nodded towards her toes, and for a moment remained subdued before perking up once more. "But, see, this proves what I was saying about him still being in love with Bella. If you're truly serious about reconciling them, you ought to discharge her from her obligations to you."

Lord deliver him from Wakefields.

"That alas, is impossible." He was never going to stand back and watch them marry. Bella belonged to him. As too did Lucerne. "Please forgive me for dismissing your request entirely out of hand. Or don't. I really don't care which."

"Lord Pennerley," she enunciated as he stalked off along the path. "A man possessed of a beneficent streak, but ultimately self-serving and rakish to his black-hearted core. It's my formal character assessment, my lord."

He didn't look back.

"You're wrong to stand between them, my lord."

"And you rattle on too much about matters you know nothing about." Frankly, he was tired of hearing how Lucerne and Bella should tie the knot. No one who knew them as well as he would ever prescribe it. They'd make the most horrid pig's ear of marriage because they would never be able to satisfy one another. Also, he refused to be the spare cock.

CHAPTER 36
LUCERNE

LUCERNE SWEPT EAST along the river bank, through the woods as far as the boundary wall in search of Leesa. It had occurred to him more than once that perhaps somebody had bundled the babe into a carriage and stolen her away. Yet who among his guests would do such a thing? The only adversary Wakefield possessed was Vaughan, and though he'd been attributed many dubious actions in his time, Lucerne refused to believe him responsible for kidnapping a child. In his wilder days, a sister, perhaps, but not an infant.

No, it made a whole lot more sense to suppose Leesa had simply toddled off somewhere, as small, improperly-supervised children were inclined to do.

Lucerne ploughed on through the woods, pushing Charles's tale of the young maiden from Reeth who'd recently gone missing from his mind. The two disappearances were in no way comparable. Little Louisa could barely string whole sentences together. The other girl had been full grown.

He blew out a breath, determined to slow his racing heartbeat and keep a level head about this.

Surely a servant would appear any moment and let him know Leesa was found and safe in her father's arms again. Any moment... The alternative that they all returned empty-handed was unthinkable.

Lucerne emerged from the wood into the paddock and shot a cautious glance at the sky. The bright sun that had enticed them all out of doors earlier had slid behind a leaden bank of clouds. The wind had picked up too, so that by the time evening arrived, he fully expected a characteristic Yorkshire deluge. The odds were against them if she was still unfound by then.

Lucerne turned east again, passing into the upper paddock, and thence into the top garden. Although he'd had the grass here clipped short when he'd first returned to Yorkshire in ninety-seven, it had rather gone to seed again in the intervening years. The grasses reached to waist height, and wildflowers were woven in fragrant clumps every few yards. It was as he plodded down slope towards the rose-covered windows of the still largely abandoned east wing that he spied a sliver of white amongst the green boughs of the vast weeping willow.

"Leesa?"

He dashed so quickly towards the tree that in several places he almost lost his footing. Managing to right his balance so as to avoid landing on his knees, Lucerne ducked beneath the drooping foliage and blundered into the space beneath. "Leesa?"

There came a rustle in response, and his heart leapt giddily into his throat. Thank God, he'd found her.

Only the figure that presented itself was rather taller than he anticipated. "Bella!" he gasped. "Hell and buggeration!"

Her expression contorted from one of deep distress into outright fury.

"Shit! I'm sorry. That didn't come out at all how I intended it. Leesa is lost. I thought you were her and that I'd found her. You've not seen her have you, Bella?"

The ferocity of her gaze softened, and whatever fire she'd meant to spit at him she instead swallowed. "I've not. Did Joanna send you to look here?"

"No. I've been out to the boundary and back. How come you to suggest it? Do you think she'd come here?"

He took a cautious step closer. Tears lay wet upon her face, and her nose bore the tell-tale signs of redness one associated with crying.

Bella inclined her head. "I showed her this cave not so long ago. She found it as enchanting as I once did."

It was akin to a gut punch to realise she no longer felt the same way. The moment of understanding they'd found a little while ago now seemed a distant memory. "I think you once told me this was where you were the first time you saw me," he said.

Bella rubbed her red nose, but also nodded. "You were with Charles, and I was here with my groom. I wasn't sure whether to be excited by your presence or horrified over your plans for my secret garden. You cut all the grass, and brought people here. Far too many people."

His first gathering at Lauwine had been ambitiously grand. It had seemed the best way to introduce himself to his neighbours, and entice those of his associates he wished to hold onto as friends from their London abodes.

"Aye, well, it grew back." He realised that unconsciously he'd allowed it to do so. From his chamber on the second floor of the east wing you could see naught but this slice of wilderness. More than once, of a night, he'd stared out at the grass and the weeping willow and imagined her in her green cave waiting for him to creep outside and meet her. "Know that I've never stopped wanting or loving you, Bella. When I dreamed of Vaughan, I dreamed of you also. This last week especially, you've never been far from my thoughts."

Bella raised her head to meet his gaze, frowning slightly, as if unsure what to make of that confession. "Do not tell me you thought of me if you didn't."

He took another step closer. "Bella, I never stop thinking of you."

She blinked at him, studying his face for evidence of deception. There was none for her to find.

"Nevertheless," he continued. "I completely understand why you wouldn't want to become involved with the pair of us in the way you once were. I doubt my own sanity for seeking it. But know it would be different. We would not rush in blindly, and each of us would know exactly what it was the others wanted."

She gave an enormously weary sigh. "What Vaughan wants hasn't changed a bit. It's you. It's always been you."

"Bella." Her blindness in this matter was truly astonishing. How had Vaughan arrived at such clarity while she had gained none? "That just isn't true. He loves you. More so than even I realised last autumn. Easily as much as he does me. Moreover, deep down, I think you know it. There is a symmetry about the pair of you that I'm both awed and scored to the bone by. If two people ever belonged more wholeheartedly together then I have not encountered them. You are his soulmate, far more so than I will ever be. Hell, at least half of his infatuation with me is borne of the fact that society will not allow him to have me in the manner he wishes, but curses us for it."

"Tis no infatuation, Lucerne. I was there. I know the sorrow you dealt him... that you dealt us."

He bowed his head. They had all suffered, but the blame was not solely his. They'd each played their parts. Still, he had taken on board Vaughan's earlier remarks about how deeply his departure had scarred her. While she was still dressing things up in terms of what wounds he had inflicted upon Vaughan, he understood that the deepest wounds were those he had inflicted upon her, but which she still practically refused to acknowledge. "Bella, he always knew where to find me."

"To face your rejection again," she huffed.

Vehemently, Lucerne shook his head. "I run. He gives chase. The result is always my capitulation. This is not the first time we've parted ways, Bella." Though he prayed it would be the last. "Vaughan believes the only reason I fly is because I'm afraid to love him and be loved by him, but that's not true. Most often the deciding factor is my fear that I'll be unable to satisfy him, and that he will realise it. It was never more obvious than last October, when it was painfully apparent to everyone but you and he that he loved you, as you love him. Bella, alone I will never be enough for him. I'm not his match, though heaven knows, I wish I were. You, on the other hand, are his perfect mirror. It stuns me that he's even prepared to consider sharing you with me."

She batted aside his remarks as if he'd waxed on about the weather, not opened a vein. "I'm a passing folly, soon forgotten when you come into view."

A thick bower of some long forgotten tree split the cave. Lucerne found a perch upon it. "It's so much easier to dismiss facts as fiction than to accept them as the truth, but it's past time you did. Know this, Bella, if you left, he'd pursue you in the way he does me, to the ends of the earth."

Bella paced back and forth before him over the fallen catkins, her teeth worrying her plump lower lip.

"Can't we at least try to fix this?"

"I want to," she said in a small voice. "Of course I do. I did think for a moment that we might, else why would I have come to you?"

"Then why the sudden change of heart? Can we, two grown adults, not reach an accord? Bella, we don't have to re-tread the same path as before. God knows, I'd rather avoid making the same mistakes anew." He gave a dry humourless huff of laughter. "If we're honest and open with one another, surely we can forge something that will bring us all the happiness and security we desire. Jealousy and petty insecurities are what tore us apart before. Cannot trust and mutual respect bring us back together?"

She drew her arms around herself. Her expression was no longer cantankerous as it had been when he'd tried unsuccessfully before to win her over, now it was contorted by a medley of longing and sorrow. "How very simple you make it all sound." It seemed to him that she leaned forward, yearning for the closeness they'd once known.

"Simple or complex, no three people can be so in love and not find a way. I won't demand your affection, nor insist upon giving you mine if you can't accept it. Though whatever you may think, I still hold you dear. I cannot imagine a future without you."

Alas, that heartfelt outpouring only made her torment intensify. She bowed her head and began agitatedly pacing again.

"I know you understand, Bella, for is it not exactly how you feel too?" Lucerne hoped beyond measure that it was, and she would finally dare to confess it. He watched her wring her hands. Such anxiety was not suited to her. Usually, she was a creature of action.

"It is," she confessed at length, sparking a moment of elation in his breast. She did love him. She did reserve a piece of her heart for him. Her devotion wasn't entirely reserved for Vaughan. Their moment in the billiards room was not an anomaly.

Sadly, the resultant euphoria proved short lived. One only had to see her expression to know that her anxieties remained. She turned away from him, so that he couldn't see her expression to read it. Not that it was necessary; her disquiet was needling his senses. Cautiously, he left his perch and took a step towards her, determined to offer comfort, though wary of being rebuked.

"What is it? Talk to me. Perhaps I'll have a solution." He dared to touch her then; placing one hand upon her upper arm. "Bella?"

She turned and crumpled against his chest, pressing her face into his clothing. At once Lucerne wrapped his arms around her and held her tight.

How incredible to feel her pressed so snugly against him once more. Memories of less difficult times flooded back, and overloaded his senses with hope. The scent of her saturated his pleasure centres, and a heady sense of excitement began to build.

Until he felt her shudder.

"What is it?" Lucerne pressed his lips to the crown of her head. "Something I have done?"

"Not you. Vaughan," she murmured.

He could not conceive of what Vaughan could have done that he himself was not also culpable for. They had made the decision to leave Stags Fell and come to Lauwine together.

"We shouldn't have left Stags Fell without probably explaining ourselves. That was unnecessarily callous."

She shook her head. "I know why you did it – why you fled last All Hallows Eve, and why you left Stags Fell. I understand, truly I do, Lucerne. If it had been I in those exact situations, I cannot swear I wouldn't have done the same. The fact is I knew where you were even without being told. I could have stormed the castle at any point. I chose not to."

"Why didn't you?" he asked, while gently smoothing a curl of hair that had come loose from her coif. He braced himself for her to abrade his heart with another rejection. "Truly, do you only have room in your heart for Vaughan now?"

Bella sighed deeply. "No. It's not that."

For a second wonderment blazed within her eyes, and diluted her frown. She seemed to smile both at him and inwardly at her own honesty. However, that brief flash of joy withered back to heartbreak almost instantly.

Lucerne gripped her a little more tightly. "Then what? What is it that convinces you that we're so ill-fated?"

Her head gave a tiny shake, then her shoulders slumped. "I realised something," she whispered into the brocade of his waistcoat. "Something that changes everything. I can see the road ahead. He'll push me away. He'll choose you. Exactly as he always does."

"He's said himself a dozen times over that he wants us both. Are you sure it is not fear prompting you to think this way?" He looked down into her eyes as he cupped her face, and chased away her tears with his thumbs. "What could possibly be so momentous as to drive such a wedge between you?"

When she didn't answer he lifted her hands and, clasped within his, brought her knuckles to his lips. "Ah, Bella, will you not confide? I can't stand to see you this upset. You're my wild Yorkshire lass – the indomitable spirit that brought light into my life and taught me to accept the truth of who I am. Without you there to convince me there was only beauty and no shame involved in it, I don't know that I'd truly have ever allowed Vaughan to inhabit my world as he does. I'd been fighting to keep him at arm's length for years."

She peeped up at him with her brows furrowed. "I never knew that you were ashamed."

"We're two men, Bella, and I allow him to sodomize me. Not only that, I enjoy it."

"So do I," she confessed. A watery smile chased across her face, gone again in the blink of an eye.

"I expect we'll all burn in hell for it."

She shrugged. "Better that than spending eternity singing choral anthems. I can't envisage anything more tedious. At least in hell, Vaughan would be with us."

He smiled. "You're right. Not that he is going to be anywhere other than with us both while we're all still here on Earth."

Sadly, she shook her head.

"This fear that has you in its grip, tell me its name, and let's see if I can't deliver you from it."

"You are sweet to try," she said, making a slow, sorrowful shake of her head. "But there is naught to be done. Fate is already set. He's yours Lucerne, no matter what I wish."

"That I will not and cannot believe." He drew her close, cradling her head against his chest.

"It's the truth, Lucerne." She lifted up onto tiptoes, and silenced his protest with a kiss. It was no small peck either, but a demand that reawakened all the desire for her he'd ever felt. Too soon, she broke away.

"I just wanted to do that one more time, before it all disintegrates."

"To the devil with it being the last time! I refuse to let it be so." He gathered her to him again and locked their mouths. Their tongues sallied, while he held her tight, one hand upon the back of her head, the other at the base of her spine. Bella's hands found their way inside his coat and clove to the muscles of his back.

Through winter, spring, and summer, he'd longed for this moment. He'd relived their parting and the last kiss they'd shared easily a hundred times over. At Pennerley, he had bid her farewell with a brush of dry lips to her brow. Their last true kiss had been on a dreary day in London, entwined between best flannel sheets with a grand fire roaring at the foot of the bed and the crumbs of toasted current buns scattered all around them. Vaughan had been gone, but the significance of his absence hadn't sunk in yet.

They'd loved one another in all the ways they'd wanted to, without interruption or direction. There'd been no shame, no strife, no existing on tenterhooks waiting for some anxiety to arise. No discord. Only love.

Three weeks later, it was all over. He'd left Pennerley heartbroken, and come home to Lauwine having left Bella and Vaughan to find one another. He didn't know how he'd ever found the strength. Being apart from them had been agony. Holding Bella in his arms again now, was the sweetest ecstasy he'd ever known. There had to be a way to allay her fears and make this work. There simply had to be.

Her tongue flicked teasingly against his and thoughts of challenges and their futures fell away, leaving in its wake thickening arousal and immeasurable gladness.

"Bella—" he began.

"Shh!" she quietened him with another kiss. "Let us just enjoy this moment."

He did not like the sentiments implicit in her words, and yet he could not help but respond to her demand for kisses.

"Just let me have this, Lucerne... Just let me have this, please."

Clinging onto one another, pretending the darkness didn't exist would not aid them, still he couldn't refuse her.

"Anything," he yielded to her caresses and the tight hold she had upon his person. Such closeness was a dream after the barren wasteland he'd endured since leaving his loves behind at Pennerley. Even his contentment at being reunited with Vaughan had not been enough to fill the hollow in his chest.

"Bella... Lord God! Bella... Just tell me what you need, and I'll give it."

He hardly needed to make the offer, for having admitted that a draw still existed between them the barrier holding her at a reserved distance had crumbled into dust. Her hands were all over him, finding ways inside his clothing, nimbly dispensing with the many buttons of his outer garments, then cajoling him with flighty, feather-like touches that teased his senses and left him buzzing all over. He was uncomfortably hard within moments; his hips rocking against hers, his hands clasped tight upon her bottom holding her fast to him. Not that such contact and movement eased his discomforts any. Rather they worsened them.

"I've missed you," he confessed. "And how once I couldn't walk past an alcove or a broom cupboard without anticipating your arms around me, drawing me into an unlooked for embrace."

"Just an embrace?"

"And a kiss or two... or three... or thirty."

She drew him into the deepest of kisses there and then. "What else did you miss?"

"Your voice, your laughter. The way you skim your hands over my skin that leaves me tingling, and how we fit together so perfectly."

"You mean how well I fit onto your cock," she said, not nearly as coy as he. "Don't pretend it isn't swiving me you've missed most of all."

"I'll not deny I've missed that. But it's not all about sex. It never has been."

He wasn't sure she was listening well enough to take heed of his words.

"Do you miss me stroking you to the point of eruption, and then begging you to fill me?" she asked.

"Bella, I miss everything about you. Every tiny detail. I've been half mad from missing you and Vaughan. Not a day went past when you weren't both in my head. The number of times I've heard you as if you were right by me, and that I've been convinced I've just seen a glimpse along a hallway or reflected in a mirror are too numerous to list. So very many times I've reached out only to discover you weren't really there."

"Do you believe me a phantasm now?"

"I hardly know what to trust."

"You mean this doesn't feel real enough to you?" Her hand covered the swell of his shaft and she began to rub him through the cloth of his breeches.

Oh, it felt real enough. He just didn't trust himself to blink, in case it all vanished. This was too much of what he'd hoped for to believe it could last. In fact, in his heart, he knew that she was bidding him goodbye. "Bella, I'm not going to let you go. Whatever you think will happen with Vaughan, whatever the reason for it, know that I'm not going to give you up again. Whatever it is, I'll stand with you. I love you, Bella."

She took no apparent heed of his words, but continued to assault his senses in a way that soon had him gritting his teeth in an effort not to spend inside his linens. "Witch, let me touch you too."

She backed away from him then, only coming to rest when her rear hit the trunk of the enormous willow.

Then she raised her hem at the front, inch by inch revealing ankles, knees, garters, and stocking tops. Finally, she offered a teasing glimpse of the split of her quim.

Lucerne dealt with the frontfall of his breeches and his shirttails. He was stiff enough to poke coals.

"Fuck me, you precious mad man."

"Yes." Lucerne lifted her so that her legs wrapped around his waist, and her back remained braced against the tree trunk. Her breaths were coming as hard little puffs against the side of his neck now, and the scent of her perfume filled his nostrils. This morning, he'd barely dared to hope for this possibility, now they were here together in this moment. Reining himself back, he held off from pushing deep, and instead found her nub with the middle finger of three. She was wet, as eager for this as he. His efforts were soon rewarded with demanding gasps for more, and the roll of her hips in time with the rhythm of his strokes.

"Lucerne, please."

"Not if this is goodbye."

"It can't be anything else," she sobbed into his shoulder.

"I said I wouldn't steal him from you, and I won't. Tell me you believe that."

"Lucerne, I believe it," she whimpered. "I know you mean it."

It was then he truly appreciated that he was no longer her biggest worry, but was in fact, incidental to why she supposed Vaughan would leave her.

Nevertheless, he insisted on making the point afresh. "I'm not letting you go," he insisted, as he pushed into her. "Not ever. I do not think you were listening before, but maybe you'll hear me now. I love you, Bella Rushdale. There's space in my heart for both you and Vaughan. There always was and will be."

Her answer was a gasp as he filled her to the hilt. Damn, the heat of her around him was exhilarating, while the rock of their bodies soon left his thoughts in tatters.

Bella mewled into his shoulder. It was all perfect. So very perfect.

Need built sharply at the base of Lucerne's cock, then seemed to pour through it as her muscles clenched tight around him as she reached her climax. Right on the verge of tipping over, Lucerne spared a brief thought as to whether he should withdraw, but Bella's hold upon him was so tight he didn't think he could have torn free of her even if he tried.

"I miss him creeping up behind you as we fuck and inserting himself into the moment as he did earlier."

She chose that precise time to tickle his anus with her fingertip. "You always come especially hard when he's breathing fire upon the back of your neck." She wiggled her finger, pushing it just a little way inside of him.

That intrusion was all it took to push him over the edge.

There was no denying the truth of that.

Spent, Lucerne sagged against Bella, his head still in a state of woozy delight. He wanted this moment to last and intended to stretch it out as long as possible in order to keep their woes at arm's length. Bella too, seemed content to linger, and concentrate on the thumps of their hearts and the heat of one another's skin.

It was hardly surprising then, that it took several moments for him to acknowledge the tug upon the leg of his breeches, and a few more for his brain to realise that it wasn't Bella who was responsible. They peeled away from each other, flushed and breathless, whereupon, he looked down. "Leesa!" Where in heavens had she cropped up from?

The bantling's tiny arms stretched up towards him. Her tiny cherubic face was red with frustration and stained with blackberry juices, and a whole thicket of vegetation was caught up in her blonde ringlets. "Mar Mar, up," she demanded, tugging on the leg of his breeches once again, and almost dragging them down. "Need byes."

Jubilant to find her safe and well, Lucerne fastened his breeches, then scooped Leesa up into his arms. She immediately wiped her nose against his cravat, and then burrowed into his shoulder.

"Ivo will have an almighty fit," Bella remarked. "Blackberry stains are beastly to remove."

"No matter." He was too thankful to have his goddaughter safe and well in his arms to fret over such trivialities as the state of his wardrobe. Or his valet's reaction.

"Does she seem all right, Lucerne?"

He smiled at Bella over the top of Leesa's ringlets. She was standing with her hands pressed fast to her abdomen as if she was holding back her sense of relief until all was confirmed as perfect.

Lucerne attempted to peel the tiny imp from his person to take a good look at her, but she locked one fist painfully tight around his hair, and made herself weigh as much as a full grown man in that peculiar way young children possessed. "Stay cud," she insisted. "Bwella cud too."

"What's that?" her godmother asked.

"She wants to con you into a headlock too," Lucerne translated. "Where have you been, little madam? We've all been searching high and low for you."

Leesa didn't reply, just pushed her thumb into her

mouth, and made some burbling noises against his shoulder.

"I should deliver her to her daddy."

Bella nodded, and back stepped away from them. Suddenly the gulf between them was back in place. "You should. You should definitely go and do that."

Come with me, he wanted to say, but couldn't stand to hear her refusal.

"Bwella come too," a sleepy voice piped up, entirely unprompted. "Bwella come tea. Bwella promised." The little imp stretched towards her godmother, who was summarily obliged to accept a grubby kiss.

Yes. Yes, that's right. You insist upon it. She might listen to you, whereas she's doing her best not to hear me.

"I'll be along in a moment," she promised.

And he intended to hold her to it.

Lucerne made a final backwards glance as he left the willow cave. Bella stood in profile to him, a shaft of green filtered light upon her, making the top layers of her spotted muslin dress translucent so that he could see all the curves of her body. She was both radiant and deeply sorrowful in that moment, but he finally understood what had such a grip upon her mind.

"Don't be long, Bella," he said. "You'll stay for dinner, so that we might talk more."

Cautiously, she nodded. "I promise; I'll be right there."

CHAPTER 37
LUCERNE

"IT'S A LONG and arduous expedition she's been on," Lucerne explained, as Wakefield and his sisters flocked around him in the grand salon. The bantling was removed from his shoulder to be petted, scolded, and sobbed over. Her daddy clung to her as if it was not possible to hold her closely enough. Gradually, worry ebbed away, while relief made all their voices shrill. Eventually, they poured into the drawing room, along with those of the remaining guests who had stayed and joined the search.

Lucerne directed the footmen to be liberal with the port, before closing the door upon them, and returning to the hallway to seek out Vaughan, and to watch for Bella coming.

As it turned out, the former presented himself immediately, albeit soaking wet.

"She's found. They're all in the drawing room," he informed Caroline who had entered with Vaughan carrying what appeared to be some kind of sodden basket and a woollen bonnet. She didn't wait for further invitation to go and join her siblings, but crossed the hall with a joyous spring in her step.

"I don't need to see the brat," Vaughan remarked. "If you'll excuse me." He headed for the stairs with Lucerne on his heels.

"You went in the river to search?" Lucerne caught the attention of a maid. "Bath water, immediately, in my chamber. Be quick about it."

"Frankly I'm astonished I'm the only one who thought to." Vaughan squelched up the stairs. "Perhaps growing up surrounded by a moat trains one to consider the adherent dangers of water. Where was she in the end?"

"The top garden on an expedition to find Bella's willow cave."

"Not so far from where she began, then."

Since Lucerne wasn't wise to where she'd begun, he couldn't say for certain. He nodded nevertheless. Not that Vaughan could see him as he was two strides ahead.

"How long ago?"

"Not long."

"Well, as naturally joyful as I am to learn that the chit is well, rather more expedience in notifying me of that fact would have been appreciated." Vaughan stopped, and rested on an old wooden trunk to pull off his soggy boots.

"You weren't overlooked deliberately. I had word sent round as promptly as I could. Come on up to my room. We can talk as you soak. A bath will help warm you through."

Clearly weary, a twinkle nevertheless appeared in Vaughan's eyes. It was banished a moment later, when another shiver wracked his body. Lucerne wrapped an arm around Vaughan's back and drew him close. There was no one around, as everyone was fussing over Leesa, so he risked giving him a kiss too.

Once inside his room, he showed considerably less reservation, drawing Vaughan into his arms to kiss more thoroughly before helping him out of his sodden clothing. "What role was Caroline playing?" he asked. Clearly, she had not waded into the river.

"Adjutant, mostly."

"Are you sure you don't mean agitator?"

"That too. Although, that more accurately describes her brother. I'm satisfied she knew nothing about Wakefield's damned matrimonial plans."

"So that was your motivation. Vaughan," he chided, pulling his lover's freezing body against him. "I'd near forgotten Wakefield even put the notion to me. You know I'm yours. Yours and Bella's."

The latter addition caused a quirking of one of Vaughan's dark brows. "Am I to deduct from that that you have spoken and some accord has been agreed?"

"Not, exactly." Lucerne guided Vaughan through to the adjoining room, where the bathtub already stood half full with warm water, and two other pails stood steaming by the hearth. The blaze stoked high to keep them hot. Ivo arrived with jugs of cold not a moment later. Lucerne ushered him away, then locked the door behind him.

"Where is she?"

Lucerne combined more hot and cold water to the tub, until he was certain the temperature was right for banishing a chill, while inwardly sighing. He kept some hot water back, so he could raise the temperature once the initial thaw had begun.

"You argued," Vaughan postulated in response to his silence.

"I hope that by now she is downstairs with the others. I had to leave her in the gardens in order to bring Leesa inside. She did agree to stay to dinner, but I suppose that will depend on Joshua's willingness to entertain the notion." Lucerne tested the water with his elbow. "You can get in."

Vaughan, naked as the day he was born, stepped into the cambric draped tub, and submerged himself completely. He raised his head above the surface again a moment later, by which time Lucerne had shed his coat, and pulled the bathing stool over to the side of the bath, so that he could lend a hand.

"If you sit, I'll scrub your back."

"I'd rather soak. But if you're desperate to get your hands on me, my front's fair game."

"I don't know if that will be very conducive to conversation. I suspect it might prove distracting."

"That depends where you put your hands."

A moment passed, without Lucerne moving, which prompted another raised brow. "Why do I feel I'm in for a berating? You're not usually this reticent about touching."

Lucerne shook his head. "I've nothing to take you to task over, besides the stupidity of submerging yourself fully clothed in a river for far too long. In truth, I'm rather delighted at you being so selfless. I know that you will hate Wakefield until the day he dies."

A snort and a splash jetted his way. "Hate requires too much effort. I don't ascribe him that much time." He sat. "You may scrub now, if you wish. I'm slightly less chilled."

Lucerne added more hot water first. Palms thoroughly laved with soap, he applied them to Vaughan's neck and shoulders. He worked in circles, kneading the stiff muscles as he cleaned the river dirt from his lover's skin. It was indicative of Vaughan's fatigue that he didn't press for the details of the discourse Lucerne had with Bella, instead closing his eyes and surrendering to the bliss of two attentive hands. The long planes of his back cleaned and caressed, Lucerne moved on to his arms, his chest and stomach, the curve of one hip and then the other. He studied Vaughan's face as he worked. He was eerily calm, drifting surprisingly close to slumber.

"You're not falling asleep on me, are you?" he asked, soaping one knee. He trailed a single finger down Vaughan's thigh.

A silky smile tweaked his lover's lips. "I doubt I could sleep through you soaping my cock if I tried. Don't," he added, as Lucerne made to do exactly that. "It wasn't an invitation." He hunched himself up to one end of the tub. "Get in."

"Wha—There's barely space."

"Stop arguing, Lucerne. Get in."

Knowing Vaughan wouldn't back down, and not wanting to cause a needless fight, Lucerne stood and shed his waistcoat and breeches. Stripping off his remaining linens took a little longer. The knot at the neck of his shirt refused to budge. In the end he wriggled out of it by stretching it to its limits, and even then he nearly lost his eyebrows to the endeavour.

He stepped into the water, and took a seat between Vaughan's spread legs. Kisses along the top of his shoulder blades and the back of his neck rewarded him. Vaughan's strong arms encircled him. "Now tell me what it is you're so desperately trying to keep a cork in."

"I don't know that there's anything specific," he began, bending the truth a little – but only a little. A whole host of things were playing upon his mind, all of which were ultimately bound to one another, so that it was wrong to attribute more emphasis to one over another.

Lucerne swallowed hard; his throat, still sore from the activities of the last few days, croaked as he tried to form a sentence. This was awkward. He needed to find the right words, present things in a way that would make sense. It wasn't easy. All he had were his instincts and a bunch of suppositions, rather than any hard evidence. A wise man would probably hold his tongue a while.

Vaughan's arms encircled him. His pointed chin, rested upon Lucerne's shoulder. "Bella has clearly said something that has your mind in a whir."

He shrugged. For she hadn't. Not really. If anything, she'd shied from saying it, exactly as he found he was doing now.

Once spoken, there'd be no pretending it wasn't real.

God's truth – he wanted to close his eyes and lose himself in Vaughan's embrace, not chew over this new dilemma. Simultaneously, he knew that way lay folly. They had to be open with one another.

"I think..." He paused and focussed his attention on a small section of the metal tub that wasn't covered by the cambric drape. "Do you ever feel you are doing the wrong thing, even when you're trying to do the right?"

Vaughan hopped out of the tub, and climbed in again, so that he was straddled across Lucerne's legs facing him. His expression was one of wary curiosity that metamorphosed almost instantly into a frown. "You scare the hell out of me whenever to take to speaking like this. It means you've got hold of some mad notion, and are about to enact an equally half-baked plan."

"I was right to leave you last All Hallow's Eve."

"It was one of many options open to us, Lucerne. You didn't have to leave. We could have worked things out in a different way."

Lucerne wasn't entirely sure about that.

Vaughan raised his hand to brush his fingers

though Lucerne's hair, only for Lucerne to back away from his touch. "I can't think properly when you're touching me."

Vaughan lowered his hand. "Very well. Then at least explain what it is that has you so agitated?"

He nodded. Sat quiet for several moments staring at the stretch of water that lay between them. "What if we can't make this work? Bella is adamant about it."

"So you did speak?"

"Aye."

"And more?"

Lucerne bit his lip, then sucked at the damage he'd wrought. "Some."

"Good," Vaughan nodded. "Now, here's the thing. Bella's head is all in a muddle. It'll remain so as long as she's resident at Wyndfell. Therefore, the best course would seem to be to head south again. Either to London or Pennerley."

Ruefully, Lucerne shook his head. "I know you dislike Freddy, but I can't up and deprive him of a home."

"He certainly isn't coming with us. Surely, he can take himself off to wherever his sisters are returning to. The property is, presumably, his? And doesn't the eldest adore her niece? There is a nursemaid provided at no cost to his purse, so he might resume his employment."

"I think he means to sell his commission."

Vaughan waved, for the matter was of no regard to him other than as a barrier to his own goals. "The alternative is that you will have the whole clan imposing upon you in perpetuity. I do not imagine that your initial rejection has eliminated his plan to palm you off with one of his sisters. Such a marriage would suit him far too well."

They were getting away from the true point of the

conversation. "He is far less mercenary than you perceive. In any case, the Misses Wakefield depart tomorrow."

"As should we."

It all felt rather uncomfortably familiar, departing after playing host to a Wakefield event. Also, in the sense that they'd be leaving with no real plan in place, and no solutions to any of their dilemmas. It had served them ill in the past, and would inevitably do so again. Nor was he convinced Bella would depart with them.

"I'm not going anywhere tomorrow. Too much is at stake. There are conversations we ought to have, the three of us, all together before we hare off anywhere."

"Then we should dress and go seek Bella. I know you said you'd invited her to stay, but I doubt Joshua will be persuaded there's a need for them to linger."

Joshua! There was an additional complication all of them could do without. Maybe Crakehall could keep him engaged. Lucerne got out of the tub and dried himself off. Clad only in a shirt, he went into his sitting room and poured a drink. He was still sitting on the sofa by the hearth when Vaughan joined him fully dressed. He threaded his fingers through the short strands of Lucerne's hair, and leaned into him. His lips brushed softly against Lucerne's, then his tongue teased between them. Lucerne groaned as he opened up to the other man's kiss. It was easy to wallow in the present, and not think about the future or their past, but long term; it was impractical to live like that.

"You taste of her," Vaughan murmured, prompting Lucerne to mutter an apology. Not that he knew exactly what it was he was apologising for.

His lover gazed at him bemused. "Devil's breath, Lucerne, spit it out! Something has you caught in a proper conundrum."

"I want a family," he said, which was evidently as

far from what Vaughan expected to hear as could be. His lover reeled back on his heels.

"You want a family?" Vaughan came around the sofa and peered intently into Lucerne's face. His violet eyes flared, white hot and intense, whether with heat or hurt, Lucerne could not quite tell. He took a steadying draft of his brandy, allowing the liquor time to burn its way down to his belly.

"I have a big old empty house and no relations left to speak of. If the Marlinscar line is to continue, then a family is rather a necessity. I miss the noise they used to make. There's something reassuring about the sound of life in other parts of the building when you're strolling around the place. Moreover, maudlin as it may appear, I'd like something of me to still exist when I'm gone."

Horror scored hollows into Vaughan's cheeks. He snatched the drink from Lucerne's hand and swallowed it down. "Christ! Please tell me you didn't lie about Wakefield's offer. It won't do to have you tied to some hideous mouse."

"She's hardly hideous, and not much of a mouse, either."

Vaughan cut him off with a mighty crash of his hand upon the mantle. Several ornaments jumped. "I absolutely refuse to share you with some brood-mare."

The best thing he could do was to maintain his composure. "I was under the impression that you intended to share me with Bella."

The silence was as profound as if a shattered crystal chandelier lay between them, or a pile of slaughtered peasants. Eventually, Vaughan drew in a breath, and seemed to take possession of his emotions. "Yes."

"So it wouldn't be unreasonable to envision a future in which I have children with her."

Vaughan stopped rolling the tension out of his

shoulders, and shot him a look of pure venom. "I don't think that would be a sensible plan."

"Because?" Lucerne rose and poured himself a second drink.

"Because you are too fucking honourable. If you got her with child, then your first instinct would be to bend the knee and make an offer, and that's... that's unacceptable. It would put immeasurable strain on our relationship. Lucerne, marriage cannot be a part of this. Nor children."

Lucerne carefully replaced the stopper in the decanter. He turned around, glass in hand. "You mean mine and Bella's cannot be a part of it." No mention had ever been made of Vaughan offering for her.

"This is ridiculous," Vaughan claimed. He began pacing again. "Seriously, how would you even know it was yours until after the birth? And even then, you are relying on the brat favouring you rather than its mother in order to tell."

No right minded individual would ever mistake his offspring for one of Vaughan's or vice versa. They were physically very different.

"I think that's entirely beside the point," Lucerne said, raising the glass to his lips. He took a sip. "Personally, I feel it would be wrong to sow such a seed and not take responsibility for it."

Vaughan regarded him incredulously for a moment. "There is a vast difference between what you are proposing and abandonment. Arrangements could be made."

"So, you'd have her give birth to a bastard!"

"Lucerne, it's not going to happen."

One had to laugh at such naivety. Nay, more like disassociation. He shook his head and then poured the rest of his drink down his throat. "That's a rather unrealistic assumption, don't you think?"

"Precautions can be taken. The three of us have already spent years entangled without the issue arising."

"Aye, because you chose to fuck her exclusively in the arse, and I..." He'd reflected long and hard on this issue and his glorious future in which he married the woman of his dreams and filled Lauwine with children. He'd concluded that's all it was, a fantasy. "I don't seem able... No fruit has ever grown from my seed—"

"Only you would interpret that as anything other than a blessing."

"—despite considerable negligence on my part with regard to active prevention."

"You've been lucky," Vaughan remarked, rolling his eyes. "Or are you suggesting you spent our time in London together actively seeking to make her quicken?" He paused. His eyelids narrowed down to slits and his mouth turned ugly. "Tell me you did not do that. Devil's teeth, Lucerne, swear that wasn't your plan. I know you, it would have given you the perfect excuse to disregard all my objections at once and claim her."

"Do you truly believe me so devoid of scruples? No, I did not plan to make her belly swell. I was altogether selfish and inconsiderate." This was something he'd never seemed able to make Vaughan understand. "My marrying Bella wouldn't have altered our relationship at all, but it would have protected her and saved her a deal of abuse. This feud with her brother need never have become a thing."

"You're not marrying her," Vaughan barked. His dark irises glinted with diamond shards.

Lucerne put his head in his hands and blew out a long breath into his palms. "What about you?" he said quietly.

"What about me?"

"Are you ready to sire a bastard?"

His lover turned his wrist dismissively. "It's not going to happen."

"Except it already has." The words were spoken, and he couldn't take them back. "Vaughan, you've already wound that clock."

They stared at one another. Vaughan's nostrils quietly flaring. "You don't know that. Bella would not tell you that, and not say anything to me."

"She didn't say anything." Lucerne let that sink in a moment before wetting his lips. "Today is the first time I've really been close to her since the christening. It's certainly the first time I've held her since last October. She's... I don't know how far along she is. Some months. I don't know that she knows for certain herself, or she even realised it until very recently. Vaughan, she's believes she's failed you because she's carrying your child. Also, I think you may be certain that seed was planted at Pennerley before you ever set north to find me."

Vaughan swung his head, as if the swish of his dark curls could dispel this notion. "It's not—"

"Possible?" Lucerne quirked a brow. "Truly, you're going to deny it?"

Vaughan turned toward the fire. He stared into the dancing flames, while his fingers whitened due to his grip on the mantle. "This has to be a mistake."

"Denying it will be a bigger one."

"I can count the occasions on one hand."

"It doesn't seem fair, does it, in light of all my episodes of 'getting lucky'."

They both fell silent. Lucerne turned all the possibilities over in his head, as he imagined Vaughan also to be doing.

"Beltane," his lover eventually mumbled. "Darleston arrived unexpectedly, and rattled over

Dovecote's marriage. He said a bunch of things that he oughtn't to have. I don't know, it unnerved... it unravelled me more than it ought. I took her out to the fields."

"And fucked her as if you were singlehandedly responsible for returning the bounty of spring to the land? My lord, if you will invoke the old gods, what in hell do you expect?"

Vaughan pressed his thumbs into his eyelids. "That was four months ago. Shit! Are you certain you're not mistaken, Lucerne?"

Lucerne replied with the only question that mattered. "What are you going to do?"

CHAPTER 38

BELLA

ELLA RETURNED TO Lauwine as promised, her mind still detached from the reality around her. The group in the drawing room were just breaking up. Leesa had fallen asleep on her daddy's shoulder and now her aunt Joanna was carrying her up to the nursery. Conversation had turned to the subject of victuals, and dressing for dinner. On seeing her, Joshua broke away from his conversation with Mr. Whistler and Stephen Crakehall and strode right up to her.

"I'd ask where you've been, but I don't suppose I'd get a sensible answer."

"Searching for Leesa, along with everyone else." It was a lie, but he wasn't to know that, and had no means of ever proving otherwise. "I had just bumped into Lucerne when we came upon her. I forgot my hat, so I was obliged to go back to collect it."

"There seem to have been an abundance of hats mislaid today. Perhaps if you all kept them perched upon your heads, instead of swinging them hither and thither, then there would be no cause to chase them."

"I don't know about any other hats," she retorted, securing hers upon her head again with a very large pin.

Joshua lifted his bony shoulders. "No matter, I see that you have it now. Thus, we're all ready to leave." He about turned her and steered her back to the marble entrance hall.

"Must there be such a hurry?" He was holding her far too tightly.

"There's no reason to remain. The child is found and well, and the farewell gathering broke up hours ago. You need only say your final goodbyes."

Bella dug in her heels. "I did say to Lucerne that we might stay to dinner." There was much that remained to be said.

Joshua's brows shot up his forehead. "What the devil possessed you to do that? We've been here far longer than necessary already. I've no desire to linger any longer. Dammit, Bella, what are you about? It's deuced awkward being here. You know perfectly well that I never wanted to come."

"I'm sorry for that, but might we not stay? Please," she coaxed, pressing a finger to his coat lapel. "Surely it would be better for us all if amends could be made. I do feel much better for having spoken to Lucerne."

"Well I don't. That is to say, I haven't and have no inclination to do so." A decisive slash of his head saw off any hope she had of his acquiescence. "It won't do, Bella. We're leaving now. You ought not to have said otherwise. Do not think me so foolish to believe there is any hope of rekindling a match between yourself and Lord Marlinscar, which would be the only possible reason for us to linger, for I know there is not. This is a ruse, I am quite certain, to enable you to consort with that confounded popinjay you prefer."

Lord, curse all brothers and their desire to do what

was best. "You mean the confounded popinjay whom you're convinced ought to take me to wife?"

"That would be the honourable thing to do, considering how freely he's made use of your assets. Not that I particularly relish him as a brother-in-law."

"You have grown into the very worst sort of hypocrite, brother."

"I have never behaved so reprehensibly."

She swirled away from him, vexed to the core. "Only because you don't afford those of lesser means the same status. You may not have bedded any one of our class, but that never stopped you debauching Em—"

"That was a financial arrangement."

"So if Vaughan were to slap a large enough payment for my services into your hand the issue would be resolved? That's despicable. And you accuse him of treating me as chattel."

"That is in no way what I implied or said." A puce stain flooded upward from beneath his cravat into his cheeks, and left his nose ruddy. His nostrils quietly flared, as he composed himself into iron-like intractability. "The strain of being here is clearly causing you to become too untethered." He hissed between his teeth. "I ask you to master yourself, then step outside to the carriage, or I will be forced to do what I have resisted all these years, and abandon you to your fate. I've no wish to lose you as a sister, but this way of conducting yourself you've indulged in, has to stop. It has to, Bella... I have heard the most scurrilous things today, or rather I wish that I could dismiss them as such, save that I know in my own heart that they are true. I have had near first hand confirmation of it from your own lips, and from Marlinscar's and Pennerley's too. It simply cannot be tolerated."

"Why not?"

"It is against the natural order of things."

457

"Says who?"

"Get into the carriage, Bella, or would you have me drag you from here?"

She bit back an angry retort. Their argument was not something she needed to offer up for public consumption, especially when it was clear that rumours and speculation enough were circulating. Still, he tried her patience to its limits.

She would have to devise another means of seeing Lucerne and Vaughan. The estates bounded one another. It could not be that difficult.

"Bella, are you leaving?" Eliza enquired, coming down the main stairs. She had been to the nursery to check upon Leesa and Joanna.

Bella bowed her head, but Eliza's attention had already transferred to Joshua. She went outside to him, to where he stood upon the steps.

Caroline came upon her from behind, and linked their arms. "Dash—we've not had a moment together. Must you go?"

"I'm afraid so. Joshua's insistent, and I doubt even Eliza can coax him to stay much longer." Already, the Rushdale carriage stood waiting, footmen at the ready, and their driver up top, while the two hackneys chomped at their bits.

"Oh, I don't know. They're very thick together, but then, so has she been with Mr. Whistler. I suppose they will go to battle over her, much like two certain gents have done for you."

Heavens, the rumours had been circulating! Bella sucked her tongue. "It wasn't like that," she said, without offering any further elaboration. "Caro, would you give Lord Marlisnscar my apologies. I did say earlier that I would stay to dinner, but... Well, as you can see, Joshua insists we leave."

"I will, and I will make it plain whose fault it is.

What a shame he is not here to see you off? Likewise, Lord Pennerley."

Quite. Bella was fervently wishing them both to arrive. Could she trust Caroline to deliver a longer message to them?

"I had the most enlightening conversation with Lord Pennerley while he was wading in the river," Caroline remarked. "It's such a pity you cannot stay so that we might discuss the twists and turns of it. I was looking forward to it." She squeezed Bella's hand. "Devil, this is most vexing. There won't be a chance to see you again before we leave tomorrow. It won't be nearly as much fun to put it all in a letter, but I suppose you must do as commanded, and likewise I."

"Wakefield has commanded you to return to Bluebell Lane?"

Caroline squeezed her arm. "Freddy, no. He never commanded anyone. Eliza insists, for practical purposes. Although one might equally suppose her to be fleeing to see if either fellow takes up the chase."

Their heads turned as one towards Eliza, who now stood a little apart from Joshua, with her arms folded and an expression of stoicism ingrained into her demeanour.

"Do hasten yourself, Bella," her brother called. "'Tis supposed to be farewell you're bidding Caroline, not agreeing the details of your next visit."

"I confess my hopes are firmly upon Mr Whistler. He's far more agreeable," Caroline sighed. She hugged Bella farewell, and walked her to the carriage steps where Joshua stood waiting. His desire to leave hung around him like a swarm of angry bees, leaving anyone in close proximity in a jangle.

"Ready?" he enquired, one foot raised to the first step.

"No, and well you know it." Bella strained her neck

for a glimpse back into the hallway, seeking out Lucerne's tall, elegant form, his silken hair – buttery-gold and spun with threads of sunlight. He was not to be found, even straining her eyes to penetrate the shadows.

"Apologies, Miss Wakefield that I've cut short your conversation. We ought to leave before the rain sets in." There was a sharp breath of cold in the air, but rain in Yorkshire was routine. The prospect of downpour was hardly a reason to make haste.

"The carriage accident that killed our parents was a result of ill weather."

Oh, truly, he'd stooped that low? He did not know that for definite. It was speculation at best, and most likely a gross misrepresentation of the facts. Their parents had been lost in a carriage accident, but the weather had most likely played very little part.

However, his goal was achieved. The remark garnered precisely the response from the Wakefields he'd aimed for, thus she was herded aboard the rickety beast.

Almost...

A caw sounded to Bella's right. Was that not someone calling her name?

"Bella...Annabella Rushdale. Wait!"

A frisson of energy burned through her chest and limbs. "Vaughan." Her purest instinct was always to go to him. At once she turned, but Joshua loomed tall behind her, blocking both her view and her descent.

"Get in," he grumbled, giving her a hefty nudge in that direction.

An overly heavy-handed nudge if she was being honest. Bella stumbled, but caught herself upon the edge of the interior seat. Pain fired upwards from her knee. She turned and tumbled onto the seat in order to rub at it, only to see a shadow loom large over her brother, and then viciously fling him aside, so that he skated across the gravel driveway, raising a cloud of white dust.

A set of broad shoulders filled the doorway, then a body occupied the tight confines of the carriage. Vaughan's eyes glittered black in the dingy interior. His dark hair was damp against his coat collar, the ringlets in the ends formed extra tightly. "Is it true?" he barked, not wasting breath on an explanation of his actions. "What Lucerne tells me, is it true?"

Bella's hand stilled upon her bruised knee. Her insides lifted and fell. Nausea tingled in her nose and at the back of her throat. How could Lucerne know? "How am I supposed to know what he has said?"

She drew both clammy hands into her lap, but the prim pose wasn't enough to deceive the man who knew her best of anyone.

"Don't play games, Bella. Not over this. I want to hear it from you, from your own lips." Behind his brusqueness lay a source of agitation he couldn't suppress. "I need to know the truth." He bent, one knee upon the carriage floor, so their heads were on a level, his hands either side of her upon the seat. "Are you increasing?"

Her first instinct was to raise her hands and cover her mouth so that there was no chance of blurting out anything she couldn't later retract, her second; denial.

"Bella, are you carrying my child?"

Vaughan rested upon one knee before her.

"If she is, this had better be a proposal, Pennerley."

Hellfire! Compelling Vaughan only made him recalcitrant.

Joshua leered at them from the doorway, rage boiling through his features, contorting them into an animalistic snarl. He climbed the carriage steps.

"Joshua, no!"

Damn him. Damn him and curse him to hell. Why must he intrude? Why must he make everything so difficult, and turn what might have been beautiful into something tawdry. When Lucerne had stood beneath the weeping willow and promised to stand by her no matter what, her mind had seized upon that notion, and her heart had declared a victory. For one clear moment, she'd glimpsed a bright future, one in which the three of them could co-exist harmoniously—a future in which she possessed not only Vaughan's love, but Lucerne's also, and more importantly one where the imminent patter of tiny footsteps was no impediment to their being as one.

She forced a laugh, even as her very instinct was to cradle her belly. "No, of course not. Whatever gave you the notion?"

Did Vaughan see the lie in her eyes? Hear it in her words? She sounded impossibly nasal, shrill, like a woman plagued with an attack of hystericism. Her gaze skewed over his shoulder again to her brother's hawkish form. She was not sure that he bought the lie either, and it was uttered for his benefit.

"I see," Vaughan said, following the line of her regard. "You'll allow us a moment, Rushdale?"

"To what end?"

Vaughan rose to his full height, which seemed impossibly tall in the confined space.

"I would speak with the lady alone," he insisted, with all the aristocratic expectation of one used to being obeyed.

He was, always, without exception. No one was stupid enough to do otherwise. Except for her exceptionally dim-witted brother.

"I cannot permit it," Joshua twittered, small and sparrow-like in his response. "You have proved over and again that your intentions are not those of a gentleman. I'm done tolerating your debasement of my sister. It's to my shame that I ever permitted this dalliance.

"Now, once again, please remove yourself from this carriage, and thence refrain from future discourse with my sister. She does not need the likes of you in her life."

"Devil beget you, Rushdale! I know your garret is not that unfurnished. You call me out as a cad, but tis presently your behaviour that's unseemly. If she is with child, then I have every right to see as much of her as I choose, and you're deluded if you think to prevent it."

"Joshua, please. Won't you give us just a moment?"

"Get out," he growled at Vaughan in response.

Vaughan turned his body back towards Bella. "Madam, now would be the time to be wholly honest with me."

Dear God, what was she to do? One way or the other, they were certain to come to blows.

Vaughan's dark gaze bore into her.

Joshua's face had lost all its humanity. He swung a punch before she managed to say anything – a right hook aimed squarely at the side of Vaughan's jaw. The smack of bone and flesh flooded her mouth with the sour taste of bile. Vaughan rocked sideways, but did not drop as she feared, but instead put his body between hers and that of her brother. They swung at one another, wrestled over the seat top, for there was precious little space. Vaughan rocked sideways, and crashed hard into the right-side window. The sudden shifting of weight caused the carriage to tilt alarmingly on its axels.

"No. Stop it! Please."

Evidently the pounding of blood in their ears deafened them to her words. Many times she'd watched Vaughan both fence and box. Her brother was no match for Vaughan's agility, his grace, his swiftness. The first punch was really the only one Joshua landed. Nimble, even in the confined space, Vaughan rebounded to retaliate with a series of low blows to the guts. Then, when Joshua bent double, he deftly turned him about and ejected him from the vehicle, so that he landed with a mighty thud on the gravel by Eliza Wakefield's feet.

"Oh, my, heaven!" she exclaimed.

"Sir, are you all right?" asked Caroline, bending to him. He sat up and wiped a streak of blood from his nose.

"Now see here," Frederick Wakefield exclaimed. "That's—"

Vaughan slammed the carriage door in his face.

"Devil take you, Pennerley."

"Really," Vaughan huffed out an extended sigh, and pushed his long hair into some semblance of order. "The lengths one has to go to in in order to secure a private tête-à-tête with a lady these days." He could not step closer to her, for he was having to hold onto the inside of the door handle, to prevent both Wakefield and Joshua rattling it. "We were, I believe, discussing the prospect of a Pennerley-Rushdale offshoot. Should I anticipate an arrival in the spring?"

Not only had he realised the truth, but he'd determined the likeliest date of conception, and extrapolated from it a likely birthing date.

"If I were to confirm such, what would it mean? Would you please my brother?"

It was impossible not to keep sliding her gaze to the window and the two men hammering on the glass.

"Pleasing your brother is the least of my concerns. I do not care for his opinion or preferences. All I desire is the answer to a very simple question. The answer is either yes or no. Which is it?"

"You say it is simple, but it does not seem that way to me. I see nothing but grimness and hostility on both sides. Answering you is akin to tossing a coin in the air, except no matter which way it lands, the outcome will land me in hot water. If I say yes, then I am a disgrace to be hidden away, and if I say no, then I'm a liar."

She shook her head, tears welling in her eyes, and causing a lump to form within her throat.

Looking down, there was Lucerne's ring, in her hands, being turned and twisted as if it were a comforter. Shocked as if it had stung her, she cast it aside, so that it rolled along the seat.

"Can you not just confess so we might end this farce?" He reached for the ring. "It's a pretty symbol."

Bella got to her feet, and reached up to reclaim the token, only for Vaughan to close his fingers around it. "Vaughan, it is mine."

"Aye, but there is likely a babe on the way that is mine, and if that's so, why would you need a ring such as this from another man?"

"I don't recall you offering me one."

The humour drained from his narrow face. "Marriage," he scoffed. "Is that what you want from me?"

"It would solve many, many problems," she said too quickly.

He bowed his head, simultaneously giving it a slow shake. It was but a moment before his gaze raked over her again. "I suppose it might silence your fool of a brother, but it would not make me any more yours than you are now. Whereas you would be my possession, to do with exactly as I saw fit. My relationship with Lucerne would not alter. I could install you in any abode of my choosing and see you only when the mood struck me. And demand anything I chose of you."

She swallowed hard, hot tears now coursed down her cheeks. "Do you think I don't know that? But it would be something, when right at this moment I have nothing, no reassurance from you, no means of supporting myself, and a brother who is ready to throw me to the dogs or else place me under house arrest."

Vaughan shook his head. He put the ring into his pocket.

"Vaughan."

"Your answer."

Every bit as stubborn as he, Bella ground her teeth. "Fine. It's true," she growled. "Is that what you wanted to hear? Are you happy now? What odds does it make? I know that I will never be enough, that no matter how much of myself I give you, you'll always prefer him, and this child will only make that even more apparent."

"Want, yes. Prefer, no. For heaven's sakes woman, would you take off the blinkers you have on. If I cared so very little, why am I here now?"

"I don't know," she sobbed, tears coursing down her face. "Why are you?"

"What is it that you want, Bella Rushdale?"

"For you to love me," she gasped. Wasn't that perfectly apparent? Hadn't it always been?

"I do," he replied, as if that too were an unquestionable truth. "Have I not been telling you so at every opportunity?"

For a second they stared at one another, a new understanding weaving its way into their psyches, stitching them together in a different way. Vaughan raised a hand to her face and cupped her cheek. "Bella, I'm yours, if you will take me. There has only ever been one sticking point, and we both know that is not truly a sticking point at all, but something we both ardently desire. He keeps us both grounded, and he will be a better father than I will ever be. He actually longs for a houseful of the dire, squalling, smelly things."

It was on the tip of her tongue to protest, that her love for Lucerne was entirely dead, but he was right, that wasn't true. There was still mending to be done. Lucerne had torn a great chunk out of her heart when he'd left, and then she'd done her damnedest to pretend it didn't exist rather than patching it. Consequently, she'd spent months slowly bleeding to death. That was done though now, all in the past. Not an hour gone, hadn't she and Lucerne taken the first steps to mending it all and understanding one another?

"I miss the three of us all snug and cosy together, a fire roaring in the hearth, and the servants scandalized by it all, and fighting to keep their stoic masks in place," she confessed.

"We can have that every day."

"I shall be enormous and round."

"I'll still want to violate you. And you'll be glad he's around in the days after the happy arrival, when I'm horn-mad with lust and all you want to do is sleep, and your teats are entirely reserved for another."

She laughed through her tears at his crude words and the image of it in her head. "You don't mind, Vaughan. You're not angry."

"I'm outraged."

"But not half as outraged as I." The carriage bowed to one side, as Joshua re-entered. "Unhand her you despicable meat-monger. You've proved beyond all doubt that you're no gentleman."

A blackbird cawed outside.

All the heat drained from Bella's body. She wanted to cover her eyes, to un-see what was before her, but dared not blink. While she and Vaughan had conversed, her brother had claimed the pair of pistols the driver kept in case of trouble on the road, and now he held them firmly, both muzzles pointed directly at Vaughan.

"Joshua, no!"

"If you don't get out this minute, I'll put a ball in

your ballocks, thereby ensuring you don't defile anyone else as you've defiled her."

"You have everything wrong, Joshua," Bella screamed. "You cannot place all the blame on him."

"Quiet. I'm sick of hearing excuses and reasons why I should tolerate this piece of aristocratic shit. I wish you to leave this carriage and our lives. You will dismount and you will close the door, and thence never try to engage myself or my sister in any way ever again. What you and Marlinscar have done – it's beyond the pale."

"Joshua, this is insane. Put the pistols down."

"I believe my instructions were clear."

"Abundantly so." Vaughan confirmed. "Regretfully, I have no inclination to obedience."

Beyond Joshua, she could see the white faces of the Wakefields and other assembled guests, and Lucerne. Thank God, he was here. He stretched a hand towards her and beckoned with the curl of his fingers.

"Go to him," Vaughan said out of the corner of his mouth.

"Sister, stay exactly where you are."

She couldn't leave Vaughan to face Joshua alone. She would stand between them no matter the risk to her person. Both men swore profusely as she stepped into the void between them. "Why are you doing this now, when everything is almost fixed?" she demanded. "Can't you understand that I wish to be with him? I'm of age, Joshua. Can I not be responsible for my own foolishness?"

"Not while I have breath in my lungs to prevent it. Now move out of the way."

"And allow you to shoot him? I will not."

"He deserves a ball in the guts. Bella, I heard what was said. God help me, I've heard what others have said too. It's unnatural and abhorrent, what has gone on. I can't know of it and willingly allow you to be part of it. They—" He swallowed hard, only for his face to screw up in utter revolt. "—fornicate with one another. Our parents would turn in their graves if they knew I'd knowingly allowed you to participate in such. Don't you see? I have to act in your best interests."

"Heavens, will you listen to yourself? How is it possibly in my interests for you to shoot the father of the child I'm carrying?"

"It will rid us of the taint."

Of all the absurd nonsense she'd heard men spout..."It will ruin us, Joshua. It won't matter as to the right and wrong of things, you'll hang for it and I'll be turned out of our home and left to raise a child alone. How exactly does that benefit anyone? He's a marquis, a lord of this country. The law will always favour him. So shove your honour and your notion of respectability, and put down the damn pistols."

"When he leaves this carriage."

"This I will not do without your sister accompanying me."

"Impossible."

Vaughan nodded.

Bella did not like the calm that had settled over him.

"You demand satisfaction, then. Hand me one of those pistols and step outside with me."

"No," Bella screamed. "No, Vaughan. Joshua." Her pleas went entirely unheeded. They both stepped down from the carriage.

"You've no bone in this, Crakehall." All of Lucerne's remaining guests had assembled, so there was no need to call for a referee. "You'll check they're both properly primed and count out fifteen paces?"

Crakehall turned his head to Lucerne, for it was his property, but Lucerne, white about the nostrils and having lost two brothers to such nonsense, took himself into the hall.

"Fifteen," Crakehall confirmed.

They moved to the opposite side of the carriage onto the grass, with all the guests stood well back. Bella refused to stand meekly to one side while they fired arms at one another. "Stop it. Stop this nonsense."

"Get her out of the way," Joshua insisted. Whereupon Charles and Mr Whistler manhandled her away from duellists. "A solution has to be found, and this is it."

"How is firing at one another going to determine anything?"

Crakehall was the one to respond. He seemed to relish his task of marshal rather too much. "The outcome will be apparent if one of them is hit."

There was a collective indrawing of breath from the assembled ladies.

"No it won't," Bella protested.

They stood back to back, Vaughan, impossibly handsome, his dark hair curling upon his shoulders, and her brother, some inches shorter, the grey wings at his temple shining in the sunlight.

"Ready?" Crakehall called.

Two "ayes" were returned.

"Then, gentlemen, on the count of fifteen you may turn and take your shots. One, two, three, four..."

They paced away from one another, while an oblivious lapwing streaked between them. At fifteen, they turned.

Bella, hands clasped tightly before her, bit her knuckles. It was too hideous to watch, but she could not turn away.

Joshua raised his arm. The shot boomed as the sound echoed off the side of the building. Vaughan tumbled left and hit the ground with a painful thud.

"No!" Bella fought the two men holding her, tore at their arms and faces, kicked and clawed until she was free. Then ran toward him heedless of the danger.

"Stay back." Vaughan had rolled partially onto one side. He raised his pistol arm. Squeezed the trigger.

That sound would forever reverberate inside her nightmares. Her brother gave a cry and dropped the pistol he was holding. Blood gushed from his hand. Bella froze between the two men, hardly knowing which way to go. Lucerne sprinted passed her, Frederick and Eliza Wakefield too. While the former ran to Vaughan, the latter pair went to Joshua.

"It's taken his finger," Wakefield gasped. The top two thirds of Joshua's little finger lay curled upon the grass like a catkin.

Eliza produced a practical, decidedly masculine handkerchief and pressed it to the stump. "Freddie, hold that tight. If the blood comes through, add another over the top, and keep the pressure on. It will have to be stitched.

"You might want to sit down," she added to Joshua, before hurrying across to where Vaughan lay. Lucerne had rolled him over and now had his head cradled against his body. The ball had hit Vaughan's leg. Bella saw Eliza wriggle a finger into the hole in his pantaloons.

Bella started in that direction too. "I can help. Let me help." Only for a wall of gentlemen to materialize before her, fronted by Stephen Crakehall.

"Go, man." He spoke over her head to her brother. "There's no place for you here now. Take yourself home, and pray he lives."

Joshua immediately took possession of the wad of blood-soaked rags pressed to his finger and headed towards the spooked hackneys.

"Your sister?" one of the men enquired.

"Put her in the carriage."

It did not seem to Bella as if they were speaking of her, until there were men all around her. "What? No, let me pass. I need to go to Vaughan. I have to see him. I can help." She was unceremoniously lifted and all the squirming and squalling in the world didn't cause them to falter. Finally, shoved into the carriage, she rose from where they'd dropped her only for the door to slam and the carriage to lurch forward.

"Vaughan!" she screamed, drumming her fists hard against the glass.

To no avail, the driver whipped the horses into froth so that they sped along the driveway and thence into the lane.

"Pass me your kerchief." Joshua said at least four times before she turned her head from the window. "I need your kerchief."

The pad around his finger was scarlet, so too were his coat cuff and one leg of his breeches.

Bella drew the tucker from around her shoulders and held it out to him. "I don't know if you have killed him."

Joshua gave a wry shrug, as he wrapped his hand. "We'll know soon enough if he dies. Crakehall will go to the Lord Lieutenant and they'll send dragoons for me."

Bella sagged, her head weighing heavily in her palms. "That is all you have to say to me. You shot him. You've ruined everything."

"Shit in your teeth, Bella! What else was I supposed to do? You wouldn't listen. There had to be an end to it."

"Not like this there didn't. You didn't need to fire pistols at one another. Maiming one another with lead never solved anything." She raised her hands, but stopped short of slapping him. "All this quarrel and nonsense just because you failed to find a wife."

Joshua sat back against the seat back with a thump.

"You're touched in the head. That has nothing to do with this."

"It had everything to do with it. And if anyone's mind is addled, tis yours. Just because you're miserable... Dammit, everything was finally coming right again. The three of us—" She pressed a hand to her belly. "—four, had a chance of building something precious together. Now I have nothing. You've stolen me away from everything I care about."

"Everything?"

She glared at him, so he did not further push it.

"Bella, you cannot love two men. Most especially not two who love each other."

"Yes," she said. "I can. I do, and if you have not killed one of them, I'll continue to do so until my very last breath. Nor do I see what difference it makes to anyone how I conduct myself. I am not advocating the same arrangement for all."

"You're unwed and flaunting your licentiousness."

"So if I were wed, it would be fine?"

Joshua shook his head. His lips had drained of colour. He looked as haggard as a ghoul. "That is not what I said. Accept that it's over Bella. We're going home to Wyndfell. You'll settle down and lead a quiet, modest life. In time, we'll look for a suitable husband for you together."

What a fool he was. Tears gathered thickly in her eyes, so that she was blinded by her efforts not to let them fall. His plan would never work. Before the snowdrops faded next spring she'd give birth to Vaughan's bastard child. No other man would ever have her, but that was fine, for she wanted no other man... men besides Vaughan and Lucerne.

"You had best put bars on my window," she advised. "It won't look good if I fall to my death, pregnant, while scrambling across the roof to be with him."

Joshua didn't reply. The shock at the loss of his finger had finally caught up with him, and he'd passed out cold.

CHAPTER 39

BELLA

I N THE DAYS that followed, Bella reflected many times on her decision to stay with Joshua and watch over him. It would have been so easy, while he was insensible, to return to Lauwine. Alas, for all his stupidity, Joshua remained her only family and she did not want to sever the ties between them, nor leave him entirely to the trust of the servants.

It was such uncertainty that prompted her to follow when the coachman and the gardener bore Joshua into the parlour between them. Bella sat in attendance while cook sewed up the end of his severed little finger like she might a bird-sized joint of meat, and then revived him with a combination of sherry and smelling salts.

Her brother's muddied gaze settled upon her. They did not speak. There was nothing to say.

He would not acknowledge the torment he had wrought with his actions, and she refused to see any evil in loving two men. What mattered was that they found happiness and fulfilled one another. She was so very certain they'd been right on the cusp of doing so.

Joshua revived and recuperated quickly enough, or

so the servants informed her. Bella kept to her room. Hence Sunday arrived and drifted into Monday. No word of anything arrived from Lauwine. Nor, thankfully, did the Lord Lieutenant and his dragoons.

At least he is alive, she told herself as she watched the rain sluice down the outside of the window pane. Though with what injuries, she didn't know. He may have lost a leg to Joshua's finger.

Mid-week two heavily embellished accounts of the duel arrived from the village, the first with the butcher's boy, the second with the baker's. Tilly whispered them to her as she huddled beneath the bedcovers, too lovelorn to even contemplate donning a dress. "The marquis has left Lauwine. He's gone south to his estate."

Surely, that was confirmation that his injury was not too severe. Alas that Vaughan had left without sending word of doing so. This time, she took little comfort in the knowledge that they often passed days without communicating.

Tilly fussed around her, sweeping a dust cloth over various surfaces and exchanging one warming bottle for another. "I heard the Wakefields are gone too; the whole lot of them, including the captain and his wee bairn. Only Lord Marlinscar remains at Lauwine. I suppose he will depart before long, too."

Bella poked her nose out from the covers. "Why so?"

"Well, miss," Tilly replied, attempting to disguise her joy at having coaxed Bella's interest by holding the duster over her mouth. "He's not rightly going to want to stay in that big old house all by himself, is he? Also, the maids that walked in from the village have been let go."

It seemed Lucerne would finally follow his lover to Pennerley, as Vaughan had once yearned for him to do.

They were leaving her.

Tilly tutted. "Lord Pennerley has served you ill, miss, and no mistake. Then, it was always said that Lord Pennerley was a wrong 'un, and now he's downright proven it."

Bella sat and plumped her pillows, which she immediately tugged several protruding feathers from. "His leaving is my brother's doing. I'll thank you to recall that. It's not like he ran off for no reason."

"Not for no reason, no. 'cause he didn't care to be saddled with a jack in the box, that's why." She stared pointedly at Bella's belly.

"Joshua shot him," Bella protested.

"For refusing to take responsibility for his actions. Oh, Miss. I'm right sorry it's come to this, but you are blind to his faults. He's a wicked, wicked man. You should have stuck with Lord Marlinscar. You'd have been a respectable lady now."

"How many walls, fences and roofs did he fix since last November to have been elevated to sainthood?" How very tiresome it had become to hear how she ought to have married Lucerne. "It's all very well saying I'd have been better off with Lord Marlinscar, but he didn't exactly offer for me. He just failed to plant a baby in my belly when he tupped me."

Tilly goggled at her, her thin little mouth fell open and then snapped closed as if she was determinedly holding onto whatever retort had come into her head.

"You're right, Til, Lord Marlinscar will leave Lauwine soon. He'll go south to be with Lord Pennerley, and they'll continue to be as notorious a pair as there's ever been. I'm telling you, and I'd know, that neither man is better than the other. They're both rogues, and I would not have them be anything else. They both bedded me a thousand times over and neither offered to waltz me down the aisle. So, you see, your assessments are all wrong. Still, at least I'll know they'll have one another while I am stuck here withering away instead of living a life of adventure." She sniffed hard. "Do go away now. I want to be alone with my misery."

CHAPTER 40
BELLA

6th September 1801

"Miss... Miss, you need to get up."

"Why?" Bella lifted her groggy head from the pillow. She had lain abed so long she could no longer be certain of the day or hour.

Tilly dragged the heavy drapes back from the window, letting the sunlight spill in and illuminate all the swirling dust motes. The sun sat fat and yellow outside. Its brilliance made Bella swear and recoil under the covers. "Go away, I don't wish to rise." There was nothing to rise for.

"Oh, but Miss, you must. There's a gig coming. Proper grand it is. Sammy saw it in the lane, and it's heading this way. Do hurry, it will be here in less than a minute."

Hurry? Fog filled her head, and her limbs would hardly obey instructions. She was so drained of vigour that she couldn't unwind herself from the sheets. What did it mean that a gig was coming anyway? Unless, the lad had misidentified Vaughan's spider phaeton?

She sat at once, and clouted the side of her head to attempt to dislodge the haze.

Tilly rattled a cup and saucer under her nose. "Drink. It'll help. I made it extra sweet."

Bella pushed it away. "I don't need tea, only aid in getting to the window." Her room overlooked the front of the house, so that if she lifted the sash, she might easily identify the caller and whether she needed to go to the effort of dressing. Could it be that Vaughan had finally come for her? Or was it the Lord Lieutenant come to arrest her brother?

She swung her legs free of the covers and rose, only to immediately find herself sitting again.

Tilly tutted, and pushed the tea cup into her hand. "Honestly, it's no wonder you're as helpless as a newborn, you've barely touched a thing for days."

She hadn't had anything because she hadn't wanted it. What purpose was there in food, in tea, or anything else, when all that you desired had been taken from you?

"Drink. All of it. I'll get you some of cook's broth too."

"No. Save the broth for afterwards." She took a hesitant sip of the tea, discovered she was thirsty, and gulped down the rest. "Help me dress."

Tilly already had an assortment of items spread across the blankets. "You're not the right shape for most of these. We might squeeze you in, but they won't be comfortable."

"I don't care about that, and I'm not so very large yet."

"How about this one?"

"Yes, yes..." Bella agreed, without paying regard to the garment. It turned out to be her old chemise de la reine; a style she hadn't worn in years. Still, true to Tilly's assessment, its drawstrings readily adjusted to her altered shape. Moreover, with a sash fastened beneath her breasts and a Kashmir shawl for her shoulders, it was not too overtly old-fashioned. She eschewed any attempt to detangle her hair, and pushed her feet into her shoes without pausing to first draw on stockings.

Her legs wobbled as she hurried downstairs. Bella gritted her teeth and clung onto the balustrade.

Broth – she would make it a priority, along with some of cook's parkin, as soon as she'd ascertained what this arrival meant.

Bella took a deep breath in the hallway. The front door already stood open, allowing more of that vicious sunlight that burned her eyes to spill onto the tiles. She blinked, waiting for her vision to adjust. Outside, Joshua was pacing back and forth like a house sparrow in search of a grub. As she'd deduced, it was not a gig that had arrived, but a phaeton. Alas, not Vaughan's spider phaeton, but a high flyer.

Not the Lord Lieutenant? Surely to God, not! She clutched her chest as a wave of panic hit.

She had to know. If Vaughan was gone, then…

She burst from the house, causing Joshua to come to a halt and the carriage driver to blurt her name. "Bella?"

"Lucerne?"

She stopped by the front wheel and stared up at him. A halo of sunlight surrounded his head. He'd dressed as she remembered him, elegantly, in a masterfully tailored coat, cut away at the front to show off his Indian silk waistcoat. There had never been a more welcome sight. Whatever troubles there had been between them, she was more than glad of his presence now.

Lucerne climbed down from the drivers perch at once and handed the ribbons to a groom. "Miss

Rushdale, good day." He bowed from the waist. "How good it is to see you. Your disposition is obviously much improved. Joshua was just explaining that you weren't receiving guests."

"Was he?" She turned her head to throw a glower in his direction.

"For all I knew, you were still abed," Joshua retorted.

"But I'm not, as you can plainly see, and would have known if you'd enquired." She gave a huff before returning her attention to Lucerne, in order to drink down every aspect of his spry appearance in case he vanished as abruptly as he'd arrived. "This is new?" she enquired of the carriage.

"It is. I called hoping your brother would allow me to take you for a jaunt about the lanes."

"You do realise she hates carriages."

"Not this sort, where the wind is in your face, only the boxed in, airless ones that jolt one all over the place."

Joshua folded his arms across his chest. His duel with Vaughan had in no way alleviated the hostility he bore Lucerne. She supposed there was no reason to suppose it would. In fact, it had been rather daring of Lucerne to come here. Only something truly important would have compelled him to do so, or else something he felt might help them all make amends.

"May I go?" she asked her brother. She meant to, no matter his opinion.

"Perhaps if we strolled around the gardens a moment or two first," Lucerne suggested, making an attempt at diplomacy. Bella failed to see what difference it made if they walked together or hared down the lanes side by side in a carriage. She was well past the point of requiring a chaperone.

Joshua shrugged. "Do as you will. Nothing I say will

make any difference." He turned about and went into the house, closing the door tightly behind him.

"I'm surprised he didn't set Campbell and the dogs onto you. You must have said something to persuade him to allow you to say whatever it is you've come to tell me." She grasped both his hands. "Vaughan – tell me. I don't know how he is. All I've heard has been garbled. His leg, it's not lost?" His mien seemed too light for him to be the bearer of ill tidings.

"Bella I cannot tell you how he is at this moment, for I haven't seen him in six days, but he was well enough when he left Lauwine. Still injured, obviously, but not in over much pain."

Bella let out the breath it seemed she had been holding onto for weeks.

"You may thank Eliza Wakefield for that miracle. She makes quite the physician, for a woman with no formal instruction."

"Eliza tended him? You did not call for Garth?"

"That quack would likely have brought his knives and taken the whole leg for no other reason than proving his credentials. Eliza dug out the ball and stitched the wound. I don't want to think too hard of where she gleaned her knowledge of anatomy, for I suspect it may be unsavoury, but I'm thankful for it nonetheless. She is quite a wonder. Who could have guessed that Wakefield had such a bluestocking as a sister?"

Bella nodded along, but even his joviality could not quite elevate her from the despair over her fortune that clung to her with tenacious, bony fingers. "Is she still with him?"

"Eliza? Of course not. Bella, really? Do you imagine Freddy would permit such a thing? She left, along with the rest of her siblings once she was certain the wound wouldn't become putrid. I sacrificed my very best brandy to that cause, and a half quart of rum."

Yes, how silly of her. Naturally, Wakefield wouldn't want Eliza associated with Vaughan, and wouldn't dream of allowing her to accompany him to his own estate. "Why did he leave? Vaughan, I mean, not Wakefield."

Lucerne offered her his arm and they strolled beneath the rose arch into the garden proper. "It seemed prudent to do so given the proximity of the two houses. Further trouble wouldn't be in anyone's best interests."

"I've so wanted to see him."

He nodded. "I think we all realised that, but such a visit could potentially have led to another skirmish. It's better that you didn't come and that he left."

She couldn't agree with him, though she saw his point.

They paused on reaching the bench that overlooked the rolling patchwork of moorland, and Bella took the weight off her feet. After a moment's hesitation, Lucerne sat beside her.

"Does he hate me, Lucerne? Is everything lost? Is that why you're here? I cannot think of another reason why Joshua would permit you to speak to me."

"None?" He clasped her hand where it rested in her lap. "Bella, Vaughan doesn't hate you, or blame you, and nor do I. We are all equally responsible for our actions. However, if you're expecting him to ride up and steal you away, I have to tell you that it won't happen. Even once he's properly on his feet again, he won't come near this place, though not from any lack of affection. Creating more strife will not help anyone."

"Yet you have come."

He jolted his head up and down in a series of tiny nods. "I didn't engage in a duel with your brother. Also,

I like to think I'm capable of diplomacy, whereas we all know Vaughan thrives on conflict. It occurred to me that I could at least attempt to fix things. Of course, I don't know that I'll succeed. It all rather depends upon where your heart lies."

"My heart?" She drew her hand through her bird's nest of hair. "With Vaughan... With you."

A smile brightened the set of his mouth. "So, there is hope for us. We might still be allies, agree a truce, work out a way of both loving him without jealousy rending us bitter?"

She shook her head. "Not allies."

He reared back a little.

"Lovers. If you still want that, knowing I'm swollen with another man's child?"

"Hell, of course, I do. I hardly dared hope."

"I still love you, Lucerne. I've tried hard not to. I wanted so badly to wash you from my world that I convinced myself that I felt nothing, that if I didn't look or poke at those feelings then they weren't real. But, the truth is that Vaughan has been right all along, we are all three better together. I want that – except we will be four." She pressed a hand to her belly. "It's taken ever such a long time to admit that you hurt me when you left. That it wasn't only Vaughan you let down. I was so angry at you for leaving, but it was easier to focus on him, to pretend all my rage was due to how you'd hurt him rather than to acknowledge what I'd lost and felt. I know it was my choice not to go with you, but it was not truly a choice I wanted to make. You were supposed to come to Pennerley and beg forgiveness... You were supposed to stay."

He took hold of her hand and squeezed it. "I was lost that day; tied up in knots, many of which were of my own making. They have all been unravelled now. The mists have lifted. I possess more clarity of vision.

There is only one thing with which I remain at odds and that is you."

She shook her head. "We are not... Lucerne, I love Vaughan with all my heart, but I love you also. All the time I've spent denying it has only created more misery for us. We could have spent the whole summer together."

"There are years of summers ahead of us, Bella."

She sighed. "All the world is against us. I am stuck here, and Vaughan is gone."

He laughed in a merry way. Unfathomably, there existed a lightness in him today that refused to be dimmed. It was as if he'd been freed from a long captivity. "Vaughan is not gone. He's only made a tactical withdrawal. We could go to him, and even if he did not wish us there, he could not run away. See, there are advantages to your brother's marksmanship."

"Joshua will not let me leave, Lucerne. If I took it upon myself to do so, we would become estranged, and for all that I am vexed beyond measure by him, I cannot risk that."

"I think we both know there are circumstances he would accept. You only need wed—"

"Vaughan won't. You saw what happened when Joshua made an attempt to coerce him."

"So don't marry Vaughan."

He slipped off the bench onto the grass upon his knees. "Bella Rushdale, I know I'm not the man you want, nor the father of your child. I, however, like to think I'm the next best thing. I want you in my life, and warming my bed, my companion, my co-conspirator, not locked away like a dirty secret. Bella, we belong together, and if there is any way to make Vaughan see that, then this is it. I should have asked a very long time ago. I didn't, but I am asking you now—" From out of his pocket he produced the ring that Vaughan had refused to return to her. "This is yours. It was always yours. Will you take it, Bella? Will you be my wife?"

"Vaughan... He won't like it. He's always been against our betrothal."

"I think he'll recognise that circumstances have somewhat changed."

Bella caught a shadow of movement out of the corner of her eye, and realised that Joshua was watching them from the parlour. If she didn't want another battle on her hands, then there was only one option available. She gazed down at Lucerne's radiant smile, and a grin came unbidden to her face. "I..." She nodded.

Lucerne slipped the ring onto her finger. Then he rose and lifted her to her feet so that he might kiss her and seal the deal. Probably it ought to have been a chaste affair, but an abundance of longing on both sides, coupled with the knowledge they were being witnessed, had them clinging fast to one another. Bella's fingers curled into the thick cloth of his coat where it pulled tight across the broad expanse of his back, while Lucerne's palm seemed to sear right though her thin dress so that it was as if he was caressing her bare skin. Their tongues sparred, and a rush like vertigo set Bella swaying merrily on her feet. Still, wasn't that a reason to cleave more closely to his strong and supple body?

Lucerne didn't kiss in the same way as Vaughan. He kissed with the intention of stoking delight, not bending her to his will. When Vaughan possessed her mouth, he bruised her with his dominance, while still always seeming to hold some part of himself back. She would never wholly know him, whereas Lucerne was only too willing to open all the doors and windows and allow her free reign of his quarters. If she wished to rifle through the cobwebby trunks stored in his attic, then he'd happily present her the keys, and chase off the spiders. I'm yours, he claimed with every caress of his tongue. Let me show you how much you please me, what a thrill it is to hold you, how very ardently I adore you.

The ring felt both alien on her finger and altogether right, at the same time. She twisted it, and dug her teeth into her lips as she gazed at it. "Is this why Joshua didn't see you off immediately?" she asked, as they strolled back to the front of the Grange, arm in arm. "You told him of your intent."

Lucerne inclined his head. "I sent a note to that effect a day or so ago. I cannot in good faith say that he was pleased to hear from me, but I've always found your brother to be immeasurably practical, when he's not allowing his emotions to rule him. When you've an unwed sister with a rapidly swelling belly, you'd have to be an idiot not to grab with both hands any offer that was made for her – especially one from a viscount."

"Practical, yes," she mused, only to then blurt; "He knows you and Vaughan are lovers."

"Mere speculation," Lucerne waved aside the notion. "Rumours of more intimacy than is seemly occurring between Vaughan and I have abounded for years, but rumours is all they are. There's no substance to them. Such speculation will cease the moment one of us ties the knot. In any case, all your brother really cares about is stilling the many waggling tongues, so he might brush the whole sorry affair under the carpet."

"You'll be branded a fool. Everyone knows that I'm carrying Vaughan's child."

"They know nothing of the sort. Gossip is not fact, and we've been practically betrothed for years. All anyone outside of this miniscule parish will say is that it's damned well about bloody time. As to those closer to home, I don't give a fig what they think. Now, come, let us go and deliver the glad tidings to your sourpuss of a brother, and then see about racing along some lanes."

In fact, there was no need to go into the parlour to address Joshua, for he was waiting for them in the hallway. He didn't speak, but lifted an eyebrow by way of enquiry.

"The answer is yes," Lucerne said.

That earned them a perfunctory nod.

"You might at least offer congratulations," Bella complained. "It's what you petitioned for over and again. Aren't you glad to have washed your hands of me and got what you wanted?"

Joshua lifted his narrow shoulders and shrugged. "If only you could have exhibited such sense earlier, then you wouldn't need to be hasty with the arrangements." He raised his gaze to Lucerne. "I won't pretend to understand your motivation. You must know her change of heart is purely down to her condition."

Lucerne ignored the remark and kept on smiling. "If it's agreeable with you, I thought Bella and I might drive by the vicarage."

Joshua nodded. "Yes, you'll want the banns read quickly. Go...go..." He shooed them away.

CHAPTER 41
LUCERNE

DECEPTION WAS VAUGHAN'S forte, not his. Lucerne kept half an eye on Bella's countenance as he guided the high-flyer along the winding lane towards Reeth. After Joshua's dismissal, they had stayed at Wyndfell only long enough for Bella to demand a hunk of bread and cheese, and to fetch her pelisse and hat. Thenceforth, she'd been silent; her gaze contemplatively fastened on his ring upon her finger.

Lucerne wasn't a fool, no matter what anyone might think. He knew necessity had motivated her acceptance, not a genuine desire to become his wife. There was a bond of love between them, but it was secondary, for both of them, to what they each felt for Vaughan. Vaughan—who would have a definite opinion upon this; most likely, a wholly negative one. How many times had he threatened, insinuated the consequences if Lucerne actually proposed.

At the crossroads he swung the phaeton left. They had barely passed the church when Bella's head jerked upward. She turned to look all about them, as if the landscape were in some way unfamiliar. "You've gone past the vicarage."

"I never said we would stop." It was Joshua who'd mentioned having the banns announced.

A short way on, he took another turn; this one set them on a southerly path across the moors. The ubiquitous drystone walls faded away, replaced by endless rolling stretches of brown, green, and purple. There were no houses, no other people, only the odd hardy, ambling sheep. It was breathtakingly lovely, and desolate. Also, wild, like the woman riding beside him.

"To where are we heading? It is not Gretna, for that is in the opposite direction."

"I have a licence," he admitted. "So a trip across the border is wholly unnecessary. Not to mention unadvisable in a vehicle such as this and without a stitch of luggage. We're going to address the question that's threatening to consume you like a flask of Greek fire."

"What question?"

Really, he was not about to spell it out, and have her feel she had to deny it.

"Lucerne? We can no more go to Pennerley than we can Gretna."

"Agreed. We are not on our way to Pennerley."

She cast him a shrewd glance. "I swear you said Vaughan had retired to his estate."

He hadn't the time to confirm or deny it, before she connected the appropriate dots for herself.

"You didn't mean Pennerley. That minor omission was for Joshua's benefit, in case he... in case he what? Protested? Refused to allow me out of his sight?"

"How about just refused?"

She nodded. "This is the Leyburn road. We're headed to Middleham. Vaughan is in Middleham, where he first intended us to stay."

"Tupgrave Park is actually a little outside of the town," he explained.

"Is he expecting us?" Her expression danced between nervousness and glee.

"Not exactly."

Bella twisted her hands, then sat upon them.

"However, when he leaves, he expects us to follow. Those are the rules, whether he's injured or not."

"You said he'd pursue me to the ends of the earth. I still don't know if that's true, but I would follow him that far." She stilled. Her attention returned to the ring upon her finger, which she lifted before her. "You don't really mean to marry me, do you?"

Lucerne halted the horses, so that he could turn and address her properly. The blue of her eyes had never seemed so bright, nor had her smile ever been so lovely. "Know this Bella Rushdale; I'd marry you in a heartbeat. Don't think it hasn't occurred to me to steal you away and wed you this very night. However, we both know that someone else has a claim upon your heart."

She shook her head and raised a finger to seal his lips. "You're a good man, Viscount Marlinscar. Too good for me, and much too good for the rogue we're bound to call upon."

CHAPTER 42

BELLA

UPGRAVE WAS A wuthering old mansion that had likely begun life as a farmstead only to be remodelled and extended by multiple generations into its current rambling configuration. It was home, Lucerne informed her, to an enviable set of stables. Horses were liveried and trained here to compete on the track at Middleham.

It was Charles Aubury who greeted them on arrival.

"You'll forgive me if I make myself scarce," he insisted while shaking hands with Lucerne. "I'm going out to watch the gallops. You'll find Pennerley among the finnimbruns in the morning room. I think they've housed him there to keep him out of sight and mind. It's such a dreadful inconvenience to the normal running of the place to have the master in residence and off his stride, don't you know."

Lucerne rolled his eyes. "I'm sure Vaughan is precisely where he wants to be," he said to Bella as he led her through the winding, dingy corridors. The house had certainly been constructed to an eccentric design. One room lead into another. Short stretches of corridor sprung out of nowhere and ended perplexingly. After only a matter of minutes, Bella was completely disorientated. To that end, she stayed fast to Lucerne's heels. Hence, they eventually found their way to their destination, at what surely must be the very back of the sprawling mansion.

Vaughan lay reclined upon a golden draped day bed, surrounded by a multitude of oddments and knick-knacks. It reminded Bella of the county fair, when everyone seemed to have some novelty to sell or exchange. There was much that was beautiful, and a deal that was not; numerous mathoms, and assorted old toys nestled together with things from far flung places.

Her lover's dark ringlets were spread against the pillows. He appeared to be sleeping, his lower body concealed by the coverlet.

"Vaughan." Lucerne approached the bed.

"So you're here at last." Vaughan responded, demonstrating his alertness without opening his eyes. "You weren't exactly hasty about it."

Lucerne bent and dropped a kiss onto his brow. "There were matters to attend before I could leave Lauwine, and you know it. I've brought someone with me you may wish to see."

A dry chuckle rumbled in his throat. "Do you think I don't recognise that which is mine, just because I have not set eyes upon it?" His eyelids flickered open. "Miss Rushdale, how delightful of you to visit."

"Vaughan," she rushed forward and clasped his outstretched hand. "How are you? I've been so worried."

"Have you now?" His lazy, penetrating gaze swept over her from head to chest. "Yes, I do believe you have. You're hideously pale. Ghastly, one might venture." He cupped his hand against her cheek, and Bella snuggled against it. "I should say, some fresh air and staunch exercise are a priority. Now, did you shimmy down the trellising, or did your oaf of a brother consent to you venturing abroad?" His gaze dropped to the curve of her abdomen.

Bella longed to take his hand and press it to her flesh. She had felt odd flutters these last few days; his son or daughter kicking her to make their presence felt. Reminding her, in ways she hadn't necessarily appreciated, that it was not only her future she had to consider. If it had only been her life, then there was no question she would have left Wyndfell at the first opportunity.

"It's Lucerne's doing that's allowed me this freedom. Not that I had any notion this is where he intended to bring me. I thought you had returned to Pennerley."

"Handicapped by this?" He rested a hand flat against his upper thigh. "Doctor Eliza worked miracles, but even she recommends bedrest and minimizing unnecessary travel. Hence I am here. Pennerley would certainly have been my preference. I've had my fill of Yorkshire."

"And Yorkshire damsels?"

He sniffed. "I confess they still hold a certain appeal."

Their gazes met and a myriad of unspoken thoughts seemed to pass between them. "I never meant for you to fight, or to get hurt," she insisted, clasping tight his outstretched hand.

"The fight was entirely my prerogative. I must remember to stick to swordplay in future." He laughed at their scowls.

Judging by the scars he bore, such endeavours in the past hadn't served him much better than pistols.

"No more duels, please."

He sucked his lips, making no promises. "So fretful," he said of them both. "I am still here, and I confess I find satisfaction in that knowledge, and knowing I made a mark upon my enemy. It might only be the tip of a finger, but he will not forget me. Mayhaps, I ought to have kept it as a trophy."

"That's savage."

"I see my humour is too bleak for you. You may calm yourself, Bella. I would have to pry the thing from Eliza Wakefield's death grip first. And I owe her too much at this point to distress her in such a way."

Eliza had Joshua's fingertip? That knowledge was equally disturbing. What in heavens did she want it for?

She had not the time to think on it though, for Vaughan raised her hand up to eye level. "While we are speaking of such things, what is this upon your finger?" He stared pointedly at the betrothal ring.

Bella touched her tongue to her lips, before shooting a hasty glance in Lucerne's direction. "It's the means by which I secured my freedom."

"This—" Vaughan said, regarding the ring, then her, and then Lucerne, "—does not look like freedom to me, but bondage. And not the sort I endorse."

"You weren't there, Vaughan." She had feared this response. "Lucerne offered a means of escape. Do not blame me for seizing it. Not when there was no other alternative."

"I concede that you were forced into a loathsome position, but still, this will not do. Lucerne—" His attention focussed over the top of her head. Lucerne stood behind her a little to the side, stiffly alert, his shoulders bowed defensively. "After our many, many discussion on this point, this cannot be what it appears. You would not be so foolish."

"I am every bit that foolish," Lucerne confessed. "Things are exactly as they appear. We're betrothed."

"No. I won't have it, goddammit! She's having my damn child."

Lucerne raised his palms. "Not an issue. You know my sentiments regarding children."

"Goddamn you! You can't just steal them."

"Sometimes one has to be practical about these things," Bella said. She turned her head to look at the man she'd blithely, perhaps foolishly agreed to marry.

Vaughan's gaze danced between them. "Is this what you want? Truly, Bella?" His breath blasted her skin like flames.

A very short while ago, little more than an hour or so, it had been. It had been the only light she could see in an increasingly dark world, but she was no longer at Wyndfell. Each step she took away from the familiar opened her mind to other possibilities. "No, not exactly," she confessed. There was such hurt in his eyes, such betrayal, it was hard to meet his gaze. Bella sighed, her head sagging limply forward. She took a deep breath. "You know what I want, Vaughan. These last few days haven't changed that. My heart hasn't changed. If anything, I'm more resolute than ever."

"It seems to me things have drastically changed. Not very long ago you told me you hated him, and now you are betrothed."

"I was lying to myself, when I said that. Wasn't it you who pointed it out, a dozen or more times? I do love him, just as I love you. I want only to be with you both. Until Lucerne arrived, it looked to me like that was extraordinarily unlikely. You may say I told you so, and brand me a fool for taking so long to admit it, if you wish. I've had much too much time to think this last sennight...fortnight." In truth she had lost track of the number of days that had past. "I was working with what options were available to me."

"That is a hint, if you cannot see it," Lucerne interjected.

Bella raised her head to meet Vaughan's violet eyes. "If you had come with that offer, then... Never mind." She shook her head. Vaughan's lips were pressed together so tightly the colour had bled from them.

"You can't marry Lucerne," he growled through gritted teeth. "You're mine. I claimed you. And he's already claimed, also by me."

A laugh came unbidden to Bella's throat. "You just wish everything your way, so that you're at the centre of things, like a great fat spider."

Vaughan stared at her as if she'd made an observation of something so universally accepted it was plain ludicrous to remark upon it. "Exactly," he eventually concurred. "So you see why this nonsense about the two of you tying the knot is impossible."

"Hardly impossible," Lucerne remarked. He had moved to stand on the opposite side of the bed from them now, so that they were gathered into a triangular arrangement. "Given I have a licence and her brother's blessing."

Vaughan raised his hand, indicating Lucerne should stop. "Cur. Hush now. Don't say another thing. Can't you see how incensed I am? This has to be the most wretched thing you've ever done."

"It's hardly my fault you're so slow to call forth," Lucerne laughed.

Vaughan pouted, so that his chin stuck out. "When exactly have I had the chance? I've been stuck here, while you've been kniving."

"Vaughan, I handed you months' worth of opportunities. Having arrived at the conclusion that you're besotted with one another, did it never occur to you that an exchange of vows might be the logical next step?"

"That would have been rather hypocritical of me, don't you think, having forsworn the possibility of the two of you tying the knot, only to then step in and wed her the moment you were out of the picture."

"I was out of the picture for that very purpose. You both had blinkers on."

"We would never have all been reunited again if Bella and I had tied the knot."

Lucerne chuckled to himself. "It's laughable, isn't it, that it's the notorious rakeshame among us that possesses such qualms about infidelity? Myself, I'm far less churlish of the notion of being a third party."

Bella strategically positioned herself between them both as they continued to glower at one another. She didn't think it would come to blows, for there remained a distinct chuckle in Lucerne's voice, and even Vaughan was struggling not to give in to a laugh. "Gentlemen, can we not settle this amicably? I'd rather not bear witness to another fight."

"Then make a choice, Bella." Vaughan settled his shoulders back against the pillows. "Marchioness or viscountess? Which is it to be?"

"What? You cannot expect me to make that choice. I don't even know what choice it is I'm making! Are you proposing to me?"

Vaughan tilted his head, seeming to consider, only for him to then blurt, "What the devil else do you imagine I'm doing? I think my child should have my name, and it's about time that people realised you're mine. It's damned tedious listening to them bleat on about how you were meant to marry Lucerne. There was no meant to about it. He was already taken – by me."

If there were any more surprises in today, Bella thought her heart might give out. As it was, it was performing some disturbing kinds of skips. "I have to say, Lucerne's proposal was a deal more romantic."

The comparison prompted another scowl. "I suppose he went down on one knee. I'm sorry, I have a gammy leg."

"But you could actually say the words."

A snort forced its way out of Lucerne's mouth. He clamped a hand over his mirth. "What? Oh, don't let me stop you," he said rolling his eyes, before adding under this breath. "You may be a masterful lover, but you're a cake when it comes to romance."

"This isn't funny," Vaughan complained. "It's a serious matter."

"No, it's bloody hilarious. I'd be an idiot not to enjoy seeing you wrong-footed for once. In any case, I think it my prerogative to find whatever humour I choose in the situation. I am, I suspect, the one about to be jilted."

Bella's brow creased. "Well, if he ever says the words." She covered her mouth. "Damn, I'm sorry, Lucerne. You don't mind, do you?"

"Mind? Quite a bit, actually," Lucerne said, his smile unwavering. "However, I have to admit, it's going to be a glorious day indeed watching this irredeemable rogue willingly embrace a pair of shackles. I do hope you're going to opt for a formal society wedding, with a full complement of groomsmen and revellers."

"You might contain your glee at least until I've got the words out," Vaughan snapped. "In fact, would you give us a moment?"

"Damn, no! I'm staying right here."

"Very well, Tommy tit." Vaughan shot Lucerne a last venomous glower, before removing all trace of distemper from his face in order to address her. "Miss Rushdale – Bella. How do you feel about growing old and ever more inappropriate together? Will you be my Persephone? Shall we rule the underworld together?"

"Well," she folded her hands into her lap. "I have given my word to someone else, so I probably ought not to say yes until he agrees to release me."

Vaughan glared at Lucerne again.

"You know he's a feckless rogue," Lucerne said, clearly finding this all far too funny. "And he'll frequently stray from the marriage bed."

It was Bella's turn to smile. "But only as far as yours, and that's what you would have done too."

"True enough," he agreed, nodding. "Bella, you know I'll never hold you to any promise you don't wish to keep. I knew when I asked you that you'd much prefer it were this devil on his knee before you, and I'll not pretend that I didn't step up with the notion in the back of my mind to force his hand by doing so."

"Knave," Vaughan muttered.

"For damn sakes just ask her and answer him," Lucerne insisted of them both. "Then, seal it with a kiss so we can get on with screwing one another. It's been an eternity since we were all together, and I, for one, would rather we spent our time fornicating than squabbling over which two of us are going to make vows to one another before a god that at least one of us doesn't believe in."

Vaughan clasped hold of Bella's hands. "Marry me?"

"I'd love to."

Lucerne whistled. "Thank the lord and all his angels for that."

Vaughan removed one of the rings from his own fingers and slid it onto Bella's so it lay beside the one Lucerne had given her. "Now come here wench," he tugged her forward until she was astride his lap. "Let's seal this deal properly, because Lucerne's right about the fucking. It's been too long."

"Wait!" Bella attempted to push him to arm's length. "Your leg. I'll hurt you."

"The hell you will. It ain't about to drop off. Now, kiss me. And Lucerne, strip."

"Bossy," both she and Lucerne chided, but that was how they both liked him.

While Lucerne undressed, Bella leaned in and brushed Vaughan's lips gently with her own.

Vaughan tolerated that dry, simpering nonsense for only a second, before his hand formed around the back of her neck and drew her into making a much deeper connection.

God, this man. It was like the whole world beyond their bodies ceased to exist when they were connected. She nipped his lip, and he bit back. A thrill soared inside her chest, while her body came alive with joy.

"Why are you wearing attire from the last century?" Vaughan asked, as he set about extracting her from it. "Don't tell me Rushdale burned your dresses."

"It's down to your basket-making, my lord. Also, as it happens, I was in a hurry."

"Well, I can't have my future marchioness swanning around in such a piece. It'll have to go."

"Truly?" She asked coyly pouting. "But there are just so many strings." She caught hold of the uppermost one at the centre of the neckline and pulled the bow loose. "What if it takes hours?"

Vaughan shifted slightly beneath her, and she felt the swell of his cock. "Then I'm sure some shears can be found to speed things along. Lucerne – a little assistance here."

Lucerne, gloriously and magnificently naked, climbed onto the bed. "Are you sure I'm allowed to fondle your bride?"

"Only if you fondle him too," Bella quipped.

"I'm sure that can be arranged." Lucerne positioned himself behind her and set about easing down the drawstring neckline of her gown until he was able to free her breasts. His hands were warm as he cradled the weight of her décolletage, smoothing his hands further down her front and over the curve of her belly. "What other services should I provide, my lord?" he asked, as his lips teased the side of her throat. "Should I dip my fingers in her honeypot and make sure she's primed for your pistol?"

"I think we need to ascertain that the pistol is primed?" Bella said.

"I know how to make sure of that."

The mattress dipped as Lucerne moved to the side of them both. He caught a handful of Vaughan's hair and used it to reel him in. It reminded her of the first time the three of them had ever made love. She had started out as silent witness, shocked, excited, and jealous of the connection between them as she'd spied on them kissing. But then they'd held out their hands to her, welcomed her into their embrace. How could she even think of resisting, both then and now?

It was Lucerne who drew the covers fully back, while Vaughan cast off his shirt exposing himself. His erection reared, pointing accusingly at her.

Lucerne cupped her face in his hands and kissed her. He nibbled at her lips, teased her breasts with loving caresses, while Vaughan urged her to rise up, straddle him, then sit back down upon his prick. She gasped into Lucerne's mouth as Vaughan filled her. Bella rocked against both their bodies as she lost herself in the rhythm of love. Vaughan was inside her, Lucerne all around. Both men seemed to find the pleasure points on her body with such surety she had to wonder if they didn't have targets painted upon them. This was how she always wanted it to be between them.

She arched her body, and upped the pace, losing herself in the sensations of oneness. When her climax hit, it seemed to rise up from nowhere to overwhelm her. As it pulsed through her body, Vaughan held her around the hips, helping her ride out every last second of pleasure. Spent, she fell forward over Vaughan's chest, breathless and tingling. He was still hard as a rock inside of her. "You and your stamina," she teased.

"I do have two lovers to content."

"Ah, yes. Of course." She made to roll to one side, but Vaughan stopped her, tangling his hands in her hair. He brought her to him, and they kissed, bodies pressed as tight as it was possible to be together.

A tickle of hair against her raised bottom alerted her to Lucerne's presence behind her. He was crouched low, and had an endearingly, mischievous grin on his handsome face.

He kissed her bottom, sending irresistible shudders through her form, but only for a moment, before he fell upon Vaughan's cock. "Damn, you taste good." He made contented noises in the back of his throat as he licked her juices from Vaughan's cock.

Bella rolled onto one side, so that she could watch Lucerne, and avoid putting pressure on Vaughan's injury. Her head nestled against Vaughan's shoulder, while he ran his long fingers through her hair.

"Will you come in his mouth?" she asked.

"He will not," Lucerne responded on Vaughan's behalf. "I've a mind to make him soil himself."

"Have you indeed," Vaughan drawled. "And how pray will you accomplish that?"

"Oh, simply enough." Lucerne caught hold of Vaughan's uninjured leg and raised it so that it was supported against his shoulder. "I happen to know of a few ways to unravel even your composure."

"Wait," Vaughan said, as Lucerne unfastened his breeches. He was hard and eager. His foreskin peeled back from the crown.

"Don't pretend you're not excited by it."

"Pass me the butter, Bella. It is just there upon the side-table."

She did as asked and returned to her former position.

"Wait," Vaughan said again as Lucerne greased his pole and worked his thumb around Vaughan's puckered entrance, but he made no attempt to escape the assault.

Bella held her breath. She had never thought to live to witness this, had in fact doubted that it was even a reality of the two men's relationship. Every time she'd witnessed them making love before, Vaughan had taken the dominant role. He was always the master of ceremonies, always bending Lucerne to his will. It was never the other way around.

"Lucerne," he reached out as his lover swapped the circling of his thumb around his opening, for the crown of his prick enacting the same dance.

"Don't you think it's time we all threw off the masks and trusted one another. She won't think any less of you for admitting you take pleasure in being overpowered once in a while."

Bella squeezed Vaughan's hand. "I want to see this very much."

"Now, tell me how much you want it. Say, fuck me, Lucerne. Sodomize me until I spend on my own belly."

He would never say that.

She watched Vaughan's angular jaw clench, so that his high-cheekbones seemed to jut out from beneath the skin. "Don't you want it, Vaughan? I'll happily slip into your place."

"No," his grip tightened in her hair. He took a deep breath, then gasped all at once. "Fuck me, Lucerne. Fuck me until I spend. Fuck me until you spend."

His lover nodded. "I'd be delighted to."

Vaughan held onto Bella with an iron grip as Lucerne slowly pushed past the muscular barrier and sank himself deep.

"Mercy, but I love being inside of you. Jesus, but you're so fucking tight. Stop squeezing you bugger."

"Fuck me," Vaughan demanded.

Lucerne shot a wary glance at Vaughan's injured thigh. The wound itself was covered with a broad linen bandage.

"It's fine. Now stop holding back."

At once Lucerne upped the pace, making them hot and breathless. He possessed Vaughan with every inch of his shaft; rode him hard, crooning out his pleasure.

 She could not truly know what either of them was feeling, but she had sense enough to make an inference, based on the heated, outpouring of curse words, and the contortion of both men's features into expressions of intense pleasure.

Lucerne fucked with his eyes wide open, gazing down adoringly at the man he was possessing. Vaughan's eyes were closed until almost the last moment, then his eyelids snapped open, and he looked up at them both, his expression full of the rapture he felt for them both.

He spent in jets over his own abdomen.

Bella lazily dipped a finger into the mess, and drew a heart upon his chest. Meanwhile, Vaughan gave a cry as Lucerne withdrew. Their golden angel trembled as he brought himself to climax with a few rough jerks of his wrist. He spent over his lover's skin, leaving Vaughan doubly soiled.

Never had she seen Vaughan so vulnerable, or so quietly content.

It was she who located a kerchief and mopped away the mess, before curling contentedly against Vaughan's side, facing Lucerne across Vaughan's chest. They lay that way, luxuriantly indolent, for a long time, none of them willing to break the spell they'd woven, until eventually Vaughan spoke.

"You really ought to marry us both," Vaughan murmured.

"That would be illegal." She squinted up at him, and saw a sly grin teasing up the corners of his lips. "Or is that your plan? Have me jailed so that you can have Lucerne bugger you without interference?"

A twinkle lit his dark eyes. "Shackled, perhaps, but I wouldn't care to see you caged. Also, I'm rather enamoured of your interference. As soon as I'm well and able enough, I intend us to make a chain with me as the middle link."

"Get well soon," she said.

She was drifting close to sleep when he spoke again. Lucerne, too, had his eyes closed and was breathing slowly and contentedly.

"Also, rather a lot of my favourite things carry that sentence. I've never allowed the law to hold me in check. It would make life so infernally dull."

"We wouldn't want that." Lucerne mumbled.

Bella laughed. "I entirely agree, but I'm still good with only saying "I do" to one of you. It's not really what the rest of society recognises that even matters, it's what we three know to be true, and that truth is that I'm yours and Lucerne's, just as you're both mine and each other's."

"Hear, hear," Lucerne agreed. "Till death do us part."

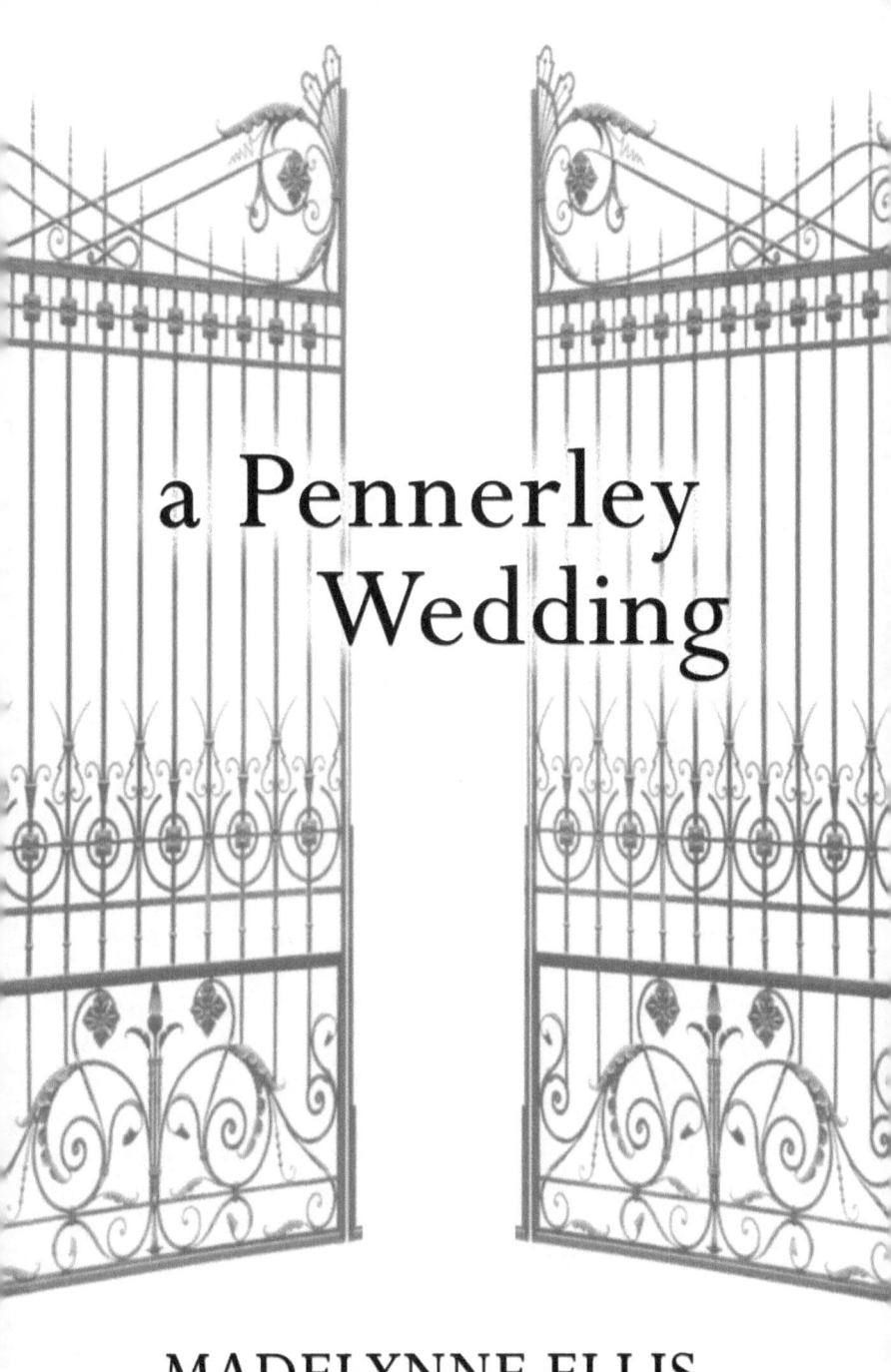

a Pennerley
Wedding

MADELYNNE ELLIS

THE NIGHT BEFORE THE WEDDING

LUCERNE

"Y OU'RE STILL UP."

Lucerne flicked his gaze up from the glass of cognac he'd been nursing for the last quarter hour to gaze at his lover's silhouette against the backdrop of the open doorway. Vaughan was down to his shirtsleeves, his dark hair curling against his shoulders.

"I thought you'd retired hour's ago," he added.

That had certainly been Lucerne's intention, but what the mind decreed sensible it didn't necessarily facilitate. He'd left the bucks to their revelling and gone to his chamber unable to put his heart into the celebratory antics. It was hard to revel over something that made you ache inside. In the isolating darkness of his chamber, he'd climbed beneath the sheets, praying that slumber would steal over him and he'd manage to sleep through the whole of tomorrow.

Only, one didn't sleep when the bed drapes were crawling with imps intent upon disturbing you with their incessant, poisonous whisperings. Lies that played into his fears, that's what they spoke, but they sibilant musings were impossible to ignore. There was no escaping the truth that the two people he loved above all others were set to tie the knot tomorrow, and hence, thereafter, in the eyes of society, would be bound to one another in a way that he never would or could be.

It was for the best, of course it was. It was the most logical solution for keeping the ne're do wells at bay. It would ease Bella's heart, and legitimize the child she carried—Vaughan's child.

Yet...

Hadn't he loved Bella first? Hadn't he offered for her first? Wasn't it he who had made the possibility of them being together again a reality? It didn't seem fair that henceforth that would make him the outsider, the interloper, the... Lucerne struggled to find the equivalent word to mistress for his soon to be newly minted position. Perhaps there wasn't a word for it, at least not any pleasant ones.

"Brandy alone is unlikely to help," Vaughan remarked, straying into the pool of light around the hearth. The observation surprised a grunt from Lucerne. It was unlike his lover to be quite so straightforwardly insightful.

"What do you recommend?"

"For the deep melancholy of the soul you're currently afflicted with? If I had a clue about that, I wouldn't be here." A wry grin flashed across his lips as he claimed Lucerne's glass and polished off the contents. His eyes were already liquid and bright enough to suggest a quantity of other beverages had been consumed in a similar way. Still, that was to be expected, when one had a houseful of stags intent on giving you a proper send off. Lucerne noticed there was a shackle clasped about one of his lover's wrists, no doubt meant to both symbolically and literally to tie him to their other lover, Vaughan's soon to be wife, Bella.

"You can't tell me that you're similarly afflicted, you're about to get everything you ever wanted."

"No," Vaughan bent forward over Lucerne's body, bracing his hands on the chair arms. He looked down into his face. "That I already have. This thing tomorrow is something else entirely. Marriage. By God! What sort of sense does it make for me to stand and make oaths in a church? I'm not convinced the almighty exists, and even if he does, I can't see that he'd be impressed to hear me solemnly swearing to forsake all others when I've no intention of doing any such thing." He dropped a kiss upon Lucerne's lips as if to prove that very point. "I'd amend the text, but I can't see that forsaking all others besides my very dear friend Lord Marlinscar would sit entirely well with the congregation, and might just give the dear reverend the sort of shock that would do for him. He's rather on the rickety side already. From what Bella's said, he's at least five hundred."

Bella had insisted they relocate Reverend Hindes from Yorkshire to Pennerley for the happy occasion. If she wasn't to be married in her home parish, then she was certainly intent upon a few home comforts.

"It would be her brother I'd be concerned over if you were to announce such a thing, not the priest. It's nothing short of a miracle that Joshua's even agreed to be here." It wasn't so very long ago the pair had shot pistols at one another.

"There's nothing miraculous about it," Vaughan scoffed. As was inevitable whenever Joshua Rushdale's name arose, Vaughan's hand strayed towards his thigh and the freshly formed scar there. "It's a simple matter of practicality. He feels he needs to be here in person to make sure the deed is done properly and there's no deception about it. Moreover, I'm funding some infernal contraption he and his cronies are building. Engines are apparently money sinks."

"You mean you twisted his arm."

"It was preferable, at least from my betrothed's point of view than twisting his scrawny neck." He failed to stifle a grimace.

Curiously, the contortion of his mouth made Lucerne long to rise up and kiss him. In fact, he was damned well going to do it. Vaughan's eyes widened a fraction as Lucerne slid a drink-weakened limb around his neck and held him steady as he leaned in. The brandy fumes on his breath tingled against Lucerne's lips as they kissed. Their tongues danced, while the stubbly shadows around their jaws rubbed together in a way that ignited tingles.

"That's certainly one solution to our dilemma." Vaughan hitched a brow, turning the remark into a question.

Lucerne hadn't meant anything by the kiss, beyond what it meant in the moment, but the possibility of sliding into Vaughan's arms and entwining himself around his lover's body hit him like a draft of Spanish Fly. Desperately excited by the prospect, yet wary, he muttered, "But you've a houseful of guests. We can't."

"That word has been excoriated from my vocabulary." Vaughan's lips turned up as he indulged in an indolent grin. "Please! I'll do as I see fit in my own abode. In any case, said guests aren't in my chamber, and are deep into their cups. Come." He clasped Lucerne's hand and tugged as if to draw him from the chair.

"Vaughan..."

"Lucerne," his lover mimicked. "Don't pretend it isn't what you want. Come, get up, or I swear I'll pick you up and carry you to my bed over my shoulder. That will certainly provide anyone who is still abroad with a tale to tell.

"Carried his own best man to bed last night, can you believe it? There's always been something untoward about those two.

"Unnatural, you mean?

"Aye, that's the word for it. Cover your ears girl, I fear... Nay, I shudder over it, but I suspect they might be sodomites?"

Lucerne rolled his eyes and let his head loll against the high chair back. "Was that supposed to compel me? Your bed is not the place I should be the night before your wedding."

"Pfft – do get over yourself." Vaughan tugged upon his hand again. "My love, it is the only place you should be. Moreover, it's where I insist you be. Now, up and get marching or I swear I'll have you here, and we all know the library is the first port of call for any midnight wanderers, especially those named Wakefield."

"I shouldn't be here," Lucerne insisted yet again as they tumbled through the door into Vaughan's chamber, his whispers comically loud. Luckily the only other chamber in this part of the castle belonged to Vaughan's sister, who was perfectly, if despairingly aware of their attachment.

"Nonsense, I cannot possibly spend tonight alone," Vaughan insisted. He shoved Lucerne towards the bed. "Strip and get in. And don't argue," he added when Lucerne came to a halt after a single step. That at least got him as far as the mattress. Vaughan shook his head at how awkwardly Lucerne sat in a space he by rights ought to be completely at home in. "Are you planning on sleeping like that?" He gestured at his lover's clothes.

"I shouldn't be here."

"Strip or I swear I'm going to peel those breeches from you."

Movement at last—he watched Lucerne shrug off his coat out of the corner of his eye as he stripped off various accoutrements of his own. Only for his lover to come to a halt after mere moments. "Now what?" Vaughan enquired.

"Strip me," Lucerne flopped backwards onto the coverlet. For a moment, Vaughan wondered if Lucerne had in fact drunk rather more than he'd supposed, and had thus passed out. But no, Lucerne smiled lazily at him. "I like it when you fondle my buttons."

"You're a contemptible scoundrel, you know." Vaughan crossed to the bed, and straddled Lucerne's prone form. "I despair of myself in worshiping you. Don't think that I don't know what this is, Lucerne. It's laziness, that's what. Your valet isn't here to do the honours, so you're co-opting me into accomplishing the task. What is it that you find so damnably hard about managing a few fastenings?"

Lucerne awkwardly pushed up onto his elbows. "If you're going to be insulting—"

"Oh, lighten up, and come here." Vaughan grasped him by the cravat and pulled him close enough to kiss. "Just how much brandy did you actually drink?"

"Nowhere near enough."

"Enough to render you out of action?"

Lucerne tilted his head in consideration, then gave it a slow shake as a grin spread across his face. "I don't think so." He rubbed his cheek against Vaughan's chest. "Are we going to fuck?"

"If I'm going to the effort of undressing you and

rolling you into my bed, then you may be certain I intend to have my wicked way with you."

Lucerne's smile grew wide again, only to die almost immediately. "I don't think you'll want to anymore after tomorrow."

Vaughan cuffed him affectionately around the head. "That's the brandy talking. Not to mention the most nonsensical thing you've ever said to me. When have I ever not wanted to bed you?"

"You'll be all tied up with Bella."

"I was thinking of tying her to you, actually. Do you think a couple of yards of ribbon will be enough, or will I need more than that?"

Lucerne squinted at him, evidently a little confused. "You're the one marrying her. That's what we all agreed." He shook his head. "What do you need ribbon for?"

"Are you sure it's only the brandy you've downed?"

"Ribbon's not so good for tying people up. You know the knots hurt. They pull too tight and dig in. Maybe something softer for your wedding night."

"Lucerne, I swear if you mention matrimony one more time I'm going to gag you with this here cravat." He pulled Lucerne's free of his collar, exposing the swell of his Adam's apple, and the pale V of skin at the base of his throat where the edges of his shirt parted.

Actually, he might yet do it anyway. The notion of his lover silenced and naked on his knees with a few red welts across his arse and maybe his wrists bound behind his back left him uncomfortably agitated.

Irresistibly drawn to turning that vision into a reality, Vaughan began by bending to brush his lips across the ridge of Lucerne's collar bone. "Nothing is going to change, Lucerne," he promised. "What happens on the morrow won't impact how we live. I'll still love you. I'll still crave you with every inch of my soul." His kisses moved to the hollow of his lover's throat, and he sucked, making his mark upon the flesh—a mark that would definitely still be there as Lucerne stood beside him in church tomorrow. Lucerne gasped and struggled a moment, only to relent and arch his neck to one side further exposing his throat. "You don't even believe all this nonsense you're spouting about me throwing you over for a nice staid marriage to Bella, you just crave a little reassurance because you're feeling left out."

"Can you blame me? Do you know how difficult it is to maintain the façade that I'm nothing more to the pair of you than a very dear friend?"

"Neither of us has asked that of you."

Lucerne's chest lifted as he gave a small huff of laughter. "The purpose of tomorrow is to calm speculation, not escalate it."

"You're mine, Lucerne, and it bothers me not at all who knows it. I'd happily exchange vows with you."

"Concentrated on making the expected ones to Bella."

Vaughan raised his head and puffed at a stray strand of hair. He cast a disarming smile in his lover's direction. "I intend to note your name alongside that of my marchioness in the family bible."

That got his lover's attention. He groaned, "Must you insist on courting scandal? It'll fuel whispers for generations."

"I intend them to be more than whispers. I trust whoever comes after knows exactly where my affections were cast. In any case, one hopes that our future society will hold a more nuanced view of such matters." He relieved Lucerne of his shirt, and proceeded to kiss his way down his lover's lean torso. "There are societies around the globe that are less prescriptive of relationships beyond those enjoyed by one man and one woman."

"None that I've heard of. I suppose you've been talking to the members of the Free Lovers Society again?"

Vaughan tutted in between kissing his way down Lucerne's chest. "While I appreciate some of their sentiments, I've no intention of sharing that which is mine. Be assured, if you give any of this,"—he covered the swell of Lucerne's cock with his palm—"to anyone besides me and Bella, then there'll be hell to pay. Some things one is induced to become aggressively protective of." He slid the buttons of Lucerne's frontfall, but to no effect. "Goddammit, Lucerne! For mercy's sakes will you stop getting Ivo to sew you into your damn breeches."

"They sit so much better."

"It's deuced inconvenient."

"It protects your assets."

"It impedes as much as it prevents." Vaughan kissed the exposed sliver of skin above Lucerne's waistband, before resorting to a sharp tug. Thankfully, the tacks gave way. Whereupon, he relieved Lucerne of both his breeches and smalls. "That's better. You're a sight to behold, Viscount Marlinscar." He would never tire of gazing at this man, at his long pale body, with his elegant limbs and the sparse smatterings of pale golden hair that invited ones touch. He drew a single finger along the narrow trail of hair down from Lucerne's navel to his loins. "Whatever am I going to do with you? With this?" He traced one digit very lightly along the side of Lucerne's prick, making it swell to its full magnificence.

"Kiss it," Lucerne suggested, raising his fingers to his mouth so that his index finger stroked along his lower lip.

"Kiss you?"

"Suck me...it."

"Suck you...?" Actually, he did have a hankering of a sort for such a thing. Vaughan sat back on his haunches. He let his fingers linger over his lover's ballocks, then fisted his cock, causing an urgent gasp to escape Lucerne's lips and his hips to buck upwards off the mattress. Unprompted, Lucerne drove his cock through the ring of Vaughan's fist.

"Please," he murmured. "I want your mouth on me. When you speak your words to Bella tomorrow, I want you to do so with a throat made hoarse from having had my cock in it."

Vaughan laughed. "Aye, I'll bet you do. This indolence is a ruse, Lucerne. You mean to punish me."

"That's not—"

"Don't waste your breath denying it. You want to fuck my mouth hard enough to make my eyes water."

Lucerne's mouth opened, as if he meant to refute the claim, but promptly shut it again.

Vaughan swept his thumb over the sensitive eye of his lover's prick. "And what do I get in return for all this larking, besides a sore throat?"

Lucerne closed his eyes then peeped at Vaughan again from beneath his eyelashes. "Whatever you demand," he said breathlessly. "Anything you want from me."

"Careful of your promises, Lucerne." His lover would indeed give him whatever he demanded, and more besides. "Very well. I'll suck you." But he wouldn't be the only one of them that wound up a little sore on the morrow. "I've a few tiny stipulations though."

"Anything." Lucerne continued to drive his staff though the ring of Vaughan's fist. "Just love me."

"That is something you never need worry about. It exists... but it's entirely separate to this. This my friend,"—he began landing kisses again upon sensitive parts of Lucerne's body—"this is about unadulterated lust. It's about theft and possession, and ownership."

"You already own me, what is it you think you're going to steal?"

"Ah..." Vaughan smoothed his free hand all over Lucerne's skin. "Your reserve, your sensibility, your cognisance of what others expect of you. In short, I'm going to make you cry out for my cock, and you're not going to care who might be around to hear that plea."

He thought he might hear a protest given Lucerne's earlier mutterings, but whether because his focus was already locked upon his aching cock, or the amount of brandy he'd drunk, Lucerne only arched further towards him. He looked up at Vaughan making eye contact as Vaughan dipped his head. There was a glaze to his eyes that made their cornflower hue that bit more vivid. "Don't make me wait" he pleaded, lips pulled wide into an easy smile. "I want you to be a beast and eat me up."

Obligingly, Vaughan dirty kissed him upon the lips until they were both bereft of breath, and their cocks were like two lead shafts wedged between them. Only then, did he reach for the cords holding the bed curtains back. As the ties fell, the curtains cocooned them in inky darkness.

"Why? Now I can't see a damn thing," Lucerne protested.

"So concentrate on feeling me."

The mattress sagged as Vaughan shifted onto his haunches. Even deprived of sight, he was feverishly aware of Lucerne's body beneath him. Nor did the dark preclude him from finding all the sweet spots on his lover's body. He tugged on his nipples, traced the seam of his ballocks, which always made Lucerne's toes curl, and only gave in to what they were both bracing themselves for when the tension between them was palpable.

"You don't need to see me to know that I'm right here. I'm going to suck you now, Lucerne." He paused, giving the other man time to feel his breath hot against the tip of his cock. "I'm going to take you right down to the root. All the way down, until my mouth and throat are completely full of you." He graced Lucerne's shaft with a kiss or two, just to ramp up the anticipation. "It's going to make you ache like you never have before. Your senses are going to be alight. The pleasure of it is going to be screaming in your brain. It's going to be agony and ecstasy all rolled into one, and your cock is going to be so damn stiff you'll fear that each and every stroke will undo you, but you're not going to come."

"I'm not?" His lover's words came out as a high-pitched croak between breaths sucked between his teeth.

Vaughan circle a wetted thumb over the crown of his cock, and those gasps got even more juddery.

"You're going to hold yourself in check, my lord. You're going to wait while your ballocks get tighter and fuller, and then only when I'm buried to the hilt inside of you are you going to spend so that your seed glues us together."

"I don't know I've the resilience."

"Find it, for it you don't... if you spend so much as a drop before I'm where I want to be, then I will make you pay."

Lucerne groaned uncomfortably. They both knew the odds were even on either outcome, and Vaughan was hard pressed to say he had a preference either way. He liked the way such manipulation wound Lucerne into a frenzy, and how it made his muscles tense so that the tendons stood out, also, how it sensitized his skin.

"Ready? You just need to say it back to me, make it clear you understand."

"Suck me while I say it."

"You'll forget how to speak."

Lucerne groaned, and pushed his cock into Vaughan's face, but failed to achieve his goal. "Fine. You're going to suck me deep, but I'm not going to come—however that's supposed to work—until you decide to bury your prick in my arse."

"Correct." He gave him a well done kiss. "You are going to hold it together now, aren't you, Lucerne. No coming in my throat, and no spurting the moment I slip a finger up your arse. I intend to fuck you hard. Hard enough that this old bed is going to creak loud enough to wake the dead in the churchyard next door, and definitely loud enough that if anyone happens to be tiptoeing by on the stairs they're going to know exactly what's going on."

"I swear you'll not be content until you get us both hanged."

"You're the one insisting on giving me a sore throat."

"So you're going to give me a sore arse in return."

"That's about the gist of it. I shan't consider my part fulfilled unless you're twitchy about sitting tomorrow, and either way I intend to bugger you right before the ceremony tomorrow."

Lucerne squirmed beneath him. "Your bride might have something to say about that."

"Well, I'd let her participate, but apparently they are some strange rules about not seeing one another."

"I believe that's what blindfolds were invented for," Lucerne remarked, the retort spilling before he'd apparently had a chance to think better of it. "And you won't be doing any such thing."

"Tell me that again later." Vaughan engulfed his

prick, which killed any contrary opinions Lucerne still had about what would and wouldn't happen on the morrow, for he was too desperately gulping air.

It was just he and Vaughan in the entirety of existence. Lucerne lay stretched taut as a bowstring across Vaughan's bed, one hand clasped within the long strands of his lover's hair. He'd lost all sense of time and space as he drove his cock into Vaughan's eager mouth. It could have been minutes since this torture began, or hours. Fact was, when it came to prick sucking, Vaughan really was second to none. Making this... He swallowed, trying to moisten his dry mouth. Well, every moment of it, was exquisite torture.

Lucerne knew damn well he was being toyed with. After all, he was on the receiving end of every trace, every whisper of breath, every flick of the tongue that had his hips jerking up off the mattress and his toes curling. He wanted this, and he wanted more... More of the sucks that threatened to draw his seed from him in an explosive gush, more of the rippling sensation against his over-sensitized skin as Vaughan swallowed. His blood was beginning to boil, and if his limbs weren't so weighty, he'd hold Vaughan's head fast to him while he fucked him without an ounce of damned restraint.

"Fuck!" he rasped. "Fuck... Goddammit Vaughan! Unless you want me to spend down your throat, release me."

"Release you and do what?" The response gave him a few seconds of respite, no more.

"You know. Your rules remember." It was a miracle

his nails weren't bloody, he was clawing at the sheets so hard.

"Say it, though. Beg me."

"Fuck me." Lucerne croaked, knowing that feeble caw would get him nothing.

"Louder."

"Fuck me," he groaned again, this time tightening his grip upon Vaughan's hair, which just prompted the bugger to intensify his efforts. Seriously, he was going to spend. He was going to fucking spend. "Vaughan!"

His lover peered up at him, only the outline of his form and the sheen of his eyes truly visible in the dark.

"Stop torturing me and put your damn prick in my goddamn arse."

"Oh what sweet temptations you offer, my lord." He drew his sinewy body up over Lucerne's, between his spread thighs until their heads were on a level. "You're ready for this, I hope." Vaughan spat into his hand.

"Oh God!"

The mattress groaned as Vaughan manipulated him into position

Blinded by the dark there was only sensation. Heat, the stretch, the resistance of muscles tensed tight for fear that any loosening of that grip would launch a volley from his own gun.

He didn't holler. His voice was gone. It was too damn much and not nearly enough. The strain was splitting him. His cock fucking ached. Pleasure and pain were entirely as one.

Heat burned through him as his muscles gave and Vaughan sunk deep.

"Are you still with me?" Vaughan passed a hand across his chest. He turned one of Lucerne's nipples between his fingers. The flash of pain almost undid him, only his lover's hand squeezed him hard around the base of his cock. "Not yet, Lucerne. Just hold it together for me a little while. I want to look at you while I'm inside of you."

He was moving, rocking, and it was so hard to take. Not that he ever wanted it to stop.

"Like you can see anything in this blasted dark."

"I can see everything that I need to. You're magnificent. Do you know that?" Vaughan rode his palms up and down Lucerne's flesh. "You're so damned ready, aren't you Lucerne. So incredibly close." His attention returned to Lucerne's prick. His touches light as a breeze, but still dangerously close to triggering Lucerne's release. "Such a pity Miss Rushdale isn't here to enjoy it. You know how much she enjoys a nice hard prick."

"Maybe you should ring and have someone fetch her," Lucerne gasped through his teeth.

"Tempting," Vaughan's lips curled. "Definitely tempting, but I think I'm just going to fuck you until you erupt."

"Is that not what you're doing right now?"

Vaughan hooked Lucerne's legs up around his shoulders. "That was us getting comfortable. This—" he said, while ramping up the pace, "—is the fucking part."

Lucerne swore he would lose it immediately, but that wasn't the case. Their bodies locked together, forming one perfectly pistoning unit. The old wooden bed frame creaked beneath them. It was as if he was too damned hard to come, so he was left skidding along a knife edge of pleasure-pain so intense he could no longer discern any difference between the two.

"Let it go now, Lucerne." His muscles were locked so tight, he couldn't do that.

Vaughan bit him. Maybe his teeth broke the skin of his throat, maybe they didn't. Either way, the exquisite agony in his throat started a chain reaction. He spent messily, all over the pair of them for what felt like at least an hour. He was just about sliding back into his own skin when he felt Vaughan come inside of him. "I love you," he said, collapsing over Lucerne's spent form. "Never doubt it. The three of us are meant to be together, and we will be. Tomorrow is how we convince society to accept that fact."

WEDDING DAY
BELLA

"YOU KNOW YOU are queer in the attic for this," Lady Niamh, Vaughan's sister, remarked as she cast her gaze over Bella. They were upstairs in Pennerley's gatehouse, with its uneven floors and crooked windows. She was not referring to Bella's attire—a dress spun of pure silk and fit for a queen—but rather her agreement to marry Vaughan. "He's a monster, much that I love him. I cannot understand why anyone would agree to belong to him. Heavens, I've been trying to escape his rule all my life."

Bella laughed as she daubed perfume behind her ears. "I know what he is, Niamh, have no fear of that. He is everything." She turned and clasped her friend's hands. "I cannot think of a single reason why I wouldn't wish him to claim me."

"Not one?" Niamh returned. Her eyebrows arched in exactly the way that Vaughan's did. She was every bit as graceful and lovely as her brother too, just void of his capacity for torment.

Bella shifted her feet, knowing exactly what Niamh alluded to, but they hadn't spoken of it, and now did not seem an appropriate time. They had only been reacquainted a matter of hours, for Niamh had been in the City and had at first supposed her brother's declaration that he was about to wed a dastardly ploy to return her home. "We'll be happy together, Niamh. I promise."

"Of course, you will, and I am glad he has finally shown some sense." Her friend smiled, and planted kisses upon both of Bella's cheeks, before turning away to busy herself picking up items of clothing and unnecessarily rearranging and folding them. "Everyone is delighted for you, though hardly anyone can quite believe it. I never dared hope that he would settle down, for it seemed impossible that he would ever love anyone besides..." She fell quiet again, and turned uncomfortably back toward the dressing table. "Are you not worried that they are still so close, Bella?"

"No—I would not have them any other way," she responded blithely, ignoring the flutter of uneasy the question raised in her stomach.

Niamh bit her lip and looked sheepishly at the floor.

"Something is praying upon your mi—"

"You should know they spent the night together caterwauling." Niamh blurted in such a rush her tongue barely formed the words correctly. "Damn Bella, I'm sorry, but I couldn't let you go through with this without knowing."

Bella's heart skipped a beat, but she curled her fists and swallowed the bile that swelled up her throat. "I thought they might," she said, taking care to keep her voice light.

Niamh stared at her, eyes liquid. "You thought they..."

Bella nodded. "Like I said, I know your brother. I know all that exists between him and Lord Marlinscar."

The only surprising part of the revelation was that they had been loud enough in their lovemaking that the sounds of it had reached Niamh's ears abed two floors above in the castle keep.

"But..."

Bella shook her head. "While he was with Lucerne last night, he will be with me shortly. Really, there's no cause for you to fret."

Niamh scrunched the shawl she had just folded, then smoothed it out again. "I don't know how you can be so calm when you are to marry someone whose heart remains tied to someone else's."

Calm wasn't entirely how she felt about it, no matter what it might appear.

"It's really quite simple. I love Lucerne just as dearly. Niamh, I know what I'm agreeing to in marrying your brother. I am, in some sense, agreeing to marry them both, and the truth is that I wouldn't have things any other way."

The other woman stared at her aghast. "Devil!" she spat. "My brother has much to answer for. This is worse than if he were asking you to acknowledge a mistress. You must know that he will spend all his time behaving reprehensibly instead of lavishing affection upon you as he should."

Bella shook her head. "Actually—and you may prefer not to know all the ins and outs of it. I know I prefer not to know all the details of Joshua's intimacies—I anticipate us spending a great deal of time together."

Niamh's jaw fell, but she nodded her head warily. "You'll excuse me if I don't think on that too hard."

Bella stood and shook out her skirts. "Your brother isn't forcing his lover on me, Niamh. I love Lucerne too."

"Yes, well, as I said, I will not think on that fact too

530

hard." She grasped Bella's hands again. "I pray you are all able to make it work."

What was there to say to that? Bella kissed her soon to be sister and shooed her towards the door. "Perhaps you'd let Joshua know that I'm ready."

Once Niamh left, Bella turned back to the cheval glass. It was quite a different woman she saw peeping back at her than the one she normally identified as herself. For once she looked regal, and perhaps even felt like a woman about to become a marchioness, rather than a wild spirit, whose hair had been teased from its pins and blown into knots by the wind. Her gown, cream with splashes of emerald green, was cleverly cut so that it sheathed her body to perfection, but also disguised her condition. While society would realise the truth soon enough, she did not want them to spoil her day with their hateful speculations. There would be rumours and such like rippling through the congregation already regarding the closeness of Vaughan and Lucerne's relationship, and the recent spat between Vaughan and her brother that had culminated in a duel. In any case, what mattered was that Vaughan's child was born his legitimate heir and that required only that vows and rings were exchanged before the mite arrived.

Bella moved away from the looking glass and perched upon the edge of the bed that she'd passed the night in alone. So, Vaughan and Lucerne had been together. She didn't know whether she was more thankful for Niamh's honesty, or vexed by the knowledge. Couldn't they keep their hands to themselves of one night?

She looked down at the betrothal ring upon her finger. It was little large, having been made for Vaughan's finger. The ring Lucerne had given her sat directly above it, holding it in place upon her finger.

Their seeking out one another was practically inevitable. She shook her head. Nor was it a cause for concern. If she'd been in Lucerne's positon, she'd have gone seeking reassurances too. Still, they might have been more circumspect about things considering the number of guests currently in residence at Pennerley, among them her brother.

While Joshua and Vaughan had so far not come to blows, as she had feared they might, things remained distinctly uneasy. Joshua was being stiffly, irritably polite, and Vaughan contemptuously welcoming. That would continue if Joshua caught wind of what cries had echoed within the keep walls last night. He might even go so far as to attempt to stop the wedding.

Damn them! She sighed into her cupped palms.

The chamber door opened.

"Joshua," she said, rising, and setting herself straight so that he wouldn't question her apparent uneasy. However, it was not her brother's form that filled the shallow doorway, but rather the man who loomed large in her mind while she cursed her betrothed's appetites. "Lucerne!" Her gaze fastened tight upon the rigid lines of his face. "Why are you here?" His place today was at Vaughan's side, as his adjutant. "I don't understand."

Lucerne ducked to enter, and closed the door behind him. He walked quietly over to her, his expression the same tight mask of joy it'd been since the guests began arriving three days back. Bella wasn't fooled; she'd seen the flashes of pain in his blue eyes as he was forced into the shadows while people offered heartfelt congratulations to her and Vaughan.

"Is there something the matter?"

For a split second, she saw it again, the heartache that was eating him alive. "Vaughan sent me."

Fear slid cold down her spine, like the steady drip

of a melting icicle. "Why?" Oh, God! He'd changed his mind. Come to his senses and realised he couldn't go through with it, because it truly was Lucerne who meant the very most to him.

"Bella?" He reached for her, clearly seeing her distress. "Oh, my love. No, that is not why I am here."

She swallowed hard, still not quite able to set aside her fears. "You're not here to tell me he's calling it off."

"Of course not. He wouldn't... I wouldn't act as his envoy to deliver such a message. No, he is ready and waiting for you in the church. Heavens, you're jumpy."

She nodded, and clasped her hands before her. "Niamh was here a moment ago, she said... You spent the night together, didn't you?"

"Ah, Bella," He sighed and caught hold of her arms. "I promise you, it was not an intentional arrangement. There was rather a lot brandy involved, and I did try to resist, but you know how persuasive he is, and I'd be lying if I said I didn't—"

"You needed the reassurance. I understand. You're free to be together whenever. It's what we all agreed." That fact didn't stop the carnal, heart-breaking images of the two men entwined, lip-locked and grinding against one another from assaulting her mind. Her heart pounded, and her stomach tossed in despair. "You don't need to apologise."

"Though I feel that I should. It was ill done of me to commandeer his attention like that."

She bowed her head, then peeped up at him, her brows quirked. "I thought you said you were persuaded."

"Persuaded, coerced... All he had to do was kiss me and crook a finger. I'm sorry, Bella. We ought to have given more thought to how it would make you feel.

"Well, as long as you don't think you can commandeer him tonight."

He shook his head. "I wouldn't dream of it. My presence or absence will be entirely up to you. I'll sit all night right outside the door if you wish it."

"That would be unnecessarily cruel. I would never force you to do that."

It remained unsaid that they both knew someone who might.

"Why has he sent you here?" she asked.

"I'm to give you what he can't, but what he wants you to know he wishes to give, if it were not bad luck for you to see one another before the ceremony."

"Do you mean he has sent you with a gift?"

"In a sense." Lucerne inclined his head again, whereupon Bella noticed that his hair was tousled on one side as though someone had fisted the longer strands, and that his skin was pink, high across his cheekbones. He sported at least one provocatively placed bite mark too, upon his throat, where its lividity was almost, but not quite hidden by his collar and cravat.

Her breath caught, before rushing out in a harried blast. "You weren't just together last night, but this morning too."

Lucerne's gaze dropped to the floor between them.

"Lucerne?" she asked, biting her lip.

He took hold of her hand and lifted it to his mouth, where he held it pressed against his warm lips. "Yes," he confirmed. "We have been together this morning."

Hurt, she jerked her hand from Lucerne's hold, and covered her face. "All morning, I suppose you mean. I don't suppose you've given me any thought, and now he's sent you here, no doubt with his seed is still warm inside of you?"

"Bella," he insisted, reaching for her again, and holding her firmly. "I promise you, you have filled both of our thoughts. In fact, it is why I am here."

"To give me a gift, as if I can be calmed with a trinket."

He drew his teeth over his swollen lower lip. "It's not a thing that he's sent. Rather it's—"

The movement he made was the tiniest of things, a slight shift in his position, the smallest repositioning of his attire, but it was enough to target her attention. As always Lucerne was spotlessly elegant, not a thread or crease where there wasn't meant to be one, that was, apart from in one distinct area.

"He's sent you," she blurted, gaze fast upon the swell of his confined prick.

"Aye."

"I thought you said he'd fucked you?"

Lucerne nodded, and dug his teeth more deeply into his lip. It was painful, she realised, his prick, not his lip. How in heavens had he walked across here and mounted the stairs? Gingerly, one presumed. She blinked, still not entirely comprehending what was being offered. "Did he mean you...That is, does he expect us to...?"

She received another nod.

"But if he's...If he's spent, inside of you, then how come...?"

"I'm this hard?"

"Mm," Bella agreed. When her two men joined themselves together, Lucerne was always the one who spent first. Always. Vaughan engineered it so.

"He didn't let me—"

It was impossible not to reach out and shape her hand around the brand pushing unrelentingly against its fabric cage. Lucerne's breath caught, then hissed out between his teeth. "God's blood, Bella! Be gentle. But don't you dare stop touching me."

"How? How is this possible? How could he...? How

was he able to prevent it?" Indeed, why had he? Why send Lucerne to her like this? A message, she supposed.

"Wait. Are you telling me that you...that your swollen prick is what he's sent me? Not pearls or a diamonds as a wedding gift, or a Kashmir shawl, but you and your ramrod?"

Lucerne shrugged. "Bella, he loves you."

Hence he'd sent her the one thing he loved above all else.

"Well, it's certainly and unusual present. Did he perhaps specify what he intended me to do with this prize, or am I to enjoy it as I see fit?"

"He's a git, what do you think?"

"I can look but I'm not allowed to touch?" Bella guessed, flouting that decree immediate, and giving her present a squeeze.

Needy and now clearly agitated, Lucerne made an aching sound low in his throat.

"Not that? Perhaps... I'm only allowed to unwrap you after the ceremony?"

Lucerne shook his head. "Not that much of a git." He breathed hard through his nose so that his nostrils flared. "I'm to fill you with it, use you hard so that when you stand by him a few minutes from now and say your vows, your nether lips will still be plump from a thorough fucking and glistening with come. They're his words, not mine."

Indeed, they were too crude, too perverse for her to think otherwise. "But what is it you think of this, Lucerne? Not everything has to be done in accordance with his whim.

A dry chuckle wormed its way from his throat. "Oh, I want you. Honestly, have you no inkling? Every breath is sheer agony at the moment. It's murder holding still and not giving in to the need to grind myself into your palm. But like Vaughan said, I don't just want to swive you; I want to fill you in a way that means you can still feel where I've been for at least the rest of the day."

Normally, Lucerne was the gentler of her lovers, the one who advocated for tenderness. Therefore it was a surprise to hear him express a desire for something else. "He really does have you wound tight, doesn't he?" She gave Lucerne's prick another squeeze, which caused him to whistle sharply through his teeth.

"Don't be cruel, Bella. I have enough of that from him."

Bella shook her head. She took a step backwards, and teasingly raised the hem of her dress, treating Lucerne to a glimpse of her silk stockings, then the blue garters holding them in place, and finally the split of her quaint. "Is this cruel? See to the door, Lucerne. Then hurry and give me my present."

From outside came the tolling of the church bells, warning they had but a little time.

Lucerne wasted no time in wedging a chair beneath the door knob, then flowing elegantly into the space between her parted thighs. "Do you realise in another hour you'll belong to him, Bella. Your body will be his to do with as he pleases. Your mind, your heart, your everything will be his to do with as he sees fit."

Bella reached up and wound her hands around his neck so that her fingers curled in the short strands of hair at the back of his neck. "He owns me anyway, just as he owns you. But you're wrong when you say all. He'll never possess the whole of me. There'll always be a part of me that's yours."

With a smile, his mouth fell upon hers, claiming her with bruising kisses. "Sometimes Bella... I swear I made the most foolish mistake. I should have insisted on keeping you. If had not been for the child kicking inside of you..."

"Shh!" She covered his lips with two fingers. "Don't…"

Lucerne sucked her fingers into his mouth.

"Don't what? Pretend that I want you? That I think I'd make a better husband? I know the path we've chosen is the right one, Bella, but that doesn't mean I don't have regrets, or that I don't sometimes imagine things were otherwise."

"I'm still yours, and I still will be when this day is over." She reached for the frontfall of his breeches. For once sliding the buttons actually released the fabric. With a victorious smile plumping her cheeks, Bella pushed aside his shirttails and claimed her prize.

Lucerne's teeth rode hard against his already wetted lips, as she palmed his bare flesh. A single brush of her thumb across his crown caused him to clasp a hand tight around her wrist so that the pinch stung all up her arm.

"Don't tease. I'm too on edge for that."

"Don't tease, or don't touch?" she counted. "You know I like to put my hands upon you."

"Bella!" Lucerne's colour heighted across both cheeks almost to the vivid red of his prick. "I'm on a knife edge. You don't understand. He was… He was inside me, Bella. His prick was nudging me in this way that normally makes the world explode, but this time he was pinching me too. He was preventing me from falling over the edge, and I don't even rightly know how. The urge, it was so insistent. It kept pounding away in the back of my brain, getting stronger and stronger, and licking through my cobs, but it couldn't rise past the pressure he was exerting." His gaze lost its focus as he seemed to fall back into the memory of being with Vaughan. His cock twitched hard within Bella's hand, and for a moment she thought he'd spend right then. If only she were privy to this magical restraint Vaughan had employed.

"He said I had to save it for you," Lucerne continued, having managed to master himself again. "I'm only to surrender once I'm deep inside your quaint, filling you as if he were here with us, swiving me as I filled you."

Of all the ways in which they melded themselves together, that still remained one of her favourites. There was something dangerously intoxicating about being part of Vaughan's efforts to possess Lucerne in aa way that made him quake like the earth was about to be rent apart and swallow them all up.

"I think you ought to do as he instructs." She inched herself upward onto the surface of the dressing table, heedless of the trinkets and potions her body sent flying. "Come to me, Lucerne." She split her legs wide, so that he could see everything. How wet she was, and how eager. "Of all the wedding gifts he could give..." She left the rest of the sentence unspoken, for he had to know, had to realise how much it meant to know that Vaughan had sent her what he could have so easily kept for himself, and had done so now, when it mattered most, because she was doubting and fearful over everything she was so certain they'd resolved. Lucerne meant the whole world to him. He'd loved him first, hardest, and for the longest, but now he was truly and willingly sharing him with her, saying "Take my lover. Take him. Love him as I love him. Let him fill you as I fill you. This marriage, it's not just a bond between you and I, but a promise made between the three of us. That promise we're about to make before witnesses, it's an oath between the three of us to love one another unreservedly until we die."

"Kiss me."

Lucerne's mouth smashed down upon hers. Almost

at the same time, his hands tightened around her hips, lifting her, tilting her so that she was angled to take his cock. That rigid staff notched effortlessly at her entrance. "Want it?" He cocked an elegant brow.

"Now who's teasing?"

"If I am it's mostly myself I'm tormenting. God, Bella! I want this to last." His teeth clamped together hard.

"Maybe if I slide gently onto you," she said, hooking her feet behind his rear, and using them to coax him closer. "Or do you think a swift sharp stroke would be better?"

"I think there's an equal chance of both getting the better of me, and leaving me with earache?"

"Earache?"

"From when you slap me in frustration."

"Lucerne, I wouldn't." She met his eyes, and saw that his pupils were hugely dilated, and that he was smiling. "Take me. Fill me," she whispered. "I don't care if you do come on the very first stroke."

"You say that, but..."

Bella clasped tight his buttocks, and rocked forward, so that he filled her to the root in one sharp thrust. The action startled grunts from them both, followed by crisp, cackles of joy as they stared at one another.

Outside, the church bell was now chiming the quarter hour. Elsewhere in the gatehouse, Bella could hear people moving about. If she and Lucerne were heard, there'd be no explaining it. "We have to be quiet."

"Yes," he agreed, as his lips crashed down hard upon hers again, and savaged her mouth. Lucerne drew back, and then slid into her again, so that their lower bodies and their teeth smashed into one another. "Yes."

Damn, he felt huge, like he was twice the size of

normal. Bella's fingers tightened in his hair. "Take me. Possess me, Imprint yourself upon me." She was definitely going to still feel this later.

It felt so good.

He was clenching his jaw.

"Are you going to come?"

"I don't want to think about it."

"I want you to come. I want to walk down the aisle with your seed still wet on my skin."

"Ah, hell, Bella." He made a desperate cry and buried his face in her neck, lips pressed tight to the pulse point there.

Bella clung to him as he stilled. Shivers raced up and down his body. He defied them, slowly tamed them.

"Together," he insisted, seeking out her pearl with thumb and stroking her with swift light brushes that made her toes curl inside of her shoes, and her inner muscles contract around his prick in eager welcome. "That's more like it. It feels like you're trying to milk me."

"Well, if you will play with that particular pearl."

He gasped, as her cunt clamped tight around him. "Dammit, Bella, that's not going to make me stop. I need to feel that again."

Another sensuous drag of his thumb and she readily obliged.

"A man could get addicted to that."

"If you keep doing that, I'm not going to be able to help myself."

"That is the idea. I want you to come all over my cock."

"I don't think you need fear over that." Her fingers curled against his flank. "Fuck me, Lucerne. I think I'm going to come."

He bowed his head and kissed her nose, before

drawing back and thrusting into her, and again, exactly how she wanted it.

The motion made the dressing table legs hammer against the uneven boards. "They'll hear us," she said.

"I don't care." Lucerne dragged them apart, and turned her around so that she was facing the mirror. He filled her from behind. "God, you're perfect. You are so damned perfect."

Within a few moments they were both panting hard. Lucerne continued to press upon her nub as he filled her with both deep and shallow strokes. There was no escaping the inevitable. Her body tightened from toes to tip as her climax overwhelmed her. Lucerne spent too the moment her inner muscles began clasping his prick. Lips draw back—she could see him in the mirror—he gasped her name as his release caused his back to arch.

He held her gently afterwards, only slowly sliding them apart. He kissed her quim, then buttoned himself up. "I should go. Vaughan's waiting."

Bella held onto him long enough to demand another kiss. "Tell him thank you for my gift." He nodded, then he was gone, leaving her grinning at her reflection.

She was still smiling inanely when Joshua arrived to play escort.

VOWS

LUCERNE

L UCERNE HAD ATTENDED his share of weddings. It was not uncommon to witness the bride's mother sniffling into a kerchief, or hastily dapping at her eyes. However, he had yet to see the chief groomsman erupt into floods. Thus, he was standing by Vaughan's side with his hands curled into fists and most likely an expression of extreme constipation contorting his features.

This was hell. It did not matter than he had held both Vaughan and Bella close that morning, or that he could still feel the impressions of their bodies upon his skin, his heart was still cracking inside his chest. What's more, it was imperative he didn't reveal that fact. Rumours about the three of them flowed in abundance already. The wedding was meant to quell such speculations.

"I believe it is I who is supposed to be the nervous one," Vaughan murmured. They were stood side by side, facing the altar.

"It's not nerves that have me in their accursed grip."

"I know." Vaughan clasped Lucerne's fingers, and gave them a squeeze. "Try to remember to breathe. The torment will be over soon enough, and then we can see about assuaging your fears. They're unnecessary, Lucerne. Did Bella not welcome you? Have I at any point today given the impression that you mean any less to me now than you did twenty-four hours ago, or a week, or month past?"

Lucerne shook his head, almost imperceptibly, all too conscious of the congregation behind them.

"Exactly, so loosen your jaw, release your shoulders, and think about how good it's going to feel when I next suck your prick."

He was not concentrating on that. Nor even letting the thought into his head. "We're in church," he hissed through his teeth.

"Where I understand one is obliged to tell the truth. I am going to suck you later; you may consider that a promise, else may I be struck down for not keeping it."

Lucerne's jaw didn't ease. His teeth were ready to crack by the time oaths were sworn and Vaughan had slid a ring onto Bella's finger. As a witness, he'd had to observe it all at close quarters, and now all was silent as the Marquis and Marchioness of Pennerley enjoyed their first kiss. Just a few more moments and then he could bolt from here.

Perhaps his absence would be noted. He no longer cared.

The guests began filing out into the autumn sunshine, ready to form an archway of hands for the new couple to pass beneath. Lucerne took a step towards the door, only for Vaughan to clasp his wrist. "A moment, please. We're not entirely done here."

Lucerne stayed, escape thwarted. "What is it?" Even Reverend Hindes had doddered along the aisle and into the daylight now.

"May I?" Vaughan asked, lifting his bride's hand. He kissed her finger, then slid the ring he had just claimed her with from her narrow finger. That set both he and Bella blinking.

The ring was an intricate thing, over large in Lucerne's opinion for a lady's finger, but as he watched, Vaughan twisted the interwoven strands of metal and the ring split into three separate circles. One he realised, as Vaughan slid only one of those pieces back onto Bella's finger, for each of them.

"You both know how I feel about the blessed Almighty, but as we have agreed he is the prime witness of today's events and assertions, then perhaps, we might prevail upon him to bear witness to this moment too."

"Vaughan, what are you doing?"

"Lucerne Aherne Meyrick Marlinscar, I love you as ardently as the woman I have just taken as my wife, and she swears she loves you too. Therefore I ask; will you be ours, to have and hold, from this day forward, forsaking all others? And, will you wear this symbol of our love, as we both will, to show our commitment and fidelity to one another?"

"You are crazy."

Vaughan obliged him with a crooked smile. "But do you accept?" He lifted Lucerne's hand and singled out his ring finger.

"Please," Bella murmured.

Lucerne nodded. "I do." Whereupon Vaughan pushed the ring onto his finger, before both he and

Bella slid the last of the three golden hoops onto Vaughan's. Then, they all clasped hands tightly, and kissed.

"Are you coming?" Niamh called from the doorway. "Everyone is waiting for you?"

They parted, but Bella looped her arm with Lucerne's as well as Vaughan's. "Breakfast, mead, and merriment," she decreed. "Come, I want to set some tongues a-wagging. And, I need to find my brother a bride.

Beetroot
and
Backache

MADELYNNE ELLIS

CHAPTER 1
LUCERNE

Pennerley, February 1802

"I'M GOING TO kill him."

"No, you won't," Lucerne, Viscount Marlinscar, said from the comfort of the armchair before the fireside. He'd been reading a book until Bella had bustled into the solar a moment ago, spitting ire. "You say that a dozen times a week, and he's still very much alive and breathing." There was no need to ask to whom she was referring. That would be their lover, the marquis, and master of this abode.

"Not this time." Bella gave an irritable huff. She eyed a chair, but seemed to change her mind about sitting.

Lucerne sighed as he pushed a hand through the long fringe of his blond hair and set his book aside, ready to listen. To be fair, she did appear to be vexed, rather than huffy because it amused her to be so.

"Am I supposed to enquire what he's done on this occasion?"

"You mean besides having burdened me with the

inability to see my own feet, stand, sit, or lie comfortably?"

Vaughan had indeed done all those things.

"Yes, besides those."

Bella fanned her pink cheeks. "Oh, well then, he has only stained my nipples purple with beetroot juice, which I wouldn't mind except that now my abigail is convinced I'm carrying the devil's spawn, rather than an ordinary baby."

Lucerne quirked one elegant eyebrow, while attempting to hold back a smile. "Oh, dear. He has? I'm both astonished he's found the time, and that you sat still for it. Or am I to believe he snuck into your chamber and attacked you thus in your sleep?"

"'twas earlier," Bella confessed, resting against the sofa back while she pressed her other hand into the small of her back, seeking relief from what Lucerne could only assume was an ache caused by the weight of the babe she was carrying. With the Pennerley heir due afore spring and the first snowdrops already dangling their heads, she was rather impressively rotund. "He conned me. I wasn't aware that he'd been eating pickled beetroot, and now I'm purple from his suckling. Not because this little beast is an imp, as Claudine seems to think. Although, I'm minded to call it one too, when it kicks me all night."

"Can you not—"

"Explain? I'd rather not get into the particulars with her, or else the details will be all around the servants' quarters and the village within the hour. Unfortunately, that means I've had to endure a rather lengthy episode of her ruminating about omens and bad blood." She rested a hand atop her belly and rubbed in a circle there. "Poor mite's already saddled with a devil for a father. It doesn't need labelling as unnatural before it even arrives."

"Then, perhaps you oughtn't to have employed a suspicious and deeply religious French woman as your aide de chambre."

"Perhaps," Bella mused, as she dug her fingers into her back again. "But they're quite the thing this season."

Lucerne nodded. Bella wasn't much of a follower of fashion, but now and then she would latch onto something and nothing else would do. Here, he suspected she'd chosen a devout catholic French woman as her abigail to irritate Vaughan. It'd backfired. Vaughan barely knew the woman existed. It was Bella who had to contend with her sour face, day in, day out.

"You realise the beetroot stains will wash off? Why don't you call and have the servants drawn up a bath for you? A nice soak will probably do the trick."

"It's not so easy clamouring in and out of a tub when you don't bend in the middle."

"Ah!" So that was the real reason she was here. "Do you need me to help?"

She smiled sweetly and cast him a flirtatious glance from beneath her eyelashes. "Would you? That'd be awfully kind of you, Lucerne."

"And I suppose you'd like me to help you wash too, given your maid's current convictions?"

"That would be good of you. Plus, you can make sure my dastardly husband has left no other devil's marks about my person."

He pushed out of the chair and strode over to her, resting against the sofa. "I believe there's one on the back of your neck."

"What? Dratted fellow."

Bella turned her head, but of course she couldn't see what he was referring to.

Lucerne traced his thumb across the angry purple blotch, which sat at the nape just beneath where the wisps of her hair hung free of the coil she'd dressed it in.

"Actually, I'm not sure it is beetroot juice." It looked more like teeth marks. "I see it wasn't just your breasts that captured his attention earlier?"

"Oh, you know Vaughan," she said with a roll of her eyes and a swish of one wrist.

"I do." He had a mark or two of his own about his person, but his valet, unlike her abigail, had been with him long enough and was wise enough not to remark upon them. "Let's get you that bath drawn."

He rang the bell for the servants.

CHAPTER 2

BELLA

T HE STEAMING WATER in the bathtub did little to ease her backache, but Lucerne's attentiveness proved an excellent distraction. Fastidious over his attire, he'd shed his coat and rolled up his shirtsleeves to assist her.

"You are rather mottled," he observed, tackling a stubborn stain on her left knee. The marks Vaughan had left behind proved rather widespread, encompassing not just her breasts, but her bottom and inner thighs too.

"I'm only surprised you haven't found his signature scrawled anyway." She gave him an idle splash.

Lucerne wiped the water from his face. "None of that now." He brandished the soap at her.

Bella gave her foot a flick, giving him a wet shirtsleeve.

"Bella," he complained, not the least bit irate. "Now I shall have to change."

"I expect so. You wouldn't want to linger about in wet clothing."

"If you'd wanted me nude, you could just have said so."

She nibbled her thumbnail, making coy faces. "I never said anything about nakedness, but there's much to admire when your shirt is off."

He obligingly shed his waistcoat and tugged the cambric over his head. "There. Happy? Might I now be allowed to finish the task I'm here to accomplish?"

"You can, yes."

"Oh, good."

He set about cleaning her of beetroot stains again, and if his hand drifted a little higher up her thighs than strictly necessary, then she didn't object, especially when he fingered her into a blissful release. She hadn't minded when he'd helped her dry off either or bent her over the bed to take her from behind in the room that was hers, but in which she rarely slept. She might have heard tales of men and husbands pushing their unshapely pregnant wives aside and even entertained the occasional dark thought that they'd abandon her in favour of one another, but her reality was that neither Vaughan nor Lucerne's ardour had been compromised by her changing shape. If anything, they revelled all the harder for it.

Once Lucerne had departed to see to his attire in his own chamber, Bella endured another round of her maid's mutterings as she dressed her.

"S o m e t h i n g … s o m e t h i n g … u n c h r i s t i a n. Something… something… Satan's spawn… mumble… Holy Mother Mary!"

Heavens, if the woman didn't learn to hold her tongue, she'd have to dismiss her.

It was notable that even though Claudine spent a great deal of time crossing herself — "Must you do that so often?" — she was never so scandalised by what went on that she gave her notice.

Of course not. They paid her well, and no doubt entertained a rapt audience relating all their wickedness both below stairs and in the surrounding locale of a night.

When Bella returned to the solar, attired and coiffed as fitted her station, she found Vaughan occupying the armchair in which she'd earlier located Lucerne. His long legs sat stretched before him, and his dark hair curled around his shoulders in a luxurious tumble.

For a moment, she paused in the doorway, admiring him. She didn't think there'd ever be a time she'd grow tired of gazing at him, nor of recalling that he was hers now as much as he was Lucerne's. The three of them had found a way to balance their relationship in a way that satisfied them all.

She must have made a noise, for he turned his head and spied her. "What have you been about this fine afternoon? I returned from my ride to find you absent from where one ought to have found you."

"I had a bath drawn."

"Hm. So I have heard, and have you given our earlier conversation thought?"

"Not particularly," she said, knowing it would irritate him.

"Bella...Bella, that is not at all acceptable. Did you not promise to love, honour, and obey me as your lawful husband?"

She considered. "'tis true, but 'tis also true that you promised to look after me in sickness and health, and I cannot comply with your desire to warm your prick for you before you do unspeakable things to Lucerne because my back is..." She groaned and attempted to rub the soreness from it. "...it's bad." The bath hadn't eased it one bit.

"Which, naturally, is my fault."

She gave him an arch look. "It very much is. You're the one who planted your seed in my belly."

Vaughan flicked his tongue across his teeth, an action that made him seem feral. "I recall you pleading for me to do so, did you not? Therefore, it is equally your fault. 'Don't put it up my bottom, Vaughan. It's unnatural'," he mimicked. "'Stick it in my puss'."

"I'm not the one who enacted a ritual to the old gods on May Eve."

"True." He graced her with a rakish smile, while his gaze took on a glaze of reminiscence. "We should reprise that ritual this year."

"I think not. This one will barely be borne. I don't intend to spend the next twenty years this shape."

"Then, I guess you're going to have a well-used arse."

She'd have objected, but that was likely what he wanted, and she honestly hadn't the energy for it. Not today. Not when she couldn't find a position sitting or standing that was remotely comfortable.

"Whatever is the matter with you? You're jiggling about like a cat in a bag."

"I have backache."

"Would you like me to rub it?"

She arched backwards as best she could. "You'd do that?" Such an offer from Lucerne was unexceptional, from Vaughan, quite the opposite.

He steepled his fingers against his sensual lips, then summoned her with a crooking of his index finger. "Come here, little dove."

"Be nice, please." She waddled over to where he sat before the fire, but there wasn't anywhere comfortable to position herself. "Can we go into your study? I could lean over your desk."

He made only a small 'hm' in response, but allowed

her to lead him through to the adjoining study in a strangely compliant manner.

While most of the castle's rooms lacked stout doors and any means of privacy, not so the study. This room was the master's domain. Thus, crowded with books, but otherwise spartan, his old oak desk devoid of ornaments except for the blotter and a single quill. There was a window, but it sat shuttered, so that daylight only peeked through the gaps by the hinges. The only other light came courtesy of the small fireplace, and whatever seeped through from the solar.

Bella positioned herself over the dark stained wood, resting on her forearms. Damn this wretched imp she was carrying; it had to have its toenails digging in her spine and its elbows in her ribs.

"Whereabouts?" Vaughan's fingers kneaded along her spine and across the top of her pelvis.

"Right there," she said, when he found a troublesome spot. The relief made her arch and purr. "Yes. And there. Oh, God! You've clever fingers. I think I shall kiss you. Oh, don't stop."

"Bella, you're sprawled over my desk. I suggest you don't rub yourself against me like a cat in heat, or it may not be your back that holds my attention."

She wriggled against him for the pure hell of it, even though it disrupted the relief he was providing. Was Lucerne correct when he said they liked nothing better than to rile one another mercilessly? There was possibly an iota of truth in that.

"Do you even have backache? Please tell me this wasn't an absurd plan to entice me to fuck you. You're more insatiable than a Covent Garden whore at present."

"I have backache, and no desire whatsoever to have you fuck me." Her grin gave away the fact that her words were a partial lie. "Lucerne satisfied every urge I had in that arena, but a little while ago."

"I see," he drawled. "Is that so?"

"It is." Her grin spread broad. Bella buried her face between her arms as he continued to work his magic on her backache, recalling the delights of Lucerne in a not too dissimilar position behind her earlier that hour. The muscles in her pussy clenched in remembrance, too. Teasingly, she rubbed her upturned rear against Vaughan's loins. It seemed her wedded husband had a pole in his pantaloons. "I hope you're not thinking of putting that anywhere it doesn't belong."

"Whatever place would that be? You're mine, if you recall." His tongue tickled the back of her neck, just above the neckline of her dress, where he'd already left a bite mark. "If you continue to wriggle like that, you'll get exactly what you deserve."

She arched her head back to spy him and found him every bit as handsome and desirable as ever. "Do you mean a spanking or a good pricking, my lord?"

"Don't tempt me, little bird. Did Lucerne fuck you before or after you'd taken your bath?"

"After. Like a thoroughbred stallion."

"And I suppose, like the wretched whore you are, you let him spend in your purse," he said, already rucking up her skirts, clearly intent on doing the same.

"Well, of course. He is my lover, and an abominably good one."

"You're a harpy sent to torment me." His hand found the bare expanse of skin above her stocking top. "I think you forget you are mine."

According to him, Lucerne was also his, but equally Vaughan belonged to them both, a fact she saw no sense in reminding him of. She had long ago realised that it was best to judge him on his deeds and not his words.

"Mine, I say. Ergo, the only cock you should

welcome into this purse is mine. The only spendings I should find dripping from your quim, mine. What say you to that, wife?"

"That I have only just got clean, and don't wish to be rumpled again quite so soon, so pray, don't get your prick out."

"You think to thwart me with such insincerity?"

"As if I would dare to thwart you o'er anything."

"You fucked my lover."

"Fear not, he can't put a bun in me, because you already accomplished that deed."

He snorted at her words. "Bella, he still spent inside you."

"Aye, he did," she mused, before shaking off her feigned fascination. "And I suppose, like a dog marking his territory, you now feel obliged to do the same."

One long, clever finger swept along the edges of her split. "I think you're near desperate for me to do the same."

Bella gave a theatrical sniff, even as a tingle of delight ran through her body. "Of course I'm not. I just said as much. What you're doing to ease my back is very nice, though."

Vaughan pressed up close to her again, letting her feel the steel of his prick all thick and eager for her. "You want me," he mouthed into her ear. "Just as you always want me. There was never a woman more eager to feel my prick than you are right now."

"I think you're categorically mistaken, my lord." If she hadn't been before, then she was definitely as eager for him now as he claimed she was. At least, she would have been if her back didn't protest so, and her cunny didn't feel as if it were filled with weights, in addition to being tingly.

"I'm going to put my whole length in you," he promised, breath warm against her neck. "I'm going to do it slowly, inch after blessed inch, and you're going to hold still like a proper lady and let me do it. No coarse remarks, no shimmying about, just dainty acceptance of the rod that rules you."

"I think your head is fogged." She teased in return. "Did you take a tumble while you were out? Come adrift of the saddle and bump your head, perhaps? I cannot comprehend why else you would desire me to be so docile and plank-like."

"Oh, Bella, I don't think you've got it in you to put on such a performance even if you were amenable enough to try. Guess a good teeth-rattling fuck will have to do."

He tugged her skirts higher and grasped her with both hands around the thighs, the better to impale her.

Only the pain in her back shot down between her legs and wriggled about inside her pelvis.

"Wait!"

"No, I think not."

"No, I mean it, Vaughan. Don't. I feel ever so queer."

"Well, I'm sure a nice pricking will set you to rights. It usually does."

The next sound she made was somewhere between a curse and a grunt. And Lord, the pain! Everything from her breasts down seemed to go rigid at once. "Oh, no. No! I think... I think it might be time." Her knuckles whitened as she tightened her grip on the edge of the desk. Another of those body-encompassing groans fled her mouth.

"Bella?" Genuine concern bled through Vaughan's voice.

She had no words of reassurance for him. It was difficult enough to hold on to her breath. A sudden gush of wet heat soaked her legs. Wet him too, causing him to make a sharp 'huh' noise. He lifted his booted foot, liquid puddled around them.

"I think the baby's coming."

"Right now?"

"Yes, now."

"That's rather inconvenient. I was about to fuck you."

She hardly knew whether to laugh or cry at the remark. "I'm sorry to upset your plans."

"I could still put it here," he said, tracing a fingertip over the curve of her upthrust rear.

She swiped at him, knowing he was being insincere, but succeeded only in knocking the blotter from the desk.

Vaughan arched a brow as it skidded across the floor. "Well, if it's time, then I had better fetch somebody. That is, if you're sure you don't want to finish what we'd started?"

"Even if I wasn't in literal agony right now," she was trembling so much she could barely keep a grip on the desk, "I hardly think the child needs baptising with your spendings on its way into the world."

"I'll fetch someone." He started to turn away, but Bella grabbed a hold of his coattails.

"Madam?"

"Don't you dare leave me."

His expression softened. "Bella, I'm sure you'd prefer the midwife's company to mine in this instance."

Her retort never left her tongue as the strength of the next contraction buckled her, but she didn't relinquish her grip on his attire. Vaughan sucked on his tongue, clearly biting back a retort or else masking a grin, perhaps both. "Perhaps I might escort you to your chamber."

"I'm not moving from this spot." She wasn't. Not for anyone. No way.

"Bella, my study is hardly an appropriate birthing chamber."

"It's not an appropriate bedding chamber either, but I swear you use this desk for that purpose more often than you do for correspondence."

"Still—"

She cut him off with a cry. "Shit. Shit. Pissing shit!"

"Your language really is—"

"That really sodding hurts!" Growling, curiously, seemed to help. As, too, did tightening her grip on Vaughan's tailoring. "Here is just fine. I say it's fine, and therefore, it is fine." Even if she'd preferred a different location, there was no way she could, especially not around Pennerley's ancient structures that were designed with defence in mind, not practicality. "Even if it isn't, I can't. Vaughan, I can't."

This time, she screamed as the contraction seized control of her body.

"I could carry you."

Physically, yes, he had proved so on several occasions. On one night he'd even borne her from one end of the castle to the other while she slept, having stolen her from her bed and moved her to his own, but at that time she hadn't been encumbered by a swollen belly, or grimacing through waves of contractions that barely gave her time to breathe between them.

"If you even attempt to upend me, I swear I'll stab you with your letter opener."

He cast a wary glance toward the nearby shelf on which it sat.

"Be reasonable, Bella. Your chamber would be far more appropriate."

"Not... going... anywhere..." she huffed as another wave of pain forced her to bear down. "I think it's coming now."

"Don't be ridiculous. These things take hours. Or so I'm told."

A curse on all men.

"I've been told that too, but I'm telling you it's happening now."

"Unlikely."

Especially argumentative, beautiful, saturnine, extraordinary marquises.

"Humour me."

"How about I summon someone to fetch the midwife?"

"Don't even think about moving," she snarled, now clinging to his coat front. "I mean it, Vaughan. Don't."

"I'm not moving."

Indeed, he wasn't. Couldn't easily, not without ripping his coat from her grip and risking her toppling headfirst to the floor.

"Bella, my coat. Maybe you'd like to take my hands instead..."

She gave her head a good shake. "No, you'll need them to catch the baby."

"Bella? Your imagination is running a little wild. Come now. I'll ring for a servant. The midwife will come. All will be well."

There wasn't time for any of that. There wasn't...

"Vaughan, I'm not moving, and I need you to look. I swear I can feel the head right between my legs."

His shoulders came up and back at that, while Bella maintained her grip on his coat front. "Must you be quite so graphic with your descriptions? The only head I care to envisage in that location is mine, or perhaps Lucerne's. Now, if you'd just release me, I think I should summon—"

"Vaughan." She gave another groan and sagged at the knees, forcing him to catch her.

"Hm, maybe if you hold on to the desk again? It's a little hard to assist in my current position."

"Stop thinking of your coat."

"I'm thinking of you and the imminent arrival."

"Don't leave me," she implored as he uncurled her fingers and helped her shuffle around so that she could brace herself against the desk again. She held on as he supported her in making an ungainly squat.

"Are you sure this is the position?"

"It's the position I'm in, so it's the position."

"As you say."

She gave another grunt. There wasn't any controlling it. Her body was doing things, and she was just along for the ride. "Oh!" she gasped at the end of another period of pushing. "I think you need to get down there and look."

"Lady Pennerley, are you asking me to lift your skirts?"

She laughed, but that hurt, and her mirth turned into a sob, and then more shuddery breaths. "Breathe, my nightingale. All will be well." He caressed her face.

"I'd rather he didn't slide out and bang his head on the floor. He needs to be pretty like his papa."

"Well, then... a cushion." He grasped the one from the chair behind his desk.

"Vaughan, please help. I need you to look."

"Very well, madam, though I'm sure I don't have a clue what I'm supposed to be looking at." He knelt and rucked up her skirts.

"What can you feel?"

His hand slid up her inner thigh. Then he was touching her, but not touching her. His hand between her legs, but it didn't feel at all like it usually did. Nothing did.

"Bella, I need to get us some assistance."

"No!" Her response was a cry of frustration, pain,

and determination. Also, surely it had been loud enough for everyone in the castle to have heard. Even if they baulked at barging in, there'd be servants scurrying about outside the door within seconds, just in case. They all knew her time was close, just not how close. All manner of people had given her all manner of dates for her lying-in time. They were all wrong. "I should never have taken that bath."

"Was it the bath or Lucerne's spendings that did it, do you think?"

She just howled at him again for trying to amuse her.

CHAPTER 3
LUCERNE

LUCERNE WAS IN the master suite in the tower when one of the footmen appeared at the top of the stairs. "Begging your pardon, Lord Marlinscar, I've been sent to tell you it's time, and that the midwife is on her way."

"Where is she now?" he asked, turning from the Cheval glass.

"The midwife, milord? She's on her way from—"

"No, man, the marchioness? Where's Bella? Has Pennerley been told?"

"I'm not sure, milord, but my lady is in the solar."

Lucerne took off at once, almost coming a cropper on the spiral stairs in his haste. He barged a couple of maids out of the way as he hurried upstairs again to the solar. Only that room lay empty. Clearly, the lad had been mistaken. Hired for looks, not brains. Only something, a near inaudible sound, caught his attention and took him through the adjoining door into Vaughan's study.

Within, Bella lay propped against the side of Vaughan's desk, clothing askew and hair tumbled around her shoulders, all loose from its pins. Her face was both tear-stained and ruddy. He dropped to his knees beside her at once. "Oh, God! Bella, what happened?"

A bloody smear streaked one cheek. Both the floor and her skirts were wet, and he noted several other bloody stains about her person. "I was told the midwife had been summoned, but—"

She reached out to him, tired but smiling. "She won't be needed."

"No?"

"No."

"It's not time?"

"It happened without her help."

At once, he reassessed the situation he'd found her in. Blood smears, water, her disorderly appearance... "Then where?" Had one of the maids taken the child? If so, why? Fearing the worst, he followed Bella's line of motion as she tilted her head toward the further adjoining room. Through the partially-open doorway, he could make out Vaughan's silhouette against the white of the window. He stood in his waistcoat, his coat bundled up in his arms.

Bella's fingers curled around Lucerne's forearm. "Give him a moment, please? He did just deliver his son. I believe they're bonding."

"He... Wait, what?"

"It all happened so fast." She shut her eyes, but a smile ate up her face. "I expect I'll be allowed another cuddle in a moment or two. I believe he's utterly besotted."

"He is?"

She nodded. "He said the boy opened his eyes and looked at him. His papa was the very first thing he saw." A joyful tear rolled over her cheek. "He should meet his other papa."

"Let's get you somewhere more comfortable first. It isn't right that you're lying on the floor."

"That would be nice." She squeezed his hand. "But I'll be fine in a moment or two. Go and meet him, Lucerne. Tell me he isn't the most perfect thing."

"Very well." He kissed her gently, then rose and tiptoed next door to Vaughan's side. "Congratulations." The child had a headful of dark hair like his father's, and eyes that were just as intense, and oddly coloured. He was staring at his papa through inquisitive eyes. "I see he favours you."

Vaughan remained focused on the child. "I have a son," he said, as if he hadn't heard Lucerne's words.

"Yes, you do," Lucerne confirmed. He leaned in and pressed a kiss to Vaughan's temple, then the baby's brow. "I'm going to get Bella moved to somewhere more comfortable. Maybe you'd like to bring the lad along. He'll want to latch on, and I think his mama would like another cuddle."

"Yes," Vaughan said, uncharacteristically agreeable. "He needs some better swaddling, too. My coat's a bit overlarge for him as yet."

Lucerne squeezed the tops of his lover's arms. "Do you have a name?"

"Sebastian Peredur."

"Sticking with tradition. It's a good name. Greetings and welcome to the world, my lord." He gave the baby a bow, and his papa another kiss, then he went and swept Bella up into his arms, and the four of them relocated to the master's chamber.

The midwife, when she arrived, was not at all

happy, having missed out on her tithe. She berated the marchioness to anyone who would listen and swore she ought to have been summoned the moment her backache started. "The marquis has no business delivering a child," she decried, but though the servants and the local farmers and villages humoured her, no one seemed much inclined to agree. Instead, they raised their tankards and doffed their caps to celebrate the arrival of the new Earl of Oswestry. Or was it Craven? No one was quite sure which of the titles the lad was saddled with yet.

ABOUT THE AUTHOR

MADELYNNE IS A **New York Times & USA Today** bestselling author. She wrote her first novel after discovering Black Lace Books in the 1990s. After escaping the Hotel California, she dived into storytelling full time. Her books are filled with bisexual bad boys who like to get down and dirty, and stories so angst-filled you know they're going to hurt.

She lives in the UK near the Welsh border, where you can find her surrounded by books, drinking rapidly cooling decaf coffee, and listening to loud music.

Come hang out with her via her newsletter, where she shares what she's reading, watching, listening to, and snippets about her current projects.